WHAT PEOPLE ARE SAYING . . .

Schuermann builds the reader's affections for the Bradbury characters in such a way that you should not be surprised to find yourself including some of these blessed souls into your own daily prayers, only to remember, embarrassingly, that these are not real souls at all. And yet, they are very real. The widows, the mother hens, the lonely singles, the gossips, the meddlers, the jilted—they are all around us. The names and faces are different, but the sins and the robe of righteousness that cover us all are the same.

—Rebecca Mayes, homeschooler, editor, and writer

Katie Schuermann gets it! . . . Not only what goes on behind the scenes— and the masks—in a congregation, not only how to negotiate the treacherous genre of Christian fiction (which is so often syrupy or contrived or idealistic), but much more important: how Christ transforms real life in a still fallen— and frequently funny!—world.

—Dr. Carl C. Fickenscher II, professor, Concordia Theological Seminary

There are a myriad of delightful qualities about this book: its humor, its bold witness to Christ, its gentle reminder of how deadly our pet sins are. One of its most endearing qualities—beyond masterful turns of phrases, twisty plot developments, and characters you are certain you have met in real life—is that it is true.

—Adriane Heins, executive editor, *The Lutheran Witness*

A Lutheran Jan Karon? Yes, Katie Schuermann! Both are great wordsmiths crafting engrossing small town tales. Both focus on town and congregational life. Both have great character development and are enlightening, spiritual, fun reads. . . . For your reading delight, for sharing, and for gifting!

—Rod Zwonitzer, director of broadcast services/KFUO, host of *BookTalk*

Anyone who has said of small town life "you can't make this stuff up" has been proven wrong by Katie Schuermann. If the people of Lake Wobegone were to fall in love with a book, it would be *House of Living Stones*, where the odors are strong, the pastor is good-looking, and the writing is all above average.

—Rebekah Curtis, housewife, author, editor, and avid reader

A delightful homage to *Anne of Green Gables*, complete with colorful characters who break the eighth commandment like pros, a heroine both sinner and saint, and a portrait of small-town life that reads like a caricature but is all too real. Katie's writing elevates "ordinary" life to the extraordinary, alternating whimsical hilarity with poignant real-life-under-the-cross moments that will have you laughing, crying, and wanting more.

—Gretchen Roberts, digital marketer, pastor's wife, avid reader of fiction, and *Anne of Green Gables* fan

How refreshing it is to read for pleasure and then to find it to be also wonderfully edifying time spent. This is Mitford plus . . . where Schuermann brings the reader into the joys and some serious challenges of a small town. You will love the writing, the story line, the characters, and the humor. Sit down with some chamomile or Merlot . . . read and enjoy!"

—Richard C. Resch, kantor and professor emeritus, Concordia Theological Seminary

Katie Schuermann's venture into fiction breathes a breath of fresh central Illinois air as her pen travels along a road less traveled. . . . Her tale of life and love, meddling and music, rebellion and reconciliation in the fictional college town of Bradbury, Illinois, is entertaining and insightful. . . . This is a delightful diversion and a helpful and practical account of living that I can't help but recommend.

—Rev. Mark A. Miller, president, Central Illinois District LCMS

A charming story about life in a small congregation in rural Illinois, with the rare feature of a choir director as a main character. The view-from-the-pew (or choir loft) perspective is reminiscent of Mark Schweizer's Liturgical Mysteries series and the down-home Lutheranism of Garrison Keillor's Lake Wobegon. Schuermann's tale is sure to draw knowing nods and smiles from readers.

—Kevin Hildebrand, kantor, Concordia Theological Seminary, St. Paul's Lutheran Church and School

House of Living Stones

KATIE SCHUERMANN

CONCORDIA PUBLISHING HOUSE • SAINT LOUIS

For my Michael,

who never fails to laugh in all of the right places.

Published by Concordia Publishing House
3558 S. Jefferson Avenue, St. Louis, MO 63118-3968
1-800-325-3040 · www.cph.org

Text © 2014 Katie Schuermann

Cover image: © iStockphoto.com
Photo (p. 5): © iStockphoto.com
Map illustration (pp. 6–7) by Dave Hill

Unless otherwise indicated, Scripture quotations from the ESV Bible®
(The Holy Bible, English Standard Version®), copyright © 2001 by
Crossway Bibles, a publishing ministry of Good News Publishers. Used by
permission. All rights reserved.

Hymn texts used in the Sunday service scenes and those marked with
the abbreviation *LSB* are from *Lutheran Service Book*, copyright © 2006
Concordia Publishing House. All rights reserved.

This is a work of fiction. Names, characters, businesses, places, and events
are either products of the author's imagination or are used in a fictitious
manner. Any resemblance to actual persons, living or dead, or actual
events or places is coincidental.

Manufactured in the United States of America

Library of Congress Cataloging-in-Publication Data

Schuermann, Katie.
  House of the Living Stones / Katie Schuermann.
    pages cm
  Includes bibliographical references and index.
  ISBN 978-0-7586-4945-4 (alk. paper)
  1. Choral conductors--Fiction. 2. Lutheran
Church--Discipline--Fiction. 3. Christian life--Fiction. I. Title.

  PS3619.C469H68 2014
  813'.6--dc23

                    2014037544

2 3 4 5 6 7 8 9 10   23 22 21 20 19 18 17 16 15 14

We are God's house of living stones,
Built for His own habitation.
He through baptismal grace us owns
Heirs of His wondrous salvation.
Were we but two His name to tell,
Yet He would deign with us to dwell
With all His grace and His favor.
(LSB 645:3)

BRADBURY

BRADBURY CEMETERY

BRADBURY DRIVE

BRADBURY COLLEGE ➤

BRADBURY DRIVE

BRADBURY HOUSE ➤

PUBLIC LIBR

CEDAR ST.

OAK ST.

THE CORNER COFFEE SHOP ➤

KOELSTER'S KITCHEN ➤

FIRST ST.

BRADBURY COLLEGE

BRADBURY HOUSE

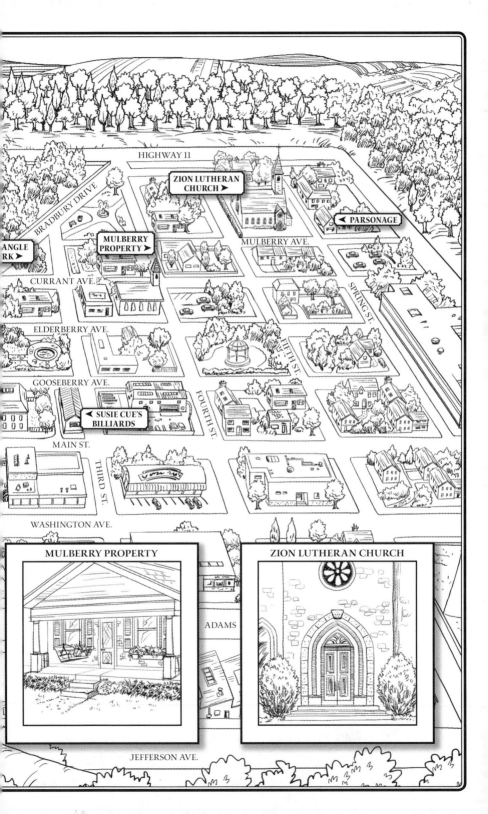

Contents

CHAPTER ONE:

MRS. SCHEINBERG IS INCONVENIENCED

Mrs. Arlene Compton Scheinberg positioned herself advantageously behind the cherrywood desk in the front office of Zion Lutheran Church. The sign out front on the church lawn announced to all the world that the Reverend Michael G. Fletcher was Zion's divinely called shepherd, but every sheep in the flock knew that Mrs. Scheinberg was the self-appointed herd dog, and she did not care for the looks of the two wolves in wrinkled suits sitting expressionless on the chairs along her east wall.

The man on the left with salt-and-pepper hair wore a blue suit coat but no tie. Mrs. Scheinberg scrutinized the exposed top button of the man's shirt over her gold-rimmed glasses while simultaneously editing the bulletin for the upcoming Sunday service. *A man should finish dressing before leaving the house,* she grumpily thought.

The young man on the right appeared to be growing a beard for the first time. The blond hair on his chin, however, was growing much faster than the hair on his red cheeks, leaving him looking oddly like a rooted sweet potato. "A job half done is a job undone," she quipped under her breath. She picked up her red pen and made a large, annoyed check on the bottom of page 2. Pastor Fletcher would expect the bulletin to be finished for printing by four o'clock that very afternoon, and Mrs. Scheinberg was not about to let these two sojourners distract her from her service to the Lord—not, at least, while so many other generous women in the congregation waited in line to steal her blessing.

Just last year, Miss Geraldine Turner, after catching a misplaced appositive in the bulletin announcements two Sundays in a row, made a point of suggesting to Pastor Fletcher that perhaps Mrs. Scheinberg would appreciate some help proofreading the bulletin every Thursday afternoon, between three and four o'clock to be precise.

"As the English teacher emeritus of Bradbury High School," Miss Turner had quipped in that tight, queenly way of hers, "I would be most happy to be of service."

Mrs. Scheinberg had kindly reminded Pastor Fletcher that the trustees had thought to provide only one chair behind the front office desk, and unless he could spare his own chair between three and four every Thursday afternoon, the benevolent Miss Turner would have no place to sit.

Miss Turner hadn't been her only critic. This past December, Mrs. Thomas Edison Bradbury III had dropped by the church office one Monday morning to express her sorrow and regret at the misspelling of her husband's ailing mother's maiden name in the prayer requests. She had even provided her own marked copy of the bulletin for Pastor Fletcher to keep, and she meaningfully handed Mrs. Scheinberg a copy of the Bradbury County Home Extension Office's recent publication, *The Life and Times of Bradbury: A Complete History.*

"Oh, no, I insist you keep it for free," Candice Bradbury had fluttered, her counterfeit smile pushing sideways against her ample cheeks. "You will find it to be a useful resource in the future. The *correct* spelling of every name of every one of my husband's relatives is in there. I know. I edited the book myself."

Mrs. Scheinberg had made sure to tie a festive, red-and-gold ribbon around Candice's miserable book before giving it to Pastor Fletcher as a Christmas present.

Even the sweet widow of the deceased Pastor Gardner had offered her proofreading services just last month. "Arlene, dear," Alice had crooned, "I couldn't help but notice the heading in last Sunday's bulletin about the fund-raiser for the food pantry on Washington Street."

Mrs. Scheinberg had not bothered to look up from the magazine she was perusing. "I double-checked the date and time, Alice. It's correct."

"Well, dear," Alice stumbled, "it's not the date and time to which I'm referring."

Mrs. Scheinberg wondered why a faithful servant of the church could not be allowed even one moment's peace in which to properly view the new line of sport coats featured in the JCPenney summer catalog. She sighed from her hips, put her glasses on top of her head, and gave Alice an eyeful of feigned civility.

"You see," Alice blushed, holding out the bulletin in question, "it says, 'Come and support our tasty food *panty*.'"

Mrs. Scheinberg hadn't missed the masculine chuckle— quickly stifled and masked as a cough—that escaped from behind the door of Pastor Fletcher's study. Even now, she scowled at the memory, her ears taking on the shade of her new, melon-colored blouse. "Everyone's a critic," she muttered aloud, causing the two dark suits to look up expectantly from their perches against the wall. She glared at them over her glasses, daring them to breathe, before slowly returning her attention to her bulletin.

The front door to the office opened just then, letting in a gust of warm air that smelled of sunned boxwood and potting soil. A young woman with rosy cheeks and serious, brown eyes floated in on the breeze. She wore a gray pencil skirt, white blouse, and quarter-length pink sweater. Her dark-blonde locks were cut short and stylishly curled around her forehead and cheeks. The two suits turned curious gazes toward the newcomer, and Mrs. Scheinberg felt oddly grateful to the young woman for the distraction. Uncharacteristic feelings of goodwill and hospitality for the ingenue stirred in the older woman.

"May I help you?" Mrs. Scheinberg smiled generously, though a bit unnaturally. She was out of practice.

"Yes, my name is Emily Duke. I have an appointment with Reverend Fletcher, though I think I may be a bit early."

"Won't you have a seat?" Mrs. Scheinberg gestured to the empty chair sandwiched between Neiman and Marcus. The young woman hesitated, scanning the room for an alternative that imposed a little less intimacy upon three total strangers. Mrs. Scheinberg followed her gaze to the rickety, three-step footstool near the floor-to-ceiling bookcase and the brass plant stand supporting an overgrown asparagus fern in the corner. Evidently finding nothing more suitable, Emily Duke lowered herself carefully onto the seat that had been proffered and hugged her elbows to her ribs in an obvious effort to keep from touching the two men.

Mrs. Scheinberg creaked back comfortably in her executive leather chair and resumed her editing, though not before taking note of the fact that the young woman now seated in the waiting room appeared refreshingly modest and pressed for a woman of her generation. She even sat with her ankles crossed. And wore hose. *Naked knees are for young children and harlots*, Mrs. Scheinberg thought with satisfaction. As far as she was concerned, Emily Duke's honor and reputation were forever secured right then and there by a simple pair of nylons.

The door to the left of her desk opened, and out stepped a man in a clerical collar. He had an ordinary face and an unassuming manner, but his dark eyes were bright with intelligence and looked as if they could crinkle into a smile at any moment, a characteristic that endeared him to everyone in his flock but the church secretary. "Mrs. Scheinberg," Pastor Fletcher said, "would you please invite Mr. Norton into my office?"

As faithful and as nice as Pastor Fletcher might be, Mrs. Scheinberg couldn't bring herself to forgive him for being under forty. It was not his fault, to be sure, but it was a fault all the same. She took off her glasses and rubbed the bridge of her nose, careful not to leave the comfort of her own chair. "Mr. Norton," she called across the room, "the Reverend Fletcher is ready to meet with you."

Pastor Fletcher's mouth twitched and his dark eyes twinkled, a sight that irritated Mrs. Scheinberg to no end. How she wished these young pastors' mothers had taught their sons to smile a little less and to comb their hair a little more! A lesson or two in ironing would have been in order as well. Why, in thirty years of faithful service, she had never once seen Pastor Gardner, may he rest in peace, step out of his home without a starched clerical on his back and a blazing white part in his hair, but this Michael Fletcher barely remembered to cut his mop of curly hair, let alone tame it; and by the end of the day, the wrinkles in his clerical wiggled and squiggled across his back like a sloppy community garden whose rows had been hoed by a five-year-old. What were the seminaries teaching these men anyway?

For the next forty-five minutes, Mrs. Scheinberg wrangled with the third page of the bulletin while simultaneously listening to the muted interviews behind Pastor's closed door, first with the unbuttoned Mr. Norton and then with the half-beard-ed Mr. Simmons. (She found it satisfying to discover that Mr. Simmons's voice was higher pitched than her own. She had guessed as much.) Then, there was also the matter of Emily Duke, who was patiently waiting for her turn. As hard as Mrs. Scheinberg tried, she could not help sneaking glances at her. The young woman had a curious yet charming tendency to sway her head back and forth ever so slightly, as if listening to music that no one else could hear, and she pursed her lips and furrowed her brow like a little girl who had lost herself in her thoughts. She could not have been a day over thirty, but even from across the room, Mrs. Scheinberg saw that there were faint lines etched around her eyes and mouth as if they were lingering shadows of laughter and smiles from years past. Disarmed by Emily Duke's mannerisms, she caught herself staring at the young woman.

Each in his turn, Mr. Norton and Mr. Simmons exit-ed Pastor's study and, subsequently, the office door. Mrs. Scheinberg celebrated the return of peace to her pasture with a desk picnic of four peanut butter cookies and one canning jar of iced peach tea. She brushed the incriminating cookie crumbs off the front of her blouse just as Pastor Fletcher ambled out of his study on his long legs. "How is the bulletin coming?" His tone was friendly, and his hands were in his pockets. Put off by his casual manner, Mrs. Scheinberg sniffed and made a large, visible check on the third page. "It would go a lot faster if there were not so many people requiring my attention and skill this morning. You *know* Thursdays are my busy days."

"Duly noted, Mrs. Scheinberg." Pastor Fletcher turned to smile warmly at the young woman. "You must be Dr. Duke."

Doctor Duke? Mrs. Scheinberg thought with approval, though she was suitably rankled to be hearing of the young woman's title for the first time. For some reason known only to Pastor Fletcher, she had not been privy to the résumés of the candidates ahead of the interviews. And that was another thing about these young pastors. They locked their filing cabinets every evening. Pastor Gardner never would have done such an untrusting thing.

"Yes," the young woman said, her smile lines blossoming in full glory. She stood and shook the reverend's hand and then walked before him into his office at his gestured invitation.

Pastor Fletcher lingered for a moment next to the secretary's desk. "Mrs. Scheinberg, would you please include a congratulatory note in the bulletin this week for Pastor Douglas? He retires a week from this Sunday."

"But he is not a member of this congregation."

"His grandchildren are."

She made a show of exchanging her red editing pen for the green writing pen in the top drawer of her desk and then looked over her glasses at the clergyman. "It seems to me that the proper place for an announcement regarding Pastor Douglas's retirement would be in his own church's bulletin. Would you like me to go ahead and call the other churches in the county to see if they have anything they would like to add?"

Pastor Fletcher, eyes sparkling, appeared as if he was resisting the urge to plant a patronizing kiss on the top of her gray head, but apparently, even youth has its wisdom. He simply stepped into his study.

"And what exactly am I supposed to say in this congratulatory announcement?" she called loudly into the great wide void.

"How about, 'We wish Reverend Douglas many blessings in his retirement,'" was the faceless reply.

Pastor Fletcher, as was his custom when meeting alone with a woman, left his door respectfully ajar a few inches, and Mrs. Scheinberg, as was her custom when sitting alone behind her desk, angled her chair and scooted a few feet closer to the door of the study to better hear every word. Although she could not see him, she could hear Pastor Fletcher sifting through the open file on his desk.

"Your résumé is impressive, Dr. Duke. I can't help but wonder why someone with your credentials would even want to interview for our part-time church choir director position."

"Thank you. I'm interested because I want to make music in a church."

"Any particular reason why you want to make music in *this* church?"

"I am a baptized Lutheran, and this is the only Lutheran church in town." Mrs. Scheinberg heard, rather than saw, Emily Duke smile.

Pastor Fletcher chuckled. "Actually, it's the only Lutheran church within thirty miles of town. What brings you to Bradbury?"

"Bradbury College hired me to teach their survey of music history courses this year."

More shuffling of papers. "Are you currently living in Bradbury?"

"Not yet. I plan to relocate from St. Louis."

"I see." Pastor Fletcher paused. "Dr. Duke, what exactly do you expect of a church choir? I mean, what situation are you used to in St. Louis?"

"Well, I've served the last three years as the senior choir director at St. Paul's in Crestwood. We average between twenty-five to thirty singers every Sunday, and we sing at both the early and late services three times a month with every fourth Sunday off. We also sing on festival Sundays and midweek services."

Pastor Fletcher's response was honest and matter-of-fact. "We have not had a consistent choir director in our employment for the last fifteen years, and we hold only one worship service every Sunday morning. It's a good week if ten singers show up for a Sunday service. I would understand if you don't find that scenario appealing."

Emily Duke's response was just as matter-of-fact. "I don't know that size is a deal breaker. 'Where two or three are gathered in My name . . .'"

Mrs. Scheinberg heard Pastor Fletcher tap his fingers on his desk, and she knew that meant he was excited. "Have you had any theological training?"

"I took a Bible and Culture class in college, but I think it hurt my theology more than helped it," Emily Duke confessed. She laughed, and the musical sound reminded Mrs. Scheinberg of a favorite wind chime her grandma used to hang on her front porch every summer.

"Honestly," Emily Duke continued, "the best theological training I ever had was in Sunday School. My teachers made sure I knew every article of the Apostles' Creed and their meanings before I finished second grade."

As she listened to the silence, Mrs. Scheinberg knew Pastor Fletcher was digesting Dr. Duke's remark. "Can you tell me a little bit more about the specific role you see the choir playing in the worship service?"

"At St. Paul's, we often sing the Alleluia Verse, sometimes the Gradual, and at other times the Psalm. Personally, I always like having the choir sing a meditative anthem or hymn during distribution or the offering."

"What are your feelings regarding traditional and contemporary styles of worship?"

Mrs. Scheinberg held her breath. One misstep here, and her good opinion of Emily Duke, nylons and all, would go the way of the sewer.

"I try *not* to have feelings on the subject," was Dr. Duke's simple reply.

Pastor Fletcher laughed. "I can appreciate that. However, what do you *think* about it?"

"Well, as a church musician, I appreciate that which promotes good order for the congregation. As a Christian, I want the music to serve the Word."

Mrs. Scheinberg let the air out of her lungs in relief.

"And what do you think as a Lutheran?" Pastor Fletcher asked, tapping away on his desk.

"I think that—"

Suddenly, the phone rang, causing Mrs. Scheinberg to drop her pen on the carpeted floor. She scrambled to pick it up and used the soles of her new Dr. Scholl's to scoot herself and her hooded, double-wheel casters back to the desk. She picked up the phone on the third ring.

"Zion Lutheran Church. This is Mrs. Scheinberg speaking," she panted.

"Oh, good, Arlene, I'm so glad I caught you," was the anxious reply. "This is Beverly. You won't believe what Irv did this morning! He dropped by the church just after breakfast to check on the leaky toilet in the men's bathroom, and he left his wallet on the counter of the sink. He told me that he set it down with his hat before going into the stall and then picked up only his hat on the way out the door. Can you go check for me real quick and see if it's still there? If it is, I can swing by and pick it up on my way to my hair appointment in town this afternoon. Seriously, I don't know what I'm going to do with that man! Just yesterday, he took one of my white dish towels out to the pig barn and . . ."

Mrs. Scheinberg rolled her eyes. Beverly Davis was the Lance Armstrong of windbags: the woman could talk longer and faster than anyone else she knew. This was going to go on for a while, so she laid the receiver down on her desk and made her way to the men's room. "As if I don't have anything better to do today," she grumbled under her breath. Adding to her irritation was the fact that she was missing precious minutes of Emily Duke's interview.

Pushing open the door to the men's restroom with her hip, she could see Irv's wallet sitting on the counter in the dark without even turning on the restroom light. She snatched it up, grumbling to herself about germs, and headed back to her office. She swung a little wide, closer to Pastor Fletcher's open office door, taking time to resituate herself comfortably at her station and rub an ample portion of antibacterial gel on her hands before picking up the phone receiver.

". . . and would you believe that he ate half of the batch before I even came back to the kitchen? Now I'm out of butter and have to think of something else to make for the VBS cookie train!" Beverly paused to take a breath, and Mrs. Scheinberg jumped at her opportunity.

"I'll be sure to keep Irv's wallet safe for you to pick up this afternoon, Bev."

"Oh, thank you, Arlene! I knew I could count on you. You're a gem! One of these days, we should—"

"I'll give you a call if there's any trouble," she barreled along. "Otherwise, plan on stopping by before three. Bye, Bev."

She hung up the phone just as Pastor Fletcher and Dr. Duke walked out of the study. Mrs. Scheinberg was so disappointed at having missed the rest of the interview that she seriously considered running Irv's nuisance of a wallet through the paper shredder.

Pastor Fletcher stopped at her desk and picked up the dog-eared church directory. He quickly found a phone number and wrote it down on the pad of paper that was kept at the ready on the corner of her desk. Tearing off what he had written, he handed it to Dr. Duke.

"Here is Alice Gardner's phone number. She owns a small rental house just down the street from here. You'll find her to be an honest and kind landlady. She may even be home this afternoon if you want to see the property before you drive back to St. Louis."

"Thank you," the young woman replied, sticking the piece of paper in her purse. "I appreciate the contact and the interview, Pastor Fletcher. Thank you, both of you." Dr. Duke beamed a sunny smile that fell directly on Mrs. Scheinberg.

"Be careful of the coffee at the Casey's on your way out of town," Mrs. Scheinberg impulsively warned. "I don't trust those teenagers who work the register to make it correctly."

Emily Duke thanked her again, letting in another fresh summer breeze as she opened the door on her way out. Mrs. Scheinberg felt oddly disappointed when the door closed behind her. She swiveled in her chair to face Pastor Fletcher's profile and said, "Please tell me that you're planning on recommending her to the council instead of one of those two gangsters."

"I am," Pastor Fletcher replied, somewhat absently. Mrs. Scheinberg noted that he was still staring at the door through which Emily Duke had left. "I already invited her to come to church this Sunday to meet Evan."

She sighed mightily, quickly regaining her natural optimism as she returned to her work on page 4 of the bulletin. "Well, I guess we can't hide him from her. God have mercy on her soul!"

"God have mercy on us all," Pastor Fletcher said as he stepped back into the quiet of his study and softly shut the door. He did not fully understand what had just happened, but he knew that half of his body wanted to jump up and holler while the other half strangely wanted to sit down and cry. Since Mrs.

Scheinberg was sitting just five feet away on the other side of the closed door, he did neither. Instead, he walked over to the window and stared unseeing at the north green lawn of the church property, quietly pondering all things intelligent, brown-eyed, and Emily Duke.

Chapter Two: Introducing Evan Ebner

‖‖‖

```
Zion Lutheran Church and Rev.
Michael G. Fletcher would like
to wish the Rev. Daniel Douglas
man blessings in his retirement
next week.
```

Emily Duke quickly closed the church bulletin and bit the inside of her cheek to keep from laughing out loud. She was sitting in the fifth pew from the back on the lectern side of Zion Lutheran Church. One of the half-dozen parishioners sitting behind her must have seen the same mistake, for she heard a masculine voice whisper indiscreetly across the aisle, "Do you suppose Pastor Douglas's wife has an opinion on the matter?" Emily looked down and covered her mouth with her hand.

In a sudden burst of musical delight, the organ bellows opened and released a joyous call to worship into the church's nave. A clear, bold reed stop sang out fragments of "Lord, Keep Us Steadfast in Your Word," while running undercurrents of flute and string stops supported and lifted the melody higher and higher into the wooden rafters of the church. The musical brilliance of the moment stunned Emily out of her suppressed laughter, and goose bumps ran up the back of her neck. She fought the childish urge to turn around in her pew and gawk at the organist and instead flipped through the bulletin to the back page and read the name: Evan Ebner.

Outstanding, Emily thought, closing her eyes and soaring with the cherubim and seraphim directly to the throne of heaven, where every knee was bowing and every voice was confessing the name of Jesus. She joined in with the heavenly host arrayed in white, coming back to earth only when the low organ pedals bid her home with their rumbling resolution.

"Amen," she whispered. When she opened her eyes again, Emily saw that a young acolyte had already lit the candles on the altar and Pastor Fletcher was turning around at the front of the church to address the congregation.

"Grace, mercy, and peace to you in Christ Jesus, our risen Lord and Savior," Pastor Fletcher greeted the congregation, his eyes crinkling as he smiled. "A couple of announcements before we begin the service this morning: Beverly Davis is still taking names of people who are willing to bake cookies for our Vacation Bible School, which begins tomorrow. If you're interested, please see her at the sign-up table in the narthex after the service. Also, the youth will be serving a sausage and pancake breakfast before next week's service to raise money for their upcoming conference, so please come early and join us in the parish hall to support them. Further details are in the bulletin." Pastor Fletcher opened his hands wide. "Let us stand and greet one another, sharing the peace of the Lord."

Emily barely had a chance to stand before the short, stout woman with graying hair who had been sitting directly across the aisle rushed over and grabbed both of her hands. "Peace of the Lord!" the woman bubbled. "You must be Dr. Duke from St. Louis! I just can't tell you how happy I am to meet you. You look just as I imagined you would. My name is Beverly Davis, and

I'm a soprano in the church choir. This is my husband, Irv," she motioned to the tall, quiet man with broad shoulders standing behind her. "He's on the church council, and he sings bass in the choir. He is the only bass. Actually, he is the only *man* in the choir."

Emily was still shaking Beverly Davis's hand when someone else greeted her.

"Peace of the Lord, Dr. Duke."

Emily turned to her left to see Mrs. Scheinberg extending her hand in Christian fellowship. She smiled at the familiar face, though it was not particularly friendly that day. Little did she know that the church secretary was grimacing as brightly as her Sunday morning toothache would allow, nor had she been privy to the preservice jibes Mrs. Scheinberg had endured earlier in the narthex from the ushers regarding Rev. Douglas's butchered retirement announcement.

"Peace of the Lord," Emily returned warmly, shaking her hand. She liked Mrs. Scheinberg and her irritated ways. What appeared on the surface to be crotchetiness and impatience was, to Emily's empathetic eyes, the honesty and world-weariness of one who has suffered. Besides, something about Mrs. Scheinberg's silver hair, golden eyeglasses, and various knitted accoutrements reminded Emily of her own grandmother.

Evan Ebner was beckoning everyone back to their pews with a prelude to the opening hymn. As she took her seat, Emily watched as congregants sifted back to their places, murmuring pleasantly and opening hymnals. She saw that Mrs. Scheinberg sat alone a few pews ahead of her on the lectern side. Emily also recognized the stooped shoulders of Alice Gardner, her new landlady, a few pews ahead of Mrs. Scheinberg. Alice was flanked by three red-headed, school-aged boys, the oldest on her right and the two younger ones on her left. An angel with strawberry-blonde pigtails in a yellow gingham dress sat primly on Alice's lap. Emily assumed that the delicate woman sitting to the left of the younger boys must be Alice's daughter, and the red-haired man sitting at the end of the line must be her daughter's husband.

Emily did not recognize any other faces in the pews of Zion, but she delighted in seeing such a variety. Most of the heads in the pews wore a crown of silver or white, but Emily was relieved to see that there were at least ten families with young children who gathered in this small house of the Lord. Young and old mingled together, some holding hymnals, others holding children.

Emily quickly swept her eyes around the nave, admiring the stained glass windows that lined each side wall. The seven windows on her right pictured events from the Old Testament, and the seven windows on her left bore images from Christ's life, death, and resurrection. A large, wooden crucifix hung directly above the freestanding, wooden altar in the sanctuary. Green paraments hung on the altar, lectern, and pulpit for the season of Pentecost. A gold processional cross stood next to the pulpit, reflecting the midmorning sunlight. Emily sighed contentedly in the rich simplicity of the scene. "Praise the Almighty, my soul, adore Him!" the congregation sang. Emily joined her voice with those seated around her. "Bless, O my soul, His holy name. Alleluia, alleluia!"

‖‖‖‖‖‖‖‖‖‖‖‖‖‖‖‖‖‖‖‖‖‖‖‖‖‖‖‖‖‖‖‖‖

Pastor Fletcher, sitting behind the pulpit in the sanctuary, looked out over his flock and let the voices of his two hundred sheep wash over him. His heart swelled with gladness and joy. He knew that even when his hair turns white and his feet begin to shuffle, he would never grow tired of hearing God's people sing. He glanced up to the balcony where Evan was working every limb of his body to support the voices below. First Evan, and now Emily Duke. He did not know why God in His wisdom had decided to bless this humble parish with two such musical treasures, but neither did he question it. He simply rose to his feet on the final stanza of the hymn and, along with the rest of the congregation, opened his mouth in thankfulness to sing:

> *Praise, all you people, the name so holy*
> *Of Him who does such wondrous things!*
> *All that has being, to praise Him solely,*
> *With happy heart its amen sings.*
> *Children of God, with angel host*
> *Praise Father, Son, and Holy Ghost!*
> *Alleluia, alleluia!*

The Word of God was preached in its truth and purity that morning, the body and blood of Christ was rightly administered, and all God's people sang, "Amen." As soon as the first notes of the postlude rang out in the church, young and old spilled out of their pews to make their exodus to the land of coffee and muffins before the Sunday School hour.

Just seven years earlier, Zion Lutheran Church had served donuts in the parish hall after the worship service and before Sunday School, but that was before Miss Geraldine Turner had stood before the church elders and accused, "Casey's donuts are a waste of our money. The Ladies Aid can bake muffins each week for the Sunday School hour. Muffins are more healthful, practical, economical, and they taste better."

Karl Rincker, the head elder at the time, had been pretty sure that Casey's blueberry cake donut looked and tasted better than any old muffin he had ever eaten, but who was he to argue with Miss Turner? She knew more words than he did. As a matter of fact, Karl and every other man in the congregation had learned early on never to contradict the women of the Ladies Aid Society when it came to the subjects of food service, kitchen organization, coffee creamer brands, liquid soap scents, altar flower arrangements, Christmas wreath placements, Bible study topics, and, well, anything and everything else.

〰〰〰〰〰〰〰〰〰〰〰〰〰〰〰〰

Emily lingered in her pew for a minute after the service, watching as Pastor Fletcher greeted each parishioner at the door to the narthex. She was standing close enough to the back of the nave to hear every exchange. She watched as the two oldest grandsons of Alice Gardner ran up to Pastor Fletcher and quickly shook his hand before scooting off in the direction of the parish hall. The youngest grandson, solemn and sober as any statesman, stood directly before Pastor Fletcher and patiently waited his turn. Pastor, just as serious, knelt down to the boy's level to hear his confession.

"I ate toast with strawberry jam this morning," Emily heard the boy say, "and I had orange juice. Mommy ran out of apple juice."

Pastor nodded his head with the propriety and authority of any judge. "No eggs, Frankie?"

"She didn't have time. Alison had an accident on the bathroom floor and made us late."

Emily watched as the rightly accused Alison pulled on Pastor's stole, smiling up at him with adoring blue eyes. She twirled her left pigtail between her fingers and held up her right arm beseechingly. Pastor was careful to shake Frankie's hand before standing and lifting Alison into his arms. The two kindred spirits touched noses in silent communion before turning to greet the rest of the parishioners together.

Emily felt a hand on her arm.

"I am so glad you could come today, dear," Alice Gardner welcomed her. "You must have started driving before the sun rose to make it to Bradbury in time for church this morning. I imagine you are exhausted."

Emily smiled down at the slight woman. "Good morning, Mrs. Gardner."

"Please, dear, call me Alice." The elderly woman fumbled around in her purse and pulled out a key tied to a silky, red ribbon. "Here, I thought you might want this. It's a key to the Mulberry property. I had it made the very afternoon you looked at the house."

"Thank you." Emily took the key and cradled it in her hand. The ribbon was sweet and delicate, just like her new landlady. "It's generous of you to let me move in this week on such short notice."

"That old house has been waiting for more than five months to meet you. There's no sense in keeping the two of you apart any longer. Besides, I imagine you are eager to get settled before the college opens up for classes in August."

Emily heard Alison's tinkly laughter echo across the pews. Irv Davis was tickling the little girl's pink cheek while Pastor listened politely to an animated Beverly. Emily turned back toward Alice when the older woman chuckled softly. "That baby girl fell in love with Pastor Fletcher at the baptismal font, you know. I've never seen anything like it. She cried and cried in her mother's arms the entire morning of her Baptism and stopped only when Pastor held her. She started crying again the moment he handed her back to Rebecca. Alison's first word was 'pastor,' would you believe it?"

Emily watched as Alison squeezed Pastor's face between her two, small hands.

"Now, tell me, dear," Alice was saying, "what are your plans for dinner?"

Emily turned to face her and started to answer, but Alice didn't wait. "I insist that you come to my house. I am making Italian pot roast, and my Rebecca is bringing a peach pie."

"Oh, well, I probably need to head back—"

"You'll need to eat first, though, won't you?" Alice persisted. "Don't tell me you would rather eat fast food over my pot roast."

Emily was outdone. "No," she smiled. "Of course I wouldn't."

"It's settled," Alice confirmed with a glint in her eye. "I may be small, but I am bossy. Come with me to Sunday School, and then you can follow me back to my house afterward for a good feeding before you hit the long road home."

"Pastor Fletcher asked me to meet with him for a few minutes after the service. I think he wants to introduce me to the organist." Emily hesitated when she saw Alice's sweet face blanch for a split second before returning to its normal pleasantness.

"Oh, of course, dear," Alice said. "I tell you what, I'll start making my way to the parish hall while you meet with Pastor and Evan. Truth be told, even with my head start, you still might make it there before this old tortoise."

"I doubt that," Emily laughed. "How about you save me a seat?"

"It's a deal." Alice patted Emily's arm, her face growing suddenly serious. "Now, don't you let that Evan Ebner sour things for you. He is an old badger, for sure, but it's not really his fault."

With that, Alice turned around and made for Pastor Fletcher, luring the bouncing pigtails away with promises of a cinnamon crunch muffin top. Emily stood in the wake of Alice's departing comment, not quite sure what to make of it.

‖‖‖‖‖‖‖‖‖‖‖‖‖‖‖‖‖‖‖‖‖‖‖‖‖‖‖‖‖‖‖‖‖‖‖‖‖

As soon as the last parishioner exited the nave, Pastor Fletcher's bright eyes quickly found those of Zion's new choir director. He came to her in the pew. "I hope your drive this morning was uneventful," he said.

"Sunshine and clear roads the whole way."

"Good, good." He glanced up over his shoulder at the balcony, then turned back to Emily. "I have about ten minutes before I need to teach Bible study. Would you mind accompanying me upstairs? I'd like to introduce you to Evan."

"Of course," Emily said. She moved as if to step out of the pew, but Pastor Fletcher's feet stayed rooted to the spot, inadvertently blocking her exit. He was staring at the floor, distracted, his brow furrowed.

"Um," he stalled, lowering his voice. "I feel a need to tell you that Evan has served this church as organist for the past twenty-five years."

Emily nodded.

"He also has served as interim choir director off and on whenever we have been . . . without a director."

Emily nodded again, waiting.

"He'll be serving as your accompanist at choir rehearsals and on Sunday mornings."

"That'll be wonderful," Emily replied. "He's an excellent organist."

"Yes. Well." He cleared his throat and looked at Emily pointedly. He wanted to say more, but some things are better left unsaid. "I hope you two will enjoy each other's musical company."

"I hope so too," Emily said cheerfully and followed him up the narrow north staircase to the balcony.

At the top of the stairs, a small, elderly man was seated and bent over his feet. He was tying the laces of his street shoes. A worn pair of organ shoes sat neatly beside him on the floor. When he sat up, he glanced first at Pastor Fletcher and then settled his cold gaze on Emily. Pastor thought he saw Emily shiver.

"Evan, thank you for the fine music this morning," he spoke sincerely. "I'll never get tired of singing stanza five of 'Praise the Almighty' as long as you're playing it."

"The Principal stop is still giving me trouble. I'm going to need to work on it again this week."

"I hope you'll call Irv to help you this time, Evan."

Evan picked up his organ shoes and walked over to a filing cabinet sitting against the north wall. He took a key from his pocket to unlock it and then put the shoes in the top drawer. He didn't bother turning around when he spoke. "Irv doesn't know what he's doing."

"But at least he can assist you," Pastor said firmly. "You can show him what to do."

Evan walked over to the organ console and picked up the neat stack of music sitting on the bench. He turned his back on Pastor and Emily again, walking over to the cabinet and silently filing the music.

Pastor Fletcher cleared his throat. "Evan, I'd like you to meet Dr. Emily Duke. She's going to be the new music history professor over at Bradbury College. At my recommendation, the council has offered her the position of choir director here at Zion."

"A pleasure," Evan replied flatly, not bothering to turn around.

Pastor Fletcher kept his voice steady, but he felt his cheeks begin to burn a bright, crimson red. He turned to Emily and smiled politely as if this were a typical introduction. "Dr. Duke, this is Evan Ebner. He has been the faithful organist of our church for the past twenty-five years. You will not find a finer musician in all of the state of Illinois."

Emily appeared uncertain as to where to look. She settled her wide-eyed gaze on Evan's back. "I am pleased to meet you, Mr. Ebner. Your prelude arrangement this morning was beautiful. I'm looking forward to working together."

Evan continued to file his music.

Pastor Fletcher's mouth pinched into a straight line. "If you have any questions for Dr. Duke, now would be a good time, Evan."

Evan's voice echoed dully off the wall. "She is already hired. What good will it do for me to ask her any questions now?"

Pastor Fletcher clenched and unclenched his hands. "Well, then, we will leave you to your filing." He turned abruptly toward the staircase, eyes ablaze. He gestured what he hoped was a polite invitation for Emily to walk in front of him.

Emily, obliging, stepped forward and reached out a shaky hand to steady herself on the staircase railing. She willed her face to remain calm, but fear was pressing against her insides like a pestle to a mortar. What in the world had she gotten herself into?

CHAPTER THREE:

A MATCH MADE IN BRADBURY

⸺⸺⸺⸺⸺⸺⸺⸺⸺⸺⸺⸺

Alice merrily poured steaming coffee into her late mother's bluebonnet china teacups. "I know you take cream, Pastor, but how do you like your coffee, Dr. Duke?"

"Just cream, please."

Alice smiled to herself. She was quite pleased with the way dinner had gone. The roast had been tender to perfection, Rebecca's peach pie had flaked in all the right places, and the boys had behaved beautifully. Well, except for the minor incident involving Alison's right pigtail and Robbie's dinner fork, but really, no one could blame the child for being left-handed. Alice had even managed to successfully invite Pastor Fletcher over for dinner after Sunday School without anyone suspecting her of a premeditated plan.

Alice did not consider herself to be a yenta, but meeting Emily Duke had brought out the matchmaker in the elderly woman. It was obvious to her that Pastor Fletcher and Emily were made for each other, and she was resolved to help point cupid in the right direction. The children were now playing happily in the backyard, Rebecca and Jeremy were washing dishes in the kitchen, and Alice, Pastor, and Emily sat nurturing their coffee in the sunroom.

"Pastor Fletcher was an English teacher before he went to seminary," Alice said. She thought it was as good a place as any to start this kind of conversation.

"Secondary English Lit," Pastor amended.

Emily smiled amicably, though Alice detected something in her manner that was quiet and removed. She tried another avenue. "You have a short volume of poetry in publication, don't you, Pastor?"

Pastor's ears turned red. "Yes, though it's very short."

"My husband always wanted to publish something, but he never seemed to be able to find time to finish what he started." Alice was all charm and hospitality.

"Parish life will do that to you," Pastor smiled. "All of your words quickly get spent in the pulpit."

"Do you like to write, Dr. Duke?" Alice gave a sweet smile of encouragement.

"I do like to write music," Emily admitted.

"Ah, what a talent!" Alice crooned. "I think it must be glorious to hear notes in your head and then be able to turn them into song."

Her guest did not take the bait. Emily kept her eyes lowered and held her coffee cup between both hands. Alice was not to be easily discouraged, however. Love was going to bloom in her sunroom that day even if she had to dig deep into the ground and loosen the soil herself. "Tell me, Dr. Duke, how did you come to study music?"

Emily's careful brown eyes met Alice's expectant green ones. "Music just seemed like the natural thing for me to do." Alice studied the young lady sitting primly in the chintz-covered occasional chair, from the way she crossed her ankles to the way she tucked a lock of hair behind her ear.

"Did you ever want to study anything else?" Pastor asked.

Emily shook her head, showing great interest in the bluebonnets on the side of her cup.

"I wanted to be a dancer when I was young," Alice sang, "but I was never very good at it."

"I wanted to be an astronaut, but the whole car-sickness thing kept me from rocket science," Pastor laughed.

"Pastor Fletcher is a musician too."

"Oh, now, musician is a strong word, Alice," Pastor corrected, "especially in present company."

"I thought you studied music when you were growing up."

"I took piano lessons for a few years but only long enough to make me dangerous."

"Well, I think it is remarkable how much you two young people have in common."

Pastor coughed into his hand. Emily continued to stare determinedly at her bluebonnets. Alice couldn't help but notice that the young woman's cheeks had turned from a lovely pink to a deeper shade of rose. This was obviously going to be more difficult than she had originally thought.

"Do you play an instrument, dear?"

Emily sipped her coffee, looking to Alice like a giant refugee ineffectively hiding behind that tiny, delicate cup. "I mostly studied voice and choral music in school. By default I play a little piano."

"I do admire singers. I have never been able to carry a tune, but my David could fill the rafters with his baritone." Alice leaned forward. "He sang to me the night he proposed, you know."

"Did he?" Pastor's eyes crinkled with delight. "Alice, I never knew that. What did he sing?"

"Oh, it is an old song. I doubt either of you two will know it."

"Alice, I spend most of my days reading texts from the first century, and Dr. Duke has a degree in music history. If there is anything we know between us, it is old."

A dimple escaped onto Emily's right cheek, and even Alice's old eyes could see that Pastor's smile widened at the sight. That was all the encouragement Alice needed.

"Well, I lived in Quincy with my parents after college," she said, "and I was in charge of serving meals to the guests who stayed at our family's inn. David was serving Our Savior Lutheran Church as pastor at the time, and he used to drop by every Monday night to help me dry the supper dishes. We usually ended up sitting out under the old willow tree on my parents' front lawn to watch the dusk settle into the riverbed below. David liked to smoke his pipe to keep the mosquitoes away. You know, I still picture hazy, lavender summer nights whenever I smell pipe smoke." Alice felt her cheeks grow warm at the memory.

"One night during the summer of '66, we sat under our willow tree, as usual, and David reached into his pocket. Only, instead of pulling out his pipe, he pulled out the ring his father had given to his mother on their wedding day." Alice absently fingered the pearl on her left hand. "He asked if he could see me wear it always, and then he sang to me." Alice's eyes grew misty with the memory of a favorite baritone. "He sang 'I Can Give You the Starlight.'"

"Oh, that's a beautiful song," Emily murmured.

Alice looked at her in surprise. "You know it?"

Emily smiled back at her. "I once wrote a paper on Ivor Novello's music. 'Starlight' is one of my favorites."

"Dad sang that song to Mother on every anniversary, didn't he, Mother?" Rebecca had been leaning against the doorway of the sunroom for the last half of the story. She walked over and kissed her mother on the head. Alice smiled up at her only daughter, who favored her so much in form, posture, and expression.

"Jeremy and I just finished the dishes," Rebecca said. "I put the china back in the hutch, but I left the silver out to dry some more. I'll come back tomorrow to help you polish it."

"Oh, thank you, Rebecca," Alice squeezed her daughter's hand. "You're not leaving, are you?"

"We need to take the kids home. Alison needs a nap like there's no tomorrow."

"Well," Alice set down her coffee cup, "the peach pie was divine, dear. I don't know how you make pastry that flakes, because you sure didn't learn it from me." Alice held her daughter's face between both of her hands and kissed her forehead.

Rebecca turned toward Emily. "I canned some peaches for your pantry. If it's all right with you, I'll drop by this week after you've moved in and deliver them in person."

Both of Emily's dimples jumped at the thought. "That is so nice. Thank you."

"It's selfish, really. You're the first woman my age to move into this town in years, and I'm determined to be best friends." Rebecca grinned at Emily and turned toward Pastor Fletcher.

"Pastor, please forgive me for not bringing Alison in to say good-bye, but Jeremy is already loading her and the boys into the car. I'm certain the world will end in a deafening scream if we try to tear her away from you this late in the afternoon."

Pastor smiled. "Understood. The pie was delicious, Rebecca."

"I wrapped the leftover two pieces for you and set them on the kitchen counter. Be sure to take them home with you when you leave."

Alice caught her daughter's hand. "Don't I get to kiss the children good-bye?"

"Robbie's pants were dripping with some mysterious, brown liquid from the backyard, and I'm not about to get it all over your clean carpets. We'll pop by tomorrow for kisses on our way to VBS." Rebecca kissed her mother one more time and waved herself out the door.

"Now, don't you two think of leaving me so soon." Alice happily passed around a plate of homemade mints. "Tell me, Dr. Duke, do you sing professionally?"

"Not anymore."

"You used to sing for a Bach society, right?" Pastor asked, popping a mint into his mouth. "If I remember correctly from your résumé, you sang a little jazz too."

Emily's posture stiffened and she quickly returned her eyes to her coffee cup. "Yes, I did."

Alice watched as Pastor studied Emily's face. She was too wise in her old age not to be aware of the careful distance the young choir director was maintaining in the conversation. Pastor, too, appeared to be sensitive to Dr. Duke's personal boundaries, but Alice detected a quiet struggle in the man's eyes. It was subtle, but it was there, like the internal flashing of opposing swords in a valiant fight between his pastoral instincts and his masculine bravado.

She couldn't help but feel a bit sorry for the young man. Zion was his first call directly out of seminary, and no woman within ten years of his own age—at least no woman worthy of his character and virtue, in Alice's opinion—had moved into Bradbury in the four years that he had occupied the parsonage.

Well, there was Shasta Kull, Don and Lois's eldest niece, but she didn't count. A two-time divorcée with a degree from the Center for the Sacred Feminine did not, Alice was certain, a proper pastor's wife make.

The Ladies Aid Society had certainly done their best to secure a mate for their pastor during the first year of his tenure. Friday night after Friday night, they had flooded his calendar with dinner invitations and social engagements, making sure single daughters, prized granddaughters, and favorite nieces were on hand to help pour the coffee during dessert. When that didn't produce a satisfactory marriage, one particular member of the Ladies Aid offered up herself for proper consideration. Alice remembered with chagrin that awkward Maundy Thursday when Miss Geraldine Turner showed up to prepare the communion bread and wine wearing a low-cut, yellow dress and enough white gardenia perfume to anoint the entire congregation. It was obvious the woman was making herself available to more than just the altar guild that night.

Alice was certain the whole, tasteless ordeal must have been a special kind of torture for Pastor Fletcher, but he graciously and patiently bore with everyone's well-intentioned, if inappropriate, interventions. Thankfully, the interest of the Ladies Aid Society slowly wore off with time, and everyone in the congregation had since grown into a comfortable acceptance of their pastor's bachelorhood. Alice, herself, had been careful to avoid such base scheming and plotting in the beginning, but the second Emily Duke stepped onto the front porch of the Mulberry property, everything changed. This Lutheran choir director was the real deal, and Alice found that she, perhaps, was not too proud to meddle for the sake of the ministry after all. Besides, if anyone knew anything about the benefits marriage could bring to a man of the cloth, it was she.

"Can I warm your coffee, Pastor?" Alice reached for the silver urn.

Pastor paused, indulging in one more look at Emily's closed face before carefully setting down his cup and saucer on the table. "Thank you, Alice, but I really must get back to the church."

"On a Sunday afternoon?"

"Oscar and Helen will be expecting me to come by with the Lord's Supper yet today, and I really want to visit Chuck at the hospital before it gets dark tonight." Pastor stood and walked over to Alice. He fondly kissed the top of her white head. "Thank you for such a delicious meal. Your pot roast never disappoints. Now, don't get up. I can easily show myself out."

Pastor turned to Emily, whose face had relaxed considerably at the mention of his leaving. "We're so delighted to have you with us at Zion. I hope you'll give me a call when you move into town. I'm good at lifting boxes."

Emily smiled at him with her eyes for the first time since leaving the parish hall. "How are you at lifting pianos?"

Pastor looked her directly in the eye. "Try me."

"Don't forget the pie on the counter," Alice reminded him.

"I won't. It has been a pleasure, ladies." With that, Pastor Fletcher disappeared through the sunroom door.

Alice pursed her lips. "You need to go too, don't you, dear?"

Emily placed her cup and saucer on the tray and smiled apologetically. "It is a long drive back to St. Louis."

"Well, Dr. Duke—"

"Please, call me Emily."

Alice clapped her hands together. "I'm pleased to do so! You know, I named my doll Emily when I was a child. It was my favorite name, second only to Rebecca, of course."

Emily stood to help her hostess out of her chair. Alice's hands were thin and fragile but warm. Emily carried the coffee tray into the kitchen, and Alice followed close behind with the plate of mints.

"You're such a dear, Emily. I do hope you and Rebecca will be good friends." Alice put the creamer in the refrigerator. "My daughter will never admit it to me, but she's been lonely for a friend ever since she and Jeremy moved back to Bradbury. God bless them, they relocated here from Chicago six years ago when David was diagnosed with colon cancer. They're both city folk at heart, but they pretend to be happy here. They do it for me. Now, where did I set your purse?"

Emily followed Alice through a narrow hallway lined with framed photographs. A small, gilded frame hanging next to an oval mirror caught Emily's eye. A young woman stood in the picture wearing a smart orange suit and holding a little bouquet of flowers. A man almost twice her size had both of his arms wrapped around her waist, and the two appeared to be laughing at a shared joke.

"That's me with my David on our wedding day." Alice stood at Emily's elbow. "My sister took that picture just before we hopped on a train for our honeymoon in the Ozarks. My mother made that suit herself. She wanted it to be pink, but I insisted it be orange. That was David's favorite color. He always joked that it was a shame the church never made more use of orange in the liturgical year."

"You must miss him so much." Emily's voice sounded very small and far away.

Alice glanced over at her, caught off guard by the shadow that had passed over the young woman's face. Something in Emily's eyes reminded Alice of a wounded bird. "Yes, I do. Life definitely lost some of its luster the day David died, but our hope has never been of this world, has it? Ah, there it is!"

Alice walked over to a small table sitting next to the front door. She picked up Emily's purse and, handing it to her, chose her next words very carefully. "Our Pastor Fletcher is a fine man, don't you think?"

Emily's face was a mighty fortress.

"Emily, dear, I hope I didn't make you uncomfortable by asking him over for dinner today. I just thought you might appreciate the chance to get to know him better, since you will be working together."

"Yes, of course," Emily murmured, looking down, fishing in her purse for her keys. "Well, I'd better be going. Thank you again for lunch. It was delicious."

Alice took hold of Emily's arms, grounding her to the spot. She looked Emily in the eye and smiled with all the kindness her age and experience could offer. "You are most welcome. I do hope it will be the first of many meals shared together. We know where to find each other now."

Emily's eyes softened and her face relaxed into a grateful smile. "Thank you for providing a home for me here in Bradbury, Alice."

"Oh, now, dear, I can't take credit for that. God provided you a home. I'm just His delivery girl." Alice squeezed Emily's hands. "Will you call me when it's time to unpack your kitchen? I may look old and rickety, but I'm perfectly capable of washing and drying your dishes as you unpack them."

"I'd like that."

Alice stood at the door, waving as Emily drove away. She liked this young woman with her serious eyes and warm smile. Most of all, though, Alice liked the way Pastor Fletcher lit up at the sight of her. Emily Duke may have built up walls around herself that were thicker than those of Jericho, but Alice knew what a little faith, marching, and trumpet blowing could do. "And the walls came tumbling down," she sang as she shut the door.

Chapter Four:

Home Is Where the Canned Peaches Are

〰〰〰〰〰〰〰〰〰〰〰〰〰〰〰

Mulberry Avenue bustled with the sights, sounds, and smells of a late June morning. Fat bumble bees lumbered clumsily from one clover patch to the next, and hummingbirds hovered near fences heavy with honeysuckle and trumpet vine. Blue jays and starlings sparred for a chance at Doris Findley's red feeder, and young Ben Schmidt could be seen further down the street mowing Mr. Dunbar's lawn. The sharp smell of fresh cut grass mixed with the sun-warmed musk of marigolds, and an occasional southwesterly breeze carried with it the vinegary scent of Cassidy Blewitt's cloth diapers drying on the line. A window was open in the front office of Zion Lutheran Church, and Mrs. Scheinberg could hear the cheers and shouts of happy children playing on the north lawn.

"Can I have some of that?"

Mrs. Scheinberg looked up from her bowl full of homemade cinnamon applesauce and stared into the wide eyes of Robbie Jones. "Mrs. Davis told you to wait in your chair," she warned. "There's no talking in time out."

Robbie slumped back over to the three chairs lining the wall and threw himself into the middle one. He pouted as he dug his hands into his pockets in defeat. Mrs. Scheinberg felt somewhat like pouting too. Vacation Bible School was not even half over, and already her office had served as a jail cell for more than six children.

The front door swung open, and Beverly Davis entered with a brown-eyed, brown-braided girl in tow. The front of the girl's pink T-shirt was stained green with grass. Beverly's own shirt was dotted with sweat spots around her middle, and her short, curly hair was plastered in gray ringlets to her damp forehead. Mrs. Scheinberg silently conceded the fact that, as trying as it might be to serve as warden of the office jail, at least she was out of the sun.

Beverly dabbed at her face with a blue bandana from her back pocket before turning to the freckled prisoner. "Robbie, do you have anything you want to say to Katelyn?"

"No."

Beverly's face was a tomb. "Then you can wait in here until you're ready to apologize."

"But I didn't do anything!"

"You tackled Katelyn on the field."

"That's because she was rounding first base!"

"You're not supposed to tackle anyone in kickball, Robbie."

"Well, that's how we play it at home with my dad." Robbie crossed his arms and furrowed his brow.

Beverly was unmoved. "As soon as you're ready to apologize to Katelyn, you may join us outside. Otherwise, you'll have to wait in here with Mrs. Scheinberg for the rest of playtime."

Mrs. Scheinberg did not appreciate being dragged into the situation.

"It's your choice, Robbie." Beverly waited one more moment before taking Katelyn's hand and heading back outside. Just before the door closed, Katelyn turned toward Robbie with a grin and stuck her tongue out at him behind Beverly's back.

Wretched, little girl, Mrs. Scheinberg thought as the door swung shut. She looked at Robbie's clouded face and softened a little toward the boy. She knew he had only been trying to play kickball the way he had learned it at home. How could anyone be expected to know all the variations of the rules that floated around the neighborhood these days? Besides, who was Beverly to think she could just drop a kid off in the office to be watched whenever she felt like it?

Mrs. Scheinberg dug around in the bottom drawer of her desk for another plastic spoon. Then, pushing back her chair and hoisting herself up, she walked over to Robbie with her bowl of applesauce extended as a peace offering.

"Here," she said, her face expressionless but her eyes dancing behind her gold-rimmed glasses. Beverly was not the queen of this castle. She was.

Robbie hesitated for one short moment before grabbing the bowl and spoon from her hands and shoveling applesauce into his mouth. A small, victorious smile played upon her lips as she walked back to her chair.

"This is good," Robbie said, his cheeks bulging and his chin slimy. "Didja make it?"

"Yes, I did."

"Well, it tastes like apple pie, only sloppier." Robbie scraped the bottom of the bowl. "What d'you call it?"

"Haven't you ever had cinnamon applesauce before?"

Robbie stopped midspoonful.

"What's the matter?" Mrs. Scheinberg asked.

Robbie stared at the dripping spoon for a moment before shrugging his shoulders and resuming his frantic shoveling. He swallowed. "Applesauce makes me poop. The runny kind. Mom told me never to eat it."

Robbie licked a few dribbles from the rim of the bowl before jumping up and returning it and the spoon to Mrs. Scheinberg's desk. He was grinning from ear to ear. "I'm ready to 'pologize now." He ran to the door and looked over his shoulder. "Don't you worry, Mrs. Shinebug. I won't tell no one 'bout the applesauce. I'll just be real quiet when it hits." With that, he ran out the door.

Mrs. Scheinberg was stunned into silence. She looked at the empty bowl on her desk, afraid to touch it. Should she tell Beverly? Should she call the boy's mother? How would she possibly explain to them what had just happened? *No*, Arlene thought. *Better just leave well enough alone.* She sat at her desk for a long moment before her shoulders began to shake. Then, her belly. She held her hand tightly over her mouth, trying to hold back the laughter, but that only made things worse. With a giant wave of spluttering and coughing, she doubled over and let out hyena-like shrieks.

Pastor Fletcher, hearing the distinct sounds of distress, ran out of his study. "Mrs. Scheinberg! Are you okay?"

Mrs. Scheinberg waved her hands at him, but she couldn't get any words out of her mouth. It seemed all she could manage was to gasp in air between howling fits. Her face was turning alarming shades of red and purple and appeared splotchy and strained.

"Do you . . . need anything?" Pastor stuttered. He had never seen his secretary in such a state before. Should he call for help?

Mrs. Scheinberg pointed at the empty bowl on her desk and then waved her arm at the open window, only to dissolve into another shrieking fit. "Robbie . . . applesauce . . . Beverly!" She gasped between each word and then doubled over again.

It wasn't until he saw her shoulders were shaking that Pastor finally realized Mrs. Scheinberg was laughing. He sighed with relief and ran his hand through his hair, the corners of his mouth twitching involuntarily. "Let me at least get you a glass of water." When he returned a few moments later, he found Mrs. Scheinberg fully recovered, but a little red faced and watery eyed.

"Thank you," she said stoically, taking a sip from the glass of water. She looked as if she was trying to pretend nothing had happened.

Cheers and hollers could be heard from outside. Pastor ambled over to the window. "It looks like Robbie just slid into home plate."

Mrs. Scheinberg spluttered into her glass, and Pastor turned just in time to see her spraying water all across her desk. He chuckled at the sight until one stern look from Mrs. Scheinberg communicated that he was not welcome to join her party. Pastor retreated to his study to work on his sermon, but throughout the next hour, he heard an occasional shriek being choked back from behind the front office desk. He nodded at the crucifix on his wall. "Still working miracles, I see."

⁙⁙⁙⁙⁙⁙⁙⁙⁙⁙⁙⁙⁙⁙⁙⁙⁙⁙⁙⁙⁙⁙⁙⁙⁙⁙⁙⁙⁙

Three houses down from the church and across the street, Emily Duke sat on the front step of 919 Mulberry Avenue. The movers had just finished closing up their empty trailer and were pulling out of the driveway. It had been a long morning of lifting and directing foot traffic, and Emily had no immediate desire to stand and go back inside. She pulled a dusty, red bandana from her hair and absently fluffed the curls that were matted to the top of her head. The front step felt cool under her legs, a warm breeze was rustling the leaves above her head, and a nearby cardinal was singing a song just for her. Emily contentedly rested her chin on her hands and let the gentle stirrings of hope and promise that often accompany new chapters in life well up in her heart.

This was her new home. This was her new town. This was her new street, and just across the way, she could see her new church. Emily squinted and noticed for the first time that morning the children playing on the lawn at Zion. She smiled at the sight of a couple of familiar redheads.

"His mercies never come to an end," she murmured. "They are new every morning."

Emily's eyes roamed around her new front yard, drinking in every little detail. Two large trees stood guard over the lawn. One was a giant, silver maple with long, supple branches that swayed from side to side in the summer breeze. It reminded Emily of a tall cheerleader with skinny arms waving pompoms of green, silver-backed leaves in the air. The second tree was a sweet gum, bright and stout. It was not as tall as the maple, but its leaves were greener and its branches were more resistant to the wind. *Sturdy and dependable*, Emily thought. She took mental note of the clusters of sweet gum balls dangling under the leaves. Those prickly pests would keep her and her trusty rake busy come next spring.

The walkway to the house was aged and cracked, but it was friendly. The mosaic of broken concrete pieces outlined with thin swatches of renegade grass reminded Emily of a stained glass window. The path meandered from the driveway to the front porch in a charming fashion, steering clear of two overgrown barberry bushes that bordered the front porch and ended near a robust azalea bush just to the west of the front steps. Emily was delighted by the azalea. She wondered what color it would bloom in the spring. It was too late in the summer to know for sure, but she was certain the delicious anticipation of its April blooms would taste sweet all winter long.

The Mulberry property itself was a small, red-brick bungalow with two big picture windows flanking the front door. A large, inviting porch spanned the entire width of the front of the house, and a wooden porch swing hung from its rafters. Emily had known from the first moment she had laid eyes on the porch swing that this house would be her home. It was just one glass of lemonade short of being perfect.

The sound of a large SUV pulling into the driveway tugged Emily from her reverie. She watched as Rebecca Jones climbed out from behind the wheel and lifted a large, cardboard box from the passenger side of the vehicle. Tucking the box under her chin, Rebecca kicked the door shut with her foot.

"Hello!" Rebecca called merrily to Emily. "I've brought you some summer rations."

Emily smiled and stood, dusting off the bottom of her shorts. She stuffed the red bandana in her back pocket. "Here, let me get the door for you."

Rebecca followed through the doorway and made a beeline through the front living room and side dining room, straight to the kitchen. Setting the box on the counter, she turned to Emily and gave her a big hug. "Welcome home!"

Home. Emily felt like laughing and crying at the same time.

"Overwhelming, isn't it? I remember when Jeremy and I packed up our house in Chicago and moved to Bradbury." Rebecca used her hands to animate every word as she talked. "It was all so new, and I already felt so tired from all of the sorting and packing and cleaning before the move. I carried the last box from the moving truck myself and proceeded to sit right down in the middle of the living room floor and cry. I'm pretty sure

I cried for a good fifteen minutes straight. How're you holding up?"

Something about Rebecca's candor made Emily forget about her own shyness. "Tired. But happy. I'm just so excited to finally be here and to have it feel so . . . good and right."

"Do you think you'll mind living in a small town?"

Emily shook her head. "No, I don't think I'll mind at all. I could actually hear the wind in the trees outside this morning. I don't know how long it's been since I've heard something outside other than a revving motor or a honking horn or a siren."

"So true! My mother is convinced that I'm unhappy living in Bradbury, but honestly, I wouldn't trade these quiet streets for all of the deep dish pizza in Chicago."

Emily smiled. She looked at the tiny fireball of a woman standing in her kitchen, and she was certain she was looking at a friend. Rebecca stood no taller than Emily herself, but her slight frame reverberated with a vim and vigor that were larger than life. Even Rebecca's blue eyes seemed plugged into some internal outlet. Emily couldn't help but be cheered by the glow. Words began to fall more freely from her mouth than her natural reserve usually allowed. "Moving has always made me feel unsettled, but I've been anticipating this move for a long time. Finally being here actually makes me feel relieved."

Rebecca nodded her head up and down, her strawberry-blonde ponytail swinging from the back of her Chicago Cub's hat as if powered by an invisible current. "I know just what you mean. It's like you can now move on from moving on."

Emily smiled. That was exactly what it felt like. "Can you stay for a little while? I can make you a cup of tea. That is, if I can find my pot."

"I'd love one, but," Rebecca was already moving toward the front door, "I actually have to scoot. Bev Davis called me from the church office a few minutes ago. Apparently, Robbie's stomach is upset, and I need to pick him up early from VBS. He probably ate too many cookies again." Rebecca stopped with her hand on the screen door latch. "Can I take a rain check?"

"Of course."

"Good. Now, be sure to open a jar of the cherry preserves as soon as I leave," Rebecca said. "It's my favorite, and it'll taste so good on the bread my mother made you. Trust me. It'll do you good to eat." She stepped out onto the porch, calling over her shoulder as the screen door shut behind her, "And Jeremy and I want to have you over for dinner soon, so check your calendar once you find it. Don't work too hard today!"

With that, Rebecca was gone. Emily stood still for a moment, a bit mystified by the immediate silence, looking through the screen door as Rebecca backed her SUV out of the driveway. Then she smiled. She liked the way Rebecca was always moving.

Emily turned and looked around at the boxes waiting for her in the living room. Their varied stacks formed what looked like a miniature city skyline along the front windows. She knew she should start unpacking before it got too late in the day, but Emily's curiosity got the better of her. She turned back toward the kitchen and tossed her bandana on the counter.

Rebecca's box turned out to be full of goodies: a jar of cherry preserves, another jar labeled as peach jam, two quarts of green beans, a plastic container of rhubarb slush, and three quarts of the promised canned peaches. A folded piece of paper was taped to the plastic container: "Be sure to freeze the rhubarb slush, and don't forget to look in the pantry." Rebecca had signed her name with a smiley face next to it.

Emily walked over to the pantry door. It was one of those pocket doors that slid back into the door frame. Humidity had made the door swell shut, so she had to jostle it a bit with both hands to get it open. Once the door slid back into its pocket, Emily gasped in surprise. She had fully expected to find the pantry just as she had left it last week when first viewing the house: completely empty. However, five of the seven pantry shelves were now stacked full from wall to ledge. Flour, sugar, salt, baking soda, yeast, pancake batter, pasta, spices, rolled oats, potatoes, a couple bottles of homemade wine, a jar of clover honey, canned beets, canned green beans, jars of pickles, canned tomatoes and tomato sauce, a bottle of ketchup, a bag of coffee beans. And there was the loaf of Alice's homemade bread.

A notecard with Emily's name was leaning against the bread. Emily reached for the card and, through eyes blurry with tears, read:

Dear Dr. Duke,

Welcome home! We wanted to give you, our new choir director, a good, old Bradbury "pounding." Each of the women in our Ladies Aid Society contributed a pound of something from her own kitchen to yours.

We thank the Lord for bringing you into our church family, and we hope it is His will that you stay with us for a long time. We pray that your transition here will be an easy (and yummy) one. See you in church on Sunday!

Your sisters in Christ,

Zion Lutheran Church Ladies Aid Society

P.S. Be sure to check in the fridge and freezer.

Emily, already overwhelmed to the point of crumbling, opened the freezer door to find four pounds of pork steaks, one pound of bacon, and two freezer bags of homemade cookies. The refrigerator door turned out to be hiding a gallon of milk, a pound of butter, one dozen eggs, a carton of orange juice, and a drawer full of fresh garden produce. A magnet stuck to the side of the refrigerator held a twenty dollar bill and a sticky note with the words "for groceries" written across it.

"Oh my!" Emily covered her mouth with both hands, unable to process the tangible, edible love that was cooling in her refrigerator and freezer and sitting on her pantry shelves. So many anonymous hearts and hands had worked to fill her kitchen! Emily's heart felt like it was going to burst with gratitude.

Thanks to Rebecca, Emily knew just what to do. She sat right down in the middle of the kitchen floor and cried for a good fifteen minutes straight.

CHAPTER FIVE: ONE SUIT AND THREE SUITORS

‖‖‖‖‖‖‖‖‖‖‖‖‖‖‖‖‖‖‖‖‖‖‖‖‖‖‖‖‖‖‖‖‖‖‖‖‖

Emily parked her bike in front of a three-story, red brick building and began tethering its front wheel shaft to a nearby bike rack. The metal rack was already hot to touch from the direct, late-morning sun.

"I don't think you'll need that."

Emily squinted up into the face of a young man with long, dark hair. He was wearing black eyeliner and an eyebrow ring in the shape of a half moon. He gestured at the bike lock.

"I'm just saying, I don't think anyone will take it."

"Oh." Emily stood, but she did not remove the lock. Small town or no, this city girl was not in the habit of trusting the advice of strangers, especially ones who wore more makeup than she did. The young man waited awkwardly for a few moments before shrugging and walking into the building. Emily followed him, hoisting her backpack higher onto her shoulders and catching the glass door before it closed. A gust of cold air hit her face like a gale and cooled the sweat on her brow. She made a hard left turn at the first hallway and knocked on the first open door on the left.

"Dr. Duke, come in!" Dr. Lauren Basset stood up from behind her desk and vigorously shook Emily's hand before proffering a worn, brown leather chair to her newest faculty member.

Dr. Basset was a slight woman with spiky, blonde hair. Her black-rimmed glasses framed eyes that were as sharp as they were blue, and her gray fitted suit was topped with a bright yellow scarf. Two of her office walls were lined with shelves overflowing with books, music scores, files, recordings, and instrument cases. A large, framed poster of Luciano Berio hung directly behind her desk, an upright piano stood along the far wall of the office, and a lone music stand holding an open folio score stood in the corner. Dr. Basset waved her hands at the stacks of file folders presently littered across her workspace. "I always thought the words *summer* and *break* were meant to go together."

Emily laughed. She had been impressed with Dr. Basset back in March, upon her initial interview for the music history position at Bradbury College, and her good opinion of the music department head had only increased with each new encounter.

"So, tell me," Dr. Basset asked, "are you settled into your new place?"

Emily nodded. "Yes, I'm renting a little house on Mulberry Avenue."

"That's a nice, quiet street. Close too. Steve and I looked for a house on that side of town when we first moved here. How do you like your office?"

"Just fine. I moved my books in yesterday."

"Do you have enough shelf space?"

"Yes, I think so."

"Great." Dr. Basset leaned back in her chair. "I went ahead and ordered the Norton text you requested for the music literature class. Your suggestion to change the textbook was spot on. The Norton listening examples are much better."

"Thank you for doing that." Emily unzipped the front pocket of her backpack and withdrew a notebook and pen. "I don't mean to keep you, but I was wondering if you know yet what my teaching load will be for the fall."

Dr. Basset pulled a blue piece of photocopy paper out from under the folders and scanned the list of classes. "I'm not sure what your final schedule will be at this point, but it's looking like you'll have at least one session of music appreciation, maybe an entry-level music lit class, history I and III, and that vocal pedagogy course we talked about. Are you still up for it?"

"Yes, I am. I think it'll be a good fit."

"That's what I like to hear."

Emily scribbled some notes. "Is there anything else I need to have in line before classes start?"

"Well, I think the vocal ped text is in at the bookstore if you want to pick up a copy on your way out today. Just have them charge it to the music department."

"Okay," Emily nodded and wrote another note.

"And I would like to have a syllabus for each of your classes on file by the department meeting on August 9th. I'll also need to know by then what office hours you'll be keeping for the students this semester."

"Mmhm." More scribbling on paper.

"Oh, and you'll want to get a faculty ID card made over at the library," Dr. Basset advised. "You can do that today before you leave, if you want."

"Good idea. I'll take care of that right now, unless there's anything else." Emily started putting away her notebook and pen.

"Not that I can think of."

Emily stood, slung her pack over her shoulder, and smiled. "I'll let you get back to those relaxing, summer break activities."

Dr. Basset laughed, standing up. "Quite right! Dr. Duke, I'm thrilled to have you on our team."

"Please, call me Emily."

"And call me Lauren. Or Basset. I answer to both." Dr. Basset grinned. "Once we get this fall semester rolling, I'd like to have you over for dinner. We can debate whether Bach or Berio is better."

Emily laughed. "You know I'm Lutheran, right?"

"Well, then, I know which side you're on." Dr. Basset followed Emily out into the hall. "While we're looking ahead, I want you to think about something. The department will probably ask you to prepare a faculty recital for the spring, and I thought it might be fun to perform a recital of flute and vocal duets together. I've never explored that repertoire. Think about it, and let me know if you like the idea."

Emily nodded her agreement. "Okay. I'll think about that."

Dr. Basset continued, "Oh, and let me know if you need to see any past syllabi from the vocal ped class. I'm sure I can find that file on my desk somewhere. Just give me a couple of days' notice!"

Emily jaunted over to the bookstore to pick up the new vocal ped text before heading over to the library for her faculty ID. The campus of Bradbury College was small and intimate, a hodge-podge of red brick and sandstone buildings scattered across two small city blocks. The sight was more inviting than impressive. It took Emily no more than three minutes total to walk from one corner of the campus to the other, a fact for which she was thankful considering the intensity of the midday sun.

The Johnson-Kilmer Library was situated just east of Thomas Edison Bradbury Field, and the media section was located in the library's basement. The service line was already eight people deep when Emily got there, so she settled in at the back and began flipping through her new textbook.

"I wish I had thought of that," a deep voice rumbled from somewhere behind Emily's left ear.

Emily startled at the sound. She turned around to excuse herself, but all words left her brain at the sight of the tall man standing directly behind her.

"The book," the deep voice spoke again, nodding toward Emily's frozen hands. "Here I am in a library, and I never thought to bring a book to keep me company while standing in line."

Emily stared mutely up into the stranger's face, unable to pull her eyes from his hazel gaze. A lock of sandy, brown hair fell strikingly across the man's forehead, and the right corner of his mouth turned up in a confident smile. Emily was suddenly—and painfully—aware of the fact that she had neglected to put on mascara that morning.

The man bent down to inspect the cover of her book. "*The Diagnosis and Correction of Vocal Faults.* Hmm. I have to admit, I would have chosen something with a little more action and adventure."

Emily recovered her voice, although her cheeks remained a little too warm and, she knew, too pink for her own comfort. "It's for a vocal pedagogy class I'm teaching this fall."

"Aha! I had a hunch you might be the new music professor."

Emily felt at a complete disadvantage.

"I'm sorry, how unfair of me." The man extended his right hand. "Zachary Brandt. I teach British Lit and whatever else they throw my way here at BC."

Emily shook his extended hand. "Emily Duke."

"We all heard that Basset had hired a new instructor. Honestly, I've been looking forward to meeting you ever since I heard the news."

Emily willed herself to say something sensible. "Have you been teaching here long?"

"I was new last year," Zachary replied. "Fresh out of Cambridge."

"You don't sound British."

"I'm not. Just obsessed with their literature. My thesis was on Joseph Conrad."

"*Heart of Darkness*?"

Zachary's eyebrows shot up with what looked like delight. "You've read it?"

"I have."

"And?"

Emily felt her shoulders relaxing in the company of this affable man. "Very dark, but true. It reminded me of Golding's *Lord of the Flies*."

"Well, if I may be so bold, I'd venture to say it's more the other way around. Conrad came first, you know."

"That may be," she agreed, "but I read *Lord of the Flies* in high school. So as far as I'm concerned, Golding came first."

"I definitely can't refute the first impressions of high school. Now, how about you?" Zachary asked. "Where did you study?"

"Washington University. Music history."

"And your thesis?"

"The theology of J. S. Bach," she said.

"The theology? How does that fall under music history?"

"I looked into Bach's choices of texts for his funeral cantatas and tried to determine stylistic changes in his music in correlation with changes in his subject matter. That's the short of it, anyhow."

"Well," Zachary's eyes glinted, "I would ask you out for a cup of coffee, but I'm not sure what a British Lit nut and a Bach historian would ever find to talk about." Zachary looked directly into Emily's eyes, openly admiring the way her rosy complexion made her eyes shine. Emily averted her own eyes, wishing more than anything that she could keep her cheeks from flaring up every other minute. She hated that she was so easy to read. She held her breath, unsure of what to say or do.

"Can I help you, ma'am?"

Emily spun around, grateful it was her turn at the counter. She let out the breath she had been holding. "Yes. I'm here to get a faculty ID."

"Here, fill out this form," the student worker said. "When you're done, I'll take your picture."

Emily stepped aside to work on the form, acutely aware of Zachary's eyes on her profile the entire time.

"What can I do for you, Dr. Brandt?" the student worker asked.

"Hi, Jamie. There should be a recording on reserve with my name on it."

The student worker turned toward a table at the back of the room. She sorted through the various items with hot pink sticky notes on them and then held up a two-disk set. "John Eliot Gardiner's recording of Bach's Mass in B Minor?"

"That's the one," Zachary confirmed.

Emily's head snapped up. Zachary, who was obviously thoroughly enjoying himself, leaned over and murmured to her, "I guess we'd have something to talk about after all."

Emily's heart raced. She looked back at the form she was filling out and tried very hard to remember how to spell her name.

"So, how about that cup of coffee? There's a nice little shop on Main Street that has the best iced lattes. Perfect for a hot, summer day." His voice was close to her ear again.

She kept her eyes on the form. "I'm sorry. I need to head back home after this."

"It would be good to support our local businesses. And I know for a fact that your class load does not start for another month." Zachary was persistent, but Emily stayed her course. This was her first day on the job, and the only relationships she felt compelled to form with her colleagues were professional ones.

"I really do need to head home. There's a stack of choral octavos on my piano waiting for my attention."

"A choral gig? Here in town?"

"Zion Lutheran Church." The words were out of Emily's mouth before she could stop them. Why was she offering up details about her life to this stranger?

The right corner of Zachary's mouth turned up again. "Well, then, Emily Duke, I will leave you to your faculty ID." He waved his CD set in the air. "I'm off to contemplate changes in Bach's style of music in correlation with changes in his subject matter. I'll let you know what I find."

Emily could not help but smile at this, and Zachary, unbeknownst to the reserved music history professor, counted Emily's dimples as a sure sign of victory. He walked away, humming Bach's Gloria theme as he left.

Emily took a steadying breath and shook her head as if to clear it of any loose parts. Zachary Brandt was definitely a force—and a handsome force at that—to be reckoned with. She finished filling out her form and allowed the student worker to take her picture. Within minutes, she had her newly minted faculty ID card in hand.

<hr>

Emily tried very hard not to think about hazel eyes or deep voices on her bike ride home, but her mind kept stubbornly finding its way back to Bradbury College's lit department. It struck her that she didn't even know where the language arts building was on the campus. The driver of a black pickup truck honked in annoyance as it passed a little too close for comfort on Emily's left. She snapped herself out of her dream world, picked up her pace, and pedaled the remaining three blocks home.

Emily was surprised to find a boy sitting on her front step when she coasted her bike into her driveway. The boy was wearing a dirty John Deere T-shirt, jeans, and grass-stained tennis shoes. His blond hair was cropped short to his head, and his face and arms were golden brown. The boy stood as Emily rested her bike on its kickstand.

"Can I help you?" Emily asked, walking up the front path.

The boy tried to look Emily in the eye, but a stray curl hanging just above her left ear was the closest he could get.

"My name is Ben Schmidt, ma'am. I was wonderin' if I could mow your lawn for you?"

Emily was taken aback. In the lone week she had been here, she had never once given a thought to the fact that her lawn would eventually need to be mowed. As a matter of fact, she did not even own a lawn mower. She looked around the yard and noticed for the first time how shaggy the grass was. She looked back at the boy and guessed him to be around eleven or twelve years old. His clothes were dirty, but his body was clean. Instinct told her that his nerves, not his attitude, kept him from looking her in the eye.

"Well, Mr. Ben Schmidt, what's the going rate these days?"

"Ten dollars for a yard this small, ma'am."

Emily nodded. "Okay. Do you use your own equipment?"

"Yes, ma'am." Ben pointed to a bicycle parked across the street. A red wagon holding an old push mower, a string trimmer, a broom, and a gasoline can was hitched up to the back of the bicycle with some wire.

Emily suppressed a smile. "Could you wait here one moment, please?"

She quickly stole inside the house, dropping her backpack on the floor by the piano on her way to the kitchen. She grabbed the twenty-dollar bill that was still stuck to the side of the refrigerator. Stepping back outside, she found Ben patiently waiting right where she had left him.

"Ten dollars for every time you mow, did you say?"

Ben nodded.

Emily smiled and handed him the twenty. "Here's cash in advance for the first two weeks."

Ben stared at the twenty-dollar bill in his hands and grinned.

"Can you come every Tuesday?" she asked.

"Yes, ma'am!"

"What will you do when school starts?"

"I'll come here right after school, ma'am."

"When can you start?"

"How about right now?"

Emily watched as Ben unloaded his mower. It was scratched and rusty on the outside, but the motor started up just fine. Ben steadily and skillfully weaved the old mower back and forth across the lawn.

Something in Emily's gut told her this boy was trustworthy. His tan lines showed that she was not his only customer, and she liked the fact that he was invested enough in his lawn business to strap a mower to the back of his bike. It would be good to support an enterprising, hard-working boy. Besides, Emily did not know a thing about how to care for a lawn herself.

It took Ben only five minutes to mow the front yard, but Emily still took him a glass of cold lemonade for a break. He downed it in three gulps. When he finished the backyard and the trimming, Ben swept the driveway and front walkway with his broom. Emily watched from inside the house as he quietly loaded his equipment back on the red wagon and then looked over his shoulder at the house once more before jumping on his bike and pedaling away.

Emily, curious, stepped outside and walked around the yard to view Ben's work. The grass looked lush and green with its scraggly ends cut off to an even plane. Ben had been careful not to scar any of the trees or bushes with his blades, and the front walkway and driveway were cleaner than they had been before he mowed the lawn.

Emily hugged herself, satisfied. The sun was setting, casting long shadows across her new, cozy, green carpet of grass. The breeze in the tree branches made the shadows bend like beckoning fingers. Emily, sorely tempted, looked around to see if any of her neighbors were watching before kicking off her sandals with abandon and digging her toes into the cool, wet blades. She closed her eyes, taking in deep breaths of the warm, fragrant air. Yes, she could get used to this small town life.

When she opened her eyes, Emily noticed a lone flower resting on her front step. It was one of the tiger lilies from the ditch across the street. Ben must have picked it and left it for her to find. Sweet boy! Emily held the bloom carefully between her fingers, admiring how its orange, black-speckled petals glowed like embers in the early evening sunshine. It was an honest, sincere gesture on Ben's part, and Emily, who considered the matter thoroughly that night while playing through choral octavos at the piano, was certain that she much preferred a tiger lily from a hard-working boy over any iced latte the lit professor could produce.

What Emily did not know was that another gentleman in a clerical collar had happened to leave his office earlier that evening right at sunset, and, as was quickly becoming his custom, he stole a glance at the Mulberry property on his walk home. The sight of Emily standing on her freshly cut lawn made the man forget himself, and he stood rooted to the spot, admiring the way her slender frame and golden hair melted into the orange sunlight. He did not think to give her a flower that evening, nor did he think to stop and ask her out on a coffee date. His only thought as he turned to walk home alone was that, somehow, he wanted to give her the world.

Chapter Six:

Squirms, Scandals, and Schisms

"The Old Testament Reading for the Seventh Sunday after Pentecost is from Leviticus chapter 19." Pastor Fletcher read from the big Bible on the lectern, "'When you reap the harvest of your land, you shall not reap your field right up to its edge . . .'"

"When is the tablecloth on the altar going to change colors?" Robbie was careful to use his inside voice, though he did not quite achieve his whispering voice. "Green is getting old."

"Shh, dear," Alice quieted him. "The paraments will change when Reformation comes."

"You mean Halloween?" Robbie felt his mother's hand reach over Davie's shoulder to rest on his own—a subtle warning. Robbie squirmed under her hand and craned his neck to look behind him. He could see that Mrs. Shinebug lady sitting just a few pews back. Boy, had her applesauce set his insides on fire! He grinned conspiratorially at her and waved his right hand in her direction. Rebecca's own hand ceased resting and promptly began pinching.

"Ouch!"

"'. . . You shall not take vengeance or bear a grudge against the sons of your own people,'" Pastor Fletcher never missed a beat, though his voiced raised considerably in volume, "'but you shall love your neighbor as yourself: I am the LORD.' This is the Word of the Lord."

"Thanks be to God!" the congregation responded as one.

"The Epistle is from Colossians chapter 1," Pastor continued. "'Paul, an apostle of Christ Jesus by the will of God, and Timothy our brother, To the saints and faithful brothers in Christ at Colossae . . .'"

"This is boring."

"Shut it, Robbie," Davie hissed.

"Boys, when Pastor speaks, you listen." Rebecca's voice was barely audible, but both boys understood her meaning clearly. Davie gave Robbie a silent look of scorn, and Robbie crossed his arms in defense. Frankie, sitting on the opposite side of his grandmother and sister, made a point of stoically leaning forward to look down, or up, rather, his nose at his older brothers. Robbie returned the favor of his younger brother's snub by crossing his eyes and sticking out his tongue.

"'. . . so as to walk in a manner worthy of the Lord, fully pleasing to Him, bearing fruit in every good work and increasing in the knowledge of God. . . .'" Pastor read.

Robbie tried his best to sit still and concentrate, but his stomach felt all empty and sloshy. "Grams, can I have some gum?"

"I want gum!" Alison, who up until that moment had been quietly and contentedly playing with the maroon and gold ribbons hanging from the spine of her hymnal, presently forgot her interest in all things silky and shiny and thought only of things chewy and sticky. Her tinker-bell voice rang clearly throughout the entire church. "I want gum, Grammie!" The hymnal, forgotten and unattended, slipped from Alison's hands and crashed onto the floor.

Robbie started to laugh.

This time, it was his father's hand that reached for him. Robbie felt himself being pulled by a firm hand past a gloating Davie and a vexed mother to be set down on his dad's far left. The pew felt cold and unwelcoming on this side.

"'. . . He has delivered us from the domain of darkness and transferred us to the kingdom of His beloved Son, in whom we have redemption, the forgiveness of sins.' This is the Word of the Lord."

"Thanks be to God."

The congregation stood, singing over the wails of a gum-less and inconsolable Alison, "Alleluia. Alleluia. Alleluia."

"The Holy Gospel according to St. Luke, the tenth chapter."

"Glory be to Thee, O Lord," the congregation responded. Robbie held the final note out a little longer than the rest of the congregation, just so there could be no mistaking his piety.

"'And behold, a lawyer stood up to put Him to the test, saying, "Teacher, what shall I do to inherit eternal life?" He said to him . . .'"

Robbie yawned and leaned against the pew in front of him. He didn't mind the singing part of church so much, but this standing and listening part did drag on so.

"Respect the Word of God, Robert," his dad whispered into Robbie's ear. Robbie recognized the almost-final warning tone and stood tall in a flash, staring straight ahead at the white, silk cross stitched onto the banner hanging just above Pastor Fletcher's head. Katelyn Bradbury had boasted to Robbie just last week that she could stare without blinking for forty seconds straight, and he was determined that by the time school started, he would be able to hold his eyes open for at least a minute. He stared with zombie-like intensity at the banner. If he could just make it to the end of the reading.

"'. . . And Jesus said to him, "You go, and do likewise."'" This is the Gospel of the Lord."

Robbie blinked his stinging eyes, and feeling the relief and gratitude of a competitive eight-year-old within reach of his young life's ultimate goal, grinned and sang with gusto, "Praise be to Thee, O Christ." The final chord of the organ echoed in the nave.

"Let us join together in reciting the Nicene Creed."

"I believe in one God . . ." the congregation spoke together. His dad was presently engaged in disciplining the Jones family's strawberry-haired angel still in want of gum, so Robbie took advantage of the moment to sneak another peek at that crusty, old Mrs. Shinebug.

For her part, Mrs. Scheinberg, who rather prided herself on her sternness with children, was not immune to the freckled charm of the young boy peeking and grinning at her over the top of her hymnal. Although she would die before ever admitting it to a gasbag like Beverly Davis, Mrs. Scheinberg was personally tickled by the little boy's attentions. She looked straight at him, never missing a word of the creed, and winked. The boy's grin flashed for a triumphant moment before his father's stern arm turned him back around.

Mrs. Sheinberg's jubilee was short lived, however.

"Please, turn in your hymnals to number . . ." Pastor's voice faltered. He stood facing the congregation with the bulletin in his hand, staring at one of the pages as his face quickly began to turn the color of the day of Pentecost. Mrs. Scheinberg heard a dainty gasp from somewhere across the aisle, followed by the snarky chuckles of a couple of teenage boys in the back. Pastor did his best to recover. "Let's sing the sermon hymn, number 845." Evan came to the rescue with the chorale prelude, the organ's fluid counterpoint covering up the rustling of paper as everyone, Mrs. Scheinberg included, opened their bulletins to find out what was the matter.

> Sermon Hymen .... *LSB* 845
> "Where Charity and Love Prevail"

Mrs. Scheinberg's insides churned as if she had eaten the entire bowl of cinnamon applesauce herself.

Bev Davis, who had stayed up way too late the previous evening watching a rerun of *Lonesome Dove* on television, already felt a little tired and loopy. The sight of Arlene's added "e" in the bulletin was more than her weary brain could handle. She bit her fist in a vain attempt to gain self-control, but she could not keep a few snorts of laughter from escaping. Irv, silent and mortified at her side, vehemently poked her in the ribs with his elbow.

Mrs. Thomas Edison Bradbury III leaned across her stoic husband and excitedly pointed out the error in the bulletin to every one of her family members, immediate and extended alike. When she had exhausted the number of people in her own pew, she openly swung her hefty frame around to point out the mistake to the innocents sitting behind her. In fact, if her husband had let her, Mrs. Bradbury, who was charitable and mission-minded as always, would have traversed across the aisle to enlighten all of those who might still be in the dark.

Miss Geraldine Turner sat rigidly behind the Bradburys with her neck aflame. She had never before in her life felt so completely horrified and justified and sanctified all at the same time. Such vulgarity! If this was not proof enough that she should take over editing the Sunday bulletin, then she would need to consider rejoining the Methodist Church after all. And on a Sunday with a visitor sitting in the pews!

The said visitor, sitting a few seats away from Miss Turner, was anything but scandalized. Quite the contrary, his hazel eyes looked around at all of the murmuring commotion with delight and considered that he had quite possibly been too hasty in assuming all Lutherans to be stodgy, old traditionalists. What had he been missing out on all of these months in the Presbyterian Church? A lock of sandy hair fell over his forehead as he looked intently across the aisle toward his favorite, rosy Lutheran.

Emily, quite oblivious to any visitors, let alone the hazel-eyed, staring one, was feeling rather sorry for Mrs. Scheinberg. She wished she had sat a few rows further up that morning, so that she could be within reach to comfort those proud, broad, royal blue shoulders. Emily was certain there would be no peace in the narthex for Mrs. Scheinberg after the service.

Mrs. Scheinberg truly felt like she was going to vomit. She could hear Bev snorting from across the aisle, and each sound felt like another punch to the gut. Her stomach flipped when she thought about facing the ushers after the service. They would be waiting for her in the narthex like rabid dogs on a coon hunt. Well, she would not break. No, she would rather be excommunicated than admit defeat to those bulletin-wielding wisecrackers. She may not be a good speller, but she most definitely was a survivor.

The sermon that day was a wash. Even Pastor Fletcher had to admit afterward that he could not remember a single word of what he had spoken. What he would never forget, though, was the sight of Bev Davis running down the aisle at the beginning of the sermon with her shoulders shaking and her face hidden behind her hand; Mrs. Bradbury's jowls swinging from side to side as she hungrily searched for virgin ears; Miss Geraldine

Turner throwing alternating glares at both Mrs. Scheinberg and himself; Rebecca Jones leaning down with a white face to explain something in the bulletin to a questioning Davie; Emily Duke blushing to beat the roses; a strange man with straight, white teeth smiling as if the occasion called for all levity and celebration; and Mrs. Scheinberg. Poor Mrs. Scheinberg, steady and regal as Venus rising from the sea in a crocheted blue shawl, her face alternating between expressions of pride and horror.

||||||||||||||||||||||||||||||||||||||||||||||||||

Sunday School packed a few of its own punches that day.

"Dr. Zachary Brandt," the confident visitor introduced himself, shaking Pastor Fletcher's hand.

"Glad to meet you, Dr. Brandt." Pastor tried to appear just as calm and at ease as the man before him, but the sight of such perfect hair standing in such close proximity to Emily Duke's dimples made him feel an odd sense of panic. He wondered what this man's relationship to his choir director might be. "Are you visiting Bradbury?"

"I teach at BC," Zachary Brandt offered. "Dr. Duke told me she was working with the choir here at Zion, so I thought I'd come over and check out what I've been missing." He turned his disarming smile toward the small circle of people standing around him. Miss Turner beamed her own Cheshire grin in return; Rebecca glanced subtly at Emily; Alice quietly studied Pastor's face; and Emily avoided everyone's eyes entirely. She looked as uncomfortable as Pastor Fletcher felt.

Brandt chuckled, "I have to admit, I always assumed that Bach was the most exciting thing ever to happen to Lutherans, but apparently I was wrong. What an exceptional service!" He turned and spoke directly to Emily. "I can see why you want to work here."

"Has anyone seen Mrs. Scheinberg?" Emily asked quietly. Rebecca and Alice shook their heads soberly, but Miss Turner spoke up with ice in her voice.

"I hope she had the good sense to go home."

At that moment, as if she was plugged into the electrical charge that was coursing through the congregation that morning, Alison let out a scream that could chip the paint off the parish hall ceiling. Everyone whirled around to find her little, red face by the muffin table, squaring off with an equally red-faced Robbie. Blueberry muffin crumbs littered the floor between them.

"Good heavens!" Alice exclaimed. Rebecca was in the war zone in two seconds flat, capturing Robbie's left hand before it could grab hold of Alison's right pigtail. Jeremy was one step behind his wife, sweeping up Alison and taking her off to a separate corner of the fellowship hall to stave off the inevitable counterattack.

Robbie, certain that his gender, age, and hair color had already convicted him of the crime, howled in defeat as his mother dragged him out of the room, "It was *my* muffin!"

Alice sighed and gestured to Davie to help her pick the crumbled casualties off of the floor. From across the room, Karl Rincker silently noted that a glazed blueberry cake donut would have broken sensibly into large pieces, unlike this muffin nonsense. Mrs. Bradbury confirmed out loud to anyone who would listen that this kind of behavior was to be expected from families who chose to have more than two children. Mrs. Scheinberg, holed up in a bathroom stall in the women's restroom, wished that she could indulge in a few screams and howls of her own. And Frankie, the trusted judge in all Jones cases, sought out his pastor to relay the solemn verdict. "Robbie is telling the truth, Pastor Fletcher. I saw Alison try to grab the muffin out of his hand. She doesn't even like blueberries."

Pastor nodded and patted Frankie on the shoulder. "We'll let your mom and dad handle it. Go on to your Sunday School class."

Pastor did his best to recover a sense of dignified scholarship in his adult Sunday School class that morning, but all hope left him when, shortly after the opening prayer, the handsome visitor raised his hand and queried, "So, why do you Lutherans keep women from the pulpit?"

Pastor Fletcher decided then and there that the devil does indeed have sandy hair and straight teeth.

Chapter Seven: Diet of Words

||||||||||||||||||||||||||||||||||||||||||||||||||||||||||||

"The general composition of the entire bulletin is lacking in uniformity. Why, I count at least six different fonts on pages 1 and 2 alone." Miss Geraldine Turner squinted as if blinded by a beam of light. "The sight practically makes my eyes cross."

"We definitely wouldn't want anyone to have a seizure." Mrs. Scheinberg made a careful note on her pad of paper. "Reduce. Font. Size."

"No, no, Arlene, not the font size. The font *style*."

"Pardon me." Mrs. Scheinberg dutifully scribbled out the last word. "Font. *Style*."

Pastor Fletcher sat behind his desk, studying the two women seated in his study. Last month, in an effort to pacify Miss Turner's righteous rage over the infamous bulletin mishap, he had decided to take the retired teacher up on her original offer to help edit the church bulletin every Thursday afternoon. It had taken him a few days to build up the courage to break the news to Mrs. Scheinberg, but surprisingly, his usually crusty secretary took the news without complaint. In fact, she had said nothing at the time; she simply stared unblinking at him over her glasses before silently nodding her head.

Since then, Mrs. Scheinberg had been nothing but obliging to Miss Turner, not even raising an eyebrow when Miss Turner suggested that her own name be listed as the Senior Editor in the bulletin itself. Pastor was equally astonished the following week when Mrs. Scheinberg readily agreed to Miss Turner's suggestion that the three of them meet every Thursday over lunch to plan the layout and flow of the announcements. "The announcements are important," Mrs. Scheinberg had conceded, turning a docile gaze to a speechless Pastor Fletcher. Now, two weeks later, Pastor found that he had somehow been volunteered to serve as one of a three-person Bulletin Planning Committee, which met every Thursday afternoon in his own study. He found himself wishing that Mrs. Scheinberg were a little less compliant these days.

Miss Turner let out a tiny snort. "What on earth are these hideous pictures next to the prayer requests?"

Mrs. Scheinberg's poker face was impenetrable. "Oh, I was thinking about what you said last week, Geraldine. You know, about trying to find ways to make the bulletin more interesting from week to week. I found these free graphics online. I think the kids will like them."

Pastor Fletcher flipped open the bulletin to the prayer requests and suppressed a snort. Next to the petition for prayers for the Koelster sisters' brother in Omaha, who was suffering from colon cancer, was a cartoon clip art of the backside of a man in an open hospital gown, holding an IV cart. Next to the prayer request for Beverly Davis's cousin, Duane Newman, now at home recovering from a recent stroke, was a bolt of lightning.

"I think we should consider the fact that there are nonreaders in the congregation who will be looking at the bulletin too." Mrs. Scheinberg was all sincerity, but Pastor Fletcher thought he caught the slightest hint of a twitch at the left corner of her mouth.

"They have to go, Arlene." Miss Turner wrinkled her nose. "They are of poor taste. It would be different if you used spiritual graphics."

"Oh, like this one?" Mrs. Scheinberg turned to the back page of the bulletin. "I really like the way the flames curl around the cross. It's almost trinitarian. Almost."

"That," Miss Turner shook her head and sighed, "is the logo of the United Methodist Church, Arlene. I mean, really, how did you ever do this by yourself?"

Pastor Fletcher waited for the inevitable blast of sarcasm, but nothing came. Mrs. Scheinberg simply shrugged her shoulders good-naturedly.

Miss Turner flipped back a few pages. "Well, Arlene, it is not all a loss. I do like that you followed my suggestion to use *The Message* translation for the Gospel Reading this week."

Pastor Fletcher's head snapped up. He cleared his throat. "Let's keep the readings as they were."

"But the wording of *The Message* is so much easier to understand than the English Standard Version," Miss Turner argued. "Don't you think so, Arlene?"

"It definitely gives a different perspective." Mrs. Scheinberg blinked innocently.

"We will keep using the ESV for the Scripture Readings." Pastor was resolute.

"Forgive me for disagreeing with you, Pastor," Miss Turner huffed, maybe even puffed. "But you have given no good reason as to why we should use the ESV. I personally find it offensive that you would give a directive without the approval of the entire committee." She swept her hand around the room for emphasis. "I am not certain we should relinquish this matter without proper discussion. Unless I am convinced by good reason, my conscience is captive to the more understandable translation. Luther said it is neither safe nor sound to act against one's conscience."

"Yes." Mrs. Scheinberg scooted her chair ceremoniously closer to Miss Turner's, barely able to contain herself. "Here we sit."

Pastor Fletcher took a slow, deep breath, counting deliberately to five. "Ladies, I am thankful for your willing hearts and ready hands to serve Zion in this capacity, but the Bulletin Planning Committee is not an approved organization of the church. It does not have the authority to make changes to the liturgical content of the Divine Service, and that includes deciding which translation of Scripture will or will not be read aloud in corporate worship. What this committee does have the authority to do is to help organize the congregation's announcements and prayer requests in an orderly, understandable format."

"Don't forget locating and correcting typos," Mrs. Scheinberg helped.

Pastor counted to five again before continuing, turning his full attention toward Miss Turner. "Geraldine, regarding *The Message*: it is a *paraphrase* of God's Word. However understandable its language may be, it often uses incorrect language. It can actually mislead you from the proper meaning of the original text. Since language is the vehicle by which God has chosen to reveal Himself to us, I, as your pastor, insist that you stick to a word-for-word translation, such as the ESV, and come talk to me about any passages you may find hard to understand."

Pastor Fletcher stood, taking full note of Mrs. Scheinberg's dancing eyes, and opened wide his office door. "Now, ladies, I think our meeting time has come to an end for this week. I trust you to pick out *one* appropriate font style, to remove all offensive and schismatic pictures, and to restore the Gospel reading to its rightly approved translation. Thank you for your help."

Miss Turner stood, picked up her bulletin, and left the room with pursed lips. Mrs. Scheinberg lingered, showing no haste in collecting her pad of paper, red and green pens, and bulletin copies. Pastor Fletcher was not immune to her posture of victory.

"There is nothing like a productive meeting," she purred as she passed through the doorway.

⁣⁣⁣⁣⁣⁣⁣⁣⁣⁣⁣⁣⁣⁣⁣⁣⁣⁣⁣⁣⁣⁣⁣⁣⁣⁣⁣

Down the street, Emily was getting ready for her own big meeting of sorts. The choir's first rehearsal of the new season was scheduled for 7:15 that evening.

"Not 7:00?" Emily had clarified with Mrs. Scheinberg in the church office earlier that day.

"Not since Janet and Dorothy Koelster joined the choir ten years ago. They can't manage a seven o'clock downbeat." Mrs. Scheinberg had rolled her eyes at the ceiling. "Janet claims it's because of the dinner rush at Koelster's Kitchen—she can't finish her shift and be here by seven—but everyone knows it's because Joe Pike comes to eat supper there every Thursday night. Janet won't leave the restaurant until he's had his dessert. She's been waiting thirty years for a ring, so she makes the rest of us wait along with her. Anyway, the Koelster sisters make up half of the alto section, so there's no point in starting without them."

Half of the alto section. Emily poured herself a glass of milk and sat at her kitchen counter with her peanut butter and jelly sandwich. Well, it was going to be an adventure. This would be like starting from scratch.

Emily scanned the piece of paper Mrs. Scheinberg had handed to her earlier on her way out the office door. It was Zion's choir roster from last year, only this was a special edition. Mrs. Scheinberg had taken the time to handwrite comments next to each singer's name.

Bass Section

Irvin Davis — *section leader; married to Bev*

Emily was relieved to see that although Zion's bass section had only one singer, it still had a section leader.

Tenor Section

Arlene Scheinberg — *section leader*

Phyllis Bingley — *has a nice singing voice, but I have honestly never heard her speak a word in my life. Sometimes I forget she is in the section, and I sit by her.*

Irene Rincker — *practically deaf, though she thinks she can hear perfectly*

Well, at least Irv stood a chance of being heard over an all-woman tenor section.

Alto Section

Janet Koelster — *section leader; cooks on the line at KK's, so will most likely come to choir smelling like fried onions*

Dorothy Koelster — *Janet's older sister; touch of vertigo*

Vertigo? In the church *balcony?*

Bev Davis — *will talk your ear off if you let her, so don't get her started during rehearsal; married to Irv*

Lois Kull — *can't find a pitch to save her life*

Soprano Section

Geraldine Turner — *section leader; will try to take your job*

Candice Bradbury — *thinks she is the section leader*

Marge Johnson — *only has one volume: LOUD!*

Why were the divas always in the soprano section? Emily took a deep breath and folded the paper in half. She felt uneasy, and it wasn't because of any name listed on the roster. It was because Evan Ebner had yet to return any of her phone calls. She had noticed when she was in the balcony earlier that afternoon that he had at least picked up the stack of choral music she had left for him on the organ bench last Sunday. Still, Emily had no other assurance that Evan would even show up for rehearsal that night. A small part of her hoped he wouldn't.

CHAPTER EIGHT: *UBI CARITAS ET AMOR*

Evan was seated at the piano bench when Emily arrived.

"Hello, Evan," Emily smiled brightly. Too brightly. Evan met her smile with a curt nod of his white head, immediately making Emily feel overplayed and juvenile. Emily cleared her throat and moved toward the music stand near the balcony railing. She set her travel mug of tea down on an empty chair and proceeded to pull a black binder of choral music out of her bag.

"I assume the choir is used to singing on the north side of the balcony?" Emily flinched at the sound of her own voice. It was too high and squeaky.

Evan conceded one more nod before picking up a novel from the piano bench, opening it to the marked page, and ignoring Emily completely.

Emily took a deep breath and turned her attention to the task at hand. The balcony hung over the back fifth of the nave, and the organ console, built into the very middle of it, completely divided the balcony into two sections. No one could walk from one side of the balcony to the other without sliding across the console bench. The south side of the balcony was filled with four short pews for congregational seating, and the north side was filled with organized chaos. An upright piano, a filing cabinet, three music stands, and twenty folding chairs were squashed into the tiny space. Why did they insist on stuffing twenty chairs together when they needed only half of them? Emily could at least appreciate the choir's optimism. She set a choir folder on each of the chairs in the first two rows.

"Since we're the first ones here, does that mean we get to choose our own seats?"

Emily turned around to see Rebecca and Alice at the top of the north stairwell. Emily clapped her hands together in surprise. "Are you two joining the choir?"

"Well, we're not here for the scenery," Rebecca teased. She helped Alice maneuver through the sea of chairs down to the front row.

"I will need a seat in the alto section." Alice smiled, but she was visibly nervous.

An almost imperceptible snort came from behind Evan's piano. Emily noted that Alice's smile flickered for an instant before returning to full voltage. "I am not the best singer, but I do try."

"Of course," Emily agreed, instinctively directing Alice to the chair furthest from Evan.

"Are the sopranos over here?" Rebecca gestured toward the chairs closest to the piano. Emily nodded her head. Rebecca chose the seat nearest Evan, which resulted in the small man fixing her with a cold stare. Rebecca returned the stare with confidence, maybe even a touch of daring. Something was happening. There was a charge in the room, but Emily could not quite place her finger on its source.

"It's good to see you, Evan," Rebecca said evenly. "I haven't gotten a chance to talk with you since the Easter breakfast. How did your summer garden turn out?"

Emily observed as Evan eyed Rebecca suspiciously, stealing a quick glance at Alice who was sitting like a statue in her chair with her eyes downcast. Evan shut his book and uncrossed his legs. "My tomatoes are still yielding."

"Are you making your famous salsa?"

"I didn't grow the habaneros this year."

"That surprises me," Rebecca leaned forward in her chair. "You are known throughout the congregation for your heat."

Evan's expression remained even. "I like it, but most people can't take it."

The conversation was disrupted by the sound of feet coming up the stairs. Mrs. Scheinberg, Miss Turner, and several unfamiliar feminine faces appeared, followed closely by Irv and Bev Davis.

"Oh, Alice, how good to see you!" Bev exclaimed. "I was sure you would never step foot in this balcony ever again."

Alice's face turned as red as Evan's tomatoes. Irv tried to steer Bev away from the defenseless Alice, but Bev plopped down in the seat right next to her. "This will be just like old times. Did I ever tell you what Dorothy Koelster said to me after you left? She said—"

"Bev," Mrs. Scheinberg interrupted, "scoot down a few chairs. You know Janet and Dorothy like to sit in the middle."

"But they're not here yet."

Emily caught Mrs. Scheinberg grimacing behind her choir folder, but the church matron reclaimed a posture of strained hospitality before welcomingly tapping the chair directly in front of her. "You haven't told me about your new car yet."

"Oh," Bev beamed with delight. She promptly forgot all about what Dorothy had said and moved to the chair in front of Mrs. Scheinberg. "Well, Irv took me to Springfield last weekend. He was hungry for a Longhorn steak, and I wanted to see . . ."

Emily watched as Alice opened her choir folder and stared unblinking at the first piece of music. Emily had no idea what had happened previously to Alice in the choir, but it was quickly becoming evident that it must not have been good for her sweet friend. Emily leaned forward and whispered, "Thank you for being here. It means a lot to me."

Alice looked up with watery eyes and smiled. "It means a lot to me too, dear."

"Am I in the right place?" The balcony grew silent at the sound of a deep voice at the top of the stairs. Emily looked up in shock to see Zachary Brandt. Out of the corner of her eye, Emily saw Rebecca quickly face forward and give her a wide-eyed look before mouthing silently, "What is he doing here?"

"Do you mind if I join you? I hear you have the best choir director in town." Zachary smiled familiarly at Emily, but his confidence faltered a bit at the sight of her alarmed expression. That was not exactly the reaction for which he had been hoping.

Miss Turner noisily clambered up from her seat in the front row, almost knocking over the director's music stand. "Of course not! Please, come in. Irv," she gestured wildly at Irv behind her, "help Mr. . . ."

"Brandt. Dr. Brandt," came the smooth response.

"Yes, that's right, Dr. Brandt," Miss Turner cooed. "How could I forget? Please forgive me." She coughed a giggle into her hand and smoothed out the front of her daffodil-colored blouse. "Irv, won't you help Dr. Brandt find a seat next to you? That is, I assume you are a bass, Dr. Brandt. Your speaking voice is so . . . low."

Mrs. Scheinberg rolled her eyes. "Dr. Brandt is not a member of the congregation."

"Oh, Arlene," Miss Turner turned around and hissed, "since when do people have to be members of the church before joining the choir?"

"Since the church was founded, Geraldine," Mrs. Scheinberg said dryly. "Sit down."

Miss Turner glared at Arlene before taking her seat. "Well, I, for one, am thrilled to have Dr. Brandt here."

"Who is Dr. Brandt?" Candice Bradbury panted from the doorway.

"That would be me." Zachary, grasping at the lone welcome, warmly extended his hand to the woman dressed in three shades of purple, four if counting the lavender scarf tied around her neck.

"Oh," Candice fluttered, "how nice. I am Candice Bradbury. My husband is Thomas Bradbury." She tossed her head to the side and forced an ironic laugh. "I imagine, Dr. Brandt, that you are probably wondering at the coincidence of our name being the same as the town's."

"I bet he isn't," Mrs. Scheinberg offered loudly enough for everyone to hear.

"It is no coincidence," Candice continued. "My husband's family founded this town five generations ago. Our son is the fourth Thomas Edison Bradbury to be born in this county, but his commemorative tree on Washington Street is actually the fifth in line. You see, my husband's grandmother was Thomasina Bradbury, the eldest daughter of Thomas Bradbury the First. Her tree is the beautiful oak on the corner of Second and Washington, right across from Town Hall."

Zachary silently contemplated the consequences of walking right back down those balcony stairs. Irv, in a sudden rush of brotherly compassion, stood up and rescued the newcomer, shaking his hand and pulling him in the direction of the bass section. Choir member or not, Irv was not about to let a fellow man get caught up in one of Candice's plots.

Janet and Dorothy Koelster came in behind Candice. At least, Emily *assumed* they were the Koelster sisters, based on the smell of onion rings that wafted across the room.

"Can someone grab Dorothy's arm, please?" Janet called out.

One of the tenors stood to grab Dorothy's left arm, helping to ease her into the empty seat next to Alice. Dorothy closed her eyes for a moment, apparently to stop the spinning.

"There, dear." Alice patted her arm.

Janet climbed down into the seat between Dorothy and Bev. She was a tall, matronly woman with dark hair, red glasses, and a fast grin. Her naturally pretty face was masked behind a thick, dusty layer of Mary Kay. Dorothy was much shorter and smaller-boned, but she had the same pear shape as her younger sister.

"How was Joe tonight?" Bev leaned over conspiratorially.

"Hungry." Janet let out a sigh of fatigue and patted Dorothy's knee. "You okay there?"

Dorothy's eyes remained closed, but she hummed an affirmative.

"Well, then," Emily called out. The choir members quieted down and turned expectantly toward their petite director. "I have not had the pleasure of meeting all of you personally, but I look forward to getting to know you better over the next few weeks. My name is Emily Duke. I hope that you will call me Emily." Emily cleared her throat and pulled a clipboard out of her bag, handing it to Alice. "I would like each of you to write your name, voice part, phone number, and email address on this sheet of paper. You will find my contact information already at the top of the page. Please feel free to copy it down for your own use."

Zachary Brandt's hand shot into the air. Emily's heart stopped as she realized that he would now have access to both her phone number and personal email account. She fought the urge to grab the clipboard back out of Alice's hands.

"Yes, Dr. Brandt?"

"I don't have a choir folder."

Emily reached back down into her bag and pulled out an extra folder.

"He's not a member," Mrs. Scheinberg reminded Emily. Miss Turner sighed in exasperation.

"I know," Emily replied quietly so that only Mrs. Scheinberg could hear. "But I'm not sure what else to do at this point. I'll talk to Pastor Fletcher about it tomorrow." Emily passed the folder back to Zachary and continued. "Let's all stand and stretch our arms high over our heads."

Everyone scuffled to their feet, setting their choir folders on their respective chairs.

"That's right," Emily coached, "stretch the tension out of your shoulders."

Dorothy stood with everyone else but got her arms only as high as her ears before veering sharply to the left.

"Quick, catch her!" Janet called out. Emily lunged forward to catch Dorothy under the arms before she could topple on top of dainty Alice. Janet leaned over to help. "That's it. Ease her down."

Emily set Dorothy down and turned around to stare at the twenty-foot drop over the balcony railing just two feet from Dorothy's chair. "Is this going to work?" she asked Janet.

"No problem," Janet assured her. "In all of our years in the choir, Dorothy has never once pitched over the railing. Maybe we'll have her sit out on the stretches, though."

Emily heard one of Evan's subtle snorts. She looked at him over the top of the piano. "May I have a D above middle C, please, Evan?"

Evan struck the pitch. Emily faced her choir members and modeled a short, five-note scale on the syllable *doo*. "Repeat after me," Emily instructed.

The choir, still standing, did as they were told. Emily watched and listened as they continued with the warm-up, instinctively going up a half step with each new repetition. It did not take Emily long to figure out who Marge Johnson was. Seated next to Rebecca, Marge's tone was at least twice as loud as any other singer in the choir. Her volume would not have been such a problem if it also had not been accompanied by the widest vibrato Emily had ever heard.

Emily also quickly picked out Irene Rincker. She was attentive enough, but it soon became clear as the choir sang through the first song that Irene could not hear a word Emily was saying. When Emily instructed the choir to sing *piano* at the entrance, Irene sang out louder than before. Mrs. Scheinberg, sitting next to her, settled the matter by resting her hand on Irene's arm. Irene immediately quieted down, and Mrs. Scheinberg gave Emily a quick wink.

Evan behaved well enough throughout rehearsal, although he persisted in reading his novel, setting it aside only whenever piano accompaniment was required. The choir members were kind and responsive, and they all seemed eager to please their new director. Emily found herself getting caught up in the delight of music making, her cheeks flushing from the experience.

"We have just one more piece to rehearse tonight. Please pull out the Duruflé." Emily continued enthusiastically while everyone found the proper octavo in their respective folders. "Duruflé's 'Ubi Caritas' is one of my favorite pieces. I think you will enjoy the chant-like movement of the vocal lines and the rich, a cappella texture. There is also something cleansing to the pallet when singing pure, Latin syllables—"

"We don't sing Latin in this congregation."

Emily was startled by the sound of Evan's voice. He had not said one word to her the entire evening. His sudden intrusion flustered her out of her musical reverie. "I'm sorry?"

"We don't sing Latin in this congregation." Evan stared at her over the piano. Emily felt everyone else staring at her too.

"I think it's okay. Pastor Fletcher approved all of these pieces."

"I am certain Pastor Fletcher assumed you would be having the choir sing the English translation of this piece."

Emily looked Evan fully in the face, taking advantage of the moment to really study him. His white hair was combed and perfectly parted. His shirt was ironed and his summer blazer, lint-free. His face was taut with resolution, and his eyes were crackling with power. For two months, he had denied her the opportunity to communicate with him, and now, in public, he was choosing to address her—no, to challenge her. Who was this man? What was he trying to prove? Whatever he was doing, Emily was certain it was not with her best in mind. Emily sensed the danger in pushing him, but experience also told her that she needed to hold her ground. Evan was not the director. She was.

"I see no problem in singing the Latin."

"No *problem*?" Evan challenged. He clicked open his binder and swiftly pulled out the Duruflé, standing up to face the choir. "Phyllis, what does '*Congregavit nos in unum Christi amor*' mean?"

Phyllis, content to forever go unnoticed in the tenor section, blanched in horror at being called out and sank lower into her chair.

"How about you, Irv?" Evan leaned toward the church's faithful trustee. "'*Et ex corde*'? Any idea?"

Irv looked evenly over his music at Evan but remained silent.

"See, Dr. Duke?" Evan proclaimed, dropping the octavo onto the piano. "That is the problem. The choir, let alone the congregation, does not know Latin. The words mean nothing to them. There is a reason Luther translated the Latin Mass into the language of the people. It was so they could rightly hear and understand the proclamation of God's Word."

"That is why we will provide the English translation in the bulletin," Emily replied calmly.

"You are assuming an awful lot from our bulletin committee," Evan quipped. "You may or may not have noticed its not-so-stellar track record."

Miss Turner sharply sucked in a breath.

"I'm sorry, chum, but you haven't asked me what any of the Latin texts mean," Zachary called out, his eyes flashing with masculine bravado. He did not like the way this mousey man was speaking to his choir director. "I would appreciate a turn."

Evan stared at the newcomer. "*Cum porci volent.*"

Zachary's eyes narrowed, but he said nothing in response.

"That is uncalled for, Evan," Alice reprimanded.

"Uncalled for?" Evan turned his poisonous stare on Alice. "*You* are going to accuse *me* of behavior that is uncalled for?"

Alice held his gaze. No one breathed. Evan stood his ground for a moment before turning coldly to Emily. "Well, I can see that twenty-five years of faithful service to this church means nothing in the face of our new, young choir director. I leave them to you, Dr. Duke."

With that, Evan slid expertly across the console bench and left the balcony by the south door.

CHAPTER NINE:

CRIBBAGE AND AN OLD CABBAGE

Pastor Fletcher tapped his fingers on his desk and stared at the phone. Surely Evan would be home by now. He picked up the receiver and dialed the number by heart. An answering machine picked up again on the other end.

"You have reached the home of Evan Ebner. Please leave a message after the beep."

Sigh. "Evan, this is Pastor Fletcher again. I want to talk to you about choir rehearsal last night. Please, call me back."

Pastor Fletcher hung up the receiver and ran his hand through his hair. He was at a loss for what to do. He knew for a fact that Evan did not have caller ID, but he was just as certain that Evan was screening calls. He might need to drive over to Evan's place tomorrow if this kept up any longer.

"Mrs. Scheinberg, did Dr. Duke pick up the key to the balcony you made for her?"

"Yesterday afternoon. Still no luck with Evan?"

Pastor Fletcher tried to push down the wave of irritation that rose up in his throat every time Mrs. Scheinberg talked freely with him about things that were not her business, professional or personal. True, she was the one who had alerted him to last night's choir fiasco in the first place, but still. There was a line. "I'm going to head out a few minutes early this afternoon."

"Big date night at the Joneses'?"

Pastor gritted his teeth. He refused to play this game, but he knew that Mrs. Scheinberg would still somehow manage to win anyway.

Mrs. Scheinberg was relentless. "Bev told me that Alice is having a sleepover with the grandkids at her house tonight, so I figure Rebecca and Jeremy must have found you a new cribbage partner. They certainly didn't ask me, and I assume Miss Turner most likely has some fundamental problem with the game that keeps her, as always, from joining in on anything fun. That leaves only—"

"Good-bye, Mrs. Scheinberg." Pastor grabbed his bag and was out the door before she could turn her afternoon's private ruminations into a full-blown public sin. He took in a deep breath of freedom in the parking lot and pulled out his tab collar. He had no intention of wearing a clerical tonight. No, he was going to relax and enjoy an evening away from his usual parish duties. Rebecca had called him on Wednesday with the news that Alice wanted a night off from their monthly cribbage game, and would he mind too terribly if Emily Duke filled in as his partner instead? Pastor picked up his pace and made a beeline for the parsonage.

iiiiiiiiiiiiiiiiiiiiiiiiiiiiiiiiiiiiiiiiiiiiiiiii

In the Joneses' kitchen, Rebecca stared a wide-eyed Emily straight in the face. "Seriously, this is not a setup."

Emily looked as if she were about to flee the scene.

"Yes, I know it looks bad, but I'm telling you the truth!" Rebecca was prepared to tackle Emily on the run if she had to. "I admit, my mother may have had an ulterior motive for scheduling a sleepover with the kids, tonight of all nights, but I promise you that is where the sneakiness ends. No one else here is expecting you and Pastor to go off on a honeymoon next month."

The doorbell rang. Jeremy could be heard greeting Pastor Fletcher at the front door. Emily looked like a deer caught in the headlights of an oncoming car.

"Don't make this into more than it really is." Rebecca shoved a plate of lettuce wraps into Emily's hands. "Here, take this and put it on the table. I'm serious, Emily. Just relax. Don't be so third grade about the fact that Pastor Fletcher is a boy."

Rebecca normally avoided hazing and stun tactics in friendship, but this time, she was desperate. She had anticipated that Emily would panic upon hearing that Pastor Fletcher was to be her cribbage partner, and for that very reason, Rebecca had waited until this moment to break the news to her. After that stunt her mother had pulled on Emily's first Sunday at Zion, Rebecca knew Emily would forever be suspicious of any social activity involving their bachelor pastor.

Emily did not look fully convinced, but she obediently turned toward the dining room to deliver the plate. Rebecca, relieved but not quite confident that she should call this a victory, followed close behind with the egg rolls and crab rangoon.

Jeremy was already in the dining room pouring wine for Pastor Fletcher. ". . . but I don't know if I would use the word *economy* to describe his writing as much as *cold.*"

"You don't think his intentional absence of descriptors serves to highlight the raw emotion in a scene?" Pastor Fletcher winked at Rebecca over his wine.

Rebecca explained to Emily, "Jeremy and Pastor are reading *A Farewell to Arms.* They read a new book every month and then spend their cribbage nights tearing it apart. They'll go at it all night if we let them."

"Aw, now, admit it," Jeremy said, passing his wife a glass of wine. "You love it when I talk literature."

"Jay, I love it when you focus on your cards." Rebecca set her glass down at her place setting and indicated that Emily should sit next to her at the table. "You know Pastor just tries to distract you from the game with all of this book talk."

"Rebecca, I don't have the slightest idea what you're talking about," Pastor grinned. He took a seat across the table from Rebecca.

"Emily, red or white?" Jeremy asked from the buffet.

"Whatever you have open."

"We love a good Cab here, and Pastor just takes whatever we give him."

"Red sounds great," Emily said with a smile.

The comfortable, easy conversation that flowed over the meal warmed Emily and slowly melted away her suspicion and anxiety. She smiled behind her hand at the brotherly banter between Pastor and Jeremy and laughed at Rebecca's animated stories of the kids' daily interactions. These friends shared a connection that seemed almost familial, no doubt built from years of confessing the same faith and living life together in Christ. They had probably been gathering to play cribbage like this for years, Emily surmised, and she began to feel silly, even selfish, for entertaining the thought that this whole night had been prearranged as a setup just for her. No, these lovely people were simply being kind in inviting her to join them at all. Emily felt that she was sitting on the outside of something wonderful and special, and she found herself wishing she could somehow be a part of it all.

"Everything goes in the dishwasher," Rebecca called out as Emily helped clear the table. "On game nights, I never cook anything that requires hand washing the dishes, and Pastor always brings dessert."

Jeremy started setting up the cribbage board, and Pastor took the plastic off of a tray of chocolate-covered fruit sitting on the buffet in the dining room. Jeremy grabbed a white chocolate-covered dried apricot and held it out for his wife. "Want a bite, my dear?"

Rebecca screwed up her face. "I refuse to let that white nonsense touch my lips."

"It's called chocolate." Jeremy popped the fruit in his mouth.

"No, *that* is not chocolate. That is some kind of pale, sad substance dreamed up to placate simple people who can't handle the real thing." Rebecca picked up a dark chocolate-covered strawberry. "*This* is chocolate."

"You are so predictable."

Pastor turned to Emily. "This is a house divided. Whatever you do, don't take sides."

"You know you love dark chocolate too," Rebecca wagged a finger at Pastor Fletcher.

"What have I ever done to convince you of such a thing?" Pastor proceeded to pull only dark chocolate-covered fruit onto his dessert plate.

"Emily, you have to try the oranges. They're Pastor's specialty." Rebecca held out a segment of a fresh, navel orange that had been half dipped in dark chocolate.

"What if she doesn't like dark chocolate?" Jeremy interjected. "She may want the white nonsense stuff like me instead."

Rebecca gave her husband an incredulous look. "Emily is a woman. Of course she likes dark chocolate."

Emily laughed and took the orange.

"Okay," Jeremy rubbed his hands together, "the Joneses take on the church staff. This should be good." He fanned out all of the cards facedown on the table. "Everyone pick a card. Low card wins the deal."

"Is the ace high or low?" Pastor inquired.

"Low."

Rebecca drew the two of hearts, the lowest card of the four drawn, winning the deal. She winked victoriously at Jeremy and shuffled the deck. However, no sooner had she dealt five cards to each player than Pastor's cell phone rang. He looked at the caller ID and politely excused himself. "I'm sorry. I have to get this."

"Use our bedroom," Jeremy offered.

Pastor stepped out of the dining room, through the living room, and down the hall to the last door, leading to Jeremy and Rebecca's bedroom. Once he had closed the door, he flipped on the light and answered the phone. "Evan."

"Pastor."

"Thank you for calling me back."

Silence.

"Do you want to tell me what happened at rehearsal last night?"

"Who told you about it?"

Pastor silently debated for a moment. "Arlene."

"Well, then, I'm sure you heard everything there is to know."

"Did you really tell the new guy 'when pigs fly' in Latin?"

"Arlene told you that?"

Pastor silently debated again. "No, that was Alice."

Evan's voice was ice. "Well, at least she's not afraid to tattle on *me*."

"C'mon, Evan. What's going on? What is this all about?"

"Michael, that Brandt guy's a joke. He's not even a member of the church. Everyone could tell he was only there for the girl."

Pastor clenched the phone. "I would be lying if I said that I didn't have similar sentiments toward the guy, but Dr. Duke was hired to handle situations like Brandt. It was not your place, Evan."

"Not my place? Since when has it not been my place to defend the teachings of my church?"

"It's not your place when it comes to Dr. Duke's rightful vocation. We hired her to direct the choir."

"You hired her."

"No, the church hired her."

"She was going to have the choir sing in Latin, Michael. For a church service! I get so tired of these young, history-worshipping musicians who insist that choral pieces be performed in their original languages. Never mind the fact that Latin is a dead language. It's all a trend, you know. It has nothing to do with the church."

"Kyrie? Sanctus? That has nothing to do with the church?"

"You know that's not what I mean. I'm talking about this ridiculous idea of introducing an entirely new text to the Divine Service in a language the congregation doesn't even understand."

Pastor was firm. "It's still not your place to challenge Dr. Duke about it in front of the choir. That's something for Dr. Duke and me to discuss in private. You were out of line."

Evan was silent on the other end.

"Look, Evan. I'm not being unfair. I'm being honest."

"I'm not apologizing to her."

"Evan, this will lead to no good—"

"And I'm not accompanying the choir."

This time, Pastor was silent for a moment. He chose his words carefully. "I don't think this is going to work the result you want, Evan."

"And what is it that I want?"

"You want peace."

Evan's voice was strained. "I'm done working with choir directors, Michael."

Pastor sighed and ran his hand through his hair. "Okay. I hear you. I know this situation is difficult for you, but it's unfair to lump Dr. Duke in with Dale. She had nothing to do with all of that."

Silence.

"Evan, you know it's a good thing for Zion to have a choir director again. It's what the congregation needs."

"I'm *done*."

"Okay, but you still need to apologize to Dr. Duke. She's your sister in Christ, and you wronged her in public. We need to live at peace with one another in the church. That's what we do. That's who we are in Christ. We're peacemakers."

Pastor was torn as he walked back down the hallway to the dining room. It was a fine line to walk when dealing with Evan. Pastor had never met a smarter man. At the same time, he had never encountered someone like Evan, who so foolishly stored up grudges like treasures. Now, he had to break the news to Dr. Duke that she had lost her accompanist.

"Welcome back, Padre." Jeremy popped another white chocolate-covered dried apricot in his mouth. "Your partner drew a five of diamonds."

Emily smiled. "It should be a good hand."

Pastor took one look at those brown eyes and felt the stress of the day melt into the background. He picked up his hand: a seven of spades, two queens, and two fives. He tossed the seven of spades in the crib and returned Emily's smile. "Yes, it should."

"You have more fives, don't you?" Rebecca moaned.

Pastor laughed and settled back into his chair. He would tell his choir director about Evan later. The only thing on his immediate agenda was to make sure he won his first game of cribbage with Emily Duke. That, and to buy Zachary Brandt a plane ticket back to England.

Chapter Ten: A Short Victory Lap

┈┈┈┈┈┈┈┈┈┈┈┈┈┈┈┈┈┈┈┈┈┈┈┈┈┈┈

The street was dark as Pastor walked Emily to her car. Normally, the Joneses' front porch threw light all the way to the sidewalk, but Rebecca had mysteriously left the exterior lights off that evening.

Pastor smiled to himself. He and Emily had won three out of the four cribbage matches, and Emily had clapped her hands delightfully at their final victory. Pastor felt like his own prize came a few minutes later when he and Emily left the Jones house at the exact same moment. Time alone with Emily Duke was better than any trophy. Pastor quickly sobered, though, at the thought of what he had to tell her.

"That was Evan on the phone earlier."

Emily slowed her step.

"I know what happened at choir practice last night, and I'm sorry. Evan was out of line. Would you like me to speak to the choir?"

Emily's voice was careful. "No. I don't think so. Although I'm not sure how to resolve this. I tried to call Evan several times today, but he never called me back."

"Well, at this point, it's Evan's place to seek you out. He's the one in the wrong."

Emily stopped and turned to look him in the eye. "Is there something I should know, Pastor Fletcher? I don't mean to pry, but there seems to be a history here that is affecting the present. I feel a bit like I'm walking in the dark without a guide."

Pastor nodded. He thought for a minute, staring down at the nearest crack in the sidewalk. "There is a history, and it does involve Evan. I was not the pastor here when it happened, but the effects of it have lasted long into my years at Zion. I was hoping it wouldn't affect you. I'm sorry that I was wrong."

Emily sighed. "I understand that you can't give me details, but can you at least tell me how I'm to work with a loose charge like Evan?"

"That problem seems to have been solved for us. Evan told me this evening that he has decided not to accompany the choir."

Emily blew out her breath slowly. "Well, that's one way to handle it, I guess. Is there anyone else in the choir who can play the piano?"

"Not well enough to serve as an accompanist. Would you feel comfortable doing it yourself?"

"I guess so, but I don't think it's best for the choir. They'll sing better if they have an actual conductor standing in front of them." Emily crossed her arms to stave off the cool, night air. "Would you or the council have any problem with my hiring a student accompanist from the college?"

"I can't speak for the council, but, considering the circumstances, I would be surprised if they said no. We have some designated funds from a sainted member's will set aside for the music program. I'll suggest that we tap into those funds to pay for an accompanist. We have a meeting next week. I can let you know after that."

Emily started walking again. "I suppose you heard about Zachary Brandt, then, too?"

Pastor walked in step with her. "Yes."

"What should I do about him?"

"Dr. Brandt should join the new member instruction class before he joins the choir."

Emily nodded. "I agree."

"Do you want me to talk to him?"

"No, I can handle it."

Pastor was careful to keep his voice light. "Do you think he wants to join the church?"

Emily shrugged. "I have no idea. I can't imagine that he would want to, but he sure keeps coming back."

Pastor was relieved to hear what he detected as a note of exasperation in Emily's voice. He took a risk. "You two aren't good friends then?"

"What? No, I barely know Dr. Brandt. I met him for the first time a couple of months ago at BC. He seems to really like Zion, though."

"I don't think it's Zion that he likes." Pastor couldn't see Emily's blush for the darkness of the street. He chuckled. "Did Evan really tell him off in Latin?"

Emily cracked a smile. "Yes, he did. It was really quite brilliant."

They had reached Emily's car. She began to fish her keys out of her purse. "Speaking of Latin, Evan had the opinion that you would object to my programming a Latin text for the church service."

"You mean the 'Ubi Caritas'? I'm fine with it as long as the text preaches Christ and there's an English translation provided in the bulletin." Pastor looked all around to make sure no one was listening before leaning closer and whispering conspiratorially, "Besides, I sang that piece in college, and I really like it."

Emily grinned at him and opened the driver's side door.

"Before you go," Pastor handed Emily a brown paper bag he had been carrying, "here is my contribution to your pantry."

Emily took the bag and curiously peaked inside. In it were a dozen oranges and two boxes of semisweet Baker's chocolate.

"The key is to make sure you use navel oranges. They have no seeds."

Emily looked up at Pastor. He was standing with his hands behind his back, rocking back and forth on his heels and toes, perfectly content. His eyes were glinting brighter than the stars above his head. Emily took an involuntary step backward toward her car. She had witnessed the kindness and generosity of her pastor several times over the past couple of months—his tenderness toward Alice, his sincerity with the Jones kids, his patience with Evan—and each of these interactions had given Emily a sense of comfort and safety to be under the staff of such a shepherd. However, something about being on the direct receiving end of Pastor Fletcher's generosity and attention made her feel like the world was closing in on her.

"Thank you." Emily's voice was more strained than polite. She hastily sat in the driver's seat, putting her key in the ignition while still holding the paper bag. "They are really good together, the oranges and chocolate. Very refreshing. I never would have thought to pair them." She reached for the car door.

"Yes, well, late-night hunger combined with an empty refrigerator calls for a little creativity." Pastor smiled easily over the car door. "Basically, all I had on hand one night after an elders' meeting were some oranges and a bar of chocolate."

"I suppose you could do worse." Emily shut her door and waved good night.

"I could, indeed," Pastor said to himself as she drove away.

Chapter Eleven: A Nightingale on a Lark

"So, tell me, Ben," Emily asked while drinking lemonade and eating peanut butter cookies with her young employee on the front step, "how does a man of your age come to own his own lawn mower?"

Ben consumed half of his cookie in one bite. "My dad works on farm equipment, and this old thing came through his workshop one day." He gestured casually at the mower cooling on the front lawn. "One of his customers found it in a pasture. Someone had junked it, I guess." Ben swallowed the remaining half of the cookie. Emily held out the plate of cookies to him, and Ben helped himself to another.

"Did your dad give it to you?"

"Sorta. He told me that if I could get it workin' again, I could keep it. He and I spent a coupla nights takin' it apart and puttin' it back together again."

Although Emily had never met Mr. Schmidt, she already liked him.

Ben's cheeks crinkled up in a shy smile. "It felt pretty good to hear that motor rev up the first time."

"When did you start mowing other people's lawns?"

"Last summer." Ben downed the rest of his lemonade. "Countin' you, I mow four lawns a week. One of 'em is Bradbury House."

"That's a pretty big business for a sixth grader."

"Yeah, well, my dad says it never hurts to start savin' up for college."

Mr. Schmidt kept sounding better and better. "Do you still have time for your school work?"

"Yep. And for baseball."

Emily sipped on her lemonade, lost in thought. She could not imagine having been able to handle so much responsibility at Ben's age. Sixth grade, as she remembered it, pretty much consisted of boys, Aquanet hairspray, and the latest Sweet Valley Twins book.

"Ben, can I ask you something?"

"Yes, ma'am."

"Do you know very much about gardening?"

Ben shrugged. "I help my mama hoe the weeds out of our garden."

In Emily's inexperienced eyes, that pretty much made Ben an expert. "I'm thinking about trying to grow some herbs. I've never done it before, and I'm not even sure where to plant them."

"You'll want full sun with herbs," Ben started sagely. "You've gotta nice, sunny spot next to your back door. That seems as good a spot as any."

"If I pay you an extra ten dollars next week, could you help me turn the ground?"

"I gotta tell ya, Miss Emily. It's a little late in the summer for planting. You won't get much of a yield, and the first hard frost'll kill all your annuals."

He could have been speaking Chinese. "Honest enough."

Ben looked at Emily's forehead, which was as close as he had yet come to looking her in the eye. "Come next spring, though, I'll help. You can count on it."

"It's a deal," Emily said.

Ben set his empty glass on the porch and stood up. "I'd better finish up your backyard. Thanks for the cookies and lemonade, Miss Emily."

Emily took the plate and glasses back inside and set them in the kitchen sink. She would wash them later. She was on a mission. Earlier that morning, Emily had finally unpacked the last three boxes that had been sitting on her living room floor, and she had come across one particular item in the second box that sparked an idea beneath those golden curls. Now, Emily felt as if she could not possibly accomplish a single thing until that idea came to fruition. She picked up a manila envelope sitting on her table, waved good-bye to Ben mowing outside her kitchen window, and locked the front door. One minute later she was peddling her bike east toward the end of town.

Alice's house was just a short ride from the Mulberry property. Emily could easily walk the one block south and four blocks east on Currant Avenue if she wanted, but there was something so liberating about pedaling down the middle of a small town road that made Emily bike everywhere she could.

"Well, dear, this is a nice surprise," Alice warmly greeted Emily at the front door. "I was just putting on some water for tea. You couldn't have timed it better."

Alice's house smelled like cinnamon and apples.

"What have you been baking, Alice?"

Alice led Emily to the kitchen. "Now, don't tell on me, but I made an apple cake all for myself. It is one of the few perks of widowhood. I can skip meals if I want and go straight for the dessert. Pull up a chair, dear, and I'll get two forks."

Emily sat at the kitchen table in front of a square, ceramic dish cooling on a trivet. She leaned over to inhale the decadent aroma of caramelized butter and sugar. Warmth was still emanating from the sides of the dish.

Alice wasn't kidding. She set two forks on the table and sat across from Emily. "Now, don't give me that look, Emily Duke. Plates are completely overrated. Besides, apple cake always tastes best straight out of the pan." To demonstrate her point, Alice stuck a fork in a corner of the cake and put the steaming bite directly in her mouth. Emily's jaw dropped.

"You'd better hurry up and claim the north corner, dear, or you may not get any." Alice took an uninhibited second bite.

Emily hesitated for one moment before timidly sticking her own fork in a virgin corner of the cake. A nervous giggle escaped her lips as she lifted the first bite to her mouth. "Oh wow, apple spice cake! And that's a caramel glaze, isn't it?"

"I told you it tastes best straight out of the pan."

Emily eyed Alice shyly. "I always like the middle the best."

"Go for the middle!"

"Oh no, I couldn't."

"Nonsense. Who says you have to eat a cake from the outside in?" Alice proceeded to stick her own fork directly in the middle of the cake. Before long, the two were digging into the middle with abandon, giggling like a couple of school girls. The tea kettle on the range began to whistle.

Alice set down her fork and stood up. "A cup of chamomile will be just the thing. Can I get one for you, Emily?"

"Yes, please." Emily leaned back in her chair, rubbing her happy belly with satisfaction.

"You know, dear," Alice started as she pulled the kettle off the burner, "that unfortunate incident with Evan at choir rehearsal was not your fault."

"I know," Emily sighed. "It still bothers me, though."

"Evan is not the easiest man to be around, but he really is not a mean soul. Milk or sugar?"

"Neither, thanks." Emily took the steaming cup of golden tea from Alice's hands. Alice brought her own cup over and sat back down at the table.

"There was a time when Evan was actually quite pleasant to be around. Oh, he has always been eccentric, mind you, and definitely opinionated. But he wasn't always so cantankerous." Alice stirred her tea absently with her cake fork. "My husband was actually the one who hired him. David heard Evan play a recital in Quincy one summer when we were up visiting family, and he convinced Evan to play for our church. Turns out Evan had a sister already living in Bradbury County, and he was looking for a chance to move closer to family. David and Evan became quite good friends. They partnered for years in the bridge club back when Bradbury still had one." Alice took a long, thoughtful sip of her tea. "Evan played the most beautiful music at David's funeral."

"Were you friends with Evan?"

Alice's head snapped up. "I still am. Always have been. Evan just doesn't realize it."

Emily didn't know how to respond to that.

Alice took a deep breath. "I stood up in his wedding, you know. I was actually the one who introduced him to his wife."

"Evan has a wife?"

"Not anymore."

Alice looked uncomfortable. Emily thought back to the way Rebecca had protected her mother from Evan's full attention at choir rehearsal. Emily also remembered Bev Davis mentioning that Alice had previously left the choir. Something had happened between Alice and Evan.

"Did Evan do something to hurt you, Alice?"

"Oh, no. I hurt him. Or rather, I was close to someone who hurt him." Alice looked at her hands. "I suppose Evan feels that hurt anew whenever he looks at me. Anyway, it's not my story to tell. It involves other people, some of whom you know and some you don't. All I can in good conscience say is my own part in the story, and that's the fact that I poorly judged a person's character many years ago."

Emily took a sip of her tea. She thought back to Evan's boorish comment to Zachary. "How did you know that Evan had insulted Dr. Brandt on Thursday night?"

Alice's eyes brightened. "I studied classics in college. You wouldn't think it to look at me, but this old girl can speak a dead language or two. That's how I caught my husband, you know. I read a couple passages from the Vulgate, and the man was hooked."

Emily smiled at the thought. "Alice, may I ask you one more question?"

"Of course, dear. You can ask me anything, anytime."

"Bev mentioned at rehearsal that you had left the choir."

"I did."

"Why?"

"It's all so silly, really. Evan told me that I couldn't sing."

Emily's face colored with anger. Those kinds of words could only come from the mouth of a director who was ignorant of how to teach people to sing.

"Now, don't get flustered. Evan is right to a point. I can barely carry a tune, and I get flustered whenever people start singing different parts." Alice sighed. "I only tried joining the choir after David died. Being a part of the music making made me feel closer to him somehow. Nights can be really lonely when you miss someone you love."

Emily reached across the table to take her friend's wrinkled hand in her smooth one. "I'm so glad you joined the choir again. Don't be afraid to sing. If you can speak, you can sing. I promise you. Oh, that reminds me!" Emily sat up and clapped her hands together. She reached down by her purse and grabbed the long-forgotten manila envelope. "Come with me."

Emily stood and led Alice to the front living room. She settled Alice comfortably in the blue, wing-backed chair next to the window.

"Now, close your eyes," Emily instructed, taking a seat at the piano and opening the manila envelope. She pulled out a tall, aged piece of sheet music, opened the lid on the Baldwin, and brushed her eager fingers over the smooth, ivory keys. Emily pressed the sustain pedal with her right foot, and gently rolled out the first chord in G major.

"I can give you the starlight," Emily sang with a tenderness worthy of her friend's precious memories. She pushed and pulled every ounce of feeling she could out of the arpeggiated accompaniment, using her voice to sing a love letter from the past. She sang of an epic love as big as the ocean, a devotion as deep and sparkling and clear as a mountain pool. She knew that her own sweet soprano could never compare with the memory of a beloved baritone, but she still poured her heart and soul into the Novello song. She knew what it was like to live with loss, and she wanted to give her friend a moment's reprieve from her pain.

As Emily slowly lifted her hands from the final chord and gently released the pedal, she turned to look at Alice. Seated in absolute stillness with her eyes shut tight, Alice held her hands clasped near her heart. Tears were streaming silently down both cheeks. Alice indulged in a quiet, private reverie behind her closed lids for several seconds before opening her eyes and looking at Emily.

"I could almost see him. He was standing there, giving me that look, the one he gave only to me. Thank you, Emily dear."

Emily was still wiping tears from her own eyes as she pulled her bike up to the Mulberry house. She smiled at the lone tiger lily waiting for her on the front step. She picked it up and took it into the kitchen, pulling out last week's wilted one from the vase on her counter and replacing it with Ben's newest offering. Then, without a second thought, she took the vase into her bedroom and set it before the picture on her nightstand. The man in the picture smiled back at her as always. He never failed to smile, but this time, Emily wanted to hear his voice. She sat, eyes closed tight, in a silent reverie much like Alice's, but the only thing Emily could hear was the sound of her own heartbeat.

Chapter Twelve: For Better or for Worse

"Be sure to leave your listening journal entries on the desk by the door on your way out." Chairs scooted noisily on the tile floor as students stood to gather their books and bags. Emily called out over the fray, "And remember to read chapters 4 and 5 over the weekend. We're moving on to the *ars nova* next week."

Freshmen filed past her desk, chatting loudly about everything under the sun except the *organum* on which Emily had just lectured. Snippets of roommate drama, dining hall cuisine, and failed ensemble auditions made it to Emily's ears. Within seconds, the classroom was empty.

They couldn't wait to get away, Emily thought with amusement as she picked up the teetering pile of journal entries. She would have a good time reading her music literature students' first impressions of early polyphony over a hot cup of tea in her office. There was always at least one student in every bunch whose entry could make her laugh out loud. Emily shuffled the papers into a neat stack before putting them in her bag. She was about to gather her things to leave when a tall, dark-haired boy walked into the room. He was holding a piece of paper.

"May I help you?"

The student handed the paper to Emily. "I saw this on the bulletin board outside Basset's office. You're Dr. Duke, right?"

Emily looked at the ad she had placed on the music department's bulletin board earlier that morning. "I am. Are you interested in the position?"

"Yes."

Emily looked closely at the young man standing before her. She recognized him as the one who had told her not to bother locking her bike on campus that hot summer day a couple of months ago. He was dressed in black skinny jeans and a tight, black shirt. He still wore dark eyeliner around his eyes, and his eyebrow ring continued to poke obnoxiously out of his pale skin. The only difference Emily could see was that he had cut short his long, black hair and styled it to look like an ocean wave rolling onto a shore. "What's your name?"

"Blaine Maler."

"Are you a piano major?"

"Yes, a junior. I'm in Ralph Bronson's studio."

"Do you do very much accompanying?"

"I usually accompany one voice studio a semester. I hope to pick up a couple of senior recitals this spring."

"Ever accompany a choir?"

"Back in high school."

Emily silently weighed the consequences of bringing Blaine Maler into the acquaintance of Mrs. Scheinberg and Miss Geraldine Turner. "Do you have a second to play for me?"

Blaine nodded. Emily reached into her bag and pulled out a couple of choir octavos she had ready. She handed him both pieces of music and gestured for him to sit at the piano near the front of the classroom. "I'd like to hear you sight-read the Brahms, when you are ready."

Blaine set the music at the console and leafed methodically through it. "The accompaniment first?"

"Yes, please."

From the first descending chords to the last phrase of "How Lovely Is Thy Dwelling Place," Blaine played tastefully, not too restrained and not too self-indulgent. He looked over his shoulder at Emily. "Now the choral parts?"

"I'd like to hear the choral parts on the Duruflé instead." Emily took a position in Blaine's line of sight. "I'll conduct this one. Let's start with the solo *cantus firmus*. I'll conduct the quarter note of the chant." Emily waited for Blaine to glance through the music and then met his eyes and gave him a preparatory beat.

Blaine breezed through the Duruflé without any hitches. His playing was clean, and he responded to all of Emily's tempo and dynamic leadings.

"Very nice," Emily was honest. "The church has offered to pay an accompanist $150 a month for an hour-long rehearsal every Thursday night and one worship service every Sunday. It's not much, but it's what they can manage. Is that satisfactory reimbursement for your time?"

Blaine nodded.

"I'd like to speak with your piano instructor before offering you the job. I just want to make sure he is okay with you taking on this extra commitment. Do you mind?"

Blaine shook his head, expressionless.

"Well, then, I'll just take your contact information, and you'll hear from me soon."

Blaine pulled a pencil out of his back pocket and scribbled his email address and phone number on the back of Emily's original ad. He handed the paper and both pieces of music back to Emily.

"How early can you start?"

"Whenever."

Emily smiled. "Great. I'll get in touch with Dr. Bronson today and try to contact you by this evening. We rehearse in the church balcony on Thursdays. Downbeat is at 7:15 p.m. Do you know how to get to Zion?"

"I ride by it on my way out of town."

Emily looked curiously at Blaine. "Say, if you're a junior, why don't I have you in any of my classes this semester?"

"I transferred in history credits."

"Oh, from where?"

Blaine started moving toward the door. "Northwestern. I transferred here sophomore year. Family stuff."

"Say, Blaine," Emily held out her hand as if to catch him before he disappeared out of sight. "There's something you should know. Zion is a small Lutheran congregation. It's pretty conservative in its doctrine and practice. Does that bother you?"

Blaine shrugged his shoulders. "Doesn't matter to me. I don't believe in any of that stuff. All I care about is the music." He stopped and narrowed his eyes. "Your church doesn't do any of that happy clappy crap, does it?"

Emily laughed, taken aback. "No, Zion is a liturgical congregation."

"Good. I'm cool, then." With that, Blaine was out the door and gone as quietly as he had arrived.

Emily took a slight detour back to her office, stopping to knock on her department head's door.

"Emily, come on in." Basset's desk, as usual, was covered with file folders. "How're you enjoying the freshmen?"

"Let's just say they would benefit from being reminded that both a subject and a verb are required to make a complete sentence."

Basset rolled her blue eyes and took off her black-framed glasses. She looked tired. "They couldn't pay me enough to work in a writing lab these days. The students' entry-level literacy keeps getting worse and worse every year. How're these kids even passing high school English?"

Emily shut the door behind her and plopped down in one of the cracked leather chairs, setting her bag on the floor at her feet. "I don't want to keep you. I just wanted to ask you about Blaine Maler."

Basset leaned back in her chair. "Good kid. Great player. Do you have him in class?"

Emily shook her head. "No, he just auditioned to be my church choir accompanist. Is there anything I should be concerned about before offering him the job?"

Basset shrugged her shoulders. "He has a good reputation with the piano studio. He transferred in last year with a clean transcript from Northwestern. I don't know very much about him otherwise. I think he keeps to himself, but I know him to be timely and responsible."

Emily nodded, thoughtful.

"Are you worried about something?"

"Oh, I don't know. He just seems pretty guarded. For someone who seems to want to keep people at a distance, he sure presents himself in a way as to draw attention." Emily stood. "But he sight-read two choral pieces cold without even flinching. I can't ask for much more than that. Thanks, Lauren."

Emily had one more stop to make before holing up in her office with her hot tea and listening journals.

||||||||||||||||||||||||||||||||||||||||||||||||

"Well, look who decided to defect to England!" Zachary Brandt rose from behind his desk, his eyes twinkling. He lifted a stack of books off a wooden chair before proffering it to Emily. He perched himself on a corner of his desk. "Did the sound of freshmen practicing their sight-singing in the hallways drive you away from McPherson Hall?"

Emily tried to manage a smile. She had been dreading this visit all day, and now that she was finally here, she found her stomach tightening in knots.

Zachary's eyes grew serious. "I'm really glad to see you, Emily. I was hoping we would run into each other today. I owe you an apology."

That was not what Emily was expecting to hear. She opened her mouth to speak, but no words came out.

"I shouldn't have come to your choir rehearsal the other night," Zachary continued. "That was too much. I admit, I'm a bit brash and bold by nature—I blame it on all of the hours I spend deconstructing the actions of protagonists in nineteenth-century literature. But I still should have given you some time and space to get familiar with your new gig before forcing myself into the plot. I fancy myself to be a Darcy, but I've been behaving more like a Wickham. Will you forgive me for playing the wrong part?"

Emily was stunned into silence. How did Zachary always manage to leave her speechless?

"How about we start over?" Zachary's smile could disarm any maiden, nineteenth-century or otherwise. He stuck his hand out toward Emily. "My name is Zachary, and I promise not to presume to know where you work, where you go to church, or what kind of music you like until you decide you want to tell me such things yourself. Is it a deal?"

Emily stared at his hand and felt herself waver. The polite thing to do, of course, was respond to his gesture with a handshake.

"And if you let me take you out for coffee tomorrow afternoon," he said, dropping her hand and resting his on the edge of his desk, "I promise that I'll stop invading your choir loft and other personal spaces until you invite me."

Emily pedaled home early that evening as the first star began to shine through the periwinkle drapery of twilight. She had managed to finish grading all of the freshmen listening journals, three of which had made her laugh. She had also managed, due to the heavy influence of some favorable terms, to secure a coffee date for tomorrow afternoon.

Chapter Thirteen:

Our Parents and Other Authorities

"You do realize that you're leaving me alone with four terrors in the pew?"

Rebecca snagged a wet dishrag from the kitchen sink to wipe some leftover oatmeal from Alison's mouth. "Only three, darling. Frankie is too pious to count."

Jeremy placed the last of the breakfast plates in the dishwasher and closed the door. "Well, you'd think the church would at least offer a support group or something for us choir widowers."

"They do, Jay," Rebecca grabbed her purse off the kitchen counter. "It's called the prayer chain."

Rebecca winked and headed out to the garage with a freshly cleaned Alison in tow. Davie and Frankie followed close behind, the former still licking peach jam from between his fingers. Jeremy grabbed the tallest redhead. "Hold it, Davie. Go wash your hands. Frankie, be sure to help your mom buckle Alison into her car seat."

Jeremy looked at his watch and bellowed down the hallway, "Robert Douglas Jones, we are going to leave without you!"

"I'm still pickin' out a book," came Robbie's muffled reply from the recesses of his bedroom.

"You've run out of time. Grab a Magic School Bus and be done with it."

"Those're for babies."

"Tough luck, then. You'll have to settle with reading the bulletin during the sermon like the other adults."

Davie smirked from the kitchen sink. "That's not as fun as it used to be."

Two minutes later, when everyone was safely buckled into their seats, Jeremy gunned the engine toward church. Rebecca turned around in her seat with the balance and ease of a stewardess. "Okay, review time. The Joneses are earning only gold stars today in Sunday School. No repeat memory work this time. Right, Davie?"

Davie turned his iPod volume up higher.

"David, don't ignore your mother," Jeremy eyed his oldest son through the rearview mirror. "I know you can hear me."

Davie sighed and took out his earbuds.

"Okay," Rebecca smiled brightly, "Alison, sweetheart, what is the First Commandment?"

Alison arched her back and grinned. "You sha' have GODS!"

"No, Ali!" Frankie moaned into his hands. "Not *gods*. Just one. We have *one* God!"

"You sha' have," Alison spread her hands wide, "ONE GOD!"

"No, Ali, it's—"

"Close enough for today, Frankie," Rebecca placated.

"I thought we have three gods," Robbie called from the back seat, chomping on a big wad of gum.

"We have one God in three persons: Father, Son, and Holy Spirit." Rebecca turned toward Frankie. "What is the Second Commandment?"

"You shall not misuse the name of the Lord your God."

"Perfect. Robbie, what is the Third Commandment?"

"Remember the Sabbath day by keeping it holy." Robbie blew a giant bubble that popped all over his face.

"Give me the gum, Robert." Rebecca held out her hand.

"I'm just trying to keep it holy." Robbie looked around and laughed. "Get it? Hole-y?"

"You're such a dweeb," Davie said.

"Don't call your brother names, David." Jeremy shot his sons a holy look in the rearview mirror. "Robert, listen to your mother."

"But this is my gum! I won it at the school carnival!"

"Well, you just lost it. Your mother told you not to blow bubbles in the car."

Rebecca extended her hand out further. Robbie scowled and stuck the soggy wad in his mother's bare palm.

"I want gum!" Alison cried.

"No one gets any gum." Rebecca wiped the chewed mess onto a napkin from the glove compartment. "Let's try another one. Robbie, what is the Fourth Commandment?"

"I already did one. It's Davie's turn."

"I'd like to hear you say this one. The Fourth Commandment, Robert."

Robbie didn't miss a beat. "Honor your father and your father."

Davie snorted. "Not in our church, you moron."

"That's it." Jeremy braked hard into the curb, stopping the vehicle and turning around in his seat. "David, you just earned yourself the honor of doing the dishes after lunch today."

"What did I do?"

"And Robert, I will give you one more chance to consider the consequence of misquoting God's Word before I tell you what you'll be doing this afternoon. Now, answer your mother. Correctly."

Robbie stared for a moment at his father, carefully weighing his options. "Honor your father and your mother."

"That's right. And since you seem to be having trouble re-membering to honor your mother this morning, you can spend the afternoon writing out the Fourth Commandment instead of playing on your X-Box." Jeremy pulled the car back out onto the road. "Now, I don't want to hear another peep from any of you for the rest of the drive."

Unfortunately for Robbie, Blaine Maler was getting out of his car just as the Joneses pulled into the church parking lot.

"Who's the freak?" Robbie hollered.

Robbie didn't say much else in the car that day. Jeremy made sure of it.

<hr />

Emily's morning wasn't going much better.

"Irv is sick," Bev explained as she came up to the balcony alone. "Food poisoning. I told him not to eat the chicken leg at the back of the fridge last night, but he wouldn't listen. I'm pretty sure it was leftover from the time we took Irv's mother to Koelster's for her birthday over Labor Day weekend."

Janet's chin shot defensively up in the air. "I'm not sure why it matters where the chicken was fried!"

"Oh, now, Janet, I'm not implying that you—"

"Because you can't blame what's coming up today on a bird that should've gone down three weeks ago." Janet's face was growing redder by the second. "That's the fridge keeper's fault, not the cook's."

Bev's nose flared indignantly. "Well, you may be able to control what goes in and out of your own refrigerator, Janet, but I am *married* and have to share my refrigerator with my *husband*."

"Married or not, ladies, we still don't have a bass this morning," Mrs. Scheinberg refereed.

Miss Turner tut-tutted from the front row, "This is precisely why we should have let Dr. Brandt join the choir."

Candice, Marge, and Lois nodded their heads in agreement. Phyllis silently studied her music. Irene simply looked around the balcony, trying to figure out what everyone was talking about.

"Evan could sing the part," Alice bravely suggested. Everyone held their breath and looked toward the console bench. Nothing came of it, though. Evan remained silent, flipping through Divine Service, Setting Three, in *Lutheran Service Book* as if nothing was happening around him.

"I can sing the part if you need," Blaine offered. He had been standing quietly at the back, looking through one of the hymnals.

"Oh, would you?" Emily begged.

Blaine shrugged. "You don't have anyone else to do it."

Emily noticed that Evan's lips pursed ever so slightly.

"Besides," Blaine added, "I know it already from rehearsal on Thursday, and the only time the piece splits into four parts is at the a cappella section in the middle. I don't even play then."

"Thank you, Blaine." Emily let out the breath she had been holding.

While Blaine made his way to the piano, Emily had the choir stand for warm-ups. Bev moved to her spot next to Janet in the alto section, making a show of not looking at her. Janet matched Bev in pathos and silent innuendo, deliberately scooting a few inches closer to Dorothy, who chose that moment to swoon.

Rebecca suddenly appeared at the top of the stairs, panting. "Sorry I'm late. We had a little situation to deal with in the van. Hey, where's Irv?"

The choir sang the Voluntary quite well that morning. There was one awkward moment during the a cappella section when Marge came in a measure early, but no one sitting in the nave seemed to think anything unusual had happened. They were used to Marge singing as if the entire choir piece were a solo.

There was also a shifty moment during the communion hymn when Bev and Janet accidentally grabbed for the same hymnal. Thankfully, Bev, feeling repentant after Pastor Fletcher's sermon on forgiveness, let go and gestured that Janet should have it. Janet, in return, shared her bulletin with Bev when the front row came up one short after communion. By the postlude, the two women were walking down the balcony stairs side by side, properly reconciled and sharing chicken noodle soup secrets. The rest of the choir followed happily behind, chatting about the success of their first choir Sunday.

|||||||||||||||||||||||||||||||||||||||||||||||||

"Hey."

Blaine, who had intentionally lingered behind to avoid the crowd of congregants leaving the church, looked up from the piano bench into a pair of curious, blue eyes floating in a sea of boyish freckles.

"Does it hurt?"

Blaine glanced nervously around the balcony. Evan was busy blasting away on the organ postlude, and no other adult was nearby to claim this kid. "Does what hurt?"

"That poker thing in your face."

"No."

"It's pretty freaky."

"So are your freckles."

The kid grinned. "Grams tells me they're angel kisses, but that's just made up."

"What are they, then?"

"They're extra brain cells."

"Brain cells?"

"Yeah. Really smart people have them."

"What about moles?"

"Oh, those aren't brain cells. Those are just stains from where bugs pooped on you when you're a baby."

Blaine actually cracked a half smile. "Where did you learn all of this?"

"My brother Davie."

"Does he have freckles?"

Robbie puffed his chest out proudly. "Not as many as me."

"Who are you, anyway?"

"Robbie Jones. Who're you?"

"Blaine Maler." Blaine scooted off the piano bench. "Should you be up here?"

"It's okay. My mom sings in the choir. How do you get your hair to stand up like that?"

"Mousse."

Robbie scrunched up his face. "You have a moose?"

Blaine shook his head. "Never mind."

"Are you a man?"

Blaine stopped and eyed his interrogator suspiciously. "Yes."

"You kind of look like a girl."

"You kind of look like a giraffe."

"Robert!" Rebecca called from the top of the stairs. "How in the world did you get up here?"

"The stairs."

"You're not supposed to run off without telling your father where you're going. Get back downstairs. *Right. Now.*" She pointed toward the stairs.

"But I was—"

"Now!"

Robbie sagged toward the doorway in defeat, each step down the stairs a heavy thud of disappointment.

Rebecca walked over to Blaine. "I'm so sorry. I have no idea what my son just said to you, but I'm sure it was inappropriate."

Blaine shrugged, saying nothing, and followed Rebecca back down the stairs.

|||||||||||||||||||||||||||||||||||||||||||||||||||

Several people were gathered in the narthex around Emily and two strangers.

"This is my father, Greg," Emily put her hand on the arm of a man with a gray mustache and then nodded toward the woman with a familiar, reserved smile who was standing next to him, "and this is my mother, Mary."

"Hail, Mary!" Candice exclaimed for all the room to hear, laughing at her own joke.

Emily's mother chuckled graciously, allowing Candice to think it was the first time she had ever heard the joke.

Alice came forward and shook Mary's hand. "Well, I have no doubt that you are full of grace, Mrs. Duke. Your daughter has your beautiful smile and kind eyes, that's for sure. My name is Alice."

"Thank you, Alice," Mary's smile lines matched those of her daughter perfectly, "but I am actually Mrs. Heath."

"Oh." Alice's confident smile faltered for a moment, but she quickly recovered her welcoming expression. Candice's eyes narrowed in Emily's direction.

"From whom does Dr. Duke get her gift of music?" Pastor Fletcher asked.

"Not from me," Greg admitted. "I can claim her brilliant sense of humor, though."

"Oh, Dad," Emily smiled.

"Are you staying for a couple of days?" Rebecca inquired.

"We came in yesterday morning and spent the night. We have to head back this afternoon."

"Well, you have to let us know the next time you're in town," Rebecca welcomed. "We'd love to show you around Bradbury."

"Be sure to stop at Koelster's Kitchen for dinner the next time you come," Bev offered enthusiastically. "They have the best fried chicken."

"Just don't take home a doggie bag," Janet joked. The two women dissolved into hysterical giggles.

As everyone filed off toward the fellowship hall, Blaine felt something tug at his shirt sleeve. He turned around to find Robbie standing at his elbow.

"Wanna see the muffins?"

"No, I'm heading out."

"You don't have to stay for Sunday School?"

"Nope."

Robbie's face reflected his covetous heart. "I can't wait to be a grown-up."

"Come on, Robbie," Rebecca called from ahead. "Leave Mr. Maler alone."

Robbie snuck one last sideways glance at Blaine's face. "You're not a freak like I thought."

"Are you disappointed?"

"A little."

Blaine nodded and mumbled under his breath, "Me too."

Chapter Fourteen: The Quilting Circle

"Greg and Mary *Heath*. Did you catch that?" Candice's eyes were bulging with emphasis.

"Careful, Candice, or your eyes will fall right out of their sockets," Mrs. Scheinberg warned from her post at the corner of the quilt.

The quilting circle of Zion Lutheran Church was a standing tradition in Bradbury County. It had its beginnings long before any of the current members could remember, but everyone knew that for more than a century, the women of Zion had been sewing quilts for the underprivileged and shipping them all over the world. The whole town of Bradbury turned out annually for the quilting circle's Fat Tuesday Flip and Fry, a pancake and sausage supper that raised funds for the circle's yearly supply of calico, batting, and thread.

Once a thriving, industrious group of more than thirty women, the quilting circle had since dwindled to a small but faithful group of eight that met every Tuesday morning in the church fellowship hall. Full-time jobs and trendier hobbies (Mrs. Scheinberg fully blamed the new scrapbooking store on Third Street) kept most of Zion's women away. This particular morning, only six women sat around the blue-and-yellow log cabin quilt that was stretched across the wooden frame that had been crafted with love and donated fifty years before by the late Dottie Burmeister's husband. Alice Gardner was sick at home with a sinus infection, and Phyllis Bingley was on vacation. Well, at least the other women *assumed* Phyllis was on vacation. Phyllis never actually talked to any of them.

"I don't understand," Nettie Schmidt squinted as she pulled a needle through her edge of the quilt.

"Emily Duke's parents have a different last name," Miss Turner explained.

"From each other?" Nettie asked.

"No, they have a different last name from Emily," Candice clucked.

"What does it mean?"

"It means, Nettie," Candice leaned in to confide, "that Emily was married. Or *still is* married."

"But she lives alone, doesn't she?" Bev pondered.

"She does now," Candice practically crowed.

Mrs. Scheinberg channeled all of her irritation into a single sigh. "Are we here to sew quilts for the military chaplains, ladies, or to indulge in idle gossip?"

"It is not gossip to clarify the facts about our new choir director," Miss Turner defended.

"Actually, Geraldine, it is gossip when our new choir director is not here to do the clarifying."

Four of the six women in attendance shifted uncomfortably in their chairs. Irene Rincker couldn't hear a thing, so she did not know to be uncomfortable.

"Well," Bev continued, "it seems odd to me that Dr. Duke wouldn't tell us herself if she were married."

"Exactly," Candice confirmed.

"Exactly, what?" Mrs. Scheinberg challenged.

"It's odd; that's all," Bev persisted.

"There is nothing odd!" Mrs. Scheinberg would have thrown her hands up in the air if someone younger had been present to chase down her thimble. As it was, it took a considerable amount of effort for her to get out of one of these tiny chairs, and she had no intention of risking her thimble flying off her finger. "Dr. Duke has told us nothing, so there's nothing to tell. End of story."

"If she is hiding something," Candice suggested, "it would be a poor play on the congregation's trust. That's for sure."

"Oh, good grief!" Mrs. Scheinberg took off her thimble and set down her needle. She leaned her bosom forward and rocked back and forth to get out of her chair. "I'm going to the kitchen to make some coffee."

Bev had enough tact to wait until Mrs. Scheinberg was out of earshot. "Do you think she's still married?"

"If she is, she must be separated," Candice concluded. "I've never seen a man come in or out of that house."

"She's never spoken of a husband," Bev argued.

"Well, she wouldn't if they were separated, would she?"

"She could be divorced," Miss Turner offered. "I've never seen her wear a ring."

"So," Nettie squinted, "you're saying that *Duke* is not Emily's maiden name, that it's her married name?"

"Yes, Nettie," Candice's voice was impatient. She wanted to get this matter settled before Arlene came back.

"Poor thing," Bev crooned.

"Poor thing?" Candice was all surprise. "There's nothing poor about her. If you ask me, the whole thing shows a want of commitment in Emily. Young women are too eager to give up on their husbands these days. It turns my stomach to think we've hired a liberal."

"Oh, now, we really don't know that she's divorced," Bev reminded everyone, mostly trying to convince herself. She did not like to think of her young director as a divorcée.

"Maybe she was adopted later in life," Nettie suggested. "I once read about that in a book."

"Why would she keep her old name if she were adopted?" Candice argued.

"Maybe she wanted to have something to remember her birth family by," Nettie romanticized. "You know, like that sweet Anne Shirley. She never took Matthew's name, even though she loved him like a father."

"What in the world are you talking about, Nettie?" Candice squinted this time.

"Or," Bev offered, "maybe her father died and her mother remarried."

"Nope," Candice nixed the notion with a swift shake of her head. "Emily distinctly introduced that man as her father after church on Sunday."

"I just thought of something." Miss Turner's face turned red hot with dismay. "If Emily is only separated, then she's still legally married. And I'm almost certain that she is dating that Dr. Brandt who showed up at the first choir rehearsal."

"How do you know?" Bev asked.

"I saw them together at The Corner Coffee Shop the other day."

Bev sucked in her breath. "He did seem awfully familiar with her at that rehearsal."

"And I remember that she seemed uncomfortable around him in front of all of us," Candice built her case. "She'd feel uncomfortable only if she felt guilty about something. To think that we have a choir director who is married to one man but dating another!"

"I think I'm going to be sick." Bev covered her mouth.

"Coffee is brewing," Mrs. Scheinberg announced, settling herself back into her chair. She chose to ignore the fact that the other women were white faced and still as statues. Except Irene, who was stitching merrily along on a bright blue log. "So, who is on the list to make muffins for next Sunday?"

Miss Turner cleared her throat, resuming her meticulously perfect stitching. "The Jones family."

"Oh, good," Mrs. Scheinberg said. "That freckled one usually puts frosting on them."

"They're all freckled," Candice quipped, "and cupcakes are frosted, not muffins."

"Speak for yourself."

"Do you know," Miss Turner sniffed, "I think last week's muffins were made from a box!"

"Why do you say that?" Bev asked.

"Did you see the corn muffins? They were canary yellow. Real cornmeal is not that bright. Only Jiffy's box mix is."

The women pondered that scandalous news for a minute in silence.

"Gas was $3.57 a gallon!" Irene hollered suddenly.

The other women looked up in surprise. Irene smiled amicably at everyone.

"Did you fill up at Casey's?" Bev asked politely.

"Phillip's not spacey!" Irene loyally defended her husband.

"No, I said . . . oh, never mind."

"What do you think of our new accompanist?" Miss Turner fished.

Bev paused for a moment. "He seems troubled, doesn't he?"

"Well, he certainly uses more hair products than I do," Candice smirked.

"Who does?" Nettie squinted.

"Blaine Maler," Miss Turner answered, "our new choir accompanist.

"Did Evan Ebner die?"

"Good heavens, no!" Bev assured. "Evan still plays the organ. He just doesn't accompany the choir anymore."

"Why not?"

Miss Turner lifted her chin ever so slightly. "Perhaps Evan simply does not approve of working with our young director."

Candice sniffed in agreement.

Mrs. Scheinberg, determined to steer the conversation away from Emily, picked the lesser of two evils. "Blaine Maler seems like a nice kid. Talented too. It was sporting of him to help out with the singing on Sunday."

"Well, I can barely look at him," Miss Turner turned up her nose. "His hair is too much for me. And that eye ornament he wears looks like something out of Dungeons and Dragons."

"I didn't know you were intimate with the details of that game, Geraldine," Mrs. Scheinberg said.

"I'm serious. Why would any decent person puncture his eyebrow? It's violent." Miss Turner pursed her lips. "I can't help but want to pull it out every time I see it."

"Now, *that* is violent," Mrs. Scheinberg pointed out.

"He needs to wash his face, if you know what I mean," Candice contributed.

"Oh, Candice," Mrs. Scheinberg sighed, "you're just saying that because he looks better in eyeliner than you do."

"Do you suppose . . . ?" Bev started.

"What?"

"Do you suppose he's a . . . ?"

"A homosexual?" Miss Turner was not too shy to say it. "Yes, I do."

"Okay." Mrs. Scheinberg had had enough. She leaned over to gather her bag and scarf from the floor and then began the laborious rocking routine of pushing herself out of her chair again. "It has been lovely, but I think I'm done here."

"Leaving so soon?" Bev was sincerely disappointed, oblivious to any damage the conversation may have caused.

"Oh, before you go," Candice fluttered, clearly not disappointed, "I have some good news. My sister's daughter, Amelia, is coming to stay with us for three months. She's going to work an internship in my husband's office. It's very smart of her, really. I think we all know that my husband's name is gold on any résumé. Anyway, we're having a party for her on Saturday, and I insist that all of you come. You too, Arlene. I'm making Great Grandmother Bradbury's apple cider punch, and Thomas Jr. has promised to play his trombone."

Mrs. Scheinberg tried to contain her excitement as she walked out to her Grand Marquis. She could think of several things she would rather do this Saturday than watch Thomas Edison Bradbury the Gazillionth pucker up his lips to a trombone. There was no getting around it, though. She would have to go, if anything, to make sure her beloved Emily Duke didn't face those flesh-eating vultures alone.

CHAPTER FIFTEEN: WELCOME, AMELIA!

The historic Bradbury House sat on an acre plot of land right in the heart of town. Surrounded by at least fifteen ancient pin oak trees, the property was a favorite target of idle college freshmen every autumn. Even now, the day of Amelia's big party, long streams of toilet paper billowed elegantly from the oaken boughs. Candice had no way of taking the tissue down herself, so she spent a good deal of time convincing her guests (and herself) that the papery drapes were a mark of fame and popularity.

"Those crazy kids," Candice smiled benevolently at her guests as if she had just received a handmade valentine. "The things they do to try to get our attention!"

Whatever the college students thought, Bradbury House was a source of continuing pride for the town. Its perfectly preserved red-brick, three-story structure was a mixture of Italianate architecture and Greek Revivalism, rare in a town so far from the Mississippi River. The original Mrs. Thomas Edison Bradbury had seen to it that her house was built facing the west. She hadn't wanted the hot afternoon sun to flood her new kitchen. The original Mr. Bradbury hadn't been too concerned about the temperature in the kitchen, but he eagerly went along with his wife's plan. He liked the idea of sitting on his front porch in the evenings and watching the sun set over his prairie farmland. Little did he know at the time that his eldest daughter would someday donate his beloved view to the Wesleyan Methodist Church to start a teacher's college. Unfortunately for Candice today, Bradbury House's front door no longer looked out over prairie sunsets but instead on Shawna Hall, Bradbury College's newest freshmen girl dormitory. The only sight Candice got to see from her front porch every evening was that of undergraduates making out in the shadows.

Emily knocked on the big front door of Bradbury House. Candice had made sure to invite all of the choir members present at Thursday night's rehearsal to Amelia's party this afternoon. Emily had hoped to carpool with Rebecca and Alice, but they were both attending one of Davie's basketball scrimmages in Hamburg that day. (The Bradbury Indians were perennial rivals of the Hamburg Comets, or the "Hamburglars," as all of Bradbury insisted on calling them.) Emily glanced nervously through the floor-to-ceiling windows that flanked either side of the door, giving view to roomfuls of guests already mingling inside. She could see Evan sitting in a straight-backed chair in a corner of the front southwest sitting room, balancing a cup of punch on his knee. Emily's stomach involuntarily lurched.

"Ah, Emily." Candice opened the door, her tone and manner unimpressed. "You came after all. This is my daughter, Caroline."

Standing next to Candice was the most uncomfortable-looking girl Emily had ever seen. She must have been at least twelve years old, but her golden hair was unnaturally curled and hung in Shirley Temple clusters around her cheeks. Judging by the way Caroline averted her eyes, Emily guessed that she had not chosen the hairstyle for herself. Nor the outfit. The knee-length, plum-colored taffeta dress would have been cute and flirty on a sixteen-year-old girl on prom night, but the spaghetti-strapped gown looked painfully inappropriate on a preteen in the afternoon light. Emily felt a flash of pity for the girl.

"Caroline made this dress herself for the Bradbury County Fair last July," Candice bragged, putting her arm around her life-size doll. "She was the only one in her 4-H group to win a blue ribbon *and* Best in Show."

"It's a very pretty color," Emily acknowledged.

Candice's cheeks pulled into a horizontal smile as she stepped back into the front hall. "Do come in, Emily. I imagine you want to see the house. Five generations of Bradburys have lived under this roof. The staircase is original, of course, and all of the light fixtures were designed specifically at Mother Imelda's request. Do be sure to notice the vaulted ceilings and original crown molding. Most people spend so much time admiring the rugs Great Grandmother Bradbury brought back from Egypt that they forget to look up. Caroline, why don't you take Emily into the dining room and help her with her plate?"

The mortified heiress led Emily past the polished wooden staircase in the front entrance hall to the dining room just off of the kitchen, situated on the southeast corner of the main floor. The dining room looked as if it could have appeared in a feature spread of *Southern Living*. The long mahogany table was dressed in lace. Silver trays and chafing dishes dotted the table, giving off tantalizing aromas of roasted meats and melted cheese. Two giant porcelain vases filled with purple asters, magenta cockscombs, and white spider mums stood guard on either end of the mahogany buffet. A full china coffee service was laid out in between the vases. Lace curtains billowed in the soft breeze at the south-facing windows. Caroline picked up a plate from the table and asked, "Brisket or chicken?"

"Oh, Caroline, thank you. I'm happy to serve myself."

Caroline nodded obediently and handed the empty plate to Emily before escaping into the kitchen.

"She looks about as miserable as I feel." Mrs. Scheinberg was leaning in the north doorway of the dining room. "Try the brisket if you like beef. Candice's smoked meat really is the best in town, but don't you dare tell her I said so."

Emily smiled, mostly in relief at seeing a familiar face in a sea of strangers. She felt nervous at parties.

"When you've filled up your plate, come find me in the northwest parlor. I've saved you a seat as far away from Thomas Jr.'s music stand as we can get."

Emily sampled the brisket as well as the mashed carrots, roasted green beans, and rosemary potatoes. She grabbed a warm, homemade oatmeal roll on her way out of the room. Then, she found Mrs. Scheinberg seated in the formal parlor next to an overgrown schefflera. An open seat next to her was being saved by a lone cup of punch.

"I thought you might need something to drink," Mrs. Scheinberg explained, picking up the cup for Emily to sit down. "That, and I'm going to break out in hives if Bev sits next to me this afternoon. She's been calling me every fifteen minutes since eight o'clock this morning to try to tell me about her mother's foot fungus appointment yesterday. I just know one of Adeline's toes fell off this time."

Emily sat in her chair, gingerly balancing her plate on her knees. "Oh, I forgot a fork!"

"No worries." Mrs. Scheinberg reached down into her green-and-yellow quilted Vera Bradley tote she used as a purse and produced a plasticware set complete with knife and spork. "I always carry a spare."

Emily took the plasticware, glancing around to see if anyone was watching. "This house is beautiful."

Mrs. Scheinberg nodded, her mouth busy with a bite of brisket.

"The wallpaper's exquisite. I've never seen anything like it."

Mrs. Scheinberg swallowed. "It's Victorian, from the Morris Tradition."

"How do you know?"

"I put it up myself." Mrs. Scheinberg shrugged at Emily's raised eyebrows. "Candice may talk like she knows the history of Bradbury, but she sure didn't live it. She grew up in Davenport and met and married Thomas in college. My grandaddy is the one who hanged the paper that was previously in this room. I was not about to let an import touch these walls."

"I have a hard time imagining Candice letting you do anything in her own home."

Mrs. Scheinberg's eyes twinkled merrily. "Oh, Candice thinks she did it herself."

"Did you bewitch her or something?"

"You're catching onto my ways, Dr. Duke. About ten years ago, Candice mentioned during quilting circle that she was going to replace the paper in the front two rooms. Now, I think we can all imagine what kind of wallpaper Candice would find appealing: open up a children's book of fairytales, turn to Cinderella, wave a purple magic wand around a few times, and— voila!—there is Candice's delicate sense of style. No one in this town would ever recover if Candice turned our pride and joy into Bippity-Boppity-Boo, so I spent a little time looking around for a respectable paper company."

Mrs. Scheinberg paused to put a round, red potato in her mouth, masterfully continuing to talk around her food. "After a little digging, I came across a company out of California that specializes in vintage paper reproductions, and, get this," Mrs. Scheinberg jabbed her left elbow into Emily's unassuming side, "the company's name? Bradbury & Bradbury! All I had to do was wave one of their catalogs around at the next quilting circle, mention that I thought there might be a connection between the company and Candice's husband's family line, and the rest," Mrs. Scheinberg sniffed with satisfaction, "is history."

Emily looked up at the fields of delicate, silver-white fern leaves climbing the grey-indigo walls. Large panels of burgundy pomegranates and yellow-orange lemons interrupted the intricate pattern, but otherwise she could find no telltale seams in the paper panels. Even the golden-brown oak leaves curling along the border near the ceiling seemed to float in an endless stream of green boxwood. "How did you convince Candice to let you hang it yourself?"

"Bradbury & Bradbury paper isn't cheap, but Scheinberg labor is."

"I can't even see where one panel ends and another begins."

"I should hope not," Candice quipped. She had made her way over to the schefflera in time to hear Emily's last comment. Candice eyed Emily's spork. "Is our silverware not good enough for you?"

"Oh!" Emily covered her mouth to hide the bite of oatmeal roll she had just taken. "No, I just missed them in the dining room, I guess."

"I see you like the rolls."

"Everything is delicious!"

"The brisket turned out a bit dry this time," Candice unsuccessfully tried to look passive as she inspected her fingernails, "but my rolls are foolproof. They come out light and moist every time."

There was an awkward silence as Emily nodded politely, unsure of what to say in response. She looked around to find Mrs. Scheinberg watching Candice warily from behind her punch cup. Their hostess had the bristly posture of a cat about to pounce on her prey.

"Did you do anything . . . *fun* this week, Emily?"

Emily looked up at Candice, startled. "Excuse me?"

"Fun? Did you do anything fun?"

"Oh, well, I . . . I started picking out music for the Christmas Eve program."

Candice forced a joyless laugh. "Oh, now, come on, Emily. That's business. I'm talking about after hours. Did you do anything *fun* this week?"

"Did *you*, Candice?" Mrs. Scheinberg demanded.

Candice turned to face her challenger. The two matrons locked gazes, a silent battle ensuing. Candice was the first one to break, her cheeks coloring slightly under her pressed powder as she looked away. "I most certainly did! Colette and I went shopping in Terre Haute on Wednesday before she headed back to Garrett and the family." Candice smoothed out the front of her violet-and-gold brocade jacket. "Well, if you'll excuse me. It's time to introduce everyone to my niece." Candice turned on her heel and walked to the front entryway, Mrs. Scheinberg's eyes following her suspiciously the entire way. She had a bad feeling in the pit of her stomach, and it was not from the brisket.

"Attention," Candice clapped her hands. "Attention, everyone!"

Clusters of guests seated in the front formal parlor and the southwest music room, both of which had clear views to the foyer, quieted down and respectfully turned to face their hostess. Roamers wandered in from the back game room, the dining room, and the kitchen to better hear what Candice had to say.

"As you all know, my sister Colette has loaned the town of Bradbury her one and only daughter, Amelia, for the next few months. Amelia is a recent magna cum laude graduate of Iowa

State University and a proud member of Rho Gamma, where she was voted 'Most Beautiful Smile,'" at which Mrs. Scheinberg coughed spastically, choking on her punch.

"Sorry!" she sputtered, waving her hands apologetically to everyone in the air. Her face was red with suppressed laughter. "Went down the wrong tube!"

Candice's flared nostrils were the only sign of her irritation. She blinked once and continued, "Of course, Amelia shares her award-winning smile with children from all across the world every summer break at Disney World's Magic Kingdom, where she works as 'Belle' from *Beauty and the Beast*."

"I wonder if they offered Candice the part of the beast," Mrs. Scheinberg whispered to Emily.

". . . Amelia is also a registered member of the Daughters of the American Revolution, an accomplished violinist, and an avid photographer. One of her photos was even recently published on a website called Flickr.com. I saw it myself last month. You will also be interested to know . . ."

Mrs. Scheinberg sighed. She was not interested. Candice had a way of talking endlessly about a person without ever actually saying anything of import. What did this girl study in school? Where did she go to church? Did she vote for Obama or not? Mrs. Scheinberg scooped up her final spoonful of creamed peas and resigned herself to the task of constructing a mental list of the similarities between Candice and Disney villains.

". . . and I think you will all agree with me that my husband's law office is the best place for a young, uprising star to serve as intern. I hope you will join me in welcoming to Bradbury my niece, Amelia Ann Grey."

Smatterings of polite applause broke out among the guests. Several of the standing roamers looked around to see where they could set down their sweating punch cups so as to free up both of their clapping hands and, finding no available surface younger than 1920, settled with slapping their free hand against a knee. A young woman with long, shiny brown hair and a refreshingly modest blush stepped forward from the stairwell and stood next to her beaming aunt. Silence hovered as everyone, Amelia included, waited to see what Candice expected to happen next. When Candice just stood there blinking invitingly at her niece, Amelia cleared her throat, looked out at everyone with her Disney-worthy smile, and said, "Thank you for having me."

Candice looked somewhat disappointed with the brevity of Amelia's acceptance speech, but her voice remained bright as a spotlight. "Well, Thomas Jr. has prepared a piece of music in honor of his cousin's arrival, and we have another family musician who has decided to make her concert debut this afternoon. If you would all please step into the music room . . ." As everyone began inching closer to the already crammed green room on the southwest corner of the house, Mrs. Scheinberg motioned for Emily to remain seated.

"It's no use. We're not all going to fit in that room." She added under her breath, "Thank God."

Emily noticed that Evan, who had previously been seated in a prime corner seat of the southwest room, presently entered the parlor from the rear. Apparently, Mrs. Scheinberg was not the only one eager to take a backseat at this concert. Emily sank back in her seat, ducking her head behind the schefflera. She immediately scolded herself for being so juvenile as to hide from Evan, but she still felt uneasy about what he might say to her in public.

Toot-like warbles suddenly blurted from the crowded music room. Evan's face physically aged ten years at the sound, and Mrs. Scheinberg immediately stuffed her napkin in her mouth. Her face was turning redder by the second. Emily could not tell if this was an effort on Mrs. Scheinberg's part to keep sound from coming in or from going out. Emily tried her best to listen attentively—the collective bleats and splats coming together to resemble something like the tune of "Be Our Guest" from Amelia's token Disney cartoon—but Emily had to look at her lap to hide her face once the singing started. A remarkably nasal, pinched voice, one Emily could only assume belonged to the tortured Caroline Bradbury, began singing in unison with the trombone.

Mrs. Scheinberg had resorted to burying the entirety of her face in her arm, her shoulders convulsing. Evan took a deep breath and held his stomach. Emily closed her eyes and prayed desperately for that poor, overexposed girl.

When it was all over, guests applauded politely enough and quickly dispersed to claim a piece of apple pie. Emily opened her eyes to find Mrs. Scheinberg digging around in her tote for a tissue. Evan was smartly facing the fireplace mantel, busily studying the painting hanging above his head as people filed past him into the dining room.

"Well, that was a butt-clenching performance if I ever heard one."

Emily didn't even have to ask Mrs. Scheinberg what she meant. She felt her own backside just now relaxing from the tension. Mrs. Scheinberg wiped her eyes with her tissue and excused herself to go get seconds on the brisket.

"May I take your plate for you?" Caroline was standing before Emily, red cheeked and somewhat relieved. She and Thomas Jr., now finished with their musical offering, were walking around per their mother's instructions to collect empty plates—and compliments, no doubt—from the guests and to take them to the kitchen.

"Thank you, Caroline," Emily smiled warmly, "especially for the music."

Caroline took the plate but didn't look Emily in the eye.

"Were you nervous?"

Caroline nodded, still staring at the plate in her hands.

"I get nervous when I sing too."

Caroline peeked at Emily's face to see if she was being mocked.

"It was very brave of you to sing in front of so many people. I don't think you forgot a single word. That was impressive!"

Caroline cracked a smile. It was smaller than her mother's but much more genuine. "I want to take voice lessons, but Mom is making me take piano instead."

"Oh, well, piano is good for you too. If you like singing so much though, maybe you and I could sing together after church sometime?"

"Oh, now, that won't be necessary, Emily." Candice had snuck up out of nowhere, putting her arm possessively around her daughter. "Caroline already has music teachers. Very honest, respectable ones."

Emily blinked, not sure what to make of that comment.

Candice released her daughter's shoulders and said, "Take that to the kitchen, Caroline. I don't want you to get any of those mashed carrots on your dress."

Emily watched Caroline weave in and out of people standing in the parlor, her head down. Pastor Fletcher appeared in the doorway from the dining room with two pieces of pie. He said something encouraging to Caroline before walking over to the fireplace and proffering a piece to Evan.

"You know, I invited Dr. Brandt to the party." Candice was still standing in front of Emily's chair. "I was sure he would come, but I don't see him."

Emily looked up into Candice's eyes, alarmed by the smoldering coals she saw there.

"Didn't he come with you?" Candice accused.

"Did who come with whom?" Miss Turner asked, saddling up beside Candice.

"Dr. Brandt with Emily."

Emily shook her head no.

"Huh. Did he tell you he wasn't coming?"

"I've never talked with Dr. Brandt about this party." Emily felt her cheeks burn, though she had no idea why.

"Oh, come now, Emily," Miss Turner's laugh was all voice and no face. "I have trouble believing that."

"What do you mean?"

"We all know you and Dr. Brandt are dating." Candice's two hot coals jumped into flame.

"I-I'm not dating Dr. Brandt," Emily stuttered. She could see the top of Bev Davis's head on the other side of the schefflera. The woman appeared to be eavesdropping on the conversation but made no immediate move to join the interrogation. Emily suddenly felt afraid. She looked around for Mrs. Scheinberg, wishing she would come back soon with her second helping of brisket.

"There's no denying it." Miss Turner's mouth was pinching unattractively. "I saw you two together at The Corner Coffee Shop last week. Was that a date, or wasn't it?"

"Well, no—I mean—it was a date, but—"

"You just said you weren't dating Dr. Brandt, but you went out on a date with him?" Candice leaned in closer, eyeing Emily hungrily like a pile of dried timber. "You can't have it both ways, so one of those statements is a lie."

Emily closed her eyes and shook her head, trying to stop the spinning. This was getting out of hand. "No. It was a date, but Zachary and I—"

"I want to know something." Candice raised her voice loud enough for the entire room to hear. "What else are you lying about, Emily Duke?"

The formal parlor hushed in an instant and faces turned toward the cluster of women planted by the schefflera. Pastor Fletcher's head snapped up in alarm. He looked around for Emily, but he couldn't see her for the human shield Candice and Geraldine made with their own bodies. Evan, however, standing just two feet to Pastor's left, had a perfectly clear view of Emily's stunned face over Geraldine's left shoulder. He stared boldly into Emily's eyes, neither smiling nor frowning. Emily shuddered. She instinctively knew Evan would not try to save her from what was coming next. She was in this alone.

"Do you know what I think?" Candice called out, her eyes throwing flames. "I think you thought you could pull one over on the small-town country bumpkins. A big city girl moving down to Bradbury all by herself, setting up a new life, all the while *still married*. That's right, Emily Duke. I am not the fool you thought. I had my husband's secretary look up your marriage certificate, filed in Shelby County, Illinois. Do you know what my secretary didn't find? A divorce certificate. Because you've never filed one! You may think you can leave your husband, throw your ring away, and start an adulterous relationship right under our noses, but that is not how we do things in Bradbury. I can't prevent you from falling into grievous sin, but I can prevent you from ever stepping into my house again!"

Mrs. Scheinberg stepped back in the parlor just then, a piece of pie in one hand and a second helping of brisket in the other, but she stopped short at the sight of a chalk-white Emily walking silently out the front door.

"What just happened?" Mrs. Scheinberg asked a heart-sick Pastor Fletcher. She didn't need an answer. Candice's victorious smile told her everything she needed to know.

Chapter Sixteen: About Emily

||||||||||||||||||||||||||||||||||||||||||||||||||

Emily was curled up in a corner of her living room couch. A cold cup of tea sat untouched on a nearby stool, and a worn copy of *Anne of Green Gables* lay unopened on the floor. The usual comforts held no appeal for her tonight. Sunset had come and gone more than an hour ago, and Emily sat unmoving in the dark, embracing the solace of evening like a forgiving friend.

A knock on the front door barely succeeded in stirring Emily from her repose. Only at the urging of a second knock did she finally get up and turn on a lamp. The heavy door groaned at Emily's touch in the late September humidity.

"It's too late for me to invite myself in, but I was wondering if you would join me out here on the porch." Pastor Fletcher stood in the doorway, the white of his clerical collar reflecting the warmth of the lamplight from inside the house.

Emily fumbled with her eyeglasses and looked down at her stockinged feet. On any other night she might have cared that her socks didn't match, but Emily felt quite cured of vanity after having spent an afternoon with the Bradburys. She gave a wry chuckle. At least her sweatpants were purple; perhaps Candice would approve of that.

Emily stepped out onto the porch, shutting the door behind her. The night air smelled of harvest corn, and the crickets were engaged in a song war. Emily sat on the front step, hugging her purple knees. She was thankful for the privacy of the night's shadows. Today's events had left her broken, and Pastor Fletcher had appeared before she could properly piece herself back together again.

"That was quite a speech Candice made this afternoon," Pastor began, sitting down a few feet from Emily. "Most of it was false, I believe."

Emily relinquished a sigh. It was late, and she was too tired to keep up her defenses. Those carefully constructed walls began to crumble. "Candice got at least one thing right."

Pastor sat quietly. Experience told him just to listen.

"I was married." Emily's voice was nasal, hinting at previous hours of crying. She passed her sweatshirt sleeve once across her nose. "Only, I didn't leave my husband. He left me."

Emily rubbed her eyes under her glasses until they stung. She would not let the tears start again. Not yet. "I met Peter my freshman year of college. He was a junior. We both made it into the same jazz lab my first semester. Peter was the seasoned pianist, and I was the green vocalist. I never stood a chance. I knew from the first major-seventh Peter played that I was going to marry him, so I worked hard to finish school in three years. We were married the summer after I graduated. That was eleven years ago." Emily shivered as a breeze blew some leaves across the sidewalk.

"We moved to St. Louis and lived the starving artist's life. It was glorious, really. The stress of scraping up a rent payment each month was no fun, but there's such freedom in having very little. You learn to value simple things, like time and music. And friendship. I'll never eat another package of Ramen noodles, though.

"It wasn't too long before Peter got a recurring weekend gig at a downtown hotel with a local trio. That was exciting. It paid well, and it was about as close as you could get to 'making it' in the local scene. Shortly after that, I got a job at a music school, teaching children's music classes during the day and giving private lessons at night. Not on Saturdays, though. I fought hard with my boss to keep those free. I wasn't going to let anything get in the way of my seeing Peter play at the Sheraton."

Emily looked at Pastor. "We were happy." Her voice was firm, and her stare was determined. She needed him to understand this. "We were young, but we were happy."

Pastor nodded. "I believe you."

Emily hugged her knees again. "It was April when it happened. A Thursday night. I was preparing my students for a spring recital, so I stayed late to rehearse. Even before I got home, I knew something was wrong. I can still see in my mind that stretch of highway near Lindbergh when I knew in my heart that something had happened. Peter had gone for a jog that morning, same as always. I had to leave for work before he got back, so I called him throughout the day to check on him. He never once answered the phone, and he never called me back."

Emily took in a sharp breath and held it. She let it out slowly, shakily. "I hate talking about this. It never feels good."

"You don't have to tell me."

"I do. You're my pastor."

"That doesn't mean you have to tell me now."

Emily looked at Pastor. "I want to. It's the only antidote to all the poison that was spread this afternoon." Emily turned her face back to the safety of the darkness. "I found Peter on the floor. He'd been sitting at the kitchen table, but he must've fallen off his chair. He was facedown. I screamed. I remember a neighbor woman from the apartment across the hall came to me. She took me into her apartment. The police came then. I don't remember much else from that night."

Emily took another deep, steadying breath. "An aortic aneurysm. Hypertrophic cardiomyopathy, that's what the autopsy revealed. He must have had it his whole life, but none of us knew. All Peter had said that morning was that he felt tired. Everything else was normal. We'd eaten oatmeal for breakfast. We'd talked about taking a bike ride in Forest Park that Saturday if the weather was nice. All of that life to live, and then he was gone."

Emily hugged herself. "Even now, it all seems unreal. We'd not even been married two years when he died. I can still see his face on the kitchen floor. I can't forget it. It doesn't haunt me, it just stays with me. It pinches me to remind me that I'm not dreaming, that my husband really died. It never gets easier to talk about that night. Some things are so hard to say out loud. Do you think I'm unhealthy?"

"No, I think you're perfectly healthy."

"I just can't imagine ever sharing something so intimate and horrifying with Candice Bradbury, no matter what kind of lies she's spreading." Emily shook her head. "I don't trust her."

Pastor turned toward Emily. "What did you do after Peter died?"

"I moved in with my parents for a year. God bless them. Can you imagine having a twenty-three-year-old widow for a daughter? They must've been terrified. I spent a summer with my sister Nicole and her family out in Colorado too. At first, it was nice spending time with my niece and nephew, but then it got hard, you know? I kept thinking about the family I would never have now that Peter was gone. I eventually applied for graduate school in Kansas City. That was a good move. New city.

New people. New life. I'm kind of amazed that after my masters, I moved back to St. Louis for my doctorate. Washington University was the right school for me, though, and I was ready to be back among my memories of Peter."

Pastor and Emily sat in silence for a few minutes, both lost in their own thoughts.

"Peter died more than nine years ago," she marveled. "I can hardly believe it. I've lived a whole other life since then. I still miss Peter, but I can hardly remember the sound of his voice."

"Time is cruel that way."

"You know," Emily continued, "I couldn't sing for the longest time. For years I couldn't get a note out for all of the tears. I guess that's why I studied conducting and history in graduate school. I kept the music without having to make it myself."

"When was the first time you sang after Peter's death?"

Emily thought for a moment. "I was in church in Kansas City. We were singing the Offertory, and I couldn't help but join in on the plea to God: 'Renew a right spirit within me!'"

Pastor leaned his elbows on his knees. "What do you want to do? About Candice?"

Emily sighed. "Ignore her."

"I'm not sure that will work in such a small town."

Emily buried her head in her hands. "Oh, I know. It just seems so unfair that the way to silence the gossip is to open up such a private part of my life to the public."

"Why are you afraid to tell people that your husband died?"

Emily started crying. "Because grief never completely goes away. Each year, it seems to stay away for longer periods of time, but it always comes back. And when it does, it's hard. I cry a lot. That bothers people. It makes them uncomfortable. They start treating me differently. I guess for once I wanted to be known as someone other than 'the young widow.'"

"But you are a young widow, and there's nothing wrong with that. It's just one part of your life story, but there's so much more to you. You are Emily, baptized child of God; Emily, choir director; Emily, teacher; Emily, friend. Are you ashamed of being any of those other things?"

"No."

"I don't think you need to be ashamed of being a widow either. True, some will treat you differently because of it, but those people are not picky in their discrimination. They'll find some reason to treat you differently whether you're a widow or not."

Emily chewed on this for a while. She still couldn't get past the accusing, fiery look in Candice's eyes earlier today. "The thought of grieving in front of Candice is so embarrassing. I just can't imagine her not beating me when I'm down. I'd rather her not know about it at all."

"Well, I can't promise that Candice will never abuse the information of your husband's death, but most of your brothers and sisters in the church will respect your seasons of grief. In fact, I think you'll find them to be understanding and empathetic, as many of them have their own grief to endure. There can be great comfort in bearing with one another in love."

Emily was silent, thoughtful.

"We can't live in fear of the Candices in life. If we do, then fear will be our rudder, not faith, and 'the righteous shall live by faith.' That means you, Emily. You are a baptized child of God, declared righteous by the blood of Jesus. You live by faith in Christ's forgiveness of sin, not in fear of sin. Honestly, the only thing to do is to let Candice know that she's borne false witness against you and then forgive her and pray for her."

"I don't know if I can forgive Candice for what she said today."

"I know you feel that way, but Christ has forgiven of you all your sins, Emily Duke. You are free—free to forgive Candice for her silly, wagging tongue."

"What if I really can't?"

"Then ask God for help. Pray to Him, 'Lord, I forgive her. Help me to forgive her.' Have faith in God's promise to help you. You may not be able to trust Candice, but you can trust Him."

Emily let out her air slowly. She turned her puffy eyes toward Pastor. "I usually feel embarrassed after someone sees me cry."

"Do you feel embarrassed now?"

"No."

"Well, I'm not just someone. I'm your pastor."

Emily nodded her head. "Thank you. I think I needed to talk about this. It's a relief not to have to hide it from everyone."

"I think you'll find most of the people at Zion to be trustworthy keepers of your sorrows and joys. None of them are perfect, but many of them are eager to love and to be loved."

"You're probably right. I need to work on that whole sharing thing." Emily looked at him suddenly, alarmed. "Are you going to tell anyone?"

"No," he said. "This is your news to tell, not mine."

Emily felt relieved. She slowly stood up and walked back to her front door. With one hand on the doorknob, she turned to Pastor Fletcher in the dark. "You know, this whole time I've been blaming everything on Candice, but she's not the only one at fault. If I'd been more forthright with people in the first place, this all might never have happened. I regret being so secretive."

"*Absolvo te,*" Pastor said, making the sign of the cross.

As he walked home that night, Pastor marveled at the gift of new life that flows from the confession and absolution of sin. Just from speaking the saving Word of Christ's forgiveness to Emily's repentant heart, her faith was restored and renewed.

She had actually smiled at him before slipping into the sanctuary of her home, and he had been afraid he might never see her smile again.

CHAPTER SEVENTEEN: *IN UNUM CONGREGAMUR*

Sunday morning was awkward. Like any family publicly confronted with the embarrassing antics of a prodigal child, the congregation simply pasted on a too-bright smile and changed the subject.

"My beans are ready. Think I'll hit the fields tomorrow if'n the rain holds."

"How about those Indians yesterday? Those Hamburglars will think twice about honking up and down Main Street today!"

"Crossed the Mason Road Bridge on the way in. Looks like those fool college students found the red spray paint at Johnson's Hardware."

Truth be told, everyone had already discussed the matter to its death over the phone the night before, and most people had the good sense not to bring the dead with them to church. Well, except Nettie Schmidt.

"Did you know Emily Duke is married?"

Men shifted uneasily from foot to foot, women avoided direct eye contact with their children, and ushers swooped in faster than the president's secret service, silencing Nettie with a bulletin and wordlessly ushering her out of sight into the nave.

Everyone abruptly gave up the small talk ruse after that and made their way to their preferred pews. Miss Turner took her time sitting down. She freely looked around in hopes of gathering looks of admiration from those who happened to notice that the Bulletin Planning Committee had turned out yet another flawless publication. No one looked up, though, let alone at one another. In fact, no one had even bothered to commend her earlier on her recent promotion to the committee's Senior Editor position. Miss Turner sighed, more than a little disgruntled. *No doubt, everyone is distracted by that disgraceful Emily Duke and her attention-getting ways,* she thought. Well, the Methodists would have handled things better, that much was certain. Not only would they have properly appreciated Miss Turner's hard work on the bulletin, they most likely would have dedicated the altar flowers in honor of her promotion.

Bev Davis was already sitting in her pew with her head bent low, her shoulders stooping under the weight of a silent burden. She was listening to a wordless sermon, and the communion rail was the preacher. Just the sight of it filled her with unbearable guilt. There, her Savior would soon set a table of His own body and blood, freely given and shed for her for the remission of her sins. Yet how could she possibly commune with all of the saints on earth and in heaven with blood on her hands? Just yesterday, she had stood by while a sister in Christ had been stoned to death with words. True, Candice had assured everyone that the killing was perfectly justified, but the look on Emily's wounded face afterward had not been one of guilt. What if—? Bev grabbed Irv's left wrist to get a better view of his watch. Five minutes to nine. She still had time. Without a word to her husband, she scooted out of the pew in search of Pastor Fletcher.

The Bradburys arrived at the perfect time: not so late as to miss the prelude but late enough to be noticed by everyone else. Candice marched up the center aisle with her family, proudly lifting her chin so as to better display the invisible laureate on her head. Caroline stepped into her family's usual pulpit-side pew halfway up the nave, but Candice grabbed her daughter's arm and steered her, instead, toward the Pharisaical third row from the front. This is where they would sit from now on. Candice had earned it.

Hardly anyone noticed Mrs. Scheinberg and Emily Duke slip into the taxpayer's pew on the lectern side.

Just ten minutes before, Mrs. Scheinberg had pulled her gold Grand Marquis unannounced into Emily's driveway. "I know you can easily walk to church," she had hastily explained from Emily's front doorstep, "but I want you to ride with me today." No other words were exchanged between the two during the block-and-a-half drive to Zion. Mrs. Scheinberg didn't dare confess that she hadn't slept a wink the night before out of guilt for having left her dear director's side at that evil party, and Emily didn't breathe a word to Mrs. Scheinberg about how scared she had been at the prospect of walking into church by herself that morning. Today was not a choir Sunday, and she was filled with dread at the thought of sitting in the pews after Candice's public condemnation yesterday.

The two women hadn't been seated in church for more than thirty seconds before a grinning Robbie skipped down the aisle, dragging a braided cherub behind him. "Mom said we could sit with you today, Mrs. Shinebug!"

Mrs. Scheinberg nodded curtly, scooting far enough to the left for Robbie to sit between her and Emily. She did her best to hide her delight, but her lips disobediently burst into a merry smile as Robbie leaned in to share her open hymnal. Emily reached down and scooped Alison onto her lap, grateful for the angel snuggles. She blinked back tears of thankfulness for the obvious gift Rebecca had express delivered down the aisle just for her.

The Divine Service was full of rich comfort for Emily that morning. She enjoyed teaching a curious Alison how to make the sign of the cross during the Invocation, remembering the new life poured out on them both in Holy Baptism; she voiced a jubilant "Amen" after Pastor Fletcher proclaimed the forgiveness of her sins during the Absolution; she confidently confessed her faith in the triune God, joining her voice with all the congregation during the Nicene Creed; she listened attentively as Mrs. Scheinberg and Robbie sang stanza one of "Entrust Your Days and Burdens," for she was too choked up at the moment to sing the words herself; she joined her voice with the angels, archangels, and all the company of heaven—her sainted husband included—when singing the Sanctus; and she ate and drank the salvation freely offered to her in Christ's Supper, the perfect answer to her fear and pain.

Thankfully, Emily had her eyes closed as she knelt and prayed at the communion rail, so she did not notice when Candice stood up to leave in holy protest of Pastor Fletcher offering communion to an adulterer. Mrs. Scheinberg noticed, though. She had kept her eyes open to monitor the wiggling bodies of Robbie and Alison on either side of her, and she marveled at how easy it was to commit murder in her heart so soon after receiving the cleansing body and blood of her Lord.

During the last phrase of the closing hymn, she and Emily discreetly slipped out the door, leaving Robbie and Alison with Pastor Fletcher to greet the congregants pouring into the narthex. Both ladies were surprised to find Bev Davis waiting for them by Mrs. Scheinberg's Grand Marquis in the parking lot.

She was twisting a crumpled tissue in between her hands, and her face bore the expression of one who had recently read her own Book of Revelation. Bev knew that God had cast her sins into the sea of forgetfulness—Pastor had assured her of this very thing before the service—but Bev was not quite ready to forget them herself. There was one more thing she needed to do.

"Good morning," Bev started nervously. She fixed her eyes determinedly on Emily. They were red from previous weeping, and it did not take long for the tears to start freely flowing again. Bev did not bother to hide them, nor did she take the time to wipe them away. She had failed to look Emily in the eye yesterday, but she was resolved to do it today.

"I just wanted to say . . . I wanted to tell you . . ." Bev's voice was shaking. She tried to take a breath to steady herself, but it resulted in a nasty hiccup.

Emily recognized a drowning soul. She reached out and took Bev's hand.

Bev tried again. "I-I wish I had followed you out the door yesterday. You know, a-at Candice's."

Emily nodded her head, encouraging her.

"I'm ashamed that I stayed. I even ate a piece of pie after you left. I'm always eating when I should be doing something else. I . . . I'm so sorry."

Emily didn't hesitate for a moment. She reached for Bev with both of her arms, hugging her sister in Christ tightly around the neck and whispering words of forgiveness and comfort into her ear.

Mrs. Scheinberg had never been more proud of Bev in her life, but all of this gushing and crying and hugging made her collar feel too tight. She acquiesced one more reconciliatory hug between the two watery women before quickly shooing Emily into the car. She did not want to risk any more surprise encounters in the parking lot this morning. Mrs. Scheinberg wasted no time in taking Emily home, but once there, both she and Emily lingered in the Grand Marquis as it idled in the driveway.

"Arlene," Emily stared straight ahead at the dashboard, "did you hear what Candice said yesterday at the party?"

"She's a fool, a self-righteous pig," Mrs. Scheinberg said and then bit her tongue. There went another murder charge.

Emily turned to look at her, and Mrs. Scheinberg could tell the young choir director was struggling against her words. "You are such a good friend to me. I want to be honest with you like Bev just was with me."

Mrs. Scheinberg held her breath, suddenly afraid of what Emily was going to say. She liked—no, more than that—she admired this young woman, and she was not sure that she wanted to know the truth.

"I was married several years ago, but my husband died of a heart aneurysm the second year of our marriage."

Mrs. Scheinberg kept silent as Emily rambled nervously on, "I should have told you months ago, but . . . I don't know. I guess I'm still uncomfortable telling people that I'm a . . . a widow."

Mrs. Scheinberg stared thoughtfully out the windshield for a moment before admitting, "I'm a widow too."

Emily blinked in surprise. "You—? I didn't know that. When did your husband die?"

"Thirty-seven years ago." Mrs. Scheinberg could have been talking about the color of paint on the garage door for all of the emotion her voice betrayed. "Dean died in a farming accident. His leg got caught in a grain auger. He was twenty-three at the time. It still bothers me to drive by the grain bins when the blowers are running."

"How did you . . . what did you—?"

"Well, I cried a good deal," the older woman confessed. "It was harvest time though, and I was a farming widow with at least a hundred acres of beans left in the fields. There wasn't a whole lot of time to sit with my head in my hands. Dean's brothers helped quite a bit even though they had their own acreage to tend. Pastor Gardner helped too. He drove the truck back and forth between the fields and the elevator for me. After the crops were in, Pastor Gardner offered me the church secretary job. Actually, he created the position for me."

Emily paused then asked tentatively, "Do you have any children?"

"Not one." Mrs. Scheinberg stared resolutely at the Jiffy Lube sticker on the top left corner of her windshield. She sniffed loudly. Blasted tears! As if Bev hadn't filled the world with enough salt water this morning. Oh well, she might as well go ahead and say it. "I always wanted children."

Emily nodded. The two sat in mutual silence for a minute, each holding a private memorial service for the dreams that had been buried deep in the ground with their husbands. Then, without warning, Emily leaned across the wide seat of the old car, threw her arms around Mrs. Scheinberg's neck, and squeezed. "Thank you."

Mrs. Scheinberg, quite inexperienced with human contact of any kind, froze with her arms stuck to her side. Emily eventually let go and moved to open the passenger door.

"Emily."

Emily stopped with her hand on the door handle. It was the first time Mrs. Scheinberg had called her by her first name.

"Don't be afraid to meet someone. You know, to get married again."

"But you didn't."

"Yes," Mrs. Scheinberg conceded, regaining her familiar tone of irritation, "but I'm not like you. I'm old. Even in my twenties, I was old. You will always be young no matter what your age. You should love someone. It suits you."

Mrs. Scheinberg drove back to the farm with her windows down; never mind the dusty roads. This was exactly how Dean had driven her home from their wedding forty years ago to the day, only then, they had been bouncing along in a blue Ford pickup truck. That was long before seat belts held newlyweds apart, and Mrs. Scheinberg had scooted across the seat in her mother's lacy wedding gown to sit directly on Dean's lap.

She sighed. Those were the good old days, but these new days were not so bad. Emily Duke had just called her a good friend, Robbie Jones had leaned against her arm all through the sermon, and there was a coconut cream pie—Dean's favorite—waiting in the refrigerator at home.

CHAPTER EIGHTEEN: THREE FORMS OF MATTER

Thunder rumbled angrily outside.

"I hope lightning doesn't strike the church steeple again," Alice shivered from her perch in the alto section. "It blows the organ out every time."

"We've been struck at least four times in the last ten years," Bev added.

Irv nodded in silent confirmation.

Emily was glad Irv was able to make it to rehearsal. She was sorry that his fields were muddy from all of the rain, but she was grateful her only bass didn't have to work the combine that night. Four days straight, it had been raining, much to the dismay of Bradbury County's farmers. It was bad news for the crops, but good news for Emily. The more it poured, the more the townspeople turned their attentions to the flooded fields instead of to the sordid life of Zion's choir director.

Even the rain, however, could not succeed in drowning out all of the echoes of Candice's acrimonious imputations. On Monday morning, Emily had overheard Candice threatening Pastor Fletcher in his study that the entire Bradbury family would leave the church if he continued to commune individuals engaged in public sin.

"Good riddance," Mrs. Scheinberg had muttered as she took the stack of choral pieces to be approved from Emily's extended hand. Tuesday afternoon, Emily happened to overhear three of her particularly silly music literature students ruminating about her supposed affair with that hot English professor. Poor Zachary had spent the entire week flooding both her office and home voicemail with concerned messages of Shakespearean proportion.

Even tonight, there were two chairs conspicuously vacant in the balcony, and no one in the choir was holding their breath for Candice or Miss Turner to return any time soon. Thankfully, Emily had been treated earlier that day to the sweetest of pardons from her assumed "scarlet *A*." Alice, Rebecca, and little Alison had shown up on her front porch holding a bouquet of yellow roses, a steaming apple cake, and four forks. When, after properly devouring the cake from the middle out, Emily had shyly admitted to her friends that she was a widow, Alice's only response had been, "Well, of course you are, dear."

Emily looked out over her faithful choir members and took a deep breath. She abhorred the very thought of public statements, especially ones regarding her own private life, but sometimes a little discomfort was worth the reward. She just wanted to get this over with.

"Well, it's been quite a week, huh?" Emily tried to laugh, but she ended up sounding something like Ben's lawn mower when it sputtered and died. She cleared her throat, gripping her music stand with both hands to keep them from shaking. Rebecca flashed her an encouraging smile, and Emily tried again. "I, um, wanted to tell you all something."

The choir went dead silent. Even Bev sat still in an attentive, listening pose.

"You all met my parents, right? Greg and Mary Heath?" Emily licked her dry lips. "Well, my name is Emily Duke."

Wow, that was dumb! Emily thought. She mentally kicked herself for not thinking to write out a statement ahead of time. How was she ever going to get through this? She took a deep breath. "What I'm trying to say is, Duke is my married name."

Bev's eyes grew wide with alarm.

Emily waved her hands frantically before her face as if to erase her previous statement. "I mean, I *was* married."

Bev's face fell to the floor in utter dismay.

"No, I mean—" Emily put her hands over her mouth and looked down at her music stand to gather her frenzied thoughts. This couldn't possibly be going any worse. She took another deep, stabilizing breath and lowered her hands to her side. When she looked back up into the faces of her expectant choir, her voice quavered slightly. "I-I'm sorry. I'm not very good at this—at talking about myself—but, if you'll bear with me, there's something important I'd like to share with all of you." Emily swallowed carefully, struggling to maintain composure. "I was married years ago. I met my husband in college, but he died a little over a year after we were married. He died of an aortic aneurysm."

"Oh, good!" Bev sighed with relief then immediately clamped both hands over her mouth. She stared wide-eyed at Emily in horror at what she had just said. "I mean—"

"I knew it," Janet Koelster announced triumphantly, turning in her seat to look pointedly at the other sections. "I knew there was a reasonable explanation. Why, I told Dot the other day, I said, 'This adultery talk is pure nonsense.'"

Dorothy Koelster nodded vigorously in agreement before gripping her forehead with a steadying hand.

Marge Johnson and Lois Kull carefully averted their eyes altogether.

"Can you believe all of this rain?" Rebecca not-so-subtly redirected the conversation.

"I almost had to build an ark to sail in for choir practice tonight," Alice jumped in to contribute.

"My umbrella broke in the parking lot," Blaine offered from underneath his sopping locks. Emily looked at him shyly. He actually smiled at her, something like camaraderie shining in his dark eyes.

Lois took the bait. "The sound of it's making me crazy. I can't sleep at night. Don and I just lie there counting drops that fall from the leak in our bedroom ceiling. It makes me sick to think of all our crops out there rotting in the ground." A big clap of thunder shook the balcony just then, and Lois winced. "I wish the Lord would see fit to let the rain fall on the unbelievers for a little while."

Emily knew there was only one way to properly start this rehearsal. "Irv, would you please lead us in prayer?" Emily bowed her head.

"Lord God," Irv began. Emily suddenly realized this was the first time she had ever heard Irv get a word in edgewise, in choir or out. She made a mental note to ask him to pray at the beginning of every rehearsal. "We thank You for the rain that waters our fields and washes our cars. Please protect the crops of all our farmers, and please bless our rehearsal this evening. In Jesus' name. Amen."

"Amen."

Everyone in the balcony opened their eyes, and Janet, who never missed an episode of *Ghost Whisperer,* let out a shrill scream. Out of the corner of her eye, she saw a scruffy man sitting in the folding chair next to Irv, and that folding chair had been empty when she'd closed her eyes a few moments before.

Everyone turned around in their seats to see what was the matter.

"Donald," Lois hollered at her husband, "what're you doing here? Don't you know you're supposed to wait outside a room when people are talking with the Lord? You near scared us all to death!"

Don Kull grinned from his seat in the back row and shrugged. He hooked his thumbs comfortably in the front of his overalls. "Rain's gone chased me outta my fields, so I'm here to spend a little time with my wife. What're we singin' tonight?"

"Songs for Reformation and All Saints' Day." Emily smiled at Don's deep voice. The blessed rain had sent her another bass, and this one was even a member of the church! She stuck her hand out invitingly over the altos. "I'm Emily Duke. I don't believe we've had a chance to meet."

"I've heard of ye," Don eyed her steadily as he shook her hand.

Emily's cheeks colored. "Well, let's get started. We'll use a hymn to warm up. Everyone open to hymn 656." Blaine rolled out the first chord, and Emily gave a preparatory beat.

"A mighty fortress is our God," the choir began with Lutheran gusto. Emily had to catch her chin to keep it from dropping onto her music stand at the sound of Don's singing voice. His appearance and grammar went down a bit hard, like moonshine, but his voice was as rich and smooth as an Irish stout. He had no problem reading the bass line, perfectly nailing the syncopation on the first try. Everyone scooted a little taller in their seats and sang a little louder at having such a strong foundation supporting them. They knew they sounded good, and by the end of the hymn the entire balcony smiled with a newfound pride.

Well, Irv wasn't smiling. He had the strangest expression on his face. Emily would have suspected that he was jealous or mad about something, but upon closer inspection she saw that his eyes were as kind and gentle as ever. Still, he was pressing his lips together and wrinkling his nose in concentration, carefully avoiding eye contact with anyone else.

"Let's try 'For All the Saints,'" Emily suggested. "Hymn 677."

"That's a good 'un," Don approved. "I love those runs at the start."

Marge jabbed Lois in the side with her elbow. "You've been holding out on us, Lois. Don's a real-life Robert Goulet."

"Robert Goulet is already 'real-life,' Marge," Mrs. Scheinberg pointed out.

Lois beamed. She was not used to being the center of attention, but she found it very much to her liking. "Don's whole family can sing, but Don's always been the best."

Don aced all of the runs. Not only that, he also sang with a natural musicality, swelling as the notes went higher on the staff and decrescendoing at the ends of phrases.

Irv was still resolutely pressing his lips together in the back row, but everyone else was excitedly chatting about their new prodigy.

"We have to try 'Behold a Host, Arrayed in White,'" Bev bubbled, wholly recovered from her earlier flub. "Don'll knock that one out of the ballpar—" Bev suddenly stopped. A funny look clouded her usually sunny features. She blinked once, cleared her throat, and plastered on her signature smile, but she forgot all about finishing her sentence.

Emily noticed that Janet had also grown quiet. She was sitting with her arms crossed, casually hiding her face behind her hand.

"Shall we try 'Behold a Host'?" Emily offered. "676."

Stanza one was soulful with Don's rumbling bass, but the altos began to poop out on stanza two. "Those martyrs stand, a priestly band, God's throne forever near," they sang, but their hearts were no longer in it. Bev and Janet looked like they were enduring some kind of private torture, and Alice had started waving an old church bulletin frantically in front of her and Dorothy's faces. By stanza three, even the tenors were fizzling. Mrs. Scheinberg's eyes were watering, Phyllis blew her nose repeatedly into an old tissue, and Irene simply got up and left without a word. Emily knew this hymn often made people emotional, but this seemed a bit extreme.

"I've a soft spot for that one," Don sighed when it was over. "We sung it at Daddy's funeral."

It was then that it hit Emily, and judging by the look on Rebecca's and Marge's faces, it hit them at the exact same moment. A heavy, pungent smell unlike any Emily had ever known suddenly overwhelmed her senses. She almost gagged at the humid odor, horrified to recognize the turgid, fruity scent of human flatus. She forced herself not to bury her nose in her sleeve like an eight-year-old, but the smell caused her to swoon. For once in her life, Dorothy reached out a hand to steady someone else.

"What's next?" Don asked eagerly, clearly not affected by the caustic odor. He and Lois were the only ones in the balcony not actively trying to filter their immediate sources of oxygen. Lois had a resigned look on her face, as if she no longer found the center of attention an enjoyable place to be.

Emily looked out over her agonized singers. At this point, Irv's face was fire-engine red, and Blaine's head was no longer visible over the top of the piano. She quickly made an executive decision. "I-I think we're done for tonight." The immediate looks of silent adoration and praise Emily received from behind each choir member's hand more than made up for all of the week's previous ills. The choir would forevermore defend their blessed Saint of the Balcony, fearless protector from Don Kull's passed gas and all other noxious foes.

"So, um, do you think you'll be joining the choir, Don?" Bev asked, trying to speak without taking in a new supply of air.

"Nah. I ain' got the time." Don put his arm around his wife and headed toward the stairs. "Tonight was just a special occasion."

"Thank God," Mrs. Scheinberg breathed, dabbing her eyes.

As soon as Don and Lois had gone, Janet helped Dorothy to her feet. "C'mon, Sis. Let's go before one of us dies of carbon monoxide poisoning."

Alice, despite the risk of losing precious stores of oxygen, leaned back in her chair and dissolved into a fit of giggles.

"Mother, what is so funny?"

Alice tried to answer, but she couldn't manage to produce even one word. She hugged her stomach as her shoulders shook with laughter.

"What is it?" Rebecca was incredulous. "C'mon, out with it."

"I was just . . ." Alice started. She coughed to clear her throat. "I was just imagining what Evan would have said if he had been here."

"What's that?" Rebecca asked, not certain she really wanted to know the answer.

Alice composed herself and lowered her voice to sound like Evan. "'Who just blew their pipes?'"

"Mother!"

Alice doubled over in her chair with laughter. Rebecca stood next to her in exasperation, unsure whether she should laugh or scold.

Emily started giggling. "'Who pulled out all the stops?'"

"Emily Duke!" Rebecca gaped at her friend. "You are no help at all."

Bev Davis couldn't help herself. "'Did the organ just blow out again?'"

Alice and Emily howled. Rebecca sat down in the nearest chair in defeat.

Mrs. Scheinberg rose stoically to her feet, tying her plastic headscarf under her chin. In her best Evan voice, "'Ladies, I think the number two stop is sticking.'"

Emily was still laughing later that night as she stood on her front porch digging through her purse for her house key. Rain was pouring in torrents from the sky, and Emily's hair was soaking wet from just the short sprint from the garage. Next time, she would remember an umbrella! As Emily stepped inside the safety of her home, the outside world lit up in a sudden flash of silvery blue. She dropped her bag on the floor to cover her ears but not before thunder rammed the outer walls of her home with its invisible force. Emily shivered, her ears ringing from the sound. That one was close.

It was six blocks close, to be exact. The bolt of lightning, uninspired by Zion Lutheran Church's pointy steeple on the north end of town, decided to strike a fourteen-year-old maple tree on the corner of Washington and Third Street instead. The tree split satisfyingly in two, one sturdy limb crashing straight through a front window of Bradbury County Bank and setting off an alarm that could be heard by the Kulls lying awake in their leaky bedroom two miles north of town. A lone strip of heated bark fell to the ground, covering up the commemorative brass plaque at the tree's foot, which read, "Sugar Maple (*Acer saccharum*)—Planted in honor of Thomas Edison Bradbury IV, April 14, 1996."

CHAPTER NINETEEN:

SOMETHING OLD AND SOMETHING NEW

||||||||||||||||||||||||||||||||||||||||||||||||||||||

The next morning, Rona Mabley, the mousy residence hall director of Shauna Hall, woke up before dawn to the muffled sound of a wildcat-like shriek. No doubt the girls in Suite 208 were staying up all night watching horror movies again. That, or McKensie Bolger had received another breakup text from her third true love of the fall semester. Rona rolled over in bed and covered her head with her pillow. Whatever the drama, it could wait for the sun.

The drama, however, was not being played out within the walls of Shauna Hall but across the street. Pat Garrison, Bradbury County Rural Electric Cooperative's hard-working technician, stood on the front porch of Bradbury House and explained to a pinstripe-pajamaed Mr. Bradbury and a yellow-robed Candice what Thomas Jr.'s tree had done to the bank power lines in the middle of the night. Candice, overcome by a fit of superstitious terror, shrieked and ran straight upstairs to her sleeping son's room to make sure his body had not been split in two along with the tree. While Junior groggily batted away his sobbing mother, Mr. Bradbury tiredly shook Pat's hand and nodded his consent to properly dispose of the tree's remains, a fact for which Candice never forgave her husband.

Candice was inconsolable. Neither of her children was allowed to attend school that day, and Amelia was forced to answer the door Saturday morning when Alice came calling with a chocolate cake in hand. Nettie Schmidt openly peeked in the front windows of Bradbury House when no one answered her knock Saturday afternoon, but Candice had already paddocked her entire family to the third story sitting room where she could keep a closer eye on them and the ceiling. Junior and Caroline's zealous protestations ceased only when Amelia snuck down to the kitchen around dinner time for some Cokes, ham sandwiches, and the chocolate cake.

Pastor checked in on the family Sunday afternoon when none of them had attended church that morning.

"We're fine," Thomas Sr. amicably assured Pastor Fletcher at the door. "No worries. Just a bit of a shock. You know Candice. She weaves these elaborate stories around the facts of life. She's always put too much into all of this family tree business. She'll wear down once the rain stops."

But even Mr. Bradbury grew concerned Sunday afternoon when his wife refused to comment on the lightning incident to a curious reporter calling all the way from *The State Journal Register* out of Springfield. It was the first time he had ever known Candice to turn down the opportunity to make the news.

The next morning, Mr. Bradbury intervened on behalf of his children. "They're going to school, and that's final."

The incessant rain had turned into incessant wind overnight, and now the farmers were concerned the cornstalks would blow over before they had a chance to get in the fields to harvest. Emily Duke was more concerned that she might blow over on her short walk across Oak Street. She shivered in the biting October wind and pulled her scarf up around her face. She had an hour break between her two Monday morning classes, so now was as good a time as any to deliver her package.

Emily knocked on the solid oak door of Bradbury House, cringing at the sting of pain that shot through her cold, bare knuckles. She shifted from foot to foot, wondering if she was making a mistake.

The heavy door swung open to reveal an almost unrecognizable Candice. At least, Emily assumed it was Candice. The woman standing in the doorway had neglected to wear any purple. Or makeup.

"Emily." It was definitely Candice.

"Hello, Candice. May I come in?"

Candice hugged her fuzzy, yellow bathrobe tighter around her middle to block out the elements. For an instant, her eyes flashed with a familiar aggression, but they just as quickly flamed out to an apathetic gray. The last four days had taken their toll on Candice, and she was too tired to fight. She simply nodded and stepped aside to let Emily into the front hall.

Emily took a good look at Candice. Her eyes, red and swollen from crying, seemed unusually small without the penciled-in garland smudged along her eyebrow bones. Emily also noticed for the first time that Candice must normally wear a wig, for the wisps of thin, graying hair hanging about her cheeks were both a different color and style from what she had ever seen Candice wear before. Emily found this understated version of Candice interesting, even beautiful, like a chair that has been stripped of its gaudy paint and restored to its natural timber.

Candice's hand flew involuntarily to her face and hair as she suddenly remembered her unkempt state. Embarrassment had always been her foe, so she pierced it through with a sword of anger.

"I'm letting you in only because the kids are in school."

Emily swallowed. This was not a time to be reactive or afraid. She silently prayed the prayer Pastor Fletcher had taught her: *Lord, I forgive her. Help me to forgive her.*

"What are you doing here?" Candice was obviously not going to invite her any further into the house.

Emily held out a brown paper bag. "I'm here because I wanted to give you this."

Candice hesitated. She had fully expected Emily to move her rook forward on the board, not backward. Was this some kind of diversion, some witty strategy to distract her from protecting her queen? Candice reached for the bag and looked inside. She lifted out a sapling in a green plastic planter.

"It's a Sugar Maple," Emily explained.

Candice stared at the baby tree in her hand, stunned.

"I don't know very much about trees, but the nursery in Hamburg said that you can plant it right now."

Candice looked at Emily with wide, conflicted eyes.

"I know it's not the same as having the original tree you planted for your son, but . . ." Emily faltered. She was feeling very flustered by Candice's persistent silence. "I heard about the lightning. It was a Sugar Maple, right? Or did I get the wrong tree? I was sure Mrs. Scheinberg had said 'Sugar Maple' on the phone, but there were so many kinds of maples at the nursery that I may have gotten confused. Do you realize how many varieties of maples can grow in Illinois? If this is the wrong tree, I can take it back—"

Emily stopped short. Candice's eyes looked pained and her chest was heaving in and out in a silent, tearless sob. Emily watched in horror as Candice struggled under the vice of some personal misery. The fight was violent, and after what seemed like minutes, Candice victoriously gasped in some air and wailed like a child. "Wh-why," hiccup, "are y-you," hiccup, "be-ing n-nice to meeeeeeee?"

Candice's tears were flowing freely now. Emily carefully took the sapling and paper bag out of Candice's shaking hands and quietly directed her into the formal parlor. Emily couldn't help but flinch at the sight of the schefflera against the wall before sitting down next to Candice on the velveteen settee.

Emily waited patiently for Candice's shudders to subside. She knew not to speak. Pastor Fletcher's example had taught her the importance of listening, of just being present to help shoulder the burden. She did reach out to take Candice's hand in her own. Surprisingly, Candice let her.

"I was s-so scared to let Thomas go to school today," Candice choked. "What if that lightning bolt was an omen? What if my Thomas is going to be struck down dead on his way home?" Candice's fear was real. She was working herself up into another fit of hysteria. "What if it's all my fault?"

Emily squeezed Candice's hand to ground her. "That lightning bolt was just lightning. Static and heat converging on a single spot. Nothing more."

"How can you be sure?"

"Think of how many times lightning has struck the church," Emily reasoned. "It hasn't burned down or anything."

Candice pondered this. "I'm a terrible person, Emily. I deserve to be punished." An idea came to Candice that made her shuddering start all over again. "What if God is going to take away my firstborn to punish me, just like He did to all of those stubborn Egyptians?"

Emily felt way out of her league. This was a kind of questioning beyond anything she had ever experienced. What was she to say? Should she even try to answer? It would be so much easier just to walk back out that front door. Oh, where was

Pastor Fletcher when you needed him? Emily silently prayed. She listened for Candice's sobs to subside again before offering timidly, "No, I don't think that will happen. God doesn't punish you for your sins. He already punished His Son on the cross in your place."

Emily held her breath. Candice stared wordlessly at the painting hanging above the fireplace, not even bothering to wipe the tears from her cheeks. When she finally spoke, her voice was remarkably small. "Do you know who that is, Emily?"

Emily followed Candice's gaze up to the painting. A large, thick woman with brown hair was sitting on a cushioned stool. The vibrant sheen of her burgundy dress shone even in the painting.

"That is my mother. I had this portrait painted from an old photo of Mother's engagement notice."

"I can see the resemblance."

"Yes, Caroline and I both have Mother's eyes and build. Colette and Amelia have her hair."

Emily waited.

"Mother died giving birth to me." That was it. The pieces began to fit together in Emily's mind. Candice's zealous family loyalty; her need to prove her worth; her unrealistic expectations; her irrational fears; her false pretenses; even her false eyelashes.

"Colette was four at the time. I get so jealous that she has memories of Mother." Candice wrapped herself in a blanket of self-pity. "I can't remember her at all."

Emily's thoughts strayed to the one whose memories had grown dim in her own mind.

"You see, I've already been punished," Candice's voice was empty. "I was punished the day I was born."

Emily was appalled to hear Candice say such things. How could Candice possibly believe that God was punishing her day after day? How could she sit in church every Sunday and not be assured of God's love for her in Jesus? How could she not recognize God's good gifts to her in a faithful husband, healthy children, a supportive community, and a caring church? Emily looked around at the wealth of history and family identity on display in Candice's home. Perhaps all of this was just evidence of how hard Candice worked to convince herself and others that she was worth being born.

"When I look at you," Emily said carefully, "I don't see someone who is being punished. I see someone who has been given a great deal."

"A great deal?!" Candice spat. "I have no mother! Oh, you couldn't possibly understand! You have *no idea* what it is like to live without someone you love."

"Yes, I do."

Candice looked at Emily skeptically. She was so full of her own misery that she had no room left to take in the suffering of others. "Who have you lost?"

Emily took a deep breath. This was the moment. This was the time to trust Candice, unproved as she may be. "My husband."

Candice squinted, trying to understand. A little bit of the old fire reappeared at Emily's audacity to compare her separation from her husband to the death of a beloved mother. Emily wasted no time in dousing that fire with a bucket of cold water. "My husband died nine years ago. He had an aortic aneurysm."

There. It was done.

Candice stared at Emily. It took a few moments for the full meaning of Emily's words to sink in, but when they did, Candice's mind dry heaved all of the false assumptions, the misdirected insinuations, and the public accusations into a vile pool at her feet.

"Dear God," Candice whispered. "I accused . . . I said . . . in front of everyone . . . in this very room . . ." She covered her face with her hands, the shame unbearable. "It *is* my fault that Thomas's tree was struck!"

"No," Emily sighed, disappointed to be back at this again. "The tree was struck because it was in a storm. The lightning had nothing to do with you or Thomas or me or any of this."

Candice cried dramatically into her hands, "I'm a monster!"

"You're a child of God."

"*I* should be hit by lightning!"

"Candice," Emily's voice held a degree of alarm, "don't say such things. You have children."

"I'm doomed to a life of regret," Candice howled into her hands, "imprisoned by my own moral bleakness!"

Wow. Emily suspected Candice might have picked up that line from a book somewhere. She could feel that they were somehow slipping from the realm of sincerity into a world of the dramatic.

"I will forever be tortured by my wrongs, looking at the world as through a window pane of guilt!"

That clinched it. Candice was obviously more interested in the sound of her own voice than in listening to anything Emily had to say. Emily leaned back against the couch, resigning herself to the ridiculous.

"Honor once lost is forever bound by the cords of time!"

What did that even mean? Emily felt an unexpected urge to laugh. She clamped a hand over her mouth, holding it in by sheer will. Candice was really working for it, though Emily was uncertain of exactly what "it" was.

"To be or not to be. That is the question!"

Zachary would have been so proud that Candice thought to include a little Shakespeare, but Emily was not about to bring up his name in this home.

"How can you ever forgive me?"

Finally, a question grounded in reality. "I do forgive you."

Candice snapped out of her poetic trance. "You do?"

"Yes, I do."

It is a very difficult thing for one who never forgives to be forgiven. Candice still felt the full weight of her own debt as a yoke around her neck. She searched her brain for some way to prove her quality to this young woman. "How can I make it up to you? I know! I'll throw you a party. I'll invite everyone. I'll make several of my twinkie cakes and set out Grandmother's tea service and hire a string quartet from the college and—"

"No," Emily interrupted. She could tell it was going to take some time for Candice to trust forgiveness's amnesia. "Thank you, Candice, but no."

"I have to do *something!*"

Emily picked the sapling up off of the floor. "How about planting a new tree for your son?"

Candice had an even better idea. She invited Emily over for dinner that night (served on Grandma Bradbury's china, of course) and then walked Emily to the corner of Washington and Third Street to plant the sapling together. As they patted down the last trowel of dirt, Candice looked at her young choir director and made a silent vow. Come rain or shine or lightning, she would find Emily a new husband.

Chapter Twenty: Something Borrowed

The corn was finally harvested the first week in November, but most of it needed to be dried and aerated before it could be delivered to Dusselbach's Elevator. Mrs. Scheinberg explained to Emily that the farmers would get docked in the marketplace if the moisture level of their corn measured too high. This resulted in all of Bradbury County running the dryers on their grain bins day and night. Mrs. Scheinberg slept with her *Celtic Woman* CD on repeat in an attempt to drown out the withering sound.

Emily enjoyed riding her bike along the country roads, marveling at the expansive view afforded by the freshly harvested fields. The world was suddenly open and wide, the sky a cobalt-blue atrium filled with flocks of birds waxing and waning with each gust of wind. She wondered why any creature would want to fly south and miss out on the sparkle and fire of late fall. The maple trees, at least those that had not lost all of their leaves in the obstinate rains and grouchy winds of October, blazed a bright red-orange, and the ginkgos rained down golden yellow confetti upon the dormant grass. The burning bushes dazzled and twinkled like red chandeliers in the autumn sunlight. Emily had already collected twelve different leaves of various sizes and colors, pressing each one between the pages of her vocal pedagogy text.

On a particularly crisp Saturday morning, Emily leaned on her rake and drank in the smell of wood smoke and overturned soil that rode in on the autumn wind. Ben was helping her herd all of the brown, yellow, and orange leaves cartwheeling across her front yard into large black garbage bags. It was a rather tedious job on such a windy day, but Ben liked working with Miss Emily. She had a way of turning all rosy and flowery in the fresh air.

Ben knelt to the ground and held a plastic bag open for Emily to rake in the ever-shifting piles. The wind was clearly opposed to his will, however, flipping, flapping, and fluttering the bag's edges with a maddening frequency. The atmosphere seemed equally opposed to the piles of leaves, scattering the paper-thin whimsies to the right and left with every gust. Emily, her curls blowing into her eyes as she looked down, blindly scraped at a particularly evasive pile, wishing it would, for once, move in a straight line toward the shape-shifting black hole. She finally abandoned her ineffective rake, bending over and picking up the fickle pile with her own bare hands.

"There!" Emily said, shoving the last of the leaves into the bag and wiping her hands on her jeans. She beamed at Ben, her face alight with victory. "The last one!"

Ben quickly tied the bag shut and tossed it next to the other three already neatly lining Emily's driveway. "I thought we'd never get those last ones inside."

"Now I understand why you eyed my box of garbage bags like it was the plague. Never again! I promise to get those sturdy paper bags next year." Emily eyed the full bags. "Now, what do I do with all of them? In St. Louis, the city always picked them up."

"My mama can take 'em," Ben offered. "She likes to mulch 'em."

"Mulchem?"

Ben nodded his head. "You know, breakin' down the leaves? They'll sit over winter and make a nice, black soil for the garden come spring."

"Ah." Emily looked up at the sweet gum tree and saw all of the prickly gumballs still dangling on the limbs. She sighed. "I suppose I'll have to bag those too."

"They should fall when the new leaves come out next spring. My mama can take 'em then too, if you like," Ben offered. "She uses 'em as filler in her ceramic pots. Those big planters get too heavy when they're filled full up with dirt."

"Genius," Emily murmured. Even these thorny pests could turn useful in the hands of the Schmidts. Emily walked over and leaned her rake against the front porch. The rain, wind, and cold had kept not only the farmers from their fields this fall, but they had also kept Ben from his lawns. It had been almost a full month since she had last seen her young friend. "How is school going, Ben?"

Ben shrugged his shoulders. "All right."

"Classes going okay?"

"Yes, ma'am."

Ben was quiet. Actually, he had been quiet all morning. Emily took a good, long look at her young helper. He had grown at least three inches since she had first met him. His face and arms were no longer as tan since the mowing season was all but over. His voice had even started to squawk occasionally at random moments. He was looking less like a boy and more like a young man. Ben noticed Emily studying him, and his neck grew red. He stuck his hands in his pockets, stared at his shoes, and cleared his throat. He started to speak three separate times before finally pushing the words out of his mouth. "I-I'm not sure what to do, Miss Emily."

"About what?"

"Well," Ben kicked his toe into the ground, "there's this girl."

Emily wisely didn't ask for her name.

"I've known her my whole life, but I . . ." Ben hesitated. He rubbed his hand on the back of his neck. "I really got to know her this summer. In 4-H. She an' I showed sheep together. You see, she kept her lamb at my house this whole year."

"What's she like?"

Ben's eyes lit up. "She's real nice. And pretty too. She's got gold hair and a real, sweet voice." Ben's chest puffed with pride. "She can hit the high note at the end of the nation'l anthem! And she can sew as good as my mom. She got Best in Show at the county fair this year!"

Caroline Bradbury! Emily tried to picture that awkward girl showing sheep.

"I was wonderin'," Ben looked at the ground again, "How to tell her, you know . . ."

Emily was certain Ben Schmidt could not possibly be any more charming if he tried, and she was just as certain that Caroline Bradbury would not be immune to his charms. "When will you see her again?"

"I see her every day in school, but I won't see her alone until I rake her yard next week." Ben smiled shyly. "She brings me drinks just like you."

That confirmed it. "The next time she brings you a drink, hand her a flower."

"There ain't no more flowers bloomin' this time of year."

That's right. Emily looked around, searching her yard for inspiration. "Hand her the prettiest leaf you can find."

Ben admitted timidly to Emily's shoes, "I gave her an orange maple leaf last week."

Emily smiled. The world needed more Ben Schmidts—that much was certain. "How about handing her a note this time?"

"What'll I write?"

"Whatever it is you'd like to tell her."

Emily had written a note of her own just a couple of weeks ago. She had avoided Zachary Brandt for as long as she could before her guilt got the better of her. It wasn't that she didn't like spending time with Zachary, but Candice's public outburst had spawned a flood of gossip around town and at the college that made Emily wary of stepping within ten feet of any man. Even after setting Candice and everyone else in her immediate circle straight on the widow situation, Emily still felt the need for a strict man-fast. However, after two straight weeks of deleting daily voicemails from Zachary, Emily realized it was rude to continue ignoring him. After all, he was her friend, and he deserved to know what there was to know.

Emily spent one of those blustery October evenings penning a letter that explained everything: her marriage, Peter's death, the recent misunderstandings, and the reasons she was not ready to date anyone at this time. Then she put the letter in campus mail and waited. Two days later, she came home to find a bag of apples and an envelope leaning against her front door. She opened the letter and read:

Dear Emily,

Thank you for telling me. I was afraid I had done something wrong, so it is a relief to be assured that your sabbatical from me is self-induced. I understand your silence and your need for space. Let me know when you are ready for some company. I'll bring Bach recordings with me.

Fondly, Zachary

P.S. These apples are from Tucker's Orchard. I picked them myself. Never fear! I did not break my vow to respect your personal space in delivering them. I stealthily dropped them by while you were teaching this afternoon. You can thank the works of Ian Fleming for schooling me in espionage.

P.P.S. I like apple pie.

Emily made proper use of the apples. She ate one that very afternoon; she walked two over to the church the next morning for Mrs. Scheinberg and Pastor Fletcher; and she baked an apple spice cake for Alice. She even tried her hand at baking an apple pie (under the careful supervision of Rebecca, of course) and delivered it to the lit department herself the next day.

"Emily!" Zachary jumped up from his desk at the sight of her. "Is that what I think it is?"

Emily, florid from both the vigorous wind outside and her perpetual feeling of self-consciousness, handed Zachary the heavy pie pan wrapped in foil, pleading, "Don't get your hopes up. This is my first pie." Zachary promised her the very next day in an email that the pie was one scoop of vanilla ice cream short of tasting like America itself.

The notes kept coming. Lauren Basset stuck a Chicago Symphony Orchestra program in her faculty box with a short message scrawled on a sticky note, "They're doing Bach's *St. Matthew Passion* next spring. What do you think? A girl's weekend?" Candice sent her a thank-you note for the sapling and a gift card for The Corner Coffee Shop "in case you need a break between classes," she wrote. Alice mailed her a note written on orange stationary that read, "Emily dear, I was wondering if you would fill in for me again at this month's cribbage tournament at Rebecca's." And Emily discovered a maple leaf taped to a piece of paper sitting under a rock on her front porch one day after work. Only three words were written in Ben's small print: "She liked it."

Emily's favorite note, though, was tucked inside the front cover of a small book sitting in her church mailbox:

Dr. Duke,

I found this at the town library yesterday. It made me think of you and your endless cup of tea. Take your time with the book. It's not due back for another three weeks.

Your fellow bibliophile,
Dr. Fletcher

Emily turned the book over: *The Engelshire Parish Ladies Society's Book of Afternoon Tea* by Cressida Langham Thompson. She opened the book to a random page and read: "Tea served in the garden is, indeed, a most welcoming diversion, but a truly elegant tea, one marked by sophistication and refinement, is best served in the parlour. Napkins should be pressed, sandwiches should be slim and crustless, individual cakes should be lighter than air, and the Victoria Sandwich, the *prima donna* of any afternoon spread, should be elevated four inches above the surface of the table." Oh, how lovely and diverting and splendid and all of those other British modifiers of Pastor Fletcher!

Emily shut the book and grinned. Her recent excursion into the world of baking had built her confidence, and she had secretly always wanted to eat crumpets and sip on a cup of Ceylon while conversing delicately with society about the weather and the price of eggs. Yes, under the tutelage of Ms. Thompson, she just might be able to pull it off. Emily rushed home and devoured the book, taking copious notes. She would host an afternoon tea, not an "unprepossessing nursery tea" or an "earthy farmhouse tea" as Ms. Thompson discriminated, but a proper, elegant, English afternoon tea complete with sandwiches of cucumber, egg, and cress.

Chapter Twenty-One: Something Blue

The morning of the tea bloomed sunny and bright, and Emily could hardly contain her excitement. She busied herself around her home, dusting furniture, sweeping floors, and polishing her grandmother Elsie's silver-plated tea service. Everything needed to be absolutely perfect. Handwritten invitations had been sent out early last week (one such invitation proved particularly difficult for Emily to pen, but deep down, she knew the best way to blot out unpleasant memories was to try making new ones), and six of her friends were expected to arrive at half past three. That gave her all day to complete her list of tasks.

Emily did not have a decorous tea table to cover with an embroidered cloth as Ms. Thompson wittingly suggested, so she had to make due by dressing up her scratched and scarred oak dining table with a white linen cloth she and Peter had received as a wedding gift. Emily, apart from any suggestions made by her British mentor, bought pink roses from the florist in Hamburg and arranged them into three short bud vases. She smiled at their sweet effect on the table.

Next came the sage-green linen napkins that Emily was borrowing from Rebecca, the silverware from Alice's silver cloth-lined chest, and the rose-embellished china from Arlene's hutch.

Emily's finger traced the delicate handle of one of the teacups, admiring the feminine lines of the bowl. It may not have been Chelsea porcelain, but it was lovely. She indulged in one last turn around the room and sighed with contentment. No English parlor with all of the marble tables and Louis XVI chairs in the world could have given her more pleasure than the sight of her humble dining room dressed in linen.

The previous evening's preparations had not gone so smoothly. Emily had thoroughly burned her homemade crumpets, and her Devonshire biscuits were so hard they could have broken through a pane of glass. In tears, she had dropped all of them in the trash and driven to Hamburg at eight in the evening to purchase new ingredients. Three hours later, Emily pulled a passable almond cake out of the oven and waved an oven mitt over the two small white cakes already cooling on a rack. She did not go to bed until the small cakes had been properly sliced, slathered, stacked, and sifted into Victoria Sandwiches and arranged on a cake plate. They were hardly regal looking, but at least they were elevated.

Three hours before her guests arrived, Emily still needed to make the cucumber and egg and cress sandwiches. "Many an excellent cup of tea has been spoiled when paired with a mundane sandwich," Ms. Thompson sagely warned. "The best sandwiches take considerable preparation, but the savory result is well worth the time and effort." Emily pulled out the day-old loaf of bread (Ms. Thompson was quite specific about this) and attempted to slice it into wafer-thin slivers.

"Not too bad," Emily mumbled to herself. The slices were not exactly uniform in thickness from top to bottom, but then, she was not a machine. She stuck a knife into the dish of homemade butter she had purchased from the Kulls and slathered each slice with the spread just as Ms. Thompson requested. Next, she meticulously applied the grated, pressed, salt-and-peppered cucumber and topped it off with another slice of bread, cutting off the crusts and slicing it into three fingers. There. That was not so bad.

Once she had used up all of the cucumber, Emily moved on to making the egg and cress sandwiches. She pulled four boiled eggs out of the refrigerator, diced them in a bowl, and mashed them with some softened butter, salt, and pepper. She spread the creamy mixture on the bread, topped it with a layer of cress, and covered the whole deal with another slice of bread. Emily didn't bother cutting the crusts off of this one, but instead devoured it in four bites. She had forgotten to each lunch.

Once all of the sandwiches were prepared and laid out in an elegant fashion, Emily moved on to making the chicken stuffed with asparagus. This was the one dish on her menu where she was going completely rogue. Nowhere in Ms. Thompson's trusty manual did she suggest providing fowl of any kind (in fact, this behavior was more in line with one of those robust farmhouse teas), but Emily, in her discouraged state of mind last night at the grocery store, had panicked and purchased the necessary ingredients for her staple home-run dish. She desperately did not want to strike out at today's tea.

Emily tenderized the chicken breasts, salted and peppered them, and deftly rolled each one around a small wedge of Colby Cheese and a petite stalk of fresh asparagus. She had done this a hundred times over the years. Emily hummed as she worked, grabbing a couple of toothpicks from the new box she had purchased the night before and sticking them in the chicken to hold everything in place. After she had properly breaded each breast, she stuck them in the refrigerator to wait. She would pop them in the oven to bake about twenty minutes before her guests arrived. Emily cleaned up the kitchen and then looked at the clock with satisfaction. One hour left before tea time—just enough time to get ready!

By half past three, Emily had showered and changed into her favorite green dress, accessorizing with only a simple strand of pearls and a frilly, white apron. The Mulberry house was filled with the aroma of baked chicken, water was reaching a boil on the stovetop, and the dining room table was spread with ample slices of almond cake, Victoria Sandwiches, and the little tea sandwiches Emily had just made.

The doorbell rang, announcing the arrival of her first guest. Emily opened the door to find Mrs. Scheinberg holding out a gift bag for the hostess.

"Oh," Emily exclaimed as she pulled out a green knitted circle, "a tea cozy! I love it!"

Lauren Basset arrived next, followed quickly by Alice and Rebecca. Bev arrived just as Emily was taking the stuffed chicken out of the oven, and Candice walked in a fashionably five minutes late. She was holding a magnificent, three-level twinkie cake on a crystal cake plate.

"It's just a little something I whipped up this morning for our little gathering," Candice trilled. She set the cake right in the middle of the table. Emily tried to hide her disappointment. The tiny cakes and sandwiches she had slaved over the past twenty-four hours looked dull and bland compared to the snowy mountain of cream and sugar towering at the center of the spread. Maybe it had been a mistake to try making new memories with Candice.

Emily pasted on a bright smile and offered, "Do sit down," coloring to realize she had inadvertently affected her voice with a slight English accent. She retreated to the kitchen in embarrassment and began the work of steeping the tea, carefully adding one spoonful for each person "and one extra for the pot," as

Ms. Thompson suggested. As the Ceylon steeped, Emily busily removed the toothpicks from the chicken and served one breast onto each plate.

"Oh, how lovely, dear!" Alice hummed.

Now, for Emily's most anticipated moment. She carefully arranged the pot of tea, the strainer, the pitcher of milk, the bowl of sugar, and the dish of sliced lemons on Grandmother Elsie's tray and covered it with a small cotton dish towel embroidered with pink and yellow flowers. (It was the closest she could come to the refined tray cloth Ms. Thompson described in her book.) Emily oh-so-carefully lifted the heavy tray and carried it into the dining room, setting it directly on the table. "Milk or lemon?" she asked each of her guests, glowing with a special kind of satisfaction and joy.

Rebecca, watching her friend closely, decided that Emily had never looked happier than at this moment.

"You never told me you could cook, Emily," Basset said, biting into an egg and cress sandwich. "Mmm, delicious. This is all quite intimidating, you know."

"Yes, what charming decor," Candice waved her hand authoritatively around the table. "It all has such a youthful, country feel to it."

"I love these!" Rebecca picked up one of the layered cakes. "They melt in your mouth. What are they called?"

"Victoria Sandwiches," Emily beamed, serving herself some tea. "That's your peach jam slathered in the middle."

"No wonder Rebecca likes them," Alice teased. "Seriously, dear, I must have this chicken recipe. I love the cheese and asparagus!"

Emily blushed with happiness. This was the first party she had hosted in her new home, and she wanted so much for it to be a success. She looked forward to calling her mother later in the evening to relay the day's events. Emily cut into her own chicken and took a big, cheesy bite. As she chewed, she looked down at her plate and almost spit her chicken right back out into her hand.

"What is it, dear? Are you okay?"

Emily nodded and forced herself to swallow. "Oh, yes. Just fine." But she wasn't. She subtly hovered her fork and knife over the cut part of her chicken, so that no one else could see the ribbon of bright blue color streaking through it.

The women chatted easily with each other while Emily silently recounted her steps in the kitchen. The tenderizing, the rolling, the toothpicks . . . the new toothpicks! Emily's stomach sank to her feet. They were appetizer toothpicks, a colored mix of red, yellow, blue, and green. The dye on the toothpicks must have bled into the meat while cooking. Emily covered her mouth with her hand.

"What's wrong, Emily?" Rebecca asked. All of the ladies froze.

"D-don't eat the chicken," Emily whispered.

"What? Why?"

Emily closed her eyes and put her head in her hands, completely defeated. "Because it's blue."

"Actually," Mrs. Scheinberg corrected pragmatically, "mine is green."

"Mine is yellow," Bev whispered.

Alice held up her hand apologetically. "Mine is red. Candy apple red."

Rebecca looked around in surprise. She, Candice, and Dr. Basset were the only three not to have cut into their chicken yet. She immediately grabbed a fork and knife and cut her breast in two, exclaiming in disbelief, "Blue!"

"It's all my fault," Emily moaned into her hands. "I accidentally bought colored toothpicks last night in Hamburg. It was late and I was tired, and I didn't know there was such a thing as stupid, colored toothpicks—"

Mrs. Scheinberg snorted at the end of the table. She held her napkin to her mouth to try her self-muting trick, but it was too late. The snigger had already gathered too much steam. Bassett soon joined her, tears of repressed laughter streaming down her face. Within moments, all of the women, Emily included, were doubled over in howls and guffaws.

The reverent elegance of the afternoon tea was lost, but the jovial camaraderie of the party only increased. Mrs. Scheinberg relayed a story of when she was a young girl and had mistaken salt for sugar when making a chocolate glaze for her father's birthday cake, and Basset admitted to having accidentally poured sour milk on her husband's cereal that very morning. "He consumed the whole bowl without telling me. I had no idea! I found out later when a curdled chunk of milk tumbled out of the carton into my coffee."

Bev giggled nonstop at everyone's stories, and tiny Alice ate every bite of her candy apple-streaked bird. "Well, it's perfectly good chicken, dear, no matter the color. In fact, I think it's quite brilliant. I'm sure the dye is food-safe. Don't you think the children would love this, Rebecca? We could call it Rainbow Chicken."

Candice sat back and wondered at the fact that a little cooking mistake could be the source of so much fun. She even felt a twinge of regret when they cut into her cake and found it without fault.

Emily did recount the day's events to her mother later that night over the phone, and she had a good laugh then too. Her afternoon tea party may not have met the refined expectations of

Cressida Langham Thompson and the Engelshire Parish Ladies Society, but it had more than exceeded her own. In fact, she and her friends had decided to make tea time in Emily's home a monthly practice, with everyone contributing a goodie or two, minus the colored toothpicks, of course.

Chapter Twenty-Two: Hail, Mary!

|||||||||||||||||||||||||||||||||||||||||||||||||||||||||||

"See it?"

Pastor Fletcher, down on all fours, craned his neck to look under the seventh pew on the pulpit side. Yvonne Roe's pew.

"Look to your right. No, back further, just inside the aisle leg."

There it was. A miniature pyramid of sand stood two inches from the inside of the pew, calculatedly out of sight. Pastor leaned back on his heels and expelled the world-weariness from his lungs. This sand pile was no diorama of Egypt. It was an all-American janitor trap. "Any idea how it got here?"

Irv gave Pastor a silent, knowing look.

Pastor closed his eyes to hide their fire. "How'd you find it?"

"Bill first called me last week, but it was pea gravel then. Same place and everything." Irv shook his head. "A vacuum won't even pick that stuff up. The sand seems to be her second go of it."

Pastor pushed himself back up onto his feet. He felt twenty years older. "What'd Bill say?"

"Not much, but he's no fool. What d'you want me to tell him?"

"Tell him to leave it. No sense in guessing. If Yvonne really planted it, well, then she'll see it here Sunday morning and come talk to me about it."

"No doubt she will." Irv's raised eyebrows punctuated his sentiment.

Pastor shook his head on his way back to his study. Of all the designing, underhanded schemes! No doubt, when it came to meddling in the congregation, Yvonne Roe took the cake.

"You've got something special in your mailbox," Mrs. Scheinberg announced as Pastor rounded the office corner.

Scratch that. Yvonne with all of the sand in the world could never outshine Zion's crowned prima meddler. Pastor Fletcher strode unseeing past his mailbox and his secretary's knowing grin to the sanctuary of his study.

"Trust me; you want to check your box," Mrs. Scheinberg sang before he could close his study door. "It'll make all of Yvonne's antics fade away."

How did she—?

Pastor Fletcher stuck his head out his door, nostrils flaring. "Any calls for me?"

"You were gone only five minutes."

Oh, for a wise, authoritative word! All Pastor could come up with was the truth.

"Mrs. Scheinberg, I don't appreciate your looking into my affairs uninvited."

Mrs. Scheinberg swiveled around in her seat and gave her young pastor a look of toleration. "I don't have to *look into* anything to see Dr. Duke walk through the front door and put a brown paper bag in your box. I sit in the middle of the church office. Would you like me to start wearing a bag over my head?"

The phone rang. Mrs. Scheinberg reached across her desk to pick up the receiver, never once breaking eye contact with Pastor

Fletcher. "Zion Lutheran Church, this is Arlene Scheinberg. How may I help you?" Her voice was syrup. "Certainly, Nettie. . . . Yes, of course, the good reverend is in. I'll put you through to him right now."

Arlene pushed the hold button on the phone and returned the receiver. "I was mistaken earlier. You do have a call. Nettie Schmidt is waiting on line one."

Pastor Fletcher turned back to his desk, shutting the door. Was he too young to start taking blood pressure pills? He picked up the receiver on his phone and leaned his heavy head on his left hand.

"This is Pastor Fletcher."

"Forgive me, Father, for I have sinned." Nettie had been watching EWTN again.

"What's bothering you, Nettie?"

Nettie cleared her throat. "You're supposed to ask, 'What is your confession, my child?'"

Pastor felt his pulse and tried to think of something other than pea gravel, swivel-back chairs, and *The Godfather*. His mind wandered to the cool oasis of a certain brown paper bag.

"I've been praying to the Virgin Mary."

Pastor snapped to attention. "What? Nettie, why?"

Nettie started whimpering. "I didn't mean to. It was an accident. All I was doing was washing the lunch dishes, and then that silly song came on. It's just so catchy, you know? I've always liked it, though I've never told anyone, not even Harold. It's just that Sister Mary Robert is so likable, you know? She's so shy, but she's really a star deep down inside. And that Whoopie woman brings it out of her, and she can't help but sing. That's how I feel. I can't help it."

"Who is Sister Mary Robert? Does she go to Blessed Sacrament?"

"No, she's the one who sings the song."

Pastor Fletcher rubbed his eyes with his right hand. Following Nettie's train of thought was like chasing smoke in a windstorm. "Nettie, what song are you talking about?"

"The one with the clapping. It comes through my window every day at noon, and I can't help but sing."

Through her window? The new carillon! Of course. Blessed Sacrament had installed a state-of-the-art carillon back in August that rang a full song at the top of every hour, and Harold and Nettie lived just three doors down from the new bell tower. All Pastor Fletcher had ever heard the carillon ring was "Let There Be Peace on Earth" on his evening walks at nine o'clock. That seemed harmless enough.

"What's the name of the song, Nettie?"

"I don't remember."

"Sing it to me."

"I can't, Pastor. I'm not Catholic."

"It's okay. You're not sinning when you sing it to me. You're just . . . helping me."

Pastor heard Nettie set down the phone and start clapping eighth notes every other beat. "Hail, Holy Queen enthroned above," she sang with a heavy vibrato, "O Ma-ri-a!"

Pastor covered his mouth. All of Nettie's ramblings suddenly fell together like pieces of an intricate puzzle. Sister Mary Robert wasn't a real person. Nettie was singing the upbeat version of a Marian hymn from the movie *Sister Act*. He stopped her before she could belt out, "*Salve, Regina!*"

"See what I mean?" Nettie whimpered again, picking up the receiver. "I'm praying to Mary!"

"No, you're not. You're just singing a song. It's okay for you to sing a song."

"I'm a blasphemer!"

Pastor heard Harold holler something from within the recesses of the Schmidt home.

"I'm talking to Pastor!" Nettie hollered back, forgetting to cover her end of the phone.

Pastor pulled the receiver away from his ear and closed his eyes.

"Pastor, what should I do?"

"Nettie, who is the mediator between God and man?"

"Jesus."

"Who intercedes on your behalf at the right hand of God?"

"Jesus."

"Who hears and answers your prayers?"

"Jesus."

"That's right. You don't pray to Mary, and you're not encouraging anyone else to pray to her. I don't think you're sinning just because your foot starts tapping along to a catchy tune. Still, maybe it would be a good idea for you to turn on the radio while doing the dishes, so your conscience won't be burdened."

Nettie sighed. "Oh, Pastor, I'm just so relieved. I could barely sleep last night, I felt so ashamed. Imagine me, Annette Marie Schmidt, a Catholic! My mother would just die. Well, she's already dead, but you know what I mean—Oh, no! Pastor, I just thought of something. Even my name is Catholic, isn't it? Maybe it's a sign, like those codes in those Italian paintings."

"Your name is nothing more than a gift given to you by your parents," Pastor reassured. "It's an honor to be named after the mother of our Lord."

Nettie sniffed. "You know what? That song shouldn't be polluting the air of Bradbury. I'm going to write a letter to the editor about it."

"Oh, please don't do that, Nettie."

"But it's noise pollution, and all pollution is bad. Harold read so on the back of the cereal box this morning."

"Our brothers and sisters at Blessed Sacrament just want to give our town the gift of music." How does one begin to reason with the unreasonable? "Have you tried wearing ear plugs?"

Not two seconds after hanging up with Nettie, the phone rang again.

"I've got it," Pastor Fletcher called to Mrs. Scheinberg, his hand still on the receiver. "Zion Lutheran Church, this is Pastor Fletcher."

"Ah, just the man I wanted!" Zachary Brandt's voice was friendlier than a golden retriever.

Pastor Fletcher felt his insides twist. Could the day possibly get any worse? "Zachary, what can I do for you today?"

"Well, I was wondering how a wandering Presbyterian signs up for new membership classes at Zion."

Yes, it could.

Five minutes later, Pastor Fletcher stood at the window, leaning his hot forehead against the cold pane of glass. He watched as the swirling November wind outside twisted the branches of a lone crab apple tree standing on the northwest corner of the parking lot. He felt a lot like that tree. It was heavy with unwanted fruit, and the *Sturm und Drang* of the season threatened to break its burdened branches.

At the seminary, professors had warned him not to be surprised by the presence of sin in the congregation. He had come into this vocation expecting there to be meddling and gossiping and ignorance, but what continually surprised him every day at this job was not the presence of his parishioners' sin, but that of his own.

Pastor Fletcher tore his gaze from the flailing crab apple tree and turned to kneel on the *prie-dieu* sitting under the crucifix hanging on the east wall of the study. As much as he wanted to pretend otherwise, he distrusted Brandt. What did a smooth-talking, networking choir stalker want with the Lutheran Confessions, anyway? Was Brandt even doing this for the right reasons?

"Forgive me," Pastor Fletcher bowed his head and prayed.

Why was he so set against Brandt? The guy was a bit light on substance, to be sure, but that didn't mean the man's intentions were false. Besides, who was he to divine the motives of another? No, he must take Brandt at his word, and Brandt had said he wanted to learn the faith. Really, this was good news, the stuff that made angels rejoice in heaven, but the thought of sitting alone in his office with Bradbury's harlequin poster child every Sunday night for eight weeks of private catechesis made Pastor Fletcher want to take up jousting.

The truth was that he was afraid—afraid that Brandt might end up joining the congregation and singing in the choir with Dr. Duke and sitting by her in the pew and who knows what else—and Pastor Fletcher knew he was supposed to be okay with that. Emily Duke was his choir director, not his maiden fair, and he was her pastor, not her knight in shining armor. He must set aside his lance for the Word and exchange his seat at the round table for a place behind the altar. It's just that, sometimes, it felt so lonely there.

It wasn't until Pastor Fletcher left for home that night that he finally retrieved the brown paper bag from his office mail-box. Mrs. Scheinberg had left two hours before, so he was safe opening the bag in the middle of the front office. He pulled out a worn book. A note tucked behind the front cover read:

Pastor Fletcher,

Thank you for the delightful encounter with Ms. Thompson. She and the Engelshire Parish Ladies Society have been properly returned to the library. In thanks, I thought I'd share with you my oldest and most favorite book in all the world. I just lived through my own version of chapter 21, though toothpicks, not liniment, were my downfall.

Best, Emily

Pastor Fletcher fingered the scuffed edges of Emily's worn copy of *Anne of Green Gables*. How long had she owned this book? How many times had she read it? Would he be able to tell her favorite pages just by looking at them? Was he the first one to be entrusted with her favorite book, or had she already lent it to Brandt? He shook the devil off his shoulder and tucked the book carefully in his bag. One thing was certain. Whenever he learned something new about his choir director, it was never enough. He always wanted to know more and more and more and . . .

CHAPTER TWENTY-THREE: WORDS AND MUSIC

"Okay, a quick review. What is good singing posture?"

Emily picked up a dry-erase marker and poised it over the white board in anticipation of her students' answers. The blood ran out of her arm before anyone bothered to speak. "C'mon, folks. We're in week twelve of the semester. Either you've got this by now, or we'll be seeing each other next fall for a very expensive review. Michelle, give me something."

"Chest should be high," Michelle spoke up from the front row. Two junior boys sitting in the back row raised their eyebrows meaningfully at each other, no doubt in appreciation for Michelle's already naturally high chest.

"Comfortably high, yes," Emily confirmed. She fixed her brown eyes on the darker-haired junior. "Bradley, why don't you come up front and demonstrate for us?"

Bradley colored respectably while his blond buddy busted up laughing.

"Stand right here," Emily gestured to her left, "and show us how to achieve a comfortably high chest."

Bradley, cheeks pink, walked to the front of the classroom and turned around to face the class.

"Arms up," Emily reminded him.

Bradley reached his fingers to the ceiling above his head.

"Now, slowly, intentionally allow your arms to fall to your side—that's it—but keep the chest elevated. Feel your spine stretch. No, don't look down—eyes level; that's right. Now, roll your shoulders back just a smidgen—good—then down a bit. Excellent."

Bradley's buddy clapped slowly and loudly.

"You're so encouraging today, Justin. How about you come up too?"

Justin ceased clapping and scowled.

"You can serve as Bradley's vocal coach." Emily turned and wrote *chest comfortably high* on the board. "Remember, before you can correct a singer's vocal flaws, you must first be able to diagnose them. That requires observation and evaluation. Justin, since Bradley hasn't begun singing yet, there are no audible clues as to his posture problems. You must go on the visible clues. What do you see?"

"A big dork," Justin said.

Bradley reached out and punched Justin in the ribs. Emily simply stared expressionless at the boys. She had learned years ago not to feed the egos of male twenty-year-olds with overreaction. Even the slightest provocation from a woman, positive or negative, seemed to fan the flame. No, apathy was the only thing she had found that properly extinguished man-cubs' fire.

"Look at his feet."

"Yeah, they're huge."

Emily blinked. "Thank you, Justin; you may sit back down. Blaine, come on up."

Blaine looked up from his book. Ten weeks ago, he had come into her office asking to audit the class "to help with my accompanying." Emily had agreed, secretly thrilled.

"His feet?" she asked again once Blaine had stepped forward.

"They're too far apart, and they're on equal planes. One foot should be slightly in front of the other."

"Yes," Emily said, turning to write *feet slightly separated, one toe in front of the other.* "What else?"

"His knees are locked."

Loose knees. "Anything else?"

"His hands are fisted. Probably so he can punch Justin."

This made the whole class laugh. Even Emily cracked a smile at the board as she wrote *arms/hands hang freely, naturally at side.* She capped the marker and set it back in the tray.

"Good. Now, teach Bradley. What suggestions can you give to him to keep his hands loose?"

"Don't sit next to Justin."

Bradley grinned. Emily noticed Michelle stealing a quick, shy glance at Blaine, and several of the other girls in the class were smiling more boldly at the piano major. Apparently, Blaine—eyeliner and piercings and all—was not hurting in the department of affections.

"Something more useful?"

Blaine shrugged.

"Anyone else?"

A red-haired senior wearing a green scarf around his neck raised his hand.

"Yes, Martin?"

"Dr. Finnegan told me to pretend like I'm holding tennis balls in my hands."

Emily nodded.

Michelle raised her hand. "He can also hold his hands together in front of him."

"Yes, as long as he doesn't clench them. Remember, excessive tension in the body is the enemy of singing. Thank you, Blaine; you may return to your seat. Okay, everyone, stand up. Bend your knees, stretch your backs, get the blood flowing. It's time to make some noise—with good posture, of course."

Emily was still humming the chorus of "At the Fair" on her bike ride home that afternoon, smiling at the memory of Justin trying to manage the top note under Martin's merciless tutelage. She'd have to remember to pair those two together more often.

Instead of taking her usual route home via Bradbury Drive, Emily veered two blocks east on Gooseberry Avenue to drop by the Bradbury County Public Library, a squat, white-stone building situated ironically next door to Susie Cue's Billiards and Brew. Emily could get just about anything her heart desired through BC's interlibrary loan, but ever since she had first stepped foot in the town library two weeks earlier to dutifully return Pastor Fletcher's loaned copy of Ms. Thomspon, she found herself returning every few days to the quirky building for the sheer pleasure of browsing the shelves of colorful, eclectic titles.

A friendly bell rang as Emily opened the front door. Lobelia Alwardt, the librarian on duty, looked up from behind her turquoise-rimmed glasses and gave a convivial wave. No sooner had Emily lifted her own hand in a return greeting than a young head the shape and color of a basketball veered round the end of the children's section and rammed straight into Emily's unsuspecting middle. Books of blue and red and green and black flew into the air like the sparks of a firecracker.

"Robbie Jones!" Lobelia cred, scaring even the dust off of the books. She jumped out from behind the counter and scurried to Emily's teetering side to lend a steadying hand. "You practically knocked Dr. Duke to the floor. How many times have I told you not to run in here?"

"At least three," answered Frankie. Emily became aware of the other two Jones boys standing on the sidelines with their book bags slung neatly over their shoulders.

"Are you hurt?" Lobelia asked, turning to Emily.

"Jus' my head," Robbie answered.

"Not you, numbskull," Davie slapped the back of his younger brother's head. "C'mon, pick up your books. Mom'll be here any minute."

"Are you okay?" Emily's voice was gentle if a bit pinched.

Robbie rubbed his head and frowned at Emily's belly button. "Your stomach hurts."

She couldn't argue with that.

Frankie bent down to help Robbie start picking up books. Judging by the rainbow of illustrated pages fluttering open on the floor, Robbie must have been carrying at least ten books when he ran into her. Emily bent over to pick up a green and black title lying at her feet. *Aliens: Are They Real?* She raised her eyebrows at the cover as Robbie took it from her hands, hastily shoving it in his bag. He glanced sideways at her before relinquishing a shrug and mumbling, "I want to know."

"Mom's here," Davie called over his shoulder, one foot already out the door. Frankie ran after his eldest brother, and Robbie messily shoved the rest of the books in his bag before sprinting outside with the top of his backpack flapping wide open.

"Tell your mom hi," Emily called out after the wind.

"He's going to lose half of those books before he even gets home," Lobelia sighed. She walked over to the door and watched to see if Robbie's books made it at least as far as the Joneses' SUV. The chiffon sleeves of her turquoise, aqua, and yellow top rippled behind her like a mermaid's tail in the ocean deep.

When Lobelia finally turned back around, she was waving her hand disgustedly in front of her face. "Ew, can you smell that? Susie must be brewing some more of her pale ale. Putrid stuff, if you ask me. Smells like vomit. At least it's still cold outside. Summertime's the worst. When it gets all hot and humid, we have to open the east windows in the ladies room, and that horrid smell wafts in like tear gas. I have to pinch my nose whenever I go to the bathroom, and that doesn't leave me enough hands to take care of the rest of my business. Even the lobby starts smelling like a brothel by late afternoon in July. Oh, I know what you're thinking, and trust me, I've told the board about it. I have, but what can they do? No one dares say a thing after the Brew War of 2003."

Emily, oblivious to any wars involving brew, was at a loss for what to say.

"Oh, that's right," Lobelia nodded her head, "you just moved here. Seems to me like you've always been here. Well, we share the parking lot with Susie's, you know? Always have, but when Susie got her liquor license seven years ago, people threw a fit. Soon as she painted the word *Brew* up on her billiards sign, the library board complained to the town council that beer and books don't go together. That's a bit extreme if you ask me, but no one ever does. Anyway, they requested a change in the zoning laws that would push Susie's business south of Main Street. Misty Jackson—she was head librarian at the time—well, she convinced the local chapter of the Daughters of the American Revolution to resurrect their old prohibition campaign from a zillion years ago to make Bradbury a dry town. Well, you can bet that once Hank Ferguson got whiff of that—Have you met Hank? No? Well, he's one of Susie's regulars.—Anyway, Hank wrote a letter to the editor calling Misty 'a book no man would ever want to read.' Isn't that funny? Well, Misty sure didn't think so. Anyway, the town council failed to pass the DAR's resolution, the zoning laws stayed stuck in the mud, Misty retired, and Hank now makes sure to send the library staff a gift certificate to Susie's every Christmas. I'm pretty sure Patty is the only one who uses it. The rest of us are left to breathe the fumes."

Emily felt a strange urge to laugh.

Lobelia stepped back behind the counter and fluffed up her curls, sending out waves of airy fabric in her wake. "Whatcha lookin' for today? Anything in particular, or just browsing?"

"Just browsing."

"Uh huh. Well we got some fancy new volumes of poetry from the Hamburg library on Monday. Just shelved them this morning. They're the pretty green books in that third aisle if you want to have a look-see."

Emily was not particularly interested in volumes of poetry, but she had nothing better in mind today. She moseyed over to aisle three.

"Holler out if you need me," Lobelia called. "I know libraries are supposed to be quiet an' all, but it's just you and me in here right now. Want some coffee? I think I'm going to put a pot on."

"No, thank you," Emily said.

"'Kay, well, tell me if you change your mind."

Emily liked Lobelia. She was a lot like the colors she wore—cheerful, bright, and loud—and she had a disarming way of eating up silence like Pac-Man on a rampage. An odd personality for a librarian, to be sure, but Emily couldn't imagine anyone else sitting behind that counter.

Aisle three was a forest of poetry volumes. Tall, sturdy hardbacks filled with children's verses and pastel pictures towered over short, stout hymnals of varying denominations. Green, cloth-covered encyclopedias of nineteenth-century poets (those must have been the implants from Hamburg) were tucked in next to a *Reader's Digest* collection of favorite rhymes. Emily ran her fingers along the spines of the books, admiring the potpourri of classics mixed with family treasures that most likely had been donated to the library by younger, unappreciative beneficiaries.

A slim blue volume, nestled between a book on medieval tropes and a paperback compendium of religious verse, caught her eye. Or rather, the name on the spine did:

    Michael G. Fletcher

Could it be? Alice had once mentioned that Pastor Fletcher had published a book of poetry, but honestly, she had forgotten all about it up to that very moment. Emily pulled the book off the shelf and stared at the cover. *Laud and Lamentation: Poetic Meditations for the Church Year* by Michael G. Fletcher, published by Mittelstadt Academic Press. Emily opened the front cover and read the author dedication:

    For my mother

Her cheeks colored. She suddenly felt as if she were peering uninvited into the private rooms of an acquaintance. What if Pastor Fletcher didn't want her to read his poems? How would she feel if he thumbed through her composition portfolio from college?

"Silly," she whispered. Pastor Fletcher's book was in print. It had an ISBN number and everything. If he hadn't intended for anyone to read his poems, he would never have published them. Emily flipped the book open to a random page.

"The Last Shall Be First"

Not a virgin favored,
Not a prophet wild,
But a dirty shepherd
Bid, "Come see the Child."

"Most unworthy servant,
Least in all the line,
Wake, for night is flying;
Greet your Christ divine."

Blinded by the glory,
Muted by the host,
Last runs first to see this Thing
Of which the heralds boast.

There, in manger lowly,
Swaddled, poor, and meek.
Lies creation's Master,
Framed in flesh so weak.

Hope, run with the shepherd.
Faith, believe His Word.
Love, proclaim, "The Christ is born,"
Till all the News have heard.

Emily stood still. Such a simple, humble poem, but that was the point, wasn't it? Who is called to first behold the Christ Child? Not the wise, not the rich—but an unsophisticated shepherd. The last is first. Emily shut the book and took it to the checkout counter just as Lobelia was returning from the break room with a coffee mug in hand.

"What'd you pick? Ah, Pastor Fletcher's poems. Pretty good, aren't they? That sweet Mrs. Gardner—Have you met her? Well, I'll never be able to call her Alice. Anyway, she donated this back when Fletcher first came to Zion. I was baptized there, did you know? Well, the first time. The second time was at Wesleyan Methodist and the third at Spirit of Life in Stalwart, but I was raised Lutheran. Confirmed by Pastor Gardner. Mrs. Gardner made my confirmation dress. My own mother couldn't work a sewing machine, but no matter. She could handle herself on any diesel that came her way."

Lobelia picked up the book and scanned it. "Your library card?"

Emily dug around in her bag in search for the piece of plastic.

"Now, Zion, that's a funny little church. I remember when Pastor Gardner first hired Evan Ebner. He was all the rage back then, rolling into town in that red Mercedes of his and that full head of black hair. Ladies nearly fell over themselves every time he played the organ. Smart too, at least smarter than anyone this town had seen since Edith Bradbury brought back that Egyptian assistant with the turban. What was his name? Yuri Babba-something-or-other. Anyway, Shirley—that's Edith's granddaughter—well, she took the biggest liking to Evan, but then you probably already know all about that. Shirley was the head librarian here before Misty Jackson, did you know?"

Emily didn't know. She tried her best to look disinterested as she handed over her library card, but the mention of Evan's name in relation to a woman named Shirley was to Emily like a frosted cupcake set before a hungry toddler. All she wanted to do was pick up the news with both hands and devour it.

"You work with Evan, don't you?"

"A little," Emily answered carefully, trying with all her might to resist the urge to ask gossipy questions. "He plays the organ on Sundays, but he resigned from accompanying the choir."

Lobelia snorted. "I bet he did. I'm surprised it took him so long. Gosh, it's been, what, fifteen years since Shirley left? I can't believe the man's stuck with it this long."

Lobelia handed Emily's card back and passed her the blue book of poetry. "Well, Dr. Duke, enjoy! It's due back the third week of December. Say, that Pastor Fletcher is still single, isn't he? Not a bad catch, that one, and he's published to boot. You look like just about the right age too, though I'm not one to talk. Never married, myself. There haven't been any more Evan Ebners rolling into town, that's for sure. Ha! Goodness knows, I probably smell like that nasty beer by now, so you'd think the men would be chomping at the bit. I suppose there's always Hank if a girl gets desperate."

Emily biked the five blocks home deep in thought. She didn't even notice Pastor Fletcher waving to her from the church parking lot as she turned into her yard. Her mind was swimming with images of Evan and a red Mercedes and—what was her name again? Shirley? Yes. Shirley Bradbury.

CHAPTER TWENTY-FOUR: RESURRECTION LILIES

Not only did Candice return to choir practice the next Thursday, but she brought Caroline and Amelia with her. Now only Geraldine was delinquent. Well, Geraldine and Evan.

"I was thinking, Emily," Candice cooed over the director's stand before rehearsal one night. "You've heard my Caroline sing. Well, I thought she might like to take some lessons, and I said to Thomas just the other day, 'You know, I think Dr. Duke would be the perfect match for our little songbird.'"

Emily remembered Candice having had a very different opinion just three months before.

"What do you think about Thursday afternoons? Say, next week?"

Emily looked beyond Candice to the golden-haired heiress sitting on a folding chair in the soprano section. Caroline was busy looking through her new choir folder, unaware that anyone was watching her. Emily could see that her eyes danced with genuine excitement as she pulled out octavo after octavo and fingered their artistic covers. Emily's heartstrings tugged for the awkward girl who wanted to learn to sing and decided to throw caution to the wind. "Well, Thursdays are already a bit hectic for me, but I could do Friday afternoons. I'm done teaching at the college by 4:00. I could pop by your place on my way home."

"Yes, yes, that should work just fine. Caroline comes home right after school on Fridays, so she would be available. When shall we start? How about tomorrow? And of course, you must stay for dinner. Did you hear that, Caroline darling? Dr. Duke is going to give you singing lessons!"

The next afternoon, Emily found herself knocking on the heavy doors of Bradbury House once again. Caroline was all grins when she answered the door.

"Are you ready to sing?"

Caroline nodded her head up and down enthusiastically. She led Emily into the southwest sitting room where a gorgeous, maplewood baby grand piano was standing. A check was waiting conspicuously for her on the bench.

"My mom wasn't sure what to pay you, since you have a doctoration and everything."

"Doctorate, darling," Candice corrected, sailing brightly through the doorway from the dining room, wiping her hands on a dishtowel. "Caroline and I are *so* excited you're here, aren't we, Caroline? (Stand up straight, darling.) Did you find your check? Will that amount be all right?"

Emily stared at the two zeros following the number one and swallowed to loosen her tongue. "Yes."

"Wonderful! Well, don't mind me. I'm just going to be in the kitchen. You're staying for dinner, right? Excellent! I hope you eat dairy. We're having chicken pomodoro with buttered risotto. I also whipped up some of Mother Bradbury's sugarplums. They're Thomas's favorite, and I've never heard anyone else complain about them. Well, now, I'll leave you to it. (Stand up straight, Caroline.)" With that, Candice veered her grand yacht-of-a-self back to the docks in the kitchen.

Emily sat at the piano and took a deep breath before turning to Caroline and smiling. "I always get a little nervous before singing in front of someone new."

"Me too," Caroline admitted.

"Right. Then there's only one thing to do. Let's get to know each other so we won't be so nervous anymore. What's your favorite kind of music?"

Emily listened intently as Caroline told her all about Taylor Swift and Carrie Underwood and Michael Bublé and John Philip Sousa (the last having been introduced to her by her trombone-playing brother) as well as the excitement of having seen *The Phantom of the Opera* in St. Louis when she was eight. Emily learned that Caroline's favorite color was yellow, that she liked baking and sewing and reading, and that she very much wanted to raise a bunny for next year's 4-H fair. Emily also learned that Caroline had dressed up as Katniss from *The Hunger Games* for Halloween—she had made her costume herself—while her brother had been Snow, and no, she had never sung in Italian before. Once Caroline was talking as if she no longer remembered to be nervous, Emily rolled a D-major chord to begin warming up Caroline's voice.

The first few minutes were rough. Caroline sang completely through her nose, making it difficult for her to sing much higher than an octave above middle C.

"Try something for me," Emily said. "Put your index fingers on either side of your jaw. Now, open your mouth wide and shut it again. Can you feel the hinges? Good, now rub them. Are they sore? Yes, I think you might have some tension there. Rub them some more; get them good and loose. Okay, now let's sing again, only this time, keep your fingers on your jaw and think about how good it feels to have all of that tension gone."

Caroline sang again.

"That's better. Try it one more time for me—you can put your hands down—and relax your jaw. Let it drop open naturally as you sing."

Caroline's brow furrowed in concentration.

"Relax your forehead. Uh huh, now, take a long breath and sing."

Caroline relaxed her face and sang, "Yah, yah, yah—"

"Let your jaw fall open."

"—yah, yahhhh."

"Good," Emily smiled. Caroline sounded a little bit more like a singer and a little bit less like a goose. "Let's do it again."

An hour later, Caroline was holding out a sparkling E above middle C when the doorbell rang.

"I'll get it," Candice trilled from the kitchen. She stuck her head through the dining room door on her way to the foyer. "You sound lovely, Caroline darling, simply lovely. Now, be a good girl and set the table for me, will you? Amelia is eating at a friend's tonight, so we'll have six at the table."

"You mean five?"

"No, six."

Caroline's brow furrowed again, but Candice steered her ship toward the front door before her daughter could say another word about it. Caroline closed the Christmas music book out of which she had been singing, but not before slipping a laminated dried leaf in between the pages to mark the spot.

"What's that?" Emily asked.

Caroline jerked her hand back as though she had been caught touching a painting in a museum. "I-it's just a little leaf I, um, found. I made it into a bookmark. We have a laminator in our sewing room."

That leaf had Ben Schmidt's fingerprints all over it; Emily'd bet her tiger lilies on it.

"Oh, Russell," Candice warbled from the foyer, opening the door, "I'm so glad you could join us! Here, let me take your coat. It's a remarkable coincidence that you're in town this evening, for we happen to have Caroline's voice teacher dining with us tonight as well. We'll make a cozy party of six tonight, three boys and three girls, to be exact."

Emily's stomach lurched. Surely not. Candice wouldn't dare.

"Come, let me introduce you." Candice stepped into the southwest sitting room before Emily could even stand up from the piano bench. A small, middle-aged man in a blue suit and red tie followed closely behind. "Russell, this is Dr. Emily Duke, our beloved choir director at Zion. She also teaches music history across the street. Emily, this is Russell Horton, my husband's partner in law. He has an office in Hamburg but comes into town every other Friday for court. I imagine you must be starving, Russell. Why don't you have a seat while I pour us some wine? Chianti is your favorite, if I remember. Emily, can I pour you a glass?"

Emily felt her face flush with mortification. She didn't even have the presence of mind to answer properly.

"I think I'll pour each of us a glass. Thomas'll want one when he gets home. It should be any minute now. He promised to pick up some aged Parmesan for me on his way home. Caroline, come with me and set the table."

Caroline, ungainly as she could be, was no idiot. Neither was she a stranger to her mother's manipulations. She gave her new voice teacher, whom she happened to like very much, an apologetic look before her mother dragged her by the elbow into the dining room.

Emily quickly busied herself by putting away her music and closing the lid on the piano. What in the world was Candice doing leaving her alone with this strange man? And why wasn't she staying in the room to help entertain her husband's business partner herself? Emily took a deep breath. Any sensible person would stand up, walk over to one of the wingback chairs facing Mr. Horton, and casually engage him in a conversation about law or Hamburg's basketball team or the price of milk, but she had never been very good at small talk. Her rigid body stayed glued to the piano bench.

Russell cleared his throat and tapped his fingers on the arm of his chair. "So, you're a music teacher?"

Emily prayed for a bear to come and eat her. Or a coyote. They had coyotes in Bradbury County, right?

"I like music," Russell continued. "Have you ever listened to those Celtic women? I have one of their recordings in my car."

Emily shook her head and stared at her hands. They were fisted into balls in her lap. She made a concerted effort to relax them.

"Oh, well, they're really good. Relaxing." Russell cleared his throat again. "Candice tells me you're from St. Louis."

Emily's head snapped up. Candice had talked about her to this stranger? What all had she told him? Anger boiled up to her ears so fast she could hear the sound of water rushing. "I'm sorry; Candice has never spoken to me about you."

Russell had the decency to color a bit around the collar. "I see. Well, I suppose you probably want to know a bit about me. I'm from the Quad Cities. I went to school with Thomas—that's how I know the Bradburys. I've been practicing law my whole career, employment and labor law, to be specific. I should tell you that I was married before."

There it was. If Emily had been uncertain as to whether or not this "coincidence" of meetings was a blind date, she no longer had any doubts. She pressed her lips into a tight line, refraining from responding. She knew she was being rude, but she didn't care.

Russell leaned forward, his elbows on his knees. "I've lost a spouse too. Candice thought we might be able to offer some comfort to each other."

Emily jumped up. "Mr. Horton, I'm sorry, but there's been a misunderstanding."

"Here we are," Candice sang, floating into the room with a tray of wine glasses. "One for you, Russell, and one for you—"

"Candice, I won't be staying for supper."

Candice blinked her eyes once, stunned. She opened her mouth to protest, but Emily did not give her a chance to speak.

"I'm sorry, but you'll have to tell Caroline to set the table for just five tonight. I've got to go." White hot fury gave Emily her legs. She picked up her bag, slung it over her shoulder, grabbed her coat, and pointed her own ship toward the horizon. "I can show myself out."

"But, Emily—"

"Give my apologies to Mr. Bradbury." Emily suddenly remembered Russell as she opened the front door. Poor man. None of this was his fault. She turned, one hand on the doorknob, and nodded her head at the speechless lawyer. "It was nice to meet you, Mr. Horton. Enjoy the sugarplums. Candice says they're really good."

With that, Emily shoved off for open water.

She was still steaming as she trudged up the stairs to the church balcony, muttering to herself about impudence and impertinence and every other word she could think of beginning with the prefix *im-*. At the top of the stairs, she flipped on the north light switch and swung open the third drawer of the filing cabinet, pulling files out by the fistful without even looking at their titles. It took a few moments before she realized she was unloading the cabinet of Lenten music.

"Oh, snap!" she groused. She awkwardly returned the files, scraping her knuckles on the metal braces in the process, and slammed the third drawer shut. She pulled out the second drawer next, being careful this time to pull only Christmas titles: "Of the Father's Love Begotten" . . . "Still, Still, Still" . . . "Cantique de Noël." The last one Emily took directly to the piano. Good, it was in the key of E-flat. Turning on the piano light, she sat down to play and began to sing:

> *O Holy Night!*
> *The stars are brightly shining,*
> *It is the night of our dear Savior's birth.*

Emily felt her shoulders relaxing under the spell of the arpeggiated eighth notes in the bass line.

> *Long lay the world in sin and error pining,*

Her shoulders tensed up again. *Sin and error, indeed!* she thought, visions of Candices and sugarplums still dancing in her head. She forced herself to relax and continued.

> *'Til He appeared and the soul felt its worth.*
> *The thrill of hope, the weary world rejoices,*
> *For yonder brinks a new and glorious morn.*

Even Candice's antics couldn't steal the thrill of singing about that glorious dawn. Yes, come quickly, Lord Jesus!

> *Fall on your knees!*
> *O hear the angel voices!*

O night divine,
O night when Christ was born;
O night divine,
O night, O night divine.

"Beautiful."

Emily jumped at the sound of a masculine voice. She turned around to see Pastor Fletcher leaning on the doorframe at the top of the balcony stairs.

"Sorry," he said, "I didn't mean to scare you."

"You really shouldn't sneak up on people like that," Emily reprimanded, still smarting from Candice's effrontery.

"I'm sorry," Pastor Fletcher apologized again. "I should have said something earlier, but I didn't want to interrupt your singing. I was just down in my office working on a sermon and heard you practicing."

Emily shut her score and turned off the piano light. The magic was gone.

"That's one of my favorite songs. Is it for Christmas Eve?"

She nodded politely but refused to look at him. Maybe if she kept staring at her music he would get the hint that she wanted to be left alone. Only the north balcony lights remained on, leaving the nave and sanctuary completely in the dark while a warm pool of golden light spilled over the piano and onto Emily's curls.

"That's the first time I've heard you sing."

Why was he still standing there? Emily felt childishly grumpy.

"Your voice is lovely."

"Thank you."

"It's rich and sweet all at the same time."

Was she now to be subjected to vocal diagnostics from an armchair musician?

"You know, my mom used to sing 'O Holy Night' in church every Christmas Eve."

Emily pressed her lips together. Apparently, she was going to have to go home to get any practicing done. Why was everyone in this church always butting into her personal space uninvited? No one at her previous church would have ever dared interrupt her while she was rehearsing in the balcony or sucker-punched her at a voice lesson with an unsolicited blind date. What was it with small-town people and their disrespect for personal boundaries? Emily picked up her music and put it in her bag.

"Her voice is different from yours though," Pastor continued, his own voice was friendly and companionable. He seemed oblivious to any irritation Emily might be feeling. "More—oh, I don't know the right words—how would you say it as a singer? Older? Or darker, maybe? Yes, that's it. You sing like a Riesling, and she sings like a Merlot."

More blasted wine! "Is she an alto?"

"I think so."

"Usually, sopranos sing 'O Holy Night.'"

"Oh, well, I don't know very much about that. My mom probably doesn't either. She just likes to sing."

Emily's conscience pricked at Pastor's words. Why was she being so mean? It wasn't his fault what happened earlier at Bradbury House, yet she seemed to be taking her frustrations out on him. She looked at Pastor and made an effort. "What I mean is that it is *special* to have an alto sing 'O Holy Night.' It's like . . . like dipping oranges in chocolate."

Pastor grinned at the imagery obviously meant for him. "No wonder my mom sounds so good. I'd sure love to hear her sing it again, but she usually goes to my brother's for Christmas."

"What about your dad?"

"He . . . he died when I was sixteen."

Emily winced. "I'm sorry."

"Me too."

Emily stared at her hands. Boy, she was really striking out this evening. She tried to think of something to say. "I read your book."

Pastor stood up straight. "My book? You mean my poems? Where in the world did you find—?"

"At the public library."

"Oh, that's right. I remember. Alice did that, I think."

"When did you write them? The poems, I mean."

Pastor stuck his hands in his pockets and leaned his back against the balcony wall. "I started writing them the year my dad died."

"How did he die?" Emily wouldn't normally ask such a personal question, but, well, she was trying.

"Heart attack."

"Was he—were you . . . ?"

"I'm the one who found him."

Emily felt disarmed by this very personal admission. More than that, she felt comforted. She was not the only one to have seen death. A warm *esprit de corps* spread throughout her chest, slowly melting away her irritation.

"I gave him CPR, but he never revived."

How awful! Emily saw past the collar to the boy who lost his father.

"I started having anxiety attacks after that. I think writing the poems came from trying to sort out all of that fear and pain. Words have always been my weapon against chaos. I think that's why I'm a pastor. The Word of God organizes the chaos in me. It creates light in the darkness. I can't help but study and preach that Word. 'In the beginning was the Word, and the Word was with God, and the Word was God.'"

Emily realized something as Pastor was talking. Small talk with him was never hard or awkward or even small. It just was. "You dedicated the book to your mother."

"Yes." Pastor shifted his weight ever so slightly, his right shoulder still leaning against the wall. "I lost my father, but my mother lost her husband. She was alone. Confused. I know you understand."

Apparently, so could a sixteen-year-old boy. What was it in men that made them so willing to die to self for a woman? Emily knew the answer was as old as Christ Himself and as deep and mysterious and unfathomable as His own self-sacrifice on the cross. "How did your poems come to be published?"

"I entered three of them in a national writing competition my first year of teaching, and the first prize was a contract for publication. No one was more shocked than I was when I won." Pastor was studying Emily. The shadows made him bold to do so. She had never taken such an interest in him before. "So what did you think of them?"

Emily looked up, startled. "Of what?"

"The poems."

"Oh. I thought—" she paused. She tried to think of the right word. "I thought they were musical."

"Musical? What do you mean?"

Emily turned to the console and flipped the piano light back on. She pulled a lone sheet of staff paper out of her bag and set it before her on the music desk. She played the simple, homophonic introduction she had sketched out on the paper and began to sing.

Be not afraid, O little lamb,
Of valley steep or river deep,
For with you is the great I AM.

You'll hunger not, O sparrow small,
Nor e'er despair of what to wear,
Who cares for thee is LORD of all.

Death has no sting, O wretched poor,
Have you not heard the blesséd Word?
The Christ who died is dead no more.

So lie and eat, O little lamb,
Enjoy the feast beside the beast,
Forevermore in perfect peace;
The Bridegroom is the great I AM.

Emily sat back and rested her hands in her lap when she finished. "That's what I mean. Musical."

Pastor stepped forward into the pool of light. "You set my poem to music?"

"I suppose I should have asked first, but this one reads like a melody from the start. It feels better sung than spoken, don't you think?"

"May I?" Pastor reached for the sheet of music. He studied the notation for a moment before shyly gesturing to sit at the piano. "If I play—or at least attempt to play—will you sing it for me again?"

Emily stood behind the piano bench and sang over Pastor's shoulder while he played. When he reached the end of the song, he started right back at the beginning again, begging, "Once more for the lyricist?"

Emily let Pastor keep the music. He seemed so delighted by the notion of his poem becoming a song that she couldn't help it. She marveled at the music that is so often born from misery. A strange paradox, to be sure, but one every Christian understands: victory is born from great sacrifice, salvation from a cross, Easter joy from Good Friday woe, and here, this very evening, the gladness of a man from the pain of a sixteen-year-old boy. Seeing Pastor Fletcher's face in the balcony had been a bit like watching that of a child waking up one summer morning to find a familiar plot of land that had been bare the day before now blanketed with resurrection lilies.

Emily wasted no time getting home that night. Another seed had begun to sprout in her curly little head, and if it was ever going to blossom this winter, she was going to need some help. She picked up the phone and dialed a familiar number.

"Alice, I have an idea . . ."

Chapter Twenty-Five:

Bless All the Dear Children

||||||||||||||||||||||||||||||||||||||||||||||||

The December sky was pregnant with snow. Nettie Schmidt took an appreciative breath of the velvety, moist air as Harold held open her car door in the driveway. The atmosphere had that frosty, magical feel to it, as if it would open its coat at any moment and unleash the snow it held within its gray folds.

This was Nettie's favorite time of year, a time thick with chocolate stars and gingerbread men and twinkling lights and Andy Williams and memories of Hank sledding headfirst down the Shelbyville dam. Oh, that boy! Hank had always been a rough-and-tumble kind of kid, taking more to his trucks and engines than to his catechism. What she wouldn't give to have her son sit next to her in church tonight, but at least he allowed them to take their grandson, Ben, to church every Christmas Eve and Easter. That was something.

Nettie plopped into the passenger seat of the car and hugged the gold-and-silver tin to her chest. It contained the divinity she had made just that morning. Hank's favorite.

As Harold swung her door shut, the carillon at Blessed Sacrament started up its sweet, six o'clock siren song for the month of December. Nettie squeezed her eyes shut and raised her shoulders to her ears in defense against the fluid notes of Gounod's "Ave Maria."

"O little town of Bethlehem," she belted out loud, "How still we see thee lie! Above thy deep and dreamless sleep . . ." It wasn't until she and Harold were well out of town on their way to Hank and Andrea's place to pick up sweet Benny that she finally leaned back in her seat and let the singing drop for good.

Across town in the Joneses' house, Rebecca discovered a handwritten note shoved between the milk and the orange juice on the top shelf of the refrigerator. The red markings on it were unmistakably the handiwork of her second son. "Robbie, what's this?"

"My Christmas list."

"Why was it in the refrigerator?"

"I wanted you to see it."

"Why not just hand it to me?"

"You were in the bathroom and I didn't want to lose it and I knew you'd find it in the fridge. You always look in there."

Rebecca couldn't argue with her son's logic, but his application wanted some refinement. She eyed the list skeptically. "You already gave me your Christmas list last month."

"This one's different."

Rebecca sighed. She started to explain that Christmas Eve was a little late to be handing *any* mother, let alone a mother of four, a wish list for Christmas morning, and that Robbie had exactly two minutes to comb his hair before they all needed to be out the door for church, when something on Robbie's list caught her attention.

MUSE

"Robbie, come here." Rebecca carefully knelt down in her black velvet skirt and pulled her green-sweatered son close to her heart. "Tell me what this says."

"Moose."

"Moose? You want a moose?"

Robbie nodded his head excitedly.

"Why do you want a moose?"

" 'Cause Blaine has one."

"Blaine has a moose?"

"Uh huh. In his hair. That's how come his head stands up so tall."

Oh, mousse. Rebecca looked Robbie in the eye for a long moment. "You want to look like Blaine?"

Robbie grinned. "Yeah, he's cool! He plays the piano. I'm going to play the piano too. And baseball. And I'm going to drive the brown truck that delivers all those big boxes."

Rebecca quietly studied her son and suddenly became aware that she no longer looked down into his eyes when she knelt beside him. His face was perfectly level with her own. When had he grown so tall? And where were the soft curves of his cheeks that she liked to nuzzle and kiss so much? They were gone, replaced by a strong, boyish chin line. Come to think of it, when was the last time he had buried his nose in her neck? He used to love doing that. And why didn't he ask for his lovey blanket before bed anymore? Rebecca blinked back a sharp sting of tears and leaned in to tenderly kiss the three freckles clustered directly below Robbie's left eye. At least those were still there.

"Wait right here, Robbie."

Rebecca disappeared down the hallway. A few minutes later, Jeremy called for his son from within the master bathroom. Robbie hesitated, afraid of what new article of clothing his parents would force on him to wear for tonight's Christmas Eve program, but when he came back down the hall to leave for church, Robbie was all grins. His shock of red hair was teased straight up into a crunchy flattop, and he looked as if he had just played a Rachmaninoff concerto, pitched a no-hitter, and been offered a job with UPS all at once.

Alas, there is no equalizer like an older sibling.

"Freak," Davie whispered in Robbie's ear as they headed out to the van.

At the church, the children were beginning to gather in the fellowship hall for the annual Christmas Eve pageant. Bev Davis walked around in circles, clipboard in hand, checking off the names of kindergarten angels and first-grade shepherds as they arrived. Mrs. Scheinberg and Marge Johnson were attempting to corral preschool sheep and cows into the appropriate flocks and herds, while Emily was upstairs in the balcony giving last-minute instructions to Blaine.

"Remember, as soon as the children finish singing 'Away in a Manger,' go right into the introduction for 'O Holy Night,' okay? Don't wait for me to come up or for the children to be seated. The Sunday School teachers have agreed to lead them back to their pews while you're playing."

"Got it."

Emily tapped her fingers nervously on top of the piano. "I have a bad feeling about this."

"The kids did great at rehearsal."

"That's just the thing." Emily shook her head. "They did too well. They peaked too soon. It's always better if they're a little nervous going into an event. You know, it keeps everyone on their toes. It's when the children are comfortable and confident that things start to happen. That's when shepherds start swinging their staffs over their heads and cows start ringing their bells."

Down in the nave, Pastor Fletcher was having his own misgivings about the night.

"Toenail clippings? Really?"

Irv nodded his head.

"But I told her when she came to me two weeks ago that you and I instructed Bill to leave that sand."

"Apparently, she didn't believe you. She's still testing him."

"But he's doing his job just fine!"

"You don't need to tell me that." Irv was as cool and calm as ever, but Pastor was a hot mess. He ran his hand through his hair, vexing his curls. There simply was no getting around it. He'd have to talk to Yvonne again before she tarred and feathered the church floor in a misguided outrage. And tonight, she'd have her sister, Yolanda, with her. Pastor almost visibly shuddered. Well, one thing was certain. There was no way he could talk about toenails in front of Yolanda, so he would have to wait until after Christmas to confront Yvonne.

"Meddy Kiss-mas."

Pastor felt a small hand tug at his alb. He looked down to see a strawberry-blonde cherub dressed in red satin smiling up at him. His heart melted into a puddle of goo at his feet.

"Merry Christmas, Alison."

"See my bow?" she chirped, twirling around for him to see her green-and-red plaid sash, which tied neatly into a bow at the small of her back.

"Very pretty," Pastor approved, reaching down and catching her midtwirl to swing her high into the air. She squealed with delight, earning an appreciative cackle from Irv.

"Okay, Miss Alison," Rebecca said, marching up the aisle to retrieve her flying daughter. "Time to get you into costume."

"I angel," Alison smiled winsomely.

"Angel?" Pastor asked.

"Not exactly." Rebecca looked pointedly at Pastor and Irv. "She's supposed to be a sheep, but a certain someone decided yesterday that wings and halos look much more appealing than wooly ears. I'm not sure how this all is going to go down."

"Wings," Alison clapped her hands. "I angel."

Upstairs, Robbie bounded around the soundboard of the piano to stick his grin directly in Blaine's face. "Hey, look at me."

Blaine eyed Robbie's turf-like do. "Nice hair."

"Yeah. Dad got me a moose for Christmas. Hey, can I play the piano?"

"Not while anyone's around to listen."

Robbie scooted onto the bench next to Blaine anyway. Evan, silent and stoic at the organ console, lifted an observant eye to the boy.

"Someday, I'm going to play the piano. Mom said I could."

"Are you taking lessons?" Blaine asked.

"Nah, I'm too young."

"No you're not."

"Your fingernails are black. Didja hit 'em with a hammer? My dad's thumbnail turned black when he built our tree house. His nail fell out and everything. Is your mom and dad here?"

Blaine's face turned pale. "No."

"Mine're downstairs. They're old, but they're cool."

"Robert," Jeremy called from the north stairwell doorway. "C'mon! Mary can't get to Bethlehem without Joseph."

Robbie jumped up and grinned, turning proudly to Blaine. "Davie was Joseph last year, but this year's my turn. Davie says costumes are for babies and morons, but he's stupid. Everyone knows it's cool to be God's dad."

The Christmas Eve service began with Evan's contemplative prelude arrangement of "O Jesus Christ, Thy Manger Is," which led directly into the opening hymn, "O Come, All Ye Faithful."

Emily processed down the aisle with the Sunday School teachers and children while everyone in the congregation sang out, "O come, let us adore Him, Christ the Lord!" She recognized the booming baritone of her father's voice somewhere off to her right—Her parents had made it, after all!—and relinquished a tiny, happy wave in their general direction.

The school-age children did an excellent job with their lines, narrating the story of Jesus' birth directly from Luke chapter 2. Caroline Bradley, especially, spoke a first-rate pronunciation of the governor's name, and Robbie Jones made a dashing bearded Joseph, leading Mary down the aisle on a four-wheeled donkey.

However, when the time came for the cows and sheep to stand and sing "In a Little Stable," Alison let out a wild shriek of gloom and doom from the front pew. She refused to walk to the front, wailing her barnyard humiliation into both of her hands. "Angel!" she shouted as her mother tried to coax her to the front, at which point Rebecca quickly whisked her grieving child away to the back row for proper consolation and discipline.

The only other noticeable mishap in the pageant was when the heavenly host stood to sing "Angels We Have Heard on High." Naomi Plueth, having arrived at church a good five minutes past call time, missed out entirely on her wings and halo. She did not seem to mind, however, as the new, sparkly gold shoes on her feet outshone the measly rounds of tinsel on everyone else's heads. In fact, Naomi was so proud of her shoes, she decided midway through the song to take them off and put them on her hands, waving them overhead with each rapturous "Glo-ria!" for everyone to see. Emily mouthed a firm "no" to her from the front pew, but Naomi did not take kindly to such instruction. She pouted her lips, stomped her stockinged feet, and proceeded to pull the hem of her dress up over her face to hide from Emily's disapproving eye.

Thankfully, Blaine never missed a beat in his playing. He flowed effortlessly through Naomi's striptease, masterfully segueing into "Go Tell It on the Mountain" before anyone could blink an eye, and per Emily's specific instructions, he went directly into "O Holy Night" when the final chord of "Away in a Manger" had faded.

This was the moment Emily had been anticipating for days. She subtly looked up from her seat in the front pew to watch Pastor Fletcher in his seat behind the pulpit. She needed to get to the balcony in time to direct the adult choir on stanza two of the song, but before she did, she wanted to see that look of gladness dawn on Pastor's face once again.

> *O Holy Night!*
> *The stars are brightly shining,*
> *It is the night of our dear Savior's birth.*

The voice floating out from the balcony was dark and mellow, like a good Merlot. Pastor Fletcher's head snapped to attention. He turned to his left to stare unabashedly at the balcony railing. There stood his mother, singing as she had done for so many Christmases past in Pastor's own childhood church. He opened his mouth, first in shock and then in wonder. Emily thought she could see the distinct glisten of tears shining in his eyes. Satisfied, she slipped down the side aisle to the north stairwell and shuffled up to the director's stand just in time to throw a happy, conspiratorial wink at Alice and to cue the choir in for the second stanza.

Mrs. Fletcher took over the melody again in the third stanza. Her phrasing was classic and simple, drawing attention to the text, not to her voice. Emily felt a private embarrassment at her own diva-like stylings with which she usually embellished the melody. Maybe it was better for an alto to sing this song after all. The choir came back in on the final chorus with Marge giving the top note everything she had. By the time Blaine had lifted the sustain pedal on the final note, Emily's own cheeks were wet with tears.

That silent, holy night, complete with sheepish wails and golden shoes, was almost Emily's favorite Christmas Eve to date. She felt a familial sense of warmth and joy for the choir members as they appreciatively bustled around Mrs. Fletcher after the service. In fact, the snapshots Emily's mind had taken throughout the evening would make a charming scrapbook in anyone's opinion if it wasn't for the dark, oily spot soiling the final page.

For, just as Evan lifted his hands and feet from holding out the closing, triumphant chord of his "Joy to the World" postlude, he turned around to find Robbie Jones, once again, peeking around the piano, talking excitedly to that foul, pierced, heathen of an accompanist. The sight was too much for the sour, old man to bear, so right then and there, in front of the choir, Mrs. Fletcher, and all the world, Evan walked right up to Blaine and said, "He's a bit young for you, don't you think?"

Chapter Twenty-Six: Old Faithful

||||||||||||||||||||||||||||||||||||||||||||||||||||||

It was one of those unfortunate days in January when the previous week's snowmelt had refrozen overnight, turning Bradbury County's roads into a luge course. Ordinary potholes and harmless, muddy tire ruts had hardened into knobby iceberg ranges the likes of which could sink the Titanic. Most people had the good sense to stay inside their homes that morning, tucked in under a warm blanket with a steaming mug of hot chocolate in hand, but Mrs. Scheinberg wasn't about to let a little ice on the roads keep her from delivering a hot-from-the-oven pan of cinnamon rolls to a person in need. Nope, if sixty years of country living had taught her anything, it was how to stay out of a ditch. She set the steaming rolls on the passenger seat of her F-150 and third-geared it all the way into town.

Earlier that morning, Emily had assured her over the phone that Blaine would be in McPherson Hall all day long. "He's preparing for his junior recital next month, so he's blocked out the entire week on the hall's calendar."

Mrs. Scheinberg pulled up in front of BC's Performing Arts Center and turned off her ignition. She could see from her vantage point in the truck that the sidewalks had been salted, but it didn't look like the salt had been there for very long. She could make out individual crystals sparkling in the bitter sunshine.

"The rolls aren't getting any warmer," Mrs. Scheinberg mumbled to herself, heaving her frame down from the heights of the Ford and landing as gingerly as a matron of sixty years possibly could on the frozen pavement. Four minutes and three close calls later, she was safely inside the building, pushing the up button on the elevator. Somewhere above her head on the second floor, she could hear a piano being pounded.

Blaine barely noticed Mrs. Scheinberg enter the hall. It wasn't that she was quiet or subtle; it was that he was lost in his own world of Bachian fugues, his neurons chasing after flighty themes that danced through a musical maze. When he paused after the first movement to mark his score, Mrs. Scheinberg dared to speak.

"Sounds difficult."

Blaine glanced up from the score, squinting across the auditorium to make out a face in the dark. "It is."

She toddled up the aisle in her Dr. Scholl's until she stood at the foot of the stage. "Hm. I think you'd better come down here. There's no way I'm making it up there."

Blaine eyed her incredulously. He had never spoken one word to this woman before, yet here she was walking into his rehearsal and telling him what to do. What was she even doing on the college campus anyway?

"C'mon. I made you cinnamon rolls. I don't believe in starving artists."

Blaine stood and rubbed his palms on his worn, black jeans, hopping easily down from the stage onto the auditorium floor. Mrs. Scheinberg proffered him a seat next to her in the third row and held out the plate of cinnamon-y goodness.

"Go ahead and grab one. They'll pull apart easily enough."

Blaine pulled on a roll—It was still warm!—and cupped his other hand under it to catch the falling granules of sugar. He took a bite, savoring the yeasty aroma, and leaned back in his chair. Once Mrs. Scheinberg was satisfied that he would swallow like a good boy, she faced forward herself and began to talk.

"Here's the way I see it. Your personal life is none of my business, but the minute you walk into my church, *you* are my business. I like you, Blaine. I like the way you play the piano. I like the way you respect Dr. Duke at the stand. I like the way you treat Robbie Jones like a human being. You seem like a sensible enough young man, maybe even smart."

Blaine took another bite of his roll, staring straight ahead while she continued.

"I have to say, I'm not sure why you wear eyeliner and style your hair to look like some kind of aquatic beast, but I'm an old lady. What do I know about such things? Maybe that's what you kids think is beautiful these days, though I have a hunch that's not why you do it."

Blaine remained silent.

"What I'm trying to say is, I think the way Evan spoke to you the other night was horrible. It was unacceptable. It said nothing about you and everything about him. I hope you realize that. Everyone else does."

Blaine leaned forward and took another roll off of the plate sitting on her lap.

"Why are you still in town during break, anyway?"

"Practicing."

"Doesn't your family have a piano at home?"

"Not like this one." "Where do you live?"

"My mom and little sister live in Lincoln with my grandma."

"Do you have a dad?"

Blaine chewed and swallowed before answering. "Yep."

"Is he in Lincoln?"

"Nope."

"Where is he?"

Blaine had finished his second roll but refrained from grabbing a third. He sat like a statue in his chair, boring a hole through a leg of the stage curtain with his eyes. His voice was cold when he finally spoke. "He's in Chicago with my piano teacher."

"What does that mean?"

"It means my father is an adulterer, as you Lutherans would say. A freaking, selfish adulterer."

Mrs. Scheinberg grabbed a roll for herself and took a bite. This was going to be harder than she thought. She held the plate out to Blaine. "Go ahead. I know you've got room. You're skinny as a wire fence."

Blaine took another roll.

"So your dad left your mom for your piano teacher?"

"That's the story."

"What'd your mom do?"

"She and my sister moved in with my grandma, and I transferred to BC. This is where my mom went to school before she met my father." Blaine swallowed the second half of his third roll. "I'm supposed to go to Chicago in a few months."

"To see your dad?"

Blaine snorted. "I never want to see him again. He chose his new life. He can live it out all by himself for all I care."

"Why go to Chicago?"

"To testify in court. For the divorce."

God love him. "How're you going to get there?"

"Drive, I guess."

That settled it. Mrs. Scheinberg took a package of wipes out of her bag and used one to clean the stickiness off her hands. She handed a clean one to Blaine. "I'm driving you."

"What?"

"I'm driving you. You're testifying at your parents' divorce trial, and there's no way you're going alone. No one is that tough, I don't care how many piercings you have."

Blaine sat motionless in his chair. "I have to be there at least a week."

"Then I guess we'll see the sights when you're not in court. I've always wanted to go to Ikea."

Blaine laughed at that.

"It's settled. I'll get two hotel rooms, one for each of us. Don't worry about the cost. I've got a lifetime's worth of savings to spend that week. You can pay me back by showing me around town. I'd like to go to one of those deep dish pizza places. And Greek town. And I've been wanting to take a picture of my reflection in that silver bean thing."

Mrs. Scheinberg left the five remaining cinnamon rolls on the plate for Blaine, making a mental resolution to fill that boy's stomach at her own table at least once a month from here on out.

When Blaine had helped her safely across the slippery sidewalk and back into the Ford, she threw her hands up in the air. "Oh, I almost forgot." She pulled a stack of envelopes out of her bag and handed them to Blaine. "Here. The choir wanted me to give you these. They each wrote one, even Irv. I think they want to make sure you come back after New Year's. Lent is our best season for music, you know."

"Mrs. Scheinberg," Blaine suddenly looked like a frightened, little boy behind his makeup. His voice broke in confession. "My piano teacher in Chicago is a man."

"I know, honey," Mrs. Scheinberg reached out and patted his hand. "I know."

|||||||||||||||||||||||||||||||||||||||||||||

Alice Gardner was also not one to let a little ice keep her down, especially when it meant a certain rascal of an organist would most likely be holed up in his own country home all morning long. If ever there was an occasion to have words with that man—and, God knows, it was time—this was the day to do it, when neither of them could run away from the other without falling on the ice and breaking a hip.

After convincing Rebecca that it would be a huge mistake to accompany her to Evan's, Alice agreed to her daughter's request that she drive the SUV with the four-wheel drive.

"And take this with you," Rebecca handed her cell phone to her mother through the open driver's side window. "If you happen to go into a ditch, all you have to do is tap on Jeremy's picture and the phone will automatically call him. He'll be there in an instant."

"Oh, how marvelous," Alice admired, turning the phone over in her gloved hands. "I feel like I'm on the Starship Enterprise."

"Call me before you head back home," Rebecca said, "and don't eat any of that man's salsa."

"Remember, dear," Alice smiled as she raised the window, "I've been driving longer than you've been alive."

As Alice meticulously steered the SUV two miles north of town and onto the Ebner property, she admired the slope of the lawn leading up to the enormous Cape Cod–style house sitting like a flagship at the very center of a frosty sea. An ice-covered, sandstone walkway wound whimsically from the driveway to the mammoth front porch, lending visitors a view of the formal knot garden, expertly designed, planted, and tended by Evan himself. The elaborate herb bed had been wintered-over for months, but a boxwood hedge outlining the rectangular plot remained green, unveiling the general skeleton of the garden's design through the frozen slush. It had been years since Alice had last stepped foot in Evan's home, at least as many years as her David had been in the grave. She cautiously scooted her way up the front walk and tapped the knocker against the red door three times.

The door opened. Evan's eyes narrowed at the sight of Alice. "Why are you here?"

"It's too cold to leave an old woman standing on your front step, Evan. You'd better let me in."

"I have nothing to say to you."

"That's okay, dear. I've got plenty to say for the both of us." Alice slipped past Evan into the foyer and began taking off her scarf. "Shall we sit in the living room or in the kitchen?"

"I've invited you to do neither."

"The kitchen then." Alice helped herself into the bright, tiled room situated at the end of the long hallway leading to the back of the house. White, winter daylight poured though a skylight onto an island countertop in the middle of the room. Alice took in the white cupboards and stainless steel countertops, noting that nothing had changed since her last visit so many years ago. She draped her scarf over the back of a black leather stool at the island and began to unbutton her coat. "I'll take a cup of chamomile if you've got some."

Evan stood in the kitchen doorway with his arms crossed over his chest. He was wearing a navy-blue housecoat and matching slippers. His hair, as always, was perfectly combed into place. "What makes you think I'm going to serve you a cup of tea in my own home?"

"You old goose," Alice replied cheerily. "You're not going to chase me away with that grumpy frown, so you might as well give it up."

Evan's expression remained disapproving, but he walked over to the floor-to-ceiling cupboard next to the refrigerator and pulled out two glass jars containing dried leaves. One was labeled "Chamomile" and the other "Spearmint."

Alice rubbed her hands together to warm them. "You've always made the best cup of tea."

"I see through your manipulations, Alice. Don't waste my time. Why are you here?"

"To talk."

"I told you, I have nothing to say to you."

"Then, maybe you could just listen."

"You have nothing to say that I want to hear."

Alice couldn't be ruffled. "Oh, Evan, you keep trying to rile me, but when are you going to realize you're the only one in this fight?"

Evan walked over to the stove and picked up a copper kettle, stopping at the sink to fill it with water from the faucet. He was careful to keep his back toward Alice. "Say what you need to say, and be done with it."

Alice sighed and sat down on the stool. He was making this so difficult. He always made things more difficult than they needed to be. She stared at his blue back, gathering her thoughts as he put the kettle on the burner and sorted leaves into a blue ceramic teapot. What she most wanted to tell him was that he'd been a rotten, selfish, boorish twerp all these years; that it was wrong and cruel of him to punish her for someone else's folly; that she had never been so hurt as when he ignored her after David's funeral; that he was not the only one Shirley had betrayed; that, because of his ridiculous, self-induced isolation, she grieved losing not just one friend, but two. She wanted to tell him all of these things and so much more, but instead, she told him the one thing he most needed to hear.

"Evan, I'm sorry. I'm just so, so sorry."

Silence.

"Won't you at least talk to me? Help me understand. Why do you keep pushing me away?"

"You betrayed me."

"No, Evan," Alice said, a deep sadness in her voice.

"You did. You lied to me. You led me to believe, to trust, to . . ."

"To love?" Alice offered. "I know, and I'm sorry you got hurt. I'm so sorry Shirley left, but, Evan," Alice put both hands on the counter and willed him with her eyes to turn around, "I wasn't the one who left. It was Shirley."

"If you hadn't introduced me to her, if you hadn't encouraged me, then—"

"Then maybe none of this would have ever happened? I know. I think about that every day. It's a bully of a thought, and it's tormented me for fifteen years."

Evan leaned on the sink with both hands, his head bent low. He was measuredly taking in deep, long breaths, but the sobs choked him in the end. Alice, tired and feeling older than ever, stood up and walked around the island to stand next to her hurting friend. She laid a tentative hand on his elbow. When he didn't pull away from her touch, she abandoned all caution and linked her arm protectively through his, squeezing hard.

"My friend, my dear, old friend. Fifteen years is a long time to be angry. Aren't you tired? Isn't it time to let it go? Look at us. We're a pair of old ding-dongs, you and me. My David is dead, and your Shirley is gone. We're both wrinkled and alone. Why aren't we spending our remaining days jawing about old memories and trying our hardest to make new ones? You're the best friend I've got now that David is dead."

Evan's shoulders shook even harder. They were bouncing up and down practically to his earlobes, and Alice almost lost her balance trying to hold on to him. She opened her mouth to suggest he try sitting down on a nearby stool, but a quick glance at his red face left her slack-jawed with shock. Somehow, in a matter of seconds—maybe moments, even—Evan's tears had turned into snickering hysterics.

"Evan Ebner! What on earth is so funny?"

Evan gasped for air and leaned against the sink for support. He held his belly with his free hand.

Alice disentangled herself. "I demand you tell me this instant!"

Evan took command of his faculties long enough to speak. "Of all the words—" gasp, "in the English dictionary—" cough, "you choose—" he snorted uncontrollably into his hand over the sink, "'*ding-dong*'?"

Alice, unmoved, narrowed her eyes at him. "It's a perfectly acceptable term."

Evan turned around for the first time and looked at Alice. "You know what it means, don't you?"

"Of course I do." Alice gave him a queenly look. "A ding-dong is, well, a fool."

"Not to a second grader."

"What are you talking about?"

"Ask your grandsons."

Alice, ignoring what she supposed to be a vulgar innuendo of the male persuasion, regally picked off an imaginary piece of lint from her sweater and sat herself down on a stool as though it was her throne of righteousness. From her lofty view, she looked down her nose at Evan and aimed her arrow straight at his big head. *"Tinnulus stultissimus es et sordidus canis!"*

Evan stopped short and stared at Alice. They held each other's gaze in a momentary stand-off of wills. Then, Evan's left nostril flared, Alice's upper lip twitched, and the two of them burst into a simultaneous fit of laughter.

Evan recovered first, wiping his eyes. "You haven't changed a bit, Alice Gardner."

Alice, immensely pleased with herself, gave a grand tilt to her chin. "You've gotten faster in your translating, Evan."

"I took to reading the Early Church Fathers after David died."

They both lost themselves for a moment in memories of David. Then, the kettle whistled a rude awakening.

"I'm adding a spearmint leaf to brighten your chamomile," Evan announced, turning to pour the steaming liquid into two blue mugs. Alice didn't bother arguing. Evan always knew best when it came to tea.

"Remember when David wrote your Christmas letter entirely in Latin?" Evan asked from the stove.

"He was such a showoff," Alice smiled, "but then you one-upped him with that ridiculous Independence Day motet you composed for his birthday."

"Ah yes, '*Semper stellae, semper laticlavia.*'" Evan chuckled. Alice marveled at the sound. It had been so long.

"Remember that year when you two insisted on speaking only in Latin on bridge nights?"

"That drove Shirley crazy," Evan admitted, sobering quickly. He stared at the cup of tea he had just poured for himself. Alice wrapped her hands around her own steaming mug.

"Why did she leave me?" Evan asked. It was clear to Alice that he had asked himself that very question a million times.

"I don't know, dear. I really don't. I think maybe she was sad."

"But I tried so hard to make her happy."

"Some people are sad in a way that can't be helped by anyone, least of all by spouses. I think Shirley always lived part of her life in her books. That's a dangerous thing to do."

"I should have seen that she was unhappy. I should have read the signs."

"I think the same thing. I do. I've always prided myself on being able to read people, but I never saw it coming with Shirley. Please, Evan, forgive me."

Evan shook his head. "You did nothing wrong, Alice. There's nothing to forgive. I'm the one who's been an ass all these years, trying to blame you for something that was my own fault."

"No, my friend. Not *your* fault. It was Shirley's fault."

Evan reflected on this for a moment before nodding his agreement. He looked up with eyes that had always been smarter and sharper than was healthy for any normal human being. "Forgive me for being a ding-dong?"

Alice couldn't help but giggle. "Forgiven."

"And for telling you that you couldn't sing?"

"Well, now, that may have been the truth."

Evan remained solemn. "I think I've been afraid to look at you. Seeing you makes me think of her."

"I understand. Sometimes I have trouble listening to you play the organ because it makes me think of David."

"I just have so much I want to say to her. But she's gone. She left before I could tell her . . . everything."

"Say it to me."

"What?"

"Say it to me. I'm not Shirley, but I'm here. And I want to listen to what you have to say. I've always wanted to listen."

Evan sat across the counter from Alice. For fifteen years, he had pushed this tender friend away, too devastated by his shattered marriage to try picking up any of the pieces, let alone putting them back together again. It had been a lonely existence, but looking into Alice's eyes, he realized he hadn't really been alone in his suffering after all. She understood. She had loved Shirley too. And David.

After a few false starts, Evan began speaking aloud the secret things—the regrets, the disappointments, the pain, even the hope—that had been festering inside of him for so long, and, as with most geysers under pressure, he spewed forth water and heat like a fountain until the force of his emotions eventually waned to a trickling sulfur spring. Only then, when his years of pent-up bitterness and resentment had been spent, did Evan's conscience turn to the new, young choir director.

"I suppose I'll need to speak with Emily."

"And Blaine."

Evan may have eaten his piece of humble pie, but he sure didn't savor the flavor. "That boy's not right."

"You're just jealous that his hair is thicker than yours."

"I'm serious, Alice. That guy pays too much attention to your grandson."

"I think it's the other way around. Blaine is incredibly tolerant of Robbie's attentions."

"I don't trust him."

"You don't trust his eye ring and his makeup. You haven't gotten to know the boy himself well enough to form a true opinion yet. You've gotten lazy in your solitude, dear." Alice was merciless in her honesty. "All this time, you've seen only what you've wanted to see, not what's really there. You're so much smarter than that."

|||||||||||||||||||||||||||||||||||||||||||||||||

By the time Alice backed out of Evan's driveway, the sun was setting and Rebecca was tearing her Cubs hat apart with worry. Not only had her mother neglected to answer any of her eight phone calls that day, she had been gone for seven hours straight. Rebecca was frantically stuffing her husband into the sedan for a momhunt when Alice pulled the SUV safely into their driveway.

"Mother! Where have you been? Why didn't you answer any of my calls? And why didn't you call me on your way home like you promised?"

"You called me, dear? How strange. I never heard the phone ring."

Truth be told, Alice hadn't thought to bring Rebecca's phone into Evan's house with her, and her heart had been too full of auld lang syne on the way home to remember any promises made earlier that morning.

"Well," Rebecca said, making an obvious effort to contain her exasperation. "I'm thankful that you're finally here. How did it go?"

Alice looked at her daughter with shining eyes, her heart in her throat. "He 'was dead and is alive again; he was lost, and is found.'"

Chapter Twenty-Seven: *Cessent Lites*

Emily finally had to face the truth. Her church choir was a mess.

Sure, they'd managed to turn out a few decent choral offerings for Sunday worship every now and then, but their confidence and morale were presently hanging lower than pants on a rapper. Between Evan's verbal abuse, Candice's meddling, Bev's motormouth, Dorothy's vertigo, Janet's kitchen romance, Zachary's exhibitions, and Don's flatulence, the choir had barely been able to make it through a rehearsal without encountering some kind of crisis.

And then there was the actual singing. If only Emily could get Marge to cease shaking her voice like a maraca; and somehow convince Irene to get hearing aids; and miraculously get Lois to sing on key; then maybe, just maybe, their tuning would improve. But what was the point? She still had only one bass, and with the soprano section practically doubling since September, their balance was shot. Listening to the choir sing in four-part harmony now was like eating a banana split without the banana.

What they all needed were a few Russian basses.

"And some vodka," Emily mumbled under her breath as she pushed open the church office door.

Mrs. Scheinberg looked up from her desk and held a finger to her lips. She motioned silently to Pastor Fletcher's door with her head. The door was cracked open six inches, and the whinnies of a disgruntled mare spilled out.

"That man hasn't polished the pews in months! I can tell because I haven't sneezed in church since April, and I *always* sneeze when I smell Murphy's Oil."

"Perhaps you haven't sneezed because you don't suffer from allergies this time of year." Pastor's voice was strained but firm.

"Don't be ridiculous, Pastor. And don't change the subject. That man is not doing his job, I'm telling you. He never vacuums the carpets."

"That man's name is Bill, and I hear him vacuuming every Tuesday morning, Yvonne."

"Then he's not vacuuming under all of the pews. I have proof. Here, look. I took a picture right here on this phone. See?"

Emily could hear Yvonne opening up her purse and passing something to Pastor.

"Yvonne, I told you. Irv and I instructed Bill to leave that pile of sand."

"I don't believe you. You're just trying to protect him."

"No, I'm not," Pastor sighed. "We asked Bill to leave it because we hoped to learn who had planted it. This has to stop, Yvonne. The rocks, the sand, the toenail clippings, everything."

Mrs. Scheinberg wrinkled her nose at Emily, and Emily blushed. She knew she shouldn't be listening, but she couldn't help herself. What was this about toenail clippings? In the church?

"Someone has to make sure the hired help is doing their job," Yvonne defended herself.

"Yes, and that someone is the congregation's trustee, not you." Emily heard sounds as if Pastor were getting up from his chair. Mrs. Scheinberg quickly picked up a pencil from her desk and feigned some kind of work. Emily, panicked, looked from left to right like a child who couldn't decide where to hide during a game. "Look, Yvonne," Pastor's voice sounded like it was getting closer to the door. "I know this must be hard. Gerald was an excellent custodian. Irreplaceable. He blessed this congregation with ten years of faithful service. But he's gone, and we still need someone to clean the church. Bill is a nice man, an honest man. He has three children, did you know? Just like you and Gerald. . . ."

Emily shook her head to stop her ears from listening. The conversation had turned too personal, too private, and too much about a kind of grief she understood all too well. Shame on her for eavesdropping! "Anything come in the mail for me, Arlene?"

Mrs. Scheinberg looked up and blinked her eyes. Apparently, she had *not* stopped listening to the conversation behind the study door, and the question caught her off guard. That, or she was deeply engrossed in her pretend work. "Oh, yes. A catalog from Concordia Publishing House and an envelope postmarked from Kansas City. I put both of them in your box."

Emily walked over to her mailbox on the wall and pulled out the catalog, a white business envelope, and a brown paper bag. She smiled knowingly, opening it up to peek inside. There was her *Anne of Green Gables* book along with a bottle of vanilla. Emily chuckled. The accompanying note read:

May all of your cakes be free of liniment.

Thank you for 'O Holy Night.' It was the best Christmas present ever.

Grateful, Pr. Fletcher

"Just so you know," Mrs. Scheinberg interrupted, leaning back in her chair to better see the bag's contents, "our white-haired rooster is currently upstairs in the balcony. He came in around five this evening to practice, but I haven't heard a peep from the organ for the last twenty minutes."

Emily's stomach dropped to her knees.

"You know, I'm thinking about getting a 'Beware of the Dog' sign to hang in the stairwell whenever Evan's around," Mrs. Scheinberg said in a show of solidarity.

Emily stuffed her mail in the brown paper bag and made her way to the north stairwell. What was Evan doing here on a Thursday night? Ever since he'd left the choir four months ago, his religious habit had been to completely avoid the church building every fifth day of the week.

Yet, there was Evan, seated straight-backed at the organ console when Emily crested the stairs.

"Ah, Dr. Duke. I was just looking through some music for Easter."

Emily stood in the doorway, eyes wide and heart pounding as if she were a frightened schoolgirl. Had Evan just *willingly* spoken to her? She didn't know what to do, so she stood stock-still and hugged her bag protectively to her chest.

"I was thinking, perhaps we could do a duet."

"On the organ?"

"No, me on the organ, you singing. I really like this *Laudate Dominum* piece. What do you think?" Evan gestured for her to come look over his shoulder.

Emily felt like she could have been shot with a stun gun for all the mobility she had in her feet. What alternate reality had she stepped into? Had she fallen down a rabbit hole? Was Evan about to pull a pocket watch out of his blazer?

Evan looked up, pausing at the sight of Emily's obvious hesitation. "Ah, yes. I can see we need to exchange words about life before music." He swung his legs to the side, dangling his feet off the north side of the bench. He proffered a nearby folding chair to her before neatly resting his hands on his knees. He looked to her a bit like a meditating monk. "Please, come sit."

Emily was certain that the Queen of Hearts must be lurking somewhere in the shadows of the balcony, waiting to cut off her head, but she dignified her fears with silence and walked to one of the empty chairs in the tenor section of the choir.

"Now," Evan started as she sat, "I owe you an apology. I was rude and insubordinate to you when first we met, and I was in the wrong. Please, forgive me."

Emily chewed on her lower lip. Evan's apology was short, maybe even sweet, but this was all happening so fast. She had trouble getting her voice to work, so she simply nodded her head.

"Thank you," Evan said. "I know I don't owe you an explanation, but I would like to give one anyway. That is, if it would not offend you?"

Emily shook her head.

"Yes, well. I do not have a good history with choir directors here at Zion, and I fear I was weak in letting the past unjustly influence the present. Our last choir director—excluding myself, of course—was also a professor at Bradbury College, and he took the liberty of running off with my wife about fifteen years ago.

I believe they now reside somewhere in the middle of Arizona or in one of those desert territories. It's a sordid story, really, the likes of which have been the plot of many a soap opera, I'm sure. But I think you'll understand when I tell you that I've struggled with bitterness and anger about the whole affair. You can also probably imagine how your own association with BC hit a bit of a nerve with me."

Evan sat quietly while Emily digested the news. He was matter-of-fact in his storytelling, detached and unmoved, as if he were merely describing the ingredients of a dish he had made for supper. When Emily said nothing, Evan continued.

"It took me five years to give Shirley the divorce she demanded, and even though I eventually signed the paperwork, it feels to me as if I'm still married but my wife is living with another man." Evan folded his hands in his lap. "I do not tell you these things because they are your business. I tell you them because I would like to give you something of myself. An exchange, if you will, for all that I have taken away from you these months."

Emily wondered at the mathematical way Evan viewed relationships. On the surface, it appeared cold and calculating, but Emily understood his use of addition and subtraction to balance human equations. She, herself, often thought of relationships like commodities on the stock exchange. No matter how much you may want to protect your assets, you eventually have to invest in people to see a good return. Even then, there's always some risk. Sometimes you win, and sometimes—with people like Candice—you lose it all.

Emily decided to take a little risk. "My husband died nine years ago."

"Yes, I heard as much through Zion's particularly exotic species of grapevine." Evan was too smart to miss Emily's investment, however, and he graciously matched her purchase share for share. "Shirley, my wife, was a good friend of Alice Gardner."

This admission helped Emily understand a good many things. She almost smiled conspiratorially at her white rabbit. "I don't want to get married again, but everyone else thinks I should."

"Shirley and that scoundrel Dale are living off the nest egg I invested from my years of working as a hospital consultant."

Emily chewed on this bit of news for a moment. She had secretly wondered what Evan had done professionally preceding retirement. He always appeared too well dressed to have been a career musician.

"Candice Bradbury tried to set me up with her husband's law partner."

"Candice Bradbury is my sister-in-law."

Emily's eyes grew wide with horror and then with delight.

"Or, *was* my sister-in-law, I suppose," Evan amended.

They both laughed at the ridiculousness of it all. Evan stood up and walked over to where Emily still sat in the tenor section, extending his hand. "Truce?"

Emily stood and looked her former nemesis confidently in the eye. She needn't be afraid of him any longer. "Truce," she said, giving his extended hand a resolute shake.

"Good, then let's get started. I think this aria will really suit your voice." Evan scooted back onto the organ bench and turned on the bellows.

"But it's in Latin," Emily pointed out.

"So it is," he said without turning.

One by one (or two by two in the case of the Davises and the Koelster sisters), the choir entered the balcony in a stupefied silence. They didn't know what to make of the sight and sound before them, for Evan—mean, malicious Evan—was accompanying their sweet Dr. Duke on the organ while she sang over his shoulder.

Blaine was particularly confused. Unsure of what to do, he hung back in the stairwell doorway until Rebecca and Alice's arrival required his stepping aside to let them pass. Mrs. Scheinberg arrived next, effectively grabbing Blaine's elbow and escorting him directly to the piano bench, but he refused to sit down.

Evan released the final chord as Emily cadenced.

"Yes, I think that will do nicely," he said, turning off the bellows and scooting to the edge of the bench to untie his organ shoes. Blaine moved as if to leave.

"Where are you going?" Evan asked, looking down at him from his perch on the console.

Blaine shrugged. "Aren't you going to play?"

Evan stood, placing his shoes neatly on the organ bench and slipping his stockinged feet into the polished leather loafers waiting beside the console. "No. We've already got a choir accompanist. A fine one too."

Alice smiled quietly into her lap. The rest of the choir stared at Evan with their mouths hanging open. Blaine said nothing, but he did sit down at the piano.

Evan, street shoes restored to their proper feet, walked over and sat down next to Irv. "May I have a folder, please?"

Emily's round eyes grew even rounder. "A choir folder?"

"Yes."

"A-are you singing with us?"

"Well, fasting is indeed fine outward training, but I don't advise any choir give up basses for Lent."

Irv's slow, deep chuckle reverberated throughout the balcony, echoing across the empty sanctuary and infecting the entire choir with an electric charge. Bev began to squeal with delight, and the entire alto section erupted into appreciative applause. Irene simply looked around in confusion, trying to figure out what all of the commotion was about.

Mrs. Scheinberg, however, was neither laughing nor clapping. She was crying. Big, sloshy tears rolled down her cheeks and splashed onto her blue polyester pants. She didn't bother hunting down a tissue to wipe her sniffles away but, instead, stood up and marched right over to the old rooster who had humbled his strut to make things right with her two favorite chicks in the pen. "Well done, Evan," she sniffled, planting a big, wet kiss on his left cheek.

Emily was still grinning as she sipped her nightly cup of hot cocoa later that evening. Not only had her soprano section doubled this year, but so had her bass section. She set down her cocoa to run a letter opener through the envelope with the Kansas City postmark. She pulled out a handwritten note, smiling as she unfolded it. She already had a pretty good idea who it was from.

⁖⁖⁖⁖⁖⁖⁖⁖⁖⁖⁖⁖⁖⁖⁖⁖⁖⁖⁖⁖⁖⁖⁖⁖⁖⁖⁖⁖⁖⁖⁖⁖⁖⁖

Emily dear:

James tells me you're doing great in Illinois. I still wish we could have convinced you to teach at Longfellow, but I understand the call of the wild. I hope you've at least found a decent cup of coffee somewhere amidst all of that corn.

Remember when I was in Berlin for my sabbatical two years ago? Well, I rubbed elbows with an arts society while I was there, and they got me involved raising funds to open an elite music school in Potsdam. I just heard from them over Christmas, and it seems they've hit it big with a couple of private donors. They've asked me to chair their instrumental studies starting next fall, and they asked me to recommend someone from the states to lead their choral program. You came to mind, of course.

I'm due for an adventure, so I'm taking the position. What do you think? Want to run away with me to Germany this summer and live the good life? Full disclosure: the society has funding drummed up for only two years of programming, so I can't promise you much outside of that. But, still. Germany for two years? Yes, please.

I've included a brochure for Potsdam Musikschule (original, huh?) with this letter. It's legit. Let me know what you think.

Deine,

Ralphe

Chapter Twenty-Eight:

A Line of Distinction

||||||||||||||||||||||||||||||||||||||||||||||||

Emily stood at the back of the media service line in the basement of the Johnson-Kilmer Library, her nose buried in a recent issue of *Opera News*.

"I wish I'd thought of that," a familiar, deep voice rumbled from behind her right ear.

Emily smiled at the sound and turned around to find Zachary standing amiably behind her right shoulder with his hands in his coat pockets. His cheeks were still ruddy from the frigid February wind outside.

"We've got to stop meeting like this," Zachary teased, his eyes twinkling. He nodded over the top of Emily's head toward the long line leading up to the checkout counter. "And I've got to remember to bring some reading material with me to the library. This line gets longer every time I come here. What's the deal?"

"It's the new DVDs." Emily said.

"What, through interlibrary loan?"

"No, the college owns them." Emily lowered her voice a notch. "Basset said that the Bradburys donated one hundred movies to BC over Christmas."

"What for?"

Emily shrugged. "She said that the family usually donates the library's annual budget for reference books and magazine subscriptions around that time, but this year they donated DVDs instead. Apparently the younger brother is a big movie buff."

"Great. So now the media counter is the new Blockbuster." Zachary shook his head. "I know," Emily commiserated. "Heaven forbid the students actually come to the library to check out books." She stepped forward as the line shortened, and Zachary followed suit.

"What're you here for?" he asked.

"Harmonic dictation recordings. I'm subbing for Mitchell's theory class next week. I figure I should at least listen to his examples on reserve before administering his exam. You?"

"Oh, I've reserved *The Aviator* and *Titanic*. I'm a huge Leo fan."

Emily couldn't tell if Zachary was teasing or not. He was often too smooth for her to read.

"No, I'm kidding!" Zachary bared his white teeth in a jovial laugh. "But, seriously, my real reason for being here is just as embarrassing."

"Why?"

"Oh, no." Zachary shook his head. "Wild horses and repeated performances of Stockhausen's *Klavierstücke* couldn't pull it out of me."

The line shortened again, and Emily and Zachary, standing side-by-side at this point, stepped forward together.

"Oh, c'mon," Emily chided him good-naturedly. "What is it?"

"No, I really don't think I can say it out loud."

"Yes, you can." Emily's inner child threatened to giggle. Zachary could be so fun.

He looked away sheepishly, his red cheeks suddenly deepening in shade without the help of any February wind. He dug his hands deeper into his pockets and shuffled his feet. His whispered response was charmingly apologetic. "I'm a closet fan of William Shatner's studio recordings."

"His what?"

"His studio recordings. You know, like *The Transformed Man*?"

"No, I don't know."

"Really?" Zachary immediately perked up. Emily didn't know if it was from relief at her ignorance of the subject or if the man smelled a mission opportunity in the air. "Well, let me tell you, Emily Duke. There is nothing so wonderful and awful and marvelous and hideous and mortifying as Captain James Tiberius Kirk reciting Shakespearean prose and Beatles' lyrics over recorded music."

Emily managed her emotions well. "Are you serious?"

"Oh," Zachary grinned, "I have never been more serious in my life."

"Do you like his recordings because they're good or because they're bad?"

"Both."

Emily laughed. "I see."

They stepped forward in line again.

"Do you think you can still be my friend?" Zachary asked, his tone jesting but his eyes sincere.

"No."

Zachary's face blanched.

"I'm kidding, I'm kidding!" Emily reassured, her own eyes glinting with fun. "Of course we can still be friends. Besides, I have something scandalous to confess to you."

"What?"

Emily peeked over the top of her magazine at Zachary, readying herself for the inevitable barrage of scorn. "I read *Pride and Prejudice and Zombies* over winter break."

"No!" Zachary cried out. "You didn't!"

"I did," Emily hid her face completely behind her magazine. "My sister gave me a copy for Christmas. It's sitting on my shelf at home next to *Persuasion*."

"Heretic! You ought to be burned at the stake."

Emily was giggling hysterically now. Oh, it felt so good to laugh!

"In all seriousness, though," Zachary continued, wiping at the damp corners of his eyes, "it's good to see you. I've missed you. Did you get my call last week?"

The cheerful warmth in Emily's heart suddenly cooled a bit. She didn't like the hard right turn this conversation had just made. Her stomach tightened in a familiar, uneasy way. She looked down at her magazine and nodded. "I did. I'm so sorry I haven't called you back. I've barely had a chance to breathe let alone think what with the upcoming recital and Lent just around the corner."

"I understand." Zachary smiled easily. He politely ushered Emily ahead of him as the line moved forward. Emily sensed him choosing his words carefully. "I'm sorry about all of that nasty business last fall. Thank you for telling me what really happened in regards to your husband. I'm so sorry."

Emily never knew what to say when people told her they were sorry Peter was dead, so she simply said the truth. "Me too."

"Are your sentiments the same?"

"What do you mean?"

Zachary turned and faced Emily straight on. His gaze was direct but not disrespectful. In fact, there was a protective kindness in his eyes that made Emily, even in her distress, feel like she was safe. "Look, I realize that this is neither the time nor the place for a serious discussion, but I hardly see you anymore. I just need you to tell me what to do. You once politely asked me to let things be. Is that still what you want?"

What Emily wanted was to never talk about this dating nonsense ever again, but words failed to pass through her centurion lips.

"What I mean is, I'd like to take you out to dinner or a movie or something—anything, really—but I don't want to keep pushing you if you don't want me to."

Emily felt physically choked by the presence of so many students in the library basement. Some were standing in line both in front of and behind her and Zachary, while others were tucked into various cubbies viewing documentaries and assigned programs for classes. Why, just three feet in front of her stood Martin from her vocal ped class! She shuddered, fearful of the ears that might be listening in on their very private conversation. The last thing she wanted was for last semester's gossip to be resurrected.

"It's okay," Zachary continued. "You can tell it to me straight. Either way, you're not going to lose me as a friend."

Emily forced herself to meet Zachary's gaze. He was such a nice man. Smart and handsome too. The real deal, as her mother used to say about Peter many years ago. In fact, the two men were quite a bit alike, and if circumstances had been any different, she might actually be tempted to give this charming man a different answer. But as it was, charm was the last thing on her mind these days. Her heart and hands were already too full with her ever-changing church choir, her spring load at the college, the upcoming recital with Basset, and the distant siren song of Germany.

"I'm not ready," was the only answer she could muster, nervously glancing around at the students.

"I understand." Zachary nodded, his eyes looking only slightly wounded. "Thank you for your honesty, Emily. I appreciate it. I appreciate *you*, actually. I do hope we can remain friends. There aren't too many people our age in Bradbury who share our interests, you know. Well, there's Pastor Fletcher. He's a great guy, by the way. Smart as a whip and good taste in music too. Did I tell you I started new member instruction with him at Zion? Yes, well, I figured if Bach devoted his life to learning the Lutheran doctrine, then there must be something to it. The Presbys can't possibly have a monopoly on God, right? Right. That's that." Zachary, for the first time since Emily had met him, actually appeared flustered. He ran his hand through his sandy hair, then patted his coat pockets. "Hm, you know what? I think I forgot my faculty ID back in my office. This line's too long anyway. I won't make my one o'clock class if I wait here any longer. I think I'll just bow out and pick up Shatner another time. Well, it was good seeing you, Emily. I've got your recital on my calendar, so expect to see me there. I'm giving my lit students extra credit points if they go. Right, well, I'm off. Do take care."

With that, Zachary was gone.

Emily stared off toward the south stairwell door through which Zachary had just escaped. The man had practically run away from her, but she really couldn't blame him. Recovery was neither easy nor elegant following such conversations, though Emily had high hopes for future encounters. Zachary was right. They shared too many interests not to be good friends in the end.

"You all right, Dr. Duke?"

The line before the media counter had finally diminished, and it was Emily's turn. She turned around and stepped forward.

"Yes, Jamie, thank you. I'm fine." She felt an unpleasant twinge of regret at Zachary's present embarrassment, but the surge of relief she felt at finally being done with all of that abhorrent relationship talk was a soothing salve to her injured conscience. Those galling knots of tension in her gut began to unravel, and she expelled the stale breath from her lungs as an easy smile played upon her lips. "You know, Jamie, I'm more than fine. I'm great."

Chapter Twenty-Nine:

Peck a Little, Talk a Little

||||||||||||||||||||||||||||||||||||||||||||||||

Herman Schmidt, Nettie's brother-in-law, fell asleep in Jesus the first Sunday in February while he was, literally, sleeping. The women of the quilting circle graciously agreed to forego their usual Tuesday morning sewing time to help the Ladies Aid Society prepare Herman's funeral luncheon. All of them were in the Ladies Aid Society anyway.

"I suppose he couldn't control it," Nettie said as she stood at the kitchen counter spooning coleslaw from a large bucket into individual cups, "but I wish Herman'd had the good sense to wait until after Ash Wednesday to die. The Flip and Fry is just a month away."

Geraldine stood like a general in front of a row of pies, consulting the yellow legal pad in her hands. "Yes, we were supposed to decide on table decorations and door prizes today, and Candice was supposed to designate shifts at the griddle. We'll just have to wait until next week to get any work done."

"And why, pray you, can't we make those decisions right now?" Mrs. Scheinberg asked, her hands submerged in dishwater at the sink.

Geraldine gave a significant look over her legal pad toward the Koelster sisters, who were busy opening the oven door and poking meat thermometers into hams. They were not members of the quilting circle.

"Oh, for heaven's sake, Geraldine," Mrs. Scheinberg rolled her eyes.

"We're ready for the pies." Candice scooted a roller cart in from the fellowship hall where she, Alice, and Irene had been arranging slices of homemade desserts on a table. Geraldine set down her pad and began serving pie slices onto individual plates, which Candice then loaded onto the cart.

"I hope we sing 'The Old Rugged Cross' today," Bev pined, stirring a giant pot of green beans on the stove.

"We hardly ever sing the old hymns in church anymore," Geraldine quipped. "I can't remember the last time we sang 'Precious Lord' or 'In the Garden' or 'Rugged Cross.'"

"Those hymns actually aren't that old, dear," Alice stood in the kitchen doorway, patiently waiting for the pie slices.

"Well," Geraldine said, "it seems that all Pastor Fletcher picks anymore are those horrible, new hymns with those appalling melodies. They're simply unsingable. What was that one we sang on Sunday?"

"'We All Believe in One True God.'"

"Yes. Ridiculous. Half the congregation wasn't even singing. He's going to chase people away with those new hymns."

"New to you, dear," Alice corrected. "That hymn is actually older than 'The Old Rugged Cross.'"

"Well, I never cared for 'The Old Rugged Cross,'" Mrs. Scheinberg admitted above the sound of running tap water.

"Arlene!" Bev was shocked. "But it's so pretty!"

"I suppose, but it goes on and on about the stupid cross."

Bev physically flinched at such blasphemy.

"I'm serious. It's creepy. It's all about how we should 'cherish' and 'love' the cross. The cross is nothing to love and cherish. It's an instrument of torture, and it wasn't the cross that saved us anyway. It was Jesus. I want my hymns to go on and on about Jesus, not about a piece of wood."

Nettie remained silent on the matter. She already had her own private struggles involving questionable lyrics.

"I like 'The Gifts Christ Freely Gives'" Alice said. "Now, that one *is* newer," she conceded to Geraldine, "but its wisdom is age-old. I told my grandchildren I would pay each of them a dollar for every stanza they memorize."

"Pies are ready," Candice sang. Personally, she wasn't about to say anything aloud regarding hymns or singing or any other subject that touched upon the music of the church. After the whole "Duke Debacle," as her husband called it at home, she had taken a vow of silence on anything and everything that could possibly link back to their sensitive choir director. Well, almost everything.

"Did you know," Candice tapped her purple fingernails on the cart handle, "that Zachary Brandt is taking adult instruction?"

"Is he joining the church?" Geraldine asked. Her face flushed at the mention of the handsome, sandy-haired professor's name.

"I'm not sure, but I saw him in Pastor Fletcher's office two Sundays ago when I dropped off all of that sale material."

"Think he still wants to get with Dr. Duke?" Janet chimed in, rinsing her hands in Mrs. Scheinberg's dishwater. Geraldine scowled. Mrs. Scheinberg did too, but for an entirely different reason.

"Maybe. I think he would make a nice match for Dr. Duke, don't you?" Candice asked.

"Candice Bradbury," Mrs. Scheinberg barked, turning around and waving a dripping finger toward the pie cart, "you leave that girl alone!"

Candice batted her fake eyelashes innocently around the kitchen. "Arlene, what on earth are you talking about?"

"I see what's going on under that wig of yours. Dr. Duke has had enough tragedy in her life without your meddling in her personal affairs."

"I would never—" Candice looked appalled, making a show of not being able to even bring herself to repeat such a heinous idea. "Dr. Duke is my daughter's voice teacher. She comes to my house every Friday afternoon. Why, we're practically family at this point. You must see how close we are, and believe me, I love her like a daughter. It's not," she coughed significantly, "*meddling* to help a daughter find a good husband."

Mrs. Scheinberg was about ready to stroke. She didn't fancy herself a bully, but she was not above a little physical altercation if the situation required it. She moved closer to Candice, dripping soapy water all over the kitchen floor. "I don't care how often you see her or how well you *think* you know her. She's an adult, not your Barbie doll to play with and manipulate."

"What Arlene is saying, dear," Alice intervened, stepping alongside Candice and putting a soothing arm around her wide shoulders, "is that no one knows Dr. Duke better than herself. It's best if we let these people work out their own relationships without our—"

"—interfering," Mrs. Scheinberg finished.

"Help," Alice corrected, settling her calming gaze on Mrs. Scheinberg.

Candice smiled brightly. "Of course! I wouldn't *dream* of— How did you put it, Arlene? Interfering? I simply care too much about Dr. Duke to let her get set up with just anybody. She's really quite a catch. At least, I've always thought so. You know, I'm not even sure that Brandt fellow is worthy of her. If you ask me, she needs someone a little more, oh," Candice dug deep for an adjective, one that sounded as if she had put some previous thought into the matter, "devout."

"How're things going in here?" Pastor Fletcher stepped into the kitchen, fully vested for the funeral. "It smells delicious."

Alice smiled, letting go of Candice. "Just trying to keep the pots from boiling over."

"Good, good. Well, the service should begin in about ten minutes. Do you ladies feel like you're at a stopping point?"

"Yes, we'll be right along after we plastic-wrap the salads."

The women finished their business in silence, steering clear of Candice and making wide circles around Mrs. Scheinberg. When they finally made their way into the nave, they all sat, as was their tradition, in the back pulpit-side pew, where they could steal out before the final hymn to man the serving line.

Candice had trouble concentrating throughout the service. Her mind was occupied with the burning question of Emily's future husband, and as hard as she tried to focus on Pastor Fletcher's sermon, she couldn't stop tending a little seed of an idea that had germinated in her imagination the very moment Pastor Fletcher had entered the kitchen. It had been years since she'd considered the fact, but Pastor was, after all, single; and he was definitely—What was that word?—oh, yes, devout; and he might even be handsome if he'd just get his hair trimmed every once in a while; at the least, he was taller than Russell. Yes, of course! Why hadn't she thought of Pastor Fletcher before?

Candice grabbed a short pencil from the pew rack in front of her and began scribbling lines across her bulletin. Geraldine, who was already feeling plenty irritated with Candice for thinking Zachary Brandt a more suitable match for that self-absorbed Emily Duke than for herself, gave the Grand Matron of Bradbury a disapproving look during the sermon, but Candice was oblivious to Geraldine and everyone else in the church. She didn't even notice when the other ladies got up before the final hymn to prepare for the luncheon, for she was too busy composing what she was certain would be the love letter of the century.

CHAPTER THIRTY: HEART OF DARKNESS

||||||||||||||||||||||||||||||||||||||||||||||||||||

Miss Geraldine Alexandria Turner was not an attractive woman. Her face and hair and figure were pretty enough, but an early frost of false promises in life followed by several hard freezes of failed expectations had killed off the sweetness of her delicate flower. What remained of her fine, feminine features was difficult for anyone else to see for the cloud of acerbic criticisms and erroneous presumptions that perpetually cumulated around her.

Perhaps it would be different if everything in life had not been such a disappointment for Geraldine, but having a delusional, superlative-spewing mother had sealed the deal early on in her childhood years growing up in the suburbs of Indianapolis.

"You're the best dancer in the class," Mrs. Turner would crow at the end of every one of Geraldine's ballet recitals. But Madame Tourigny, after six years of laborious instruction, sang a different tune to the underperforming wunderkind.

"You'll never be a good dancer with that turn-out."

No matter; Mrs. Turner was certain her daughter would be a celebrated artist someday. "You must enter this in the art fair," she crooned about every drawing Geraldine sketched in her art lessons. "Your balance and composition are simply the best, darling." Yet, despite Geraldine's artistic eminence, she never won best in show.

The most humiliating season of Geraldine's life had been when Mrs. Turner insisted on enrolling her daughter in local beauty pageants. "You're the prettiest girl in town," Mrs. Turner had pronounced, "and everybody knows it. There's no sense in wasting all of that beauty behind a book." However, as Geraldine never made it past the talent portion of the competitions, even the overly optimistic stage mother had to relinquish her maternal dream for the crown.

Never mind; Mrs. Turner became convinced that music was actually Geraldine's hidden talent. Hadn't her grandmother been a respected soprano in the Harris County Chorus for twenty years? "We'll start you in clarinet lessons next week."

The only time Geraldine ever saw her mother's confidence in her superiority falter was when, after a particularly memorable clarinet audition, Indiana University politely but firmly declined Geraldine entrance into the School of Music.

"I simply can't understand what's wrong with these people," Mrs. Turner had fluttered. "Who is the Dean of Music these days? I'm going to ring him up and let him know he's hired a bunch of clowns to run his school."

"I want to be a teacher" was all Geraldine had said at the time.

"Good heavens, girl. What good did any of your teachers ever do in this world? No, you're too bright for that," Mrs. Turner had pursed her lips. "You'll be a writer. Yes, your language skills have always been excellent, and goodness knows, you've spent your whole life inside of a book."

Geraldine's mother had been right about one thing. Her daughter's language skills were excellent, maybe even the best, and Geraldine excelled in her grammar and composition cours-es. Creative writing, however, much to her mother's chagrin, never proved to be Geraldine's rising star, and not a single news-paper or magazine accepted her stories for publication; so, when a small school district in south central Illinois announced an opening for a secondary English teacher mid-term, Geraldine, who had finished her coursework one semester earlier than her classmates, applied for the job. In a rare display of indepen-dence, she told her mother about it only after she had accepted the position and purchased a one-way train ticket to the Land of Lincoln.

Yet, a little bit of yeast leavens the whole loaf, and Geraldine's self-regard had risen much higher than was healthy for any sin-gle, working woman living in a new community. While she was an excellent teacher, Geraldine tolerated no disrespect, real or imagined, in the classroom. Her vanity simply couldn't take it, so she distanced herself from her students' personal interests and hobbies as well as any subject that might put her at a disad-vantage as an authoritarian. With her colleagues, she refused to concede any points of contention in pedagogical discussions at faculty meetings, and she quickly gained a reputation for being stubborn and conceited. During parent-teacher conferences, she was quick to point out the shortcomings in each of her students while never admitting to any flaws in her own character or abil-ities.

The biggest blow for Geraldine was not having her mother there to pet her ego. To compensate, she began filling the void with self-proclamations of her own gifts and talents, quickly dowsing any sparks of social interest others might have taken in her. The result was a sad social life limited to whatever meager opportunities were offered by the community or the church she attended at the moment.

Geraldine switched churches regularly. Upon moving to Bradbury, she first joined Wesleyan Methodist on Main Street. They were advertising a Thursday night social club for singles called SAM (Single and Methodist), but none of the men who wandered in and out of the program ever took an interest in Geraldine—not from any lack of worthiness on her own part, of course.

Then there was the time, in the mid-eighties, when that tall, red-haired Mr. Springer got hired on as the basketball coach and physical education instructor at Bradbury High. Geraldine followed him to Bradbury Presbyterian. He was nice enough to her—even waved across the church parking lot a time or two— but he soon moved north to greener pastures and larger stadiums in Joliet.

When Dale Westfield and his Tom Selleck mustache started directing the Zion Lutheran Church choir, Geraldine immediately signed up for adult instruction; but Dale turned out to prefer older, wealthier women and ran off with that cougar of a librarian, Shirley Ebner. Geraldine had stayed at Zion, holding out a candle of hope for the jilted church organist, but in fifteen years of singing in the choir, Evan had spoken directly to Geraldine only twice—once to tell her she was sharp and another time to tell her to stop singing altogether.

The new dark-haired pastor seemed promising at first, but all it took was one year of Sunday School classes for Geraldine to determine that he was far too Lutheran to be marriageable.

It was then that Geraldine's mother died, leaving her a rather large inheritance. Really, it was the nicest thing Mrs. Turner had ever done for her daughter, for Geraldine, who detested children at heart, was able to take an early retirement at the ripe old age of fifty and begin reorganizing her closets and repapering her bathroom like she had always wanted. Geraldine was even able to indulge in a weekly water aerobics class at the community civic center in Hamburg, although she was careful to always enter the ladies locker room via the south entrance to avoid walking past the adult ballet class, which met down the hall.

Geraldine had actually been considering retiring her membership at Zion when Dr. Zachary Brandt sat down in her pew. Finally, a man worthy of her expectations—well-read, witty, handsome, good hygiene, and perfect teeth! He was a bit young for her, some might argue, but hadn't Shirley been able to snag a younger man? And Shirley wasn't nearly as attractive or as accomplished as herself.

Zachary, however, seemed perfectly content to look at that silly flit of a choir director, Emily Duke. In fact, the entire church seemed to always be looking at her, and it was nauseating the way everyone coddled her and fawned over her just because she'd lost a husband. What about all of the women who had never even had *one* husband?

Geraldine was particularly hurt the Sunday she looked up at the balcony and saw Candice sitting there. Apparently, her best friend had decided to rejoin the choir without even bothering to tell her. Then there was that elitist tea party Emily had hosted in her own home. Of course, Geraldine, on principle, would have most certainly turned down an invitation had she received one, but it still turned her stomach to think of Candice and everyone else sitting around a festive table without her. They were always doing things without her.

Honestly, all of the people at church had become simply unbearable since Christmas. It was ridiculous the way Arlene's grammar and syntax needed babysitting every week, and Nettie's conversation burned about as bright as a 40-watt bulb. Bev never said anything worth hearing, and Alice and Evan had suddenly become thick as thieves. Why, just the other day, she had seen them having coffee together at The Corner Coffee Shop—at their age!

Yes, if she weren't needed so badly at Zion to edit the bulletin, she would transfer back to Wesleyan Methodist this very minute. After all, just this past Thursday, Arlene had attempted to include in the bulletin a prayer request for Arnold Hamilton "whose wife is going through menopause" as well as a request submitted by that wretched, potbellied, donut-advocating swine Karl Rincker that read, "Please pray for all of the people going hungry during the Sunday School hour." If she, personally, wasn't there to bring some sense to the Bulletin Planning Committee every week, who knew what Arlene would do?

Geraldine's resolve solidified as Karl Rincker, who happened to be ushering that Sunday morning, handed her a bulletin with his suit coat unbuttoned. His stomach hung over his belt buckle like a scoop of vanilla ice cream melting over a cone. Yes, her vocation was clear. She must remain at Zion and protect the muffin line, or Karl would surely have his way and die of a heart attack within the year. Staying on at Zion was mercy work, really.

Geraldine was more than pleased to find Zachary sitting in her pew again that morning. She shimmied past him to sit on his right, politely excusing herself. She was thankful she had chosen to wear her yellow wool pantsuit this morning. It was her best color.

"Do you have any plans for Valentine's Day?" Zachary whispered congenially.

Geraldine's heart skipped a beat. Maybe Emily Duke wasn't the only woman Zachary looked at, after all. "I've kept my calendar open this year. And you?"

Zachary smiled. "I thought I'd go to Dr. Duke's faculty recital that night. The one for flute and voice."

Geraldine's face soured. "Oh, I hadn't heard about that."

That was a lie. She had heard about it, or overheard about it, as Candice was just moments ago jabbering on and on in the narthex about her plans to host a post-recital reception at Bradbury House for Emily and all of the other choir groupies.

Zachary started chuckling as he eyed the last page of his bulletin. "Hey, look at this."

Geraldine obligingly pulled out her glasses and slipped them onto the tip of her nose, smiling triumphantly. He had finally noticed her title of Senior Editor in the bulletin! She had been wondering when he would actually say something about it; however, as Geraldine leaned over to harvest his praise, she saw that he was actually pointing to the service portion of the folder.

"It looks like someone left out a 'g' this week."

Geraldine's face went red as a cherry. She pulled off her glasses as fast as she could and resisted the urge to retch, for there, after the Pax Domini—where the Lord's blessed, sacrificial title should have been proclaimed with all reverence and dignity—were the unfortunate words "Anus Dei."

"A bit irreverent, I know, but funny, isn't it?"

Blast that Arlene! If only she hadn't distracted her with all of those ridiculous prayer requests last Thursday, Geraldine was certain she would have caught this apostasy. And there sat Zachary, laughing at her as if she had put the Lord's rear end in print on purpose.

"How dare you laugh at me!" Geraldine ripped the bulletin out of Zachary's hands and gave him a dirty look.

Zachary, shocked at Geraldine's reaction, sobered in an instant. He watched as the woman in yellow jumped up from her seat and flitted from pew to pew like a spooked canary, tearing bulletins out of people's hands and stuffing them in her purse. Karl Rincker lumbered up the aisle to put a stop to her paper tyranny, but Geraldine simply rent the stack of remaining bulletins from his hands too and darted out of the church.

Zachary shook his head in silent amazement. He had suspected for some time that the Turner woman was teetering on the brink of some kind of crazy, but her present parade of madness confirmed it.

"And she 'was hollow at the core,'" he murmured under his breath.

Chapter Thirty-One: Baby Carrots

|||||||||||||||||||||||||||||||||||||||||||||||||||||||||||||||||

"Caroline's keepin' the white doe," Ben said, pointing to a fuzzy piece of white fluff hovering in a back corner of the cage. "She named her Frosty."

Emily leaned down to get a better look inside the wire box sitting on top of the Schmidts' workbench. Ben had invited her out to the farm for the afternoon to meet his new rabbits, and he was practically hopping with excitement. "So Caroline convinced her mom to let her have one, huh?"

Ben grinned and nodded. "Long as we keep her here."

A second, sandy-colored bunny with floppy ears hopped over to lie next to Frosty while a third bunny, this one white with sandy-colored splotches, plopped over on his side near the food dish. "Can I pet them?"

"Sure." Ben opened the front door of the cage, and Emily stuck her hand in to gently stroke their warm, velvety ears. The splotchy bunny licked her hand.

"Dad says I can breed 'em when they're old enough."

"When will that be?"

Ben shrugged. "I haven't got that far in the manual yet."

"They're so soft!"

"Which one's your fav'rite?"

Emily studied the three downy cushions. She reached out her hand again to pet the splotchy one, admiring the calico pattern of color that framed his dark-brown eyes. He looked like a woolly paint horse. "This one."

"Then he's yours."

"What?"

Ben blushed with excitement. He'd been waiting all day to tell her this. "I thought you might be needin' a pet."

"You got me a bunny?"

"It don't seem right for a lady to live alone."

Emily was speechless. Ben reached into the cage and scooped up the splotchy bunny, cradling him like a baby in his hands. "Here. Hold him."

Ben pushed the bunny into Emily's arms, immensely pleased with himself. "He's a Holland Lop. That's why his ears are so floppy. And he's called a broken tort buck. Buck is 'cause he's male, tort's his color, and broken means he's got some white in there too."

Emily still didn't know what to say. On the one hand, she was already falling in love with this soft, little fluff ball, but on the other hand, she was not much of a pet person. And she knew nothing about rabbits.

"He don't need any shots, and he'll be easy to potty train."

"I have to potty train him?"

"It's easy, Miss Emily. He'll want to go in the same spot every time, so all you gotta do is leave him in his cage until he shows you where he wants to go. Then you put his litter box in that spot."

Emily's head was spinning. Litter box? She didn't even have a cage. And what do rabbits eat and how much and—

"I found this really cool cage online," Ben read her mind. "You build it yourself with these wire shelf units and hold it together with plastic ties. Dad and I already got the parts and everything. We can make it before you go home."

"What does he eat?"

"Hay, pellets, and some greens. You can get the hay and pellets at the Rural King in Hamburg, and I thought we could plant some greens in your garden this summer." Ben was looking at Emily with puppy dog eyes, eager to please. "I'll help you, Miss Emily. Just like with the yard."

Emily looked down at her furry bundle. She had to admit it. The bunny was pretty cute, and it might be kind of nice to come home to floppy ears and fuzzy snuggles every night. "How much does he cost?"

"Nothin'. He's a gift. From me and Caroline."

Emily marveled at the generosity of youth. "Really? Ben, thank you!"

"What are you goin' to name him?" Ben asked.

Emily looked down at the reddish-brown tufts of hair spiking above the bunny's floppy ears. His irregular blots of the same color looked like giant freckles on his snow-white coat, reminding her of her favorite heroine. She knew just the name. "Carrots."

"Hey, Carrots," Ben said, petting the bunny's dark brown nose. He merrily reached into the cage and picked up Carrot's brother buck. "I'm namin' this one Cinnabon. Or Dr. Zaius. I can't decide."

Emily drove home that afternoon with a bunny, a homemade cage, a bag of Timothy hay, a pound of pellets, a bucket of paper litter, and one of Mrs. Schmidt's old plastic tubs. "Just cover it with a plastic bag, honey, and it'll make a perfect litter box," Mrs. Schmidt had assured her with a wink.

Emily barely had time to deposit the bunny and all of its accoutrements in the kitchen before it was time to turn around and get ready for the recital. She felt bad leaving her little friend alone so soon, but she had no choice. She and Basset had been rehearsing their flute and vocal duets since Christmas break, and tonight was their big performance. She quickly hopped in the shower, brushed on some mascara, pinned back her side curls, and put on the red dress she reserved for special occasions.

"You look like a valentine," Basset said, saluting Emily with her flute as she walked up the recital hall aisle.

"Nice shoes," Emily returned, admiring Basset's patent leather red pumps. "I'm glad we're doing this. It'll be good for the students."

"Forget the students," Basset laughed. "It's good for me. I can't remember the last time I played a recital with someone who doesn't live in a dorm."

Twenty minutes before seven o'clock, students, faculty, and friends began bubbling over the threshold of the recital hall like champagne over the brim of a glass. Lobelia Alwardt took her place at the door to hand out programs, and Mrs. Scheinberg, Alice, and Rebecca claimed seats together in the front row. Emily peaked through a leg of the curtain and saw that Candice's entire family, Thomas Sr. included, had come out for the event. Zachary, too, was in attendance. Even Evan had come. He was sitting in the second row directly behind Alice, chatting familiarly with Clarence Mitchell, BC's notorious theory instructor. Emily felt a twinge of disappointment at not seeing Pastor Fletcher in the crowd, but truth be told, she had never formally invited him, and he had never mentioned an intent to come.

Candice also noticed Pastor's absence from the hall. She dug around in her purse in search of her phone, but the curtain rose before she could indulge in any impulsive calls of intervention.

The recital program was musically pleasing, if a bit unorthodox. Dr. Basset and Emily performed Corigliano's *Three Irish*

Folksong Settings for voice and flute as well as the mad scene from the finale of Donizetti's *Lucia di Lammermoor*, but that was where they parted with tradition. Dr. Basset stood her C flute upright on its stand and picked up her alto flute, playing the mezzo counterpart to Emily's soprano in *"Christe eleison"* from J. S. Bach's Mass in B Minor as well as keeping it in hand for *Psalmody*, a song cycle for alto flute, soprano, and piano she had composed herself. Blaine joined his professors on stage for the last three pieces, and Mrs. Scheinberg, in spite of Alice's incessant elbow jabbing, clapped vigorously at the end of each song.

"You're supposed to clap only at the end of a work, dear," Alice whispered in the middle of the song cycle.

"That's what I'm doing."

"No, you're clapping at the end of each song. The work's not complete until the final song of the cycle has been sung."

"What?"

"Shhh!" Clarence Mitchell reprimanded sharply from behind.

"Oh, never mind."

Emily stared out over the audience and lightly touched the string of pearls at her neck. She had forgotten how thrilling it was to sing alongside musicians the caliber of Basset and Blaine, and her voice felt so good that night. The recital happened to fall on one of those magical evenings when everything—the humidity, the acoustics of the room, the repertoire, her health and energy level—all came together to create an effortless, buoyant sound. Basset winked at her appreciatively before beginning "New Song," the final movement in the cycle.

"'He put a new song in my mouth,'" Emily sang, bouncing on ascending dotted eighth notes to a luminous high C, "'a song of praise to our God.'"

Evan leaned back in his seat and closed his eyes, basking in the warm radiance of Emily's tone. Hers was the special breed of soprano created by God to float Bachian *melismata* across church rafters and to spill gentle lullabies into the ears of sleepy children. Her brilliant command of pitch and rhythm incited confidence in her listeners, no one doubting whether or not she would stick her landings after each long run of vocal gymnastics. Evan particularly enjoyed Emily's use of dynamics, the way she pushed and pulled at each musical phrase until it shimmered and flashed in the air like a billowing satin banner. And so it was with deep, professional respect that Evan stood to his feet after the final note and belted *"Bravo! Bellissimo!"* to the rosy diva on stage.

Zachary, too, jumped to his feet, holding his program under his arm and clapping until he lost all feeling in his hands. "Encore!" he shouted from the balcony. "Encore!"

Only one person in the hall failed to stand. Pastor Fletcher, sitting discreetly in the back right corner of the auditorium, remained in his seat. He almost felt embarrassed to look at Emily. She looked so beautiful in that red dress, her cheeks flushed from the exertion of expanding and contracting her intercostal muscles for an hour straight, and every time she smiled her bright sunbeam down onto the audience, something in him—something he couldn't keep from showing on his face or in his eyes—came undone.

"Are you leaving so soon?" Lobelia called after him as he pushed through the lobby door. "The Bradburys are hosting a reception for Emily's friends and family." "I've got to go," was all Pastor could manage, gripping a folded piece of paper hidden in his coat pocket as he hustled down the stairs.

At Bradbury House, Alice cupped Emily's face in her hands and kissed her cheek. "You were splendid, dear."

"I've never heard anything so beautiful," Rebecca agreed, handing her friend a bouquet of yellow roses. "And you, Dr. Basset," she said, turning to the spunky woman dressed in a black suit and red heels, "are amazing! To think we have a real composer right here in Bradbury!"

Steve Basset grinned and put a proud arm around his wife's waist.

"That song cycle was an inspiration," Zachary confirmed. "How did you choose which Psalms to use?"

Emily smiled politely as Basset explained to the small gathering of people at the Bradburys' reception the process of choosing texts for musical settings, but her mind was elsewhere. She glanced around the northwest parlor in hopes of sighting a certain clerical collar, but her search came up wanting. He hadn't come.

Candice, too, seemed disturbed by Pastor's absence. She whispered into Emily's ear, "Have you seen Pastor Fletcher? I was sure he'd be here."

"No," was all Emily could manage in response.

"Did he call you or anything?"

"No."

"I don't understand. He had to've seen it by now."

Emily gave Candice a puzzled look, but her hostess was already moving on to continue her hunt in the southwest sitting room.

After staying at the Bradburys for a polite thirty minutes and drinking an obligatory cup of Great Grandmother Bradbury's punch, Emily managed to pull away from the reception without offending Candice too terribly. Her feet hurt from standing all night, and all she really wanted to do was put on her comfy, purple sweatpants and check on Carrots. There was to be no rest for the weary that night, however, for no sooner had she pulled her car into the driveway of the Mulberry property than she spied the missing clerical collar, bundled inside a wool coat and hat, seated on the top step of her front porch.

Pastor Fletcher rose to his feet as Emily came up the walk, extending a red rose to the celebrated soprano. "Your singing was beautiful."

"You were there?" Emily asked. She graciously accepted the flower and nestled it against Rebecca's yellow bouquet.

"Yes, though a bit late. I apologize. Irv was taken to Regional this evening. Don't worry," Pastor quickly reassured, "he's just fine. He's got a new cast on his right arm, that's all. Broke it catching himself on a fall in the IGA parking lot. He's more irritated than injured."

Emily shivered in the cold. All she was wearing over her red dress was the black shawl her mother had given her for Christmas. "Would you like to come in? I was about to make myself some hot chocolate."

Pastor hesitated. As a rule, he never entered the homes of single women by himself unless it was a pastoral emergency. Emily colored, suddenly realizing the predicament in which she had put him.

"May I take you out for a cup of cocoa instead?" Pastor quickly asked. "You know, to celebrate?"

She hesitated. Her feet were throbbing, and all she wanted to do after an evening of performing and shaking hundreds of hands was to get out of her dress and into her sweats. "I'm really tired."

"Of course." Pastor looked down at his feet. He stuck his hands in his coat pockets and then pulled them out again when he realized Emily was standing there coatless. "Look, I don't

mean to keep you, but . . . I mean, there's something I'd like to
. . . what if we sat in the living room with the blinds open?"

Emily nodded, trying to hide her own discomfort. This
whole situation was just so awkward. She let herself into the
house, turning on every light she could find and opening blinds
and curtains so all the world could be their chaperone.

"Before you sit down," she said, turning to Pastor Fletcher,
"can I show you something in the kitchen?"

Emily walked through the dining room and flipped on the
overhead kitchen light. A little fuzzy nose turned up and wiggled at her. "Pastor, meet Carrots."

"You have a bunny?"

"Ben Schmidt and Caroline Bradbury conspired to get me a
pet," she answered with a smile.

"How in the world do you take care of a bunny?"

Emily stared into the cage with all sobriety. "I've no idea."

They both burst out laughing at the awful truth. The stress
and fatigue of the day were catching up with Emily, and her
laughter felt dangerously close to hysterics. She busied herself
finding vases for the flowers she had received that evening,
while Pastor leaned down to inspect the floppy-eared fur ball.
"Carrots, huh? He or she?"

"He."

"He's so tiny."

"I know. You can pick him up, if you want. He's friendly."
Emily felt a flash of embarrassment at the sight of all the round
poo pellets covering the floor of the cage. How could such a tiny
creature create so much waste in such a short amount of time?
"He's still potty training."

"Doesn't he need water?"

"What?" Emily turned around to look at the cage. "Oh, good grief! I completely forgot. Poor guy. What should I do? It's too late to call Ben."

"Have you got a spare bowl?"

"In the cabinet to the right of the sink."

Pastor opened the cabinet, took out a low, ceramic bowl, and filled it with water. Emily removed a metal clip from the top of the cage. "Here, you can set it down by his food."

Pastor lowered the water down through the open panel, and Carrots immediately hopped over to his water dish to start drinking.

"I'm a terrible pet owner. Don't laugh! It's not funny."

Pastor was snickering behind his hand. "Actually, it is."

Emily couldn't deny the humor of the situation, but her face remained serious. Her mind was stuck on those comfy pants, and she wanted nothing more than to excuse herself and politely slip down the hall to her bedroom. But it felt inappropriate changing clothes while Pastor was in the house, so instead, she modestly crossed her arms over her chest and asked, "Was there something you wanted to talk about?"

"How about that cup of cocoa first?"

A few minutes later, Pastor and Emily were seated in the living room, each with a steaming mug of hot chocolate in hand. Pastor was staring into his as if he could teleport its contents with his gaze alone. In reality, he was simply trying not to look at his hostess. He was still afraid his eyes might reveal too much of himself, and now that the time had come for him to ask his question, he was terrified. What if she said no?

"Did you, um," he false-started, still looking into his cocoa. "Did you by any chance write me a note this week?"

Emily's brow furrowed. "You mean the one I put in my Anne book?"

"No, a different note. All by itself."

Emily shook her head. "No."

Pastor's heart sank.

Emily's brow furrowed even deeper. "And that was at least a couple of months ago. Did you get a note this week?"

Pastor nodded.

"From me?"

Pastor hesitated before nodding again, daring to look at her this time.

Emily sat up straight, almost spilling her cocoa all over her dress. She set the sloppy mug down on a coaster and held out her hand. "I want to see it."

Pastor most definitely did not want her to see it.

"If you received something counterfeit in my name, then I have the right to see the evidence."

Pastor sighed and reached into his pants pocket, pulling out a folded piece of paper. Emily leaned over, snatched it from his hand, and began smoothing it out. The paper was cut in the shape of a heart.

Dearest,

For that is what you are, the dearest and best. I can no longer hide from you how I feel. In the deepest part of myself, I know you are the one. If you feel the same, please come to my recital and tell me.

Sincerely, reverently, devoutly yours,

Emily

Emily's nostrils breathed fire. What vile nonsense! She would *never* have written a note like this. Who in the world would dare—? Emily gasped and looked up from the note, her hands shaking with anger and her face burning with flames of injustice. Oh, she knew exactly who would dare. That manipulative, interfering monster of a woman! That deceiving, conniving reptile! There was not a punishment in the world sufficient for the sins of Candice Bradbury, of that much Emily was certain.

"What is it?"

"Candice." Emily's voice shook with fury.

"What about Candice?"

"She did this. I'm certain of it."

Pastor ran his hands through his hair, alarmed at Emily's rage. This was all coming down the pipe too fast for him to contain. "I'm sorry. I never should have come here tonight."

"This is Candice Bradbury's doing," Emily repeated, conviction ringing in her voice.

"I shouldn't have shown you the note. I knew you couldn't possibly have written it, but I still—I guess I just . . . I should have just let it be." Pastor held his repentant head in his hands.

Emily dropped the note on the coffee table as if it were laced with poison. "Does the woman not have a shred of decency in her? Is there not one brain cell in her head that acknowledges the laws of God and man?"

Pastor reached for the note, quickly wadding it up and sticking it back in his pocket. Out of sight, out of mind, he hoped. He made a mental note to burn it as soon as he got home. "I think she's trying to help you."

"*Help* me?" Emily turned toward Pastor. "What kind of help does she think I need that she would forge my own name?"

Pastor looked at Emily, his eyes an open portal to all of the things he had been trying so hard to hide, but she was too enraged to see past her own nose.

"She lied to you too, you know." Emily Duke, sweet and fair, was under wrath's evil spell. Her heart had hardened against compassion, readily trading mercy for retribution. She looked like a ruthless, prosecuting lawyer making her closing statement before a jury. "Candice lied to you about my feelings. Do you understand? She was willing to make a fool of you and of me for the sake of her little game. Doesn't that make you angry?"

Pastor wasn't angry. He was crushed. He looked at his feet, wounded and silent.

"Why aren't you upset about all of this?"

He looked up into Emily's steely face, a thousand unspoken words on his lips. He had been silent for so long, but silence had gotten him nowhere. He took a deep breath and screwed his courage to the sticking place. "I guess I am a fool, because I came here tonight hoping that letter really was from you. I knew it wasn't, but I still wanted it to be true."

There. He'd said it.

He stood and walked to the front door, stopping with his hand on the doorknob. He didn't bother turning around when he spoke. "I'm so sorry I came. Good night."

And then he was gone.

Chapter Thirty-Two:

Stricken, Smitten, and Conflicted

░░░░░░░░░░░░░░░░░░░░░░░░░░░░░░░░░░░░░░

Emily was a disaster. She tossed and turned the entire night, alternately crying then seething then weeping then stewing then bawling then second-guessing then crying some more. Why had Pastor Fletcher shown her that stupid note? And why on earth had he said all of those things before he left? He'd ruined a perfectly good friendship, that's what, and now they'd never be able to be friends again. A fresh wave of anger washed over her.

At 5:30 in the morning, Emily finally got out of bed and took her soggy, crusty self to the kitchen for a cup of tea. It was too early to call anybody, so she sat down on the cold linoleum floor for a proper heart-to-heart with the biggest pair of ears in the house.

"Why did I ever move to this town?" Emily moaned.

Carrots wiggled his nose sympathetically.

"I'm just so sick of it all. The gossip, the lies, the fake letters, the setups, the . . . the Candices!" Even speaking her name aloud made Emily's blood boil all over again. "If I have to see Victorian wallpaper ever again, I'm going to vomit. I should take Ralphe up on his offer and move to Germany."

Carrots clamped his teeth on a stray piece of hay and chomped away.

"And how does Pastor Fletcher get off saying what he said and then walking out the door like that? Why does everyone have to—Oh, bunny boy! I didn't give you any greens last night, did I?" Emily scrambled to her feet and threw open the refrigerator door. She grabbed a plastic container of spinach. "Here, have some of my spinach. Can you even eat spinach?"

She held a single leaf through the front of the cage. Carrots sniffed it curiously, licked it twice and then grabbed it in his front teeth and gobbled it up. Emily gave him another and another and another.

"We're a rotten mess, you and I. I've got a husbandmonger for a neighbor, and you've got a ditz for an owner. We'd both be better off somewhere else."

Emily reached a hand through one of the wire squares and scratched the top of Carrots's head. He jumped straight up in the air, wiggling his ears. Emily laughed in spite of her misery, and Carrots rewarded her with another happy, fluttery jump.

"You probably need more hay, don't you?" As she leaned over to open the top panel of the cage, the stinging scent of ammonia almost knocked her backwards. Her hand involuntarily went to her nose. "Whoa, Carrots. That's some strong urine."

A brownish wet spot stained the newspaper in the back left corner of the cage. Apparently, Carrots had chosen his potty spot. Not knowing what else to do, Emily picked up the newspaper, threw it in the trash, and reset Carrots's litter box to where the urine stain had been. When she stood back up, she looked at the clock above the kitchen sink. Six o'clock. It was still too early to call anyone in polite society, but this was an emergency. Emily picked up her phone and texted an SOS to the only person she felt she could trust in this situation. Twenty minutes later, a giant SUV pulled into her front drive.

"I'm moving to Germany," Emily announced as soon as she opened the front door.

"What?" Rebecca, still groggy and more than a little confused, pushed her way into Emily's living room and walked straight back to the kitchen as if it was her own. "Emily Duke, what in heaven's name is a rabbit doing in your kitchen?"

Emily followed her as far as the dining room before succumbing to tears. She crumbled onto a chair and buried her face in her arms on the table. Rebecca was too busy making a racket in the kitchen to notice. "You text me at six-freaking-o-clock in the morning, and you don't even have a pot of coffee going? Are you trying to kill me? Where's your Keurig?"

"I don't have one," Emily whimpered through her arms.

Rebecca stuck her head around the kitchen door and eyed the swampy situation suspiciously from under the rim of her Cubs hat. "No coffee pot? And you want to move to Germany, the land of *Milchkaffee*? C'mon then. Where's your coat?"

"Where are you taking me?" Emily cried as Rebecca pulled her up from the table by her elbow.

"Casey's."

"But I'm in my pajamas."

Rebecca gave the curly-haired diva hanging at the end of her arm a look of motherly forbearance, the one she usually reserved for Robbie. "So am I."

Ten minutes later, Rebecca and Emily sat in the northeast corner of Casey's parking lot while Rebecca nursed a black coffee. Emily stared dismally out the car window toward one of the Scheinberg acres north of the station.

"Now, what is this about Germany?"

Emily sniffed.

"Spill it, Duke."

Emily crossed her arms over her chest and pouted like a stubborn six-year-old, but she told Rebecca the truth. All children tell Rebecca the truth. Emily poured out every detail, starting with Candice's pirate letter and ending with Ralphe's job offer.

"So, let me get this straight. Candice wrote Pastor Fletcher a love letter from *you*?"

"Yes."

Rebecca started laughing.

"It's not funny!"

Rebecca snorted into her left hand. "Yes it is. That ridiculous woman! In what universe did she think that would ever work?"

"Well, your sneaky mother tried to set me up with Pastor Fletcher too, remember?"

"Fair enough."

"And Arlene. She's never said anything, but I see the way she eyes the things Pastor leaves in my box."

"Pastor leaves you things in your box?"

Emily felt strangely caught. "They're nothing. Just some books and things."

Rebecca turned a serious face toward her friend. "Honey, be honest with yourself for a second. You really think Pastor Fletcher leaves 'books and things' for other people?"

Emily shrugged. "Sure. He's a pastor."

Rebecca stared hard at Emily's profile. "Tell me again what Pastor said to you last night."

Emily remained silent. Her stomach felt empty and sick.

"Why are you trying so hard to pretend the man doesn't like you? What're you afraid of?"

"I'm not afraid of anything."

"Yes, you are. Look at you. You should be sleeping in the morning after your big recital, but instead, you're here, sitting in a gas station parking lot in your pajamas, crying."

"That's because you dragged me here."

"That's not what I mean." Rebecca set her coffee in a cup holder and turned sideways in her seat to better look at Emily. "Think about it. You're crying over this stupid letter and actually considering taking that position across an ocean from everything and everyone you love. You're running from something."

"Okay, fine. I'm running from Candice. I'm running as far and as fast as I possibly can."

"No," Rebecca shook her head. "Candice is harmless. She's a piece of work—don't get me wrong—but everyone knows she's a fool. She's not why you're running."

Emily's eyes watered until they spilled over onto her cheeks.

Rebecca softened at the sight. "Look, Em, I don't know what it's like to lose a husband. I've tried to imagine it. Out of love for you, I really have, but even the thought of losing Jay makes me want to die. I just can't do it."

Emily cried into her hands.

"It must be so scary, the thought of loving and losing again."

"Why can't everyone just let me be?"

"Because they love you, honey. They look at you and see all of the life you have left to live, and they don't want you to be alone. And I think, deep down inside, they feel that you don't really want to be alone either."

"I can't do it again."

"I know." Rebecca pushed aside a lunchbox, a bag of coloring books, and a box of Fruit Roll-Ups to scoot closer to her friend. She wrapped a protective arm around her shoulders and hugged hard. "As far as I'm concerned, you never have to get married ever again. Just promise me that whatever you do, you'll do it because you're running toward something, not away from it, okay?"

Emily took a deep, shaky breath and wiped at her cheeks. The sun was just unfolding its petals above a low rim of blue clouds on the southeastern horizon. It was going to be a sunny day. Cold, certainly, but still sunny. "Rebecca?"

"Hm?"

"Thank you."

||||||||||||||||||||||||||||||||||||||||||||

Emily decided to let Candice's letter die without a memorial. What was the point in trying to talk about it, anyway? Rebecca was right. Fools will be fools, and Candice will be Candice. And Pastor Fletcher was the only other person who knew about the letter. If she dared mention it to Candice, the woman would know Pastor had talked to her; and Emily, as desperate as she was to get Candice off her trail, was not about to lure that bloodhound straight to Pastor's front door. No, silence was the best funeral for this kind of forgery.

Still, silence cultivated its own strain of discomfort. Pastor kept his study door closed most days at the church, and Emily started emailing her choir business to Mrs. Scheinberg rather than dropping it by the office. Sundays presented more of a challenge in the art of avoidance, but Emily managed to busy herself in the pew with her purse every week until Pastor had finished greeting everyone else in the receiving line and had moved on to the fellowship hall. Only then did she get up to leave.

Mrs. Scheinberg seemed to be the only one who noticed any change.

"Everything okay?" she asked Emily over her choir folder one night at rehearsal.

"Of course," Emily assured, digging intently through her bag to avoid those golden spectacles.

Cribbage night posed the biggest problem. Pastor and Emily were polite enough to each other over the table, but their lack of conversation was excruciatingly obvious to their hosts. Rebecca did her best to fill the silence with stories of Alison's swimming lessons at the civic center and Frankie's latest theological queries, but even Rebecca found herself grasping at conversational straws toward the end of the night.

"Any news from Germany?"

Emily's head shot up in alarm.

"Germany?" Jeremy looked back and forth between Pastor and Emily and Rebecca over his cards. "What's in Germany?"

Rebecca's cheeks drained of their color. She shot a look of contrition toward her friend, realizing her mistake. "Oh, no one, really. Just a little music school Emily was telling me about."

Jeremy, unaware of the panicked undertones vibrating between the ladies in the house, grabbed hold of the new topic and held fast in support of his exhausted wife. "Sounds interesting. What's it called?"

"Potsdam Music School," Emily surrendered.

"I've never been to Germany. Czech Republic, yes—on business, believe it or not—but never Germany. What's this school?"

"Whose turn is it?" Rebecca asked brightly.

"Yours, honey," Jeremy answered, turning right back to Emily. "A music school? Did you study there at some point?"

"Seven for thirty-one," Rebecca called out triumphantly, setting down a seven of spades. "Look at that, Jay! Another two points."

"Mark 'em on the board, babe," he said, not about to be diverted from the topic at hand. He looked at Emily over his cards. "Do you send some of your BC students over there?"

Emily saw that she was not getting out of this. She picked up her stack of cards and resorted them carefully in her hands, stalling up to the very last moment. "No. It's a new school. I've never been there, but the chair of instrumental studies is a friend of mine."

"Where is it?"

"Just outside of Berlin."

"I dealt, so you go first, Pastor." Rebecca stood up and walked toward the kitchen, chatting the entire time. "I'm thirsty. Anyone else need a drink? Pastor, you've been to Germany, haven't you? You know, Jay, we really should go. Maybe we could get a church group together for a tour or something. I've always wanted to see the Wartburg. Speaking of castles, have you heard of that new princess movie coming out in theaters? I'm thinking about taking Alison to see it. Want to come, Emily?"

"Rebecca mentioned some news or something," Jeremy persisted, ignoring his wife's talk of the Wartburg and every other castle, real or pretend. "Does the school want to do an exchange program with BC or something?"

Emily squinted at her cards.

"Team America's not trying to trade you to Team Germany, are they?" Jeremy teased.

Emily set down her cards in resignation. "I've been offered a position with their choral department."

This time, Pastor's head shot up. He stared at Emily, looking her in the eye for the first time in weeks.

"Seriously?" Jeremy was no longer teasing.

"Well, we've been waiting for the right time to tell you two," Rebecca swept in from the kitchen, a fresh glass of ice water in hand, "and I think now's the time." She tapped Jeremy on the shoulder, nodding significantly, and then turned to Emily, wide-eyed and penitent. She was desperate to make things right.

"What, you want to tell them *now*?"

"Yes, Jay, now."

"But—"

"It's getting late. They're going to have to leave soon. I think now is the perfect time."

Pastor was still looking searchingly at Emily, but Emily looked up at Rebecca in confusion. What was going on?

"Okay, well," Jeremy stood and put his arm around his wife, clearing his throat. "You two are our closest friends, and we wanted to let you know before we told anyone else at church that, well, the rabbit died."

"Jeremy, that's awful!" Rebecca socked her husband in the gut with her elbow. "Emily has a bunny, so that's not funny. C'mon, be serious."

Jeremy kissed his wife's cheek and grinned at his friends. "God be praised, Rebecca and I are expecting our fifth child."

Emily's hands flew to her mouth.

Pastor stood and shook Jeremy's hand. "That's the best news! Praise be to God for His good gifts!"

Rebecca was still looking at Emily, a pleading look in her glistening eyes. At the least, she had managed to swipe Germany off the table for a bit.

Emily stared back at her friend, a mixture of happiness and wonder coloring her insides, but there was something else in there too. A surprising flash of green. An emerald monster of discontent hovered just beyond the rainbow, threatening to crash their sweet celebration with its poisonous envy. Emily kept the beast at bay long enough to stand up and hug Rebecca across the table. "I'm so happy for you!"

As usual, Pastor walked Emily to her car that night, but he didn't chatter and he certainly didn't linger. He did allow himself one question while holding open her car door. "Are you really considering this offer from Germany?"

"I-I don't know," she answered honestly.

"I believe that is a yes. Good night, Emily." Pastor softly shut her door and turned down the street toward his own car.

Emily sat with her hands on the wheel, her heart and conscience battling it out in an epic civil war. Why did Rebecca get to live in a house with a husband and children while she always went home to an empty house? Why did Rebecca get to spend her days making memories with her family while she had to carve out a living teaching classes and lessons to other people's children? Why did Rebecca get to drive an SUV full of Cheerios and comic books while she drove a little Honda coupe full of nothing? Emily glanced mournfully over at the empty passenger seat and then back out the windshield toward Pastor Fletcher's retreating back. The snowmelt from her frozen heart pooled behind her eyelids and cascaded down her cheeks in shiny rivulets of grief.

Maybe Alice and Candice and Mrs. Scheinberg and everyone else in Bradbury were right. Maybe she really didn't want to be alone after all.

Chapter Thirty-Three: Silly Rabbit

Something was wrong with Carrots. He had stopped eating, and he no longer hopped around his cage and wiggled his ears at the sight of Emily. Instead, he sat balled up in his litter box with his feet tucked tightly under his belly.

"He keeps grinding his teeth," Emily explained to Ben over the phone.

"Sounds like gastric stasis, Miss Emily."

"Is that bad?"

Ben purposefully didn't answer. "You need to take him to the vet."

Emily drove to Hamburg with Carrots in the passenger seat so she could lean her hand against his cheek the whole way to the vet's. She felt sick that her sweet bunny was in pain. "I'm so sorry, Baby Carrots. I'm going to make everything better, okay?"

Carrots squeezed his eyes shut and ground his teeth.

"It's gastric stasis," Dr. Boyer confirmed.

"What does that mean?"

"It means his digestive system has stalled."

"Why?"

Dr. Boyer shook her head. "There's no way to know for sure. It just happens sometimes with bunnies. They're very sensitive.

It could've been caused by a change in his diet, a stress of some kind, or nothing at all. What've you been feeding him?"

"Hay, pellets, some spinach. The usual."

"He's pretty young for greens, let alone spinach."

Emily winced. She had meant to check out a book on rabbits from the library, but she'd been so consumed by her own troubles the last month she'd never actually gotten to it.

"Is he going to die?" Her voice broke on the last word.

Dr. Boyer was a kind woman, but she didn't offer false hope. "He might."

"What do I do?"

"You're going to have to force feed him."

Emily nodded. Anything. She'd do simply anything to help her sweet, little Carrots.

"And I'll give you some liquid antibiotics to help counteract the bile festering in his system."

Emily took Carrots home armed with a special food formula, a syringe, antibiotics, and a fierce determination. Iron had entered her blood. Carrots was not going to die; not on her shift, at least. She called Basset and cancelled her classes for the day. Then she called the Schmidts.

"I've been readin' in my manual, Miss Emily, and it says a bunny's body temperature drops when it's sick. You need to hold him to keep him warm."

"Okay."

"And keep him hydrated."

"Right."

"And try rubbin' his belly. See if you can't work out some of his gas."

"Hold him, hydrate him, and rub him. Got it. Can you come over today to help me with the feeding?"

"I can't, Miss Emily. I would, but I have school."

"Of course, of course. Don't worry about it, Ben. I'll find someone."

Emily called Rebecca next.

"I'm so sorry, Em, I can't. Frankie's home from school with a fever."

Alice wasn't home to answer Emily's call, and neither was Bev. Emily stared at her phone, then looked at her bunny. Carrots's belly was so swollen, and he kept making that horrible grinding sound with his teeth. He would die if she didn't get some help rebooting his digestive system. She steeled herself and picked up the phone again.

"Zion Lutheran Church, this is Pastor Fletcher."

"Oh. I was looking for Mrs. Scheinberg."

"She's home with the flu."

"Okay." Emily sat still, staring at Carrots's taught face. This was no time for pride. "I need some help. Can you come over?"

Pastor Fletcher was at her door in two minutes flat.

Emily held Carrots out to him. "If you can hold him, I'll force the syringe down his throat."

"How do I hold him?"

"I don't know." Emily's face blanched. "I forgot to ask."

"It's okay. We'll figure it out." Pastor took Carrots in his arms.

"I told you I'm a terrible pet owner," Emily confessed, her voice wavering. She was dissolving faster than a pillar of salt in a rainstorm.

"We'll figure it out," Pastor assured her again. "Now, do you have an old towel or something I can wrap around him? I've a feeling this is going to be messy."

Pastor was right. Every time Emily tried to stick the tip of the syringe into Carrot's mouth, he resisted.

"Try from the side instead of the front."

Emily poked the syringe into the side of Carrots's mouth, accidentally smearing his cheek with the pasty nutritional food mix.

"I think you're going to have to hold down his head, Emily."

"I can't."

"Yes you can. He has to eat to get better, right? Sometimes you have to hurt those you love to help them. Now, grip his head and hold back his cheek, so you can see where to shoot the food."

Emily grabbed Carrots's face in her left hand and shot some food into the gap behind his front teeth. Some of it went down, but most of it squeezed out the other side of his mouth. She had squeezed too hard.

"Try again, just not as much this time."

Bit by bit, Emily managed to squeeze the rest of the strong-smelling formula down into Carrots's stomach. By the time she was done, the fur on his face was wet with the grainy paste. He looked like he'd been in a mud fight, but Emily didn't care. Hot tears of relief stung her eyes. They'd done it. Now, all they could do was wait. She stuck her nose up against her bunny's cheek and nuzzled his dirty face. "I'm so sorry, Baby Carrots, but this is what you need."

Thankfully, Carrots took to the antibiotics much better. He lapped up the pink liquid from the syringe with his paper-thin tongue.

"I'll come back for the next feeding, okay?" Pastor said as he passed Carrots back to Emily.

True to his word, Pastor returned at noon, letting himself in the front door. He found Emily on the kitchen floor sitting with her back against the sink cabinet. Carrots was wrapped in a towel on her lap, and a bowl of water and a syringe lay next to her on the floor.

"Have you been sitting there all morning?"

Emily nodded.

"Here, I brought you a sandwich and some tea from The Corner Coffee Shop." He set the food on the counter and reached for Carrots. "I'll hold him while you eat."

Emily stood up and stretched her back. She noticed a small stack of books on the counter next to the sandwich bag. "What're these?"

"Just a few books I picked up from the library. Thought you might enjoy reading a bit while you hold Carrots."

Emily bowed her head at Pastor's thoughtful gesture. Why was he being so nice to her? It hadn't been so long ago that she'd basically called him a fool to his face. She hid her own face behind her tea and looked through the stack of books. The top one was on rabbit care, the second was a biography of Eleanor of Aquitaine, and the third was a tour book of northern Germany. A pang of guilt stabbed at her heart.

"Go ahead and eat," Pastor prodded. "We'll feed Carrots after you're done."

Pastor stayed to hold Carrots while Emily pushed another syringe full of the nutritional formula down his throat. They even managed to get a few ounces of water into him after that. Still, his belly looked sickeningly swollen, and he continued to lie limp in her arms. Emily thought his breathing looked more labored too.

"He still hasn't poo-ed yet," Emily admitted, her voice tight with concern.

"I think it's going to take some time. I'll come back to help around dinnertime."

"Wait!" Emily said. "It's Thursday. I totally forgot about choir. I'm going to have to cancel rehearsal."

"Why?"

"I can't leave Carrots, or his body temperature'll drop."

"No, it won't. I'll hold him."

"What?"

"I'm going to hold him tonight, so you can direct the choir."

Emily looked up into Pastor's face. He met her gaze full-on, just as he had that very first Sunday in Alice's sunroom so many months ago. Emily felt herself blush under the directness of his gaze.

"It's settled then," he said. "I'll come back around five-thirty. Will that give you enough time to eat and get ready for choir? We can give Carrots his final feeding after you get home from rehearsal."

Emily nodded. She had to admit that it felt good having someone help her take care of Carrots—but it felt even better having someone take care of her.

|||||||||||||||||||||||||||||||||||||||||||||||

After choir practice, Emily found herself seated once more beside Pastor Fletcher on the kitchen floor while forcing formula into her bunny's tummy.

"Thank you," Emily said, meeting Pastor's eyes over the top of Carrots's head.

"You're welcome."

Emily wiped Carrots's slimy cheek with a wet paper towel. She cleared her throat. Now was as good a time as any. "I owe you an apology."

"No, you don't."

"I do. I lost my temper the night of the recital, and I'm sorry."

"You're forgiven."

"And I called you a fool."

"Actually, you didn't. You said Candice was willing to make a fool of me. Even if you had called me a fool, it wouldn't have been a sin. You were just trying to tell me the truth that night."

Still, Emily colored in shame. However Pastor had taken it, she knew how she had meant it.

Pastor handed Carrots back to Emily. "I was telling you the truth that night too, you know."

There was that bold look again.

"The thing is," he continued, standing up and stretching his legs, "I wanted that letter to be from you. I know that makes you uncomfortable, but I wish it didn't."

Emily sought respite in her bunny's face.

"I'm not going to just walk out the door this time, Emily. Please, say something."

Emily forced herself to speak. "I'm not ready."

"Ready for what?"

"I-I don't know."

Pastor nodded. "But you're ready to move across an ocean?"

"I didn't say that."

"You don't say a lot of things."

Emily's temper flared a bit. "Why does everyone keep pushing me?"

Pastor smiled knowingly at Emily. "Because you need a little pushing."

"You have no idea what I need!"

Pastor stared down at Emily's flushed face for a long moment, and Emily's breath caught in her throat. Something had changed in this man since that awful night in February. He was no longer afraid. He grabbed his coat off the counter and said, "I think I do know what you need, Emily Duke. I'll see you tomorrow morning for Carrots's feeding."

Emily's heart was racing when Pastor walked away, only this time, it wasn't from anger or frustration. This time, it was from something else, something she was afraid to name.

Chapter Thirty-Four: Spring Fever

<hr />

The azalea bush bloomed pink.

Not a puny, sickly pink or a tacky, bubblegum pink, but a flaming, magenta pink that threatened to light Emily's entire porch on fire with its blaze. Purple crocuses crouched beside the front step, leaning against the knees of fragrant white and pink hyacinths, and yellow daffodils served up cups of sparkling dew alongside the front walk. The midmorning sun gently warmed the vibrant bouquet of early spring, and Emily drank in its sweet perfume one delicious sip at a time.

Ben and Caroline were busy raking sweet gum balls into paper yard-waste bags, while Emily worked beside them, scooping up prickly balls and delivering them to the large ceramic pot Mrs. Schmidt had given her for growing spearmint and peppermint.

"Don't plant them in your garden," she had warned. "They'll shoot runners across your whole yard if their feet touch the ground."

Emily carried the half-filled pot to the back stoop and set it down next to her freshly mulched herb bed that Ben had helped her spade earlier that morning. It was still too early in the season to plant anything, but the smell of the overturned earth alone was enough to make Emily grow a few inches taller herself.

"All done, Miss Emily!" Caroline called out happily from the front yard.

"Time for cookie, then." Emily took off her gloves, dropped them on the back step, and headed into the house via the kitchen door to retrieve the tray of peanut butter cookies and lemonade she'd prepared earlier that morning. She paused for a moment by the pantry door, remembering with a sweet sadness the cage that used to sit there. She would forever miss seeing Baby Carrots's floppy ears and wiggly nose greet her every time she entered the room.

"But you're much happier out here, aren't you Big Bunny Boy?" Emily cooed to the half-grown buck lounging in his new cage on the living room floor as she carried the tray out to the front porch. A few weeks ago, Pastor Fletcher had helped her move Carrots closer to the windows in the front room, where he could enjoy more natural sunlight while she was gone during the days. "I'll come back to let you out in a minute."

Emily pushed open the screen door with her hip and delivered the well-earned refreshments to her hard workers. "How much do I owe you?"

"Nothin'," Ben replied, his mouth already around a cookie.

"Oh, come, now. You two worked all morning long. That's at least twenty dollars each."

"Nope," Caroline said, "we're counting it toward our community service hours for 4-H. Besides, we've got a favor to ask of you."

Emily hid a grin behind her hand. There was no mistaking which child was the lawyer's.

"You see, Miss Emily," Ben began, "Carrots has the prettiest coat. He's skinnier, sure, but—"

"But he's our best bet for the fair," Caroline finished.

"You want to enter Carrots in the county fair?" Emily asked.

"No, Miss Emily, the state fair," Ben corrected.

Emily's eyebrows shot up. "Can you do that?"

"Sure, if *you* sign him up."

"Me?"

"Uh huh," Caroline nodded enthusiastically, her blonde bangs flopping up and down a bit like a bunny's ears. "It'll be fun. Ben and I'll enter Cinnabon and Frosty, and you can enter Carrots, and then we can all go to the fair together!"

"Oh, I don't know, you guys. Carrots was so sick just a month ago. I mean, I'm sure he'd be fine and everything, but, well, what if he gets stressed and his stomach stops up again? I think maybe this is not the best year to push him."

Caroline and Ben exchanged a significant look. Ben nodded his approval, and Caroline turned around to begin negotiations.

"What if Ben mows your lawn for free this summer?"

"What? Absolutely not. He earns the wage, and I pay it. That's how business works."

"What if I practice singing one hour every day?"

Emily raised her eyebrows knowingly and asked, "Aren't you doing that already?"

"Okay, two hours then."

She gave Caroline a doubtful look. "Even I don't practice two hours a day."

"What if I go to church every Sunday with my grandma?"

Emily stopped short. She stared at Ben. He looked serious enough. "Church is too important to joke about, Ben."

"I know. That's why I'm offerin' it up on the table."

Emily crossed her arms. "So if I enter Carrots in the state fair this summer, you'll go to church every Sunday with your Grandma Schmidt? For a whole year?"

Ben nodded solemnly.

"Starting when?"

"Startin' this Sunday." Ben rose to his feet and stuck his hand out toward Emily. "Deal?"

Emily wasted no time grabbing her young gardener's hand and giving it a firm shake. "Deal!"

Caroline squealed and clapped her hands. Emily laughed nervously, wondering what exactly Carrots would need to be able to do by this summer, and Ben smiled sheepishly at the porch floor. He was pleased about Carrots and all, no question about it, but he couldn't help feeling a bit like he'd just pulled a fast one over his favorite employer; he'd already promised as much about church and everything to his Grandma Nettie earlier that very week. Maybe Emily didn't need to know that, though.

<hr/>

Across the street, Mrs. Scheinberg was locking up the church office filing cabinet and tossing explicit instructions over her shoulder to Pastor Fletcher.

"Now, I should only be gone a week, but Geraldine'll attempt a full-blown mutiny before I get back, no doubt about it. Remember, that is *my* chair, and those are *my* pens. Under no circumstance is she to use either. If she wants to use the blue pencils in the canister by the door, that's fine, but she's to pull up one of the chairs from along the wall to edit the bulletin. Don't give me that look! I'm serious. One moment in that chair and she'll never give it back, I promise you. You think I'm a hazard in here, but trust me. One week with Geraldine, and you'll be begging me to come home from Chicago."

Mrs. Scheinberg rubbed the back of her leather chair absentmindedly. "I don't know. Maybe I won't come back. Maybe city life is just what this old broad needs. I'd retire in a heartbeat if I thought this place wouldn't fall apart without me, but I guess Blaine'll need me to drive him back to BC either way."

"It's a nice thing you're doing for Blaine," Pastor said, leaning against the wall with his hands in his pockets. Mrs. Scheinberg hated when he did that. It made him look even younger than he already was.

She shrugged her shoulders. "Blaine's a nice boy. Seems a shame anyone has to live through what he's endured."

Pastor often thought the same thing about Mrs. Scheinberg, though he never dared speak it aloud. That would spell certain death for their already tenuous office peace treaty.

Mrs. Scheinberg tapped her finger on a sheet of yellow copy paper tucked neatly under the stapler on her desk. "Here're the additional prayer requests for Sunday's bulletin. All Geraldine needs to do is key them into the template, and then she can alphabetize them or color-code them or whatever else it is she does that makes her feel like she's in charge."

"I'll make sure Geraldine gets the prayer requests. We'll be fine, Mrs. Scheinberg. You go and take care of Blaine."

Mrs. Scheinberg nodded her head, picking up her quilted bag and turning around for one final note. "I'm sorry to be leaving you during Holy Week. I feel rotten about it, but this is when the Malers' case came up. Heaven forbid our insidious government show a little respect for the Church and her holy days. Okay, I'm outa here."

"Drive safely."

As the door closed behind her, Pastor picked up the piece of yellow paper and scanned the typed prayer requests: there was one for Hattie Plueth, who got laid off from work this past week; one for Dorothy Koelster, whose vertigo was acting up again; one for Evan's sister, who was undergoing tests at Memorial;

and at the bottom of the page, written by hand in a familiar shade of green ink, was a special request that God would protect the hearts of children from broken families.

Pastor smiled as he carefully reset the paper under the stapler. Mrs. Scheinberg, as much as she tried to hide it, was a Baby Ruth Bar at heart: salty and crunchy on the outside with a sweet, soft chewy center.

Chapter Thirty-Five: Christ Is Risen!

For Geraldine, the root of all evil wasn't money but Mrs. Scheinberg, so it was with much rejoicing that the Senior Editor of the Bulletin Planning Committee took a seat in the front office leather chair on Maundy Thursday to edit the prayer requests for Easter Sunday's bulletin. Finally, Geraldine was convinced, there would be peace in the valley and in the bulletin for Zion.

"Arlene's gone to Chicago with that cabaret act," Geraldine murmured over the church office phone to Candice that afternoon, indulging in a little trumpet blowing.

"Poor woman," Candice pitied. "She's getting desperate for attention."

Geraldine tried sitting upright in Mrs. Scheinberg's leather chair, but the permanently dimpled seat cushion kept propelling her unnaturally forward. Arlene really needed to lay off the cookies. Geraldine opened the top drawer of the desk and began rearranging the various trays of paper clips, staples, and pens. The drawer would function much better if the taller containers sat toward the back.

"Is Pastor Fletcher there?" Candice asked conspiratorially. "I've been trying to get that man to take a look at Emily Duke for weeks, but he's hopeless. A complete waste when it comes to romance. Religion does that to a man, I think. Too much praying."

Always Emily Duke! Geraldine scowled. "It's Emily who's a waste. She's too much absorbed with her own reflection in the mirror to notice anyone else. I think it's simply appalling the way that girl left Russell hanging at your house. You know, ever since I saw her mother and father, I've suspected that her raising was slim, but now I'm certain of it."

"I've tried to help, Geraldine, God knows I've tried, but Russell won't hear of giving her a second chance, and that Brandt fellow is hard to read."

"Zachary is too old for her."

"You think so?"

"Oh, yes." Geraldine had spent a good deal of time convincing herself of this truth, so it was pittance convincing the likes of Candice. "Dr. Brandt's traveled around the world. He needs someone who's lived a little. Emily is practically a baby in his eyes."

"Well, I've run out of ideas. This town's grown too small, that's what. I've told Thomas a thousand times that Bradbury needs to build a shopping mall to attract more young people. Maybe," Candice mused, "I should create a profile for her online with one of those dating services."

Geraldine balanced the phone in between her right ear and shoulder while attempting to key the new prayer requests into the bulletin template on Arlene's computer. She didn't dare put Candice on speaker, not with Pastor Fletcher sitting just a few feet away in his study.

"Anyway," Candice sighed, "Thomas and the kids are grabbing dinner at Koelster's tonight in between play practice and church. Thomas knows I refuse to eat there, but he insists on going. He says it's to support local business, but he really just wants to eat Janet's biscuits and gravy. Janet won't admit it, but I'm certain she uses Crisco in her biscuits. Egregious!" Candice had just learned that word earlier in the week while checking Junior's vocabulary homework, and she had made a point of using it in every conversation since. "I simply can't support the Koelsters as long as they use trans fats. It's a matter of principle, you know? What're you eating tonight?"

Geraldine paused after typing in Hattie's name. She usually didn't eat supper on Thursdays (or Tuesdays, for that matter), but she could smell the yeasty aroma of opportunity baking in the air. If she played her cards right, she might actually score a night out with Candice. "I was thinking about trying that new Chinese restaurant in Hamburg."

"Oh, Geraldine! I've heard about that place. You know, we should go together. If we leave now, we can make it back in time for church tonight. No, wait. We'd never make it back by seven with that roadwork on Route 11. Hm, well I suppose it wouldn't hurt if we missed one night. It's not like there won't be more services this week. Yes, we can make it up tomorrow. Good Friday's the important service anyway. That's when Junior's acolyting. Can you be ready in five minutes? I'll swing by the church and pick you up."

Geraldine didn't need to be asked twice. She hurriedly finished typing up the prayer requests and did a cursory look-through of the announcements before powering off the computer.

In the months ahead, the tiny part of Candice's conscience that was still active speculated about whether or not things might have been different for Geraldine if she'd just left her alone that day. However, since Candice's conscience rarely ever visited her thoughts, let alone judged them, it was easy to simply ignore those pesky little pricks whenever they arrived.

||||||||||||||||||||||||||||||||||||||||||||

Easter Sunday dawned a rosy gold, unfurling bright ribbons of yellow, pink, and purple across the morning sky. Emily could barely contain her alleluias as she walked over to the church. She was wearing a brand new yellow sundress from her favorite catalog as well as Grandma Elsie's white cloche she had inherited the year her grandmother died. Earlier in the week, Alice had clued her in on the women of Zion's longstanding tradition of wearing hats on Easter Sunday, and Rebecca had popped by her house the evening before to help her wrap a wide yellow ribbon around the cloche and fashion a feminine bow just above its subtle rim. Emily fingered the ribbon happily as she dropped a package off in the church office and climbed the north balcony stairs.

The balcony could have been a flower market for all of the colors and blooms sprouting from the heads of the women that morning. Alice smiled gaily from beneath the wide brim of her orange organza swinger hat, and Rebecca delicately adjusted the lily she had pinned to the band of her understated gray felt kettle. Marge's cheerful pink pillbox looked like it had been purchased the same decade as Jackie Kennedy's, and the dark purple netted veil hanging down the front of Candice's lavender wedding hat looked equal to the task of catching fish as well as one of her false eyelashes. Even Caroline and Amelia joined in on the fun, wearing short, white bucket hats adorned with stargazer lilies. The Koelster sisters sported matching bowlers, one snow white and the other navy blue but both with pink roses lining their satin bands, and Geraldine's bright yellow fascinator with the peacock feather plume was pinned dangerously close to the cliff of her forehead.

Geraldine, who had decided she'd rather suffer singing under Emily's baton than miss out on viewing the Easter parade of hats from the balcony, pinched her lips together in a self-satisfied smile at the sight of her choir director. She thought Emily bore a rather ridiculous resemblance to Shirley Temple on the Good Ship Lollipop with her curls popping out from under her silly vintage headpiece. However, Geraldine would have benefitted from a quick glance at her own profile in the mirror that morning. What she'd intended to be a stylish tribute to the royal wedding of the century actually turned out to be an absurd millinery mistake, for her feather plumage looked dangerously similar to that of the dead bird Lois had dislodged from the windshield of Don's truck yesterday. Lois was practically retching into her choir folder at the memory.

It was Bev's hat, however, that beamed the brightest and best of the stars that morning. Measuring at least two-and-a-half feet wide from shoulder to shoulder, the ruffled brim of her cornflower blue cartwheel sunhat looked remarkably similar to the umbrellas that covered the patio tables at the Kuhl Whip Stand on the corner of First and Adams, across the street from the town hall quad. The entire alto section had to scoot their chairs a good ten inches to the left just to keep the mammoth hat from knocking Janet in the eyebrow every time Bev took a breath to sing.

Pastor Fletcher had his own scrimmage with Bev's headgear that morning. As Bev knelt at the railing during the Service of the Sacrament to receive the body and blood of her Lord, she bowed her head in pious reverence, effectively blocking all access to the field goal. The Super Bowl-wide brim succeeded in intercepting every pass Pastor Fletcher attempted of the host and common cup, and Irv eventually had to nudge Bev in the ribs with his elbow to get his wife to look up to complete the play. Even then, she had to bend her neck back an extra forty-five degrees to score a sacramental touchdown. Few people noticed the Davis fumble, however, as most had their scarlet faces buried deep in their bulletins, where a particularly colorful Easter egg had been delivered in the prayer requests.

```
Please pray for Hattie Plueth, who
    got laid this week.
```

"Egregious!" Candice spoke aloud from the balcony, hoping and praying her purple netting was effective in hiding her suppressed laughter. It wasn't. And poor Geraldine, mortally wounded that her best friend would commit the ultimate blasphemy, flared her nostrils in tortured pride and silently returned her choir folder to Emily's director stand before they had even sung their anthem. She would no longer cast her pearls before these Lutheran swine. Without a word, she turned on her yellow heel and imperiously launched herself and her peacock plumage down the north stairwell and out of Zion.

Emily was busy singing Evan's chosen *"Laudate dominum"* during distribution and didn't notice Geraldine's flight until the entire choir stood after the benediction to sing the "Hallelujah Chorus."

"Where's Geraldine?" she whispered frantically to Rebecca.

"Halfway to the Methodist Church, I'd imagine."

The show must go on and the youth group's Easter egg casseroles must be eaten, so Emily gave a preparatory beat to Clarence Mitchell at the piano (who was graciously filling in for Blaine while he was in Chicago) and hoped for the best. Thankfully, the soprano section managed just fine without Geraldine. In fact, the entire choir sang as if they were forty voices thick rather than one soprano short. They attacked each entrance with a confidence and gusto that made Emily's spine tingle with excitement. Maybe it was the festal spirit of the Resurrection Day, or maybe it was having Evan and Zachary—who had joined the church on Palm Sunday—singing bass with Irv. Whatever the reason, her tiny sanctuary choir sounded like a heavenly chorus bouncing joyous hallelujahs across the rafters and down onto the congregation standing below. When the final "Hallelujah" was sung and Evan had resolved his glorious Handelian postlude on the same theme, he turned to Emily with a nod of the head and said, "Christ is risen!"

"He is risen indeed," Emily returned, a huge smile on her face. "Alleluia!"

Evan quickly replaced his organ shoes with his loafers and chivalrously offered Emily his left arm, a mischievous glint in his eye. "My dear director, if you'll allow an old man to escort you down to the fellowship hall, I made a special apple streusel coffee cake for the church brunch this morning. Alice informed me of your culinary preferences, so I paid the youth an extra ten dollars to set aside the middle piece just for you."

Emily, slim as her upbringing was, did not hesitate in taking Evan's arm and coyly replying, "Oh, I'm sorry. You were misinformed. I eat it only directly out of the pan."

After the youth brunch dishes had been washed, dried, and put away (and the final two pans of cinnamon rolls had been sent home with the Plueth family as a peace offering), Pastor Fletcher draped his suit coat over his arm and ambled back to his study. The Easter service and brunch had been a success in spite of Geraldine's pornographic prayer requests, and he was looking forward to a leisurely afternoon of reading books and hunting eggs with the Jones kids. A conspicuous brown paper bag, however, caught his eye as he rounded the corner of the front office. Pastor dropped his coat on Mrs. Scheinberg's empty chair and reached for the bag sitting in his mailbox. He pulled out a navel orange, a bar of dark chocolate, and Emily's worn copy of *Anne of Green Gables*. A sticky note was marking a page in the very last chapter. Pastor quickly opened the book and read the two lines Emily had meticulously underlined the night before:

```
. . . there was a smile on her lips
and peace in her heart. She had
looked her duty courageously in the
face and found it a friend — as duty
ever is when we meet it frankly.
```

Pastor didn't bother with his suit coat or his briefcase or the orange or the chocolate bar. He walked straight out of the office door and on down the street to the Mulberry property. He knocked loudly on Emily's front door, his heart pounding with hope.

When Emily opened the door, he held the book before her eyes.

"Does this mean what I think it means?"

Emily looked at Pastor through her lashes, blushing a new shade of pink she had patented just for him.

"You're staying?"

Emily moved her lips to speak an affirmative, but she never got a word out. Michael Fletcher made sure of it.

CHAPTER THIRTY-SIX:

MRS. SCHEINBERG IS SATISFIED

Mrs. Scheinberg leaned back comfortably in her midback executive leather chair and waved the two service men toward the back of the church. "The stairs to the balcony are down that hallway, gentlemen."

The men nodded their appreciation as they lugged heavy equipment on a dolly down the hall.

"Sorry, Candice, you were saying?"

Candice waved last week's bulletin before her flushed face like a fan, the afternoon heat of early June sprouting beads of sweat on her caked brow. She had come in to the office to serve a formal complaint to the church staff about the suspicious omission of Junior's upcoming trombone recital from last week's bulletin announcements, but strange men kept coming in and out of the office door and interrupting her rant. "I was saying that I specifically emailed you about Junior's recital last Tuesday, and there was no mention of it in Sunday's bulletin."

"Oh, yes." Mrs. Scheinberg took the bulletin from Candice's hand and pretended to look interested. "I can't imagine how that happened."

Candice stood as tall as her husky shoulders would allow and put her fisted hands on her hips. "Geraldine may be gone, Arlene, but I can just as easily keep my eye on you. I might have to suggest to my husband and the voters that we organize a Bulletin Task Force in the congregation. In fact, I'm perfectly capable of coming in every week to make sure *all* of the announcements get published in the bulletin. I took advanced English in high school, you know."

"Oh, now that would be an *egregious* mistake, Candice. I mean, Geraldine is one of a kind. Irreplaceable, really." Mrs. Scheinberg pulled out every large vocabulary word she knew for show-and-tell. "How many times does a church get to have a paragon of pedagogy edit the bulletin? Geraldine was peerless, the quintessence of wordsmiths, the epitome of editors! We should be retiring her jersey and paying her the respect a deft player is due, not attempting some kind of subversive replacement."

Candice eyed Mrs. Scheinberg warily at first, but then conceded a nod of her head. She wasn't exactly sure what Mrs. Scheinberg was talking about, but her conscience was experiencing one of those irritating pin-pricks at the mention of Geraldine's name. Whatever those words meant, surely Geraldine was all of them and more.

"Personally," Mrs. Scheinberg continued, sealing the deal, "I've often thought we should frame Geraldine's clever Easter edition of the bulletin and hang it in a place of honor over the copier, but I suppose we'd need to ask the Plueths for permission first. How is Geraldine, anyway?"

Candice shifted uncomfortably. "I haven't heard from her in a while."

"Oh, I thought you two were best friends. Well, she found a house in Indianapolis close to her brother. I've got a letter from her right here requesting a release of membership. She's apparently joining First United Methodist, north of the city. Just like her, isn't it? No seconds and thirds for Geraldine, only the first and the best. Well, God bless her. We'll never be the same without her, that's for sure." Mrs. Scheinberg looked up innocently while subtly slipping the forgotten bulletin into the recycling bin at her feet under the desk. "Tell me, how is Amelia getting along at the firm? Will she be loaning her smile to Disney this summer?"

Candice ran after the stick like a dog playing fetch. Her hands grew animated as she described Amelia's unparalleled success under her husband's tutelage, and, no, Disney would have to manage without her this summer. Amelia was going on a two-week trip to England as an assistant to Dr. Brandt for some college research project involving some dead writer. Neither Amelia nor Dr. Brandt had admitted as much to her with actual words, but Candice fully expected the two to be engaged by the time they came back. They were both too good looking not to fall in love around all of those castles.

Apparently, Candice had transferred her crazy matchmaking energies to her niece. Mrs. Scheinberg offered up a silent prayer of thanks on Emily's behalf. But still. Poor Amelia.

As Candice talked on and on about Junior and his trombone lessons and Caroline's ribbon-worthy sewing projects, Mrs. Scheinberg let her mind wander to Geraldine. Bev had informed her over the phone of how Geraldine had fled from Zion that Easter morning. Sure, the ushers would have teased that anguished woman mercilessly after the service had she stayed, but Mrs. Scheinberg was just as certain everyone else would have rallied around Geraldine for making such a human mistake. An openly flawed Miss Turner was so much more likable, refreshing even, after that horribly hypocritical persona she'd insisted on pushing down everyone's throats over the years. All of that false piety was a turnoff. It stank of self-righteousness, and Jesus came to save sinners, not the righteous, after all. As much as Mrs. Scheinberg reveled in no longer having to share the office with Geraldine every Thursday afternoon, she still felt sad for the woman. Geraldine carted around that heavy burden of unforgiveness wherever she went, and in refusing to forgive the mistakes of others, it seemed she was unable to forgive her own.

"Lord, have mercy." Mrs. Scheinberg found herself praying out loud.

"What?" Candice asked.

Mrs. Scheinberg stammered for a cover. Thankfully, one of the two uniformed men peered around the corner just then. "Sorry to interrupt, ma'am, but the door to the steeple's locked."

"Oh, the key!" Mrs. Scheinberg opened her top drawer and took out a massive key ring loaded with at least thirty pokes of metal stabbing out in a circle like the spokes of a wheel. She worked to remove an older, worn key and worked to remove it from the tightly packed ring. "Here, this one should work."

The man tipped his head in thanks and disappeared back around the corner.

"Arlene, what in heaven's name is going on around here?"

"The new carillon."

"New carillon? I don't remember anything about a carillon, and I certainly never saw one listed on the treasurer's report at last month's voters' meeting."

"That's because it wasn't."

Candice planted a fist on a purple hip and challenged the propriety of the action. "Pastor Fletcher'd better not be sneaking money out of the sewing circle budget. Instruments should come out of the music budget. And a purchase that large should be brought before the voters' assembly."

"It's not an instrument, Candice. It's an electronic speaker. And it wasn't purchased; the Schmidts donated it. They're giving the carillon to the church with the stipulation that it be pointed directly toward their house. Seems we're going to have dueling carillons with Blessed Sacrament. That'll smooth the Reformation over, for sure. Anyway, it's one of those new, fancy digital models that can be programmed to play a song every hour on the hour."

Candice was even less interested in digital carillons than she was in other peoples' thoughts and feelings, so she soon found an excuse to leave the office. After the door had shut behind Candice's lavender capris, Mrs. Scheinberg contentedly leaned on her desk and adjusted the framed picture sitting next to her computer monitor. It was of her and Blaine standing in front of that shiny Cloud Gate in Chicago. She couldn't help but smile at the memory.

Things seemed to be going better for Blaine. At least, so it seemed to her. He now came over to her house for dinner every Tuesday night, and he had made a point of inviting her to his junior recital. He had even begun giving piano lessons to that rascally Robbie Jones every Thursday afternoon in the church balcony. Mrs. Scheinberg made a point of sneaking into the nave and sitting in a back pew to listen during the lessons. That Jones boy turned out to be a pretty good piano player.

"Mrs. Scheinberg?" Pastor Fletcher called from within the bowels of his study. "Did you call in the donut order for Sunday?"

"Yes. Fifty glazed, twenty-five iced cake donuts, and twenty-five assorted cream-filled."

"We need some sugar-and-cinnamon ones too. Karl was adamant about that."

Mrs. Scheinberg sighed loud enough for Pastor Fletcher to hear. Since when did Karl Rincker get to personally order his donuts? Well, she couldn't blame the man. After all, she wasn't the only one to have suffered oppression under Geraldine's imperious reign. In fact, as soon as Geraldine had rescinded her crown Easter morning, Karl came armed to the next voters' meeting with a proposal to return to donuts in the fellowship hall on Sunday mornings. It took only twenty seconds for Karl to pitch his idea, gather a move and a second from the floor, and pass the resolution with a unanimous vote.

"I'll make sure Casey's tosses in some sugar-and-cinnamon donuts too," Mrs. Scheinberg promised.

Pastor Fletcher stepped out into the office, his portable communion set in hand. "I'm off to visit Oscar and Helen. Do you need anything from me before I leave?"

"Nope."

"Then I'll see you later tonight."

Mrs. Scheinberg tried to hide her delight at his last statement, but she couldn't keep a tell-tale tide of happy color from creeping up the back of her neck at the thought of what fun was in store for later that evening. She tried to sour the embarrassing scene with a sharp reprimand. "You really should get a haircut. You look like a twelve-year-old."

Pastor Fletcher grinned and, abandoning all caution and reserve to satisfy a particularly stubborn, ornery itch, leaned over to deliver a patronizing kiss on top of his dear secretary's head. "You *do* care, Arlene."

Mrs. Scheinberg's neck grew even hotter. She would have swung out at him with her green pen if he had not wisely jumped to the side and scooted on out the door. Still, she couldn't stay mad at the man for long. She was pretty certain her beloved

Emily Duke was sweet on the preacher, and anyone Dr. Duke admired was a winner in her book. In fact, Mrs. Scheinberg would never breathe a word of it to anyone, but she had noticed Pastor Fletcher staying late in his study Thursday nights in order to walk Emily home after choir rehearsals. The two tried to be discreet, for sure, but one Thursday night in May—when she had been a bit late getting to her car after double-checking her email from the office computer—she'd spied a certain man in a clerical collar sweetly taking the hand of a certain choir director as the two passed under a street lamp on Mulberry Avenue.

The office phone rang. "Zion Lutheran Church, this is Arlene."

"Oh, good! I was hoping to catch you," Bev chattered away on the other end of the line. "I'm in crisis, Arlene. Utter, complete crisis. You'll never guess what happened this morning. Irv delivered two dozen eggs to Mother, and one of her toes was green again with—"

Mrs. Scheinberg immediately held the receiver away at arm's length and squeezed her eyes shut. She simply couldn't take it anymore. One more story about Adeline's afflicted toes and she'd never be able to sleep again. She tentatively, carefully held the receiver in front of her mouth and cut Bev off short.

"Bev, I've got to go."

"Why?"

"The carillon installers are here. They need me."

"What for?"

"To . . . find the right key for the steeple door." Mrs. Scheinberg felt a twinge of guilt at the little white lie.

"Just give them the key ring. They'll find the one that fits. Besides, I was wondering if you wanted to go to Koelster's with me and Irv tonight."

"I can't."

"Why?"

Mrs. Scheinberg glowed with a quiet, warm pride. Should she tell Bev? She hadn't told anyone else about her plans yet, but it was all too good to keep to herself. She simply had to share the news with someone. "Blaine and I are partnering up for a cribbage tournament at the Joneses' tonight."

"Oh. How about that! Who else is going?"

While Bev Davis was often silly, Mrs. Scheinberg had never known her to be jealous. She didn't hesitate in answering. "The usual. Jeremy and Rebecca and Pastor and Emily. Evan and Alice are coming too."

"Good for you, Arlene!" Bev's voice radiated a smile across the phone line, relaying a genuine happiness for her friend. "That sounds like so much fun! You know, Irv and I used to play cribbage. It was years ago, back before we had the pigs, but I still remember the night we lost one of those little red pegs. I thought I'd suffocate under the couch trying to find it. I still had all of my baby weight from Johnny, and I remember my pants wouldn't button. No, wait! I had on my green dress pants, not my jeans. That's right, it was those green-and-yellow-striped pants. Do you remember those, Arlene? I think I got them at Dickey Bub's down in . . ."

Mrs. Scheinberg settled back in her chair, a satisfied smile on her face. Bev really wasn't such a bad egg in the end. Sure, she talked a lot, but she was generous with more than just her words. Hadn't she been looking after her ailing mother all of these years? No wonder the old girl needed to talk. Adeline's toes would push anyone into needing therapy. Besides, there were rare moments in life, like this one, when the heart was too full and rich and merry to hang up the phone. Life was for sharing, after all, and Mrs. Scheinberg thought she might try her hand at being a little less alone this summer.

"What was that you were saying about your mother, Bev?"

‖‖‖‖‖‖‖‖‖‖‖‖‖‖‖‖‖‖‖‖‖‖‖‖‖‖‖‖‖‖‖‖‖‖‖‖‖‖‖

LATIN TRANSLATIONS

- *Ubi caritas et amor* (where charity and love are)
- *Congregavit nos in unum Christi amor* (love of Christ has gathered us into one)
- *Et ex corde* (from the heart)
- *Cum porci volent* (when pigs fly)
- *Absolvo te* (you are absolved)
- *In unum congregamur* (gathered into one)
- *Cessent lites* (let controversy cease)
- *Tinnulus stultissimus es et sordidus canis!* (You're a ding-dong and a dirty dog!)
- *Semper stellae, semper laticlavia* (Stars and Stripes Forever)

DISCUSSION QUESTIONS

1. What is the "House of Living Stones" referred to in the title?

2. Gossip is poison in the life of a congregation. How is this evidenced at Zion?

3. What characteristics in Emily make it difficult for her to form and maintain relationships?

4. Is the misunderstanding about Emily's marital status Emily's fault or Candice's?

5. Emily needs a little pushing in order to take risks in life. Which people in Bradbury help her do this?

6. Why is Zachary unsuccessful as a suitor for Emily?

7. Is Evan justified in his behavior toward Emily at the first choir rehearsal? What about his behavior toward Alice?

8. What makes Alice such a good friend to Evan, Emily, and so many other members at Zion?

9. Candice keeps interfering in Emily's personal life. What different choices could she make to finally earn the friendship, respect, and trust she so craves from Emily?

10. Why is Candice unable to accept the forgiveness of others?

11. What is Geraldine's fatal flaw when it comes to relationships?

12. Who is right about Blaine? Alice or Evan?

13. Why do you think Mrs. Scheinberg never remarried?

14. Do you think Emily will remarry? Why?

ACKNOWLEDGMENTS

Thank you to . . .

Peggy Kuethe, my faithful editor and friend, for giving this book its wings; Elizabeth Pittman for directing its flight plan; Lisa Clark for treating this manuscript with such tender, professional care; Zeke, Jack, Via, Lydia, Braden, Lily, Mia, Abby, and all of the children in my life who generate genius plot material on a daily basis; every overworked church secretary for providing inspiring bulletin flubs; Kara for letting me walk with her in her grief; Lisa for inspiring the character of Basset; the Rev. Dr. Benjamin Mayes and the Rev. Heath Curtis for being my Latin consultants; Emily for her medical assistance; Sara for the vertigo; Rebekah, Rebecca, and Dr. Everett for making me a better writer; my patient focus-group readers: Mom, Grandma, Kristi, Lucy, Lisa, Tony, Emily, Eliza, Sara, Pauline, Gloria, Addie, Nora, Steve, Mary Ann, Jan, Wendy, and Micheal; Cindy Roley, my talented mother and English teacher, for keeping me classy and for introducing me to chocolate-covered oranges; Bob Roley, my creative father and brainstormer, for serving as my farming advisor and my map renderer; Michael, my ever-ready, ever-patient techie, my long-suffering listener, and my beloved husband: thank you for giving me the best writing advice I've ever received—to write what I know and to write something I want to read.

Soli deo gloria.

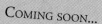
COMING SOON...

The Choir Immortal

Excerpt from
CHAPTER ONE: THE BIG DAY

Zion Lutheran Church roasted in the late August sunshine like a crock in a convection oven. Ripples of hot, humid air rose from the asphalt parking lot in waves, and Beverly Davis, dressed in her favorite cobalt-blue frock with the embroidered portrait collar, heaved her sticky frame out of her Buick and onto the sweltering pavement. She fanned herself frantically, shaking out her pleated skirt in a desperate attempt to create wind where there was none, but her efforts were to no avail. Beads of sweat sprouted on her powdered forehead and threatened to stream down her cheeks in erosive rills as she crossed the black, oily expanse and entered the church office door. Irv, her husband and Zion's faithful trustee, was waiting for her there.

"Here," Bev panted, shoving a metal tool into his hand while dabbing at her face with a clean hankie. "I found it in the shed like you said. It was hiding under those bags of fertilizer we bought on sale last week at Big R."

Irv simply nodded his thanks before quickly disappearing down the hall with his adjustable wrench. The stoic man had never been one to waste words, but the present crisis called for all brevity and efficiency. In less than one hour, Zion was hosting Bradbury's wedding of the century, and the church's air conditioning was a bust.

||||||||||||||||